Praise for Nicola Cornick

"I was hooked from the first pages... I can't remember when I last read a book so fast, just to find out what happens next. A twisty and deceptively clever book...[with] a wonderfully satisfying conclusion."

—Gill Paul, bestselling author of *The Secret Wife*

"A fascinating tale with intriguing twists which kept me reading late into the night."

—Barbara Erskine, *Sunday Times* bestselling author

"Atmospheric and compelling, I was gripped from beginning to end."

—Sarah Morgan, *USA TODAY* bestselling author

"A rising star."

—*Publishers Weekly*

"Nicola Cornick is the mistress of keeping you up way beyond lights out because you just can't put it down. Brilliant!"

—Katie Fforde

"A gorgeous novel, so fresh and original. And the tension! I was on the edge of my seat."

—Jenny Ashcroft

"With its intriguing premise and engaging characters, this fresh take on the time-slip novel completely won me over."

—Kate Riordan

"A lively, entertaining read... The story kept me turning the pages right to the very end."

—Katherine Webb

Also by Nicola Cornick

THE WOMAN IN THE LAKE
THE PHANTOM TREE
HOUSE OF SHADOWS

NICOLA CORNICK

THE
FORGOTTEN
SISTER

GRAYDON
HOUSE

GRAYDON
HOUSE®

Recycling programs
for this product may
not exist in your area.

ISBN-13: 978-1-525-80995-8

The Forgotten Sister

This edition published by arrangement with Harlequin Books S.A.

Graydon House
22 Adelaide St. West, 40th Floor
Toronto, Ontario M5H 4E3, Canada
www.GraydonHouseBooks.com
www.BookClubbish.com

Printed in Italy

This book is dedicated to my grandmother
Doris Clark, whose shelf of Tudor-set
historical novels started me on my journey.

THE
FORGOTTEN
SISTER

PROLOGUE

❀

Amy Robsart, Cumnor Village

THEY CAME FOR me one night in the winter of 1752 when the ice was on the pond and the trees bowed under the weight of the hoar frost. There were nine priests out of Oxford, garbed all in white with tapers in hand. Some looked fearful, others burned with a righteous fervour because they thought they were doing the Lord's work. All of them looked cold, huddled within their cassocks, the one out ahead gripping the golden crucifix as though it were all that stood between him and the devil himself.

The villagers came out to watch for a while, standing around in uneasy groups, their breath like smoke on the night air, then the lure of the warm alehouse called them back and they went eagerly, talking of uneasy ghosts and the folly of the holy men in thinking they could trap my spirit.

The hunt was long. I ran through the lost passageways

of Cumnor Hall with the priests snapping at my heels and in the end, exhausted and vanquished, my ghost sank into the dark pool. They said their prayers over me and returned to their cloisters and believed the haunting to be at an end.

Yet an unquiet ghost is not so easily laid to rest. They had trapped my wandering spirit but I was not at peace. When the truth is concealed the pattern will repeat. The first victim was Amyas Latimer, the poor boy who fell to his death from the tower of the church where my body was buried. Then there was the little serving girl, Amethyst Green, who tumbled from the roof of Oakhangar Hall. Soon there will be another. If no one prevents it, I know there will be a fourth death and a fifth, and on into an endless future, the same pattern, yet different each time, a shifting magic lantern projecting the horror of that day centuries ago.

There is only one hope.

I sense her presence beside me through the dark. Each time it happens she is there too, in a different guise, like me. She is my nemesis, the arch-enemy. Yet she is the only one who can free me and break this curse. In the end it all depends on her and in freeing my spirit I sense she will also free her own.

Elizabeth.

I met her only a handful of times in my life. She was little but she was fierce, always, fierce enough to survive against the odds, a fighter, clever, ruthless, destined always to be alone. We could never have been friends yet we are locked together in this endless dance through time.

I possessed the one thing she wanted and could not have and in my dying I denied it to her forever. For a little while I thought that would be enough to satisfy me.

Yet revenge sours and diminishes through the years. All I wish now is to be released from my pain and to ensure this can never happen again.

Elizabeth, my enemy, you are the only one who can help me now but to do that you must change, you must see that the truth needs to be told. Open your eyes. Find the light.

1

Lizzie: Amelia and Dudley's Wedding, 2010

EVERYONE WAS DRUNK. They had broken into the wedding favour boxes early and were downing champagne directly from the quarter-bottles, lobbing chocolates at each other and throwing the beribboned scented teabags into the swimming pool. Amelia, the bride, who had personally chosen the Rose Pouchong and Green Jasmine teabags to match the scented candles, had stormed off in tears. Dudley, instead of going after his new wife, had jumped fully clothed into the pool, laughing maniacally.

Lizzie thought boy bands were the pits, especially Dudley's band, Call Back Summer, whom she secretly believed were just talentless entitled rich boys. She would never say that to Dudley, of course. He was her friend. But she wrote and played her own music and before they'd split up, her band had been way more successful than Dudley's.

Lizzie didn't drink. She hated it when Dudley behaved like her father, ringing her up when he was pissed, slurring his words as he told her she was his best friend in the world, that he'd love her forever. It was only because they'd known each other since the age of six that she put up with it. She had no idea why he had married Amelia anyway unless it was for publicity. He'd said he was in love but Dudley was always falling in love with someone. It was a stupid idea to get married when you were only eighteen. Lizzie didn't intend to marry anyone, ever.

She stood up, unpleasantly aware of the sweat sliding down her back and turning her lace mini dress transparent as it stuck to her skin. Kat, her godmother, had told her it was bad taste to wear a white dress to a wedding but Lizzie hadn't cared. The June sun was dropping towards the horizon now and the marquee cast long shadows across the lawn. Not a breath of wind stirred the sultry air. A band was playing on the terrace but no one was paying any attention. Lizzie knew the partying would carry on long into the night. Dudley seemed to have an inexhaustible capacity for drink and drugs but she was bored.

Stepping out from beneath the jaunty poolside umbrella, she was hit by the full heat of the day. She hated being too hot; it didn't agree with her redhead's pale, freckled skin. Suddenly the water looked very tempting. Dudley, seeing her hesitate on the edge of the pool, waved a soaking arm in her direction.

"Lizzie!" he shouted. "Come on in!" Beside him a number of girls splashed around, screaming. One was Amelia's younger sister, Anna, who had jumped in wearing her bridesmaid's dress. Another was Letty Knollys, the girlfriend of one of Dudley's bandmates whom Lizzie privately thought was an even bigger groupie than Amelia.

Lizzie smiled and shook her head. Her curls would go even frizzier if she got them wet and there were bound to be paparazzi hiding in the trees to capture the wedding reception for the papers. Dudley would have made sure of that. She didn't want to be all over the red tops with mad hair and a wet see-through dress. She was too careful of her reputation for that.

She wandered off in the direction of the luxury portaloos. Evidently the plumbing at Oakhangar Hall, the ridiculously ostentatious wedding present that Amelia's father had bought for the bride, was not up to coping with two hundred celebrity guests. Nevertheless, the cool darkness of the entrance hall beckoned to her.

It took her eyes several seconds to adjust when she took off her sunglasses and then she almost fell over the enormous pile of wedding presents spilling across the floor. Beyond the gift mountain the flagstones stretched, smooth and highly polished, to the base of a grand staircase that curved up in two flights to a balustraded gallery. The soaring walls were panelled in dark wood and hung with tapestries. The whole effect was consciously mock-medieval and rather over the top but Lizzie could see that it suited Amelia's Pre-Raphaelite style.

A huge black grand piano skulked in a corner beside the stair, its surface playing host to a vast display of lilies more suited to a funeral than a wedding in Lizzie's opinion. She muffled a sneeze as the pollen tickled her nose. In contrast to the roar of the party outside, the house was sepulchrally quiet. Except... Across the wide acreage of

floor came the cascading melody of a harp, the notes res-
onating for a couple of seconds then dying away.

Lizzie spun around. There was no sign of a harp, no sign
of any instrument other than the piano. The cadence came
again, higher, wistful, a fall of notes that sounded like a
sigh. She moved towards the sound and then she saw it,
on a little shelf to the right of the door, a crystal ball held
in the cupped palms of a stone angel.

The crystal swirled with a milky white mist.

Touch me.

Lizzie stopped when her hand was about an inch from
the crystal surface.

No. The urge was strong but she knew what would
happen if she did. Ever since she had been a small child,
she had had an uncanny knack of being able to read objects. It was something she had grown up with so at first
it had seemed natural; it was only when she had first mentioned it to Kat, who had looked at her as though she was
a changeling, that she realised not everyone had the gift.
"It's just your imagination running away with you," Kat
had said, folding her in her embrace and stroking her hair,
trying to soothe and normalise her, to reassure herself as
much as Lizzie. "You see things because you want to see
them, sweetie. It doesn't mean anything..."

Lizzie had never mentioned it to her again after that but
she had known Kat was wrong. Later, when she looked
it up, she saw it was called psychometry. She used it carefully, secretly, to connect with her past and the mother
she had lost as a child. The rest of the time she tried not
to touch anything much at all if it was likely to give her a
vision. She really didn't want to know.

The crystal was calling to her. She rubbed her palms

down her dress to stop herself reaching out to obey the unspoken whisper.

"What did you see?"

Lizzie jumped. A boy was standing on the bottom step of the vast staircase, dwarfed by its height and breadth. He was staring at her. It was disconcerting; she hadn't known anyone was there.

"Nothing," she said. "I didn't touch it." She sounded defensive, which was ridiculous. She'd done nothing wrong and he was only a child. Deliberately she relaxed her face into the smile she used for the public.

"Hi, I'm Lizzie."

The boy looked at her as though he was trying to make some sort of private decision about her. It was an odd expression for such a young child; wary, thoughtful with a flash of calculation. It hinted, Lizzie thought, at a rather terrifying intelligence.

"I'm Johnny." He came forward and stuck out a hand very formally. Lizzie shook it.

"You're Amelia's brother. I saw you at the wedding." She recognised him now from the church, traipsing in behind the flower girls in Amelia's wake, looking as though he'd rather be somewhere else. Amelia's family had turned out in force for the wedding. They were all very close, a situation which Lizzie secretly envied.

"They made me be a pageboy." Johnny sounded disgusted. He looked down at his miniature three-piece suit with loathing. Lizzie could hardly blame him. It was horribly twee. "I hated it," he said. "I'm six years old, not a baby."

Lizzie smothered another smile. "Life lesson, Johnny.

People are always trying to make you do stuff you don't want to do. You have to stand up for your rights."

"Arthur says sometimes you have to do what other people want to make them happy," Johnny said.

"That's true," Lizzie acknowledged. She wasn't great at putting other people's happiness first. She'd had to struggle too hard for her own. She thought Arthur, whoever he was, sounded a proper goody-goody. "It's complicated," she said. "Next time, though, ask Arthur whether he'd like to be a pageboy instead of you."

Johnny giggled. "Arthur's too big to do that." He cocked his head to one side. "Did you really see nothing in the crystal?"

"Not a thing," Lizzie said lightly. She remembered now that Amelia liked all the flaky stuff, though with the amount of drugs she and Dudley took sometimes they didn't need a crystal ball to see things. Lizzie didn't do drugs. She'd grown up seeing her father offer Ecstasy to his dinner guests along with coffee and mints. No thank you.

"The crystal called to you," Johnny said. "I heard it."

OK, so he was an odd child, Lizzie thought, but then so had she been. She felt a tug of affinity with him.

"I thought I heard a harp playing," she said, "but it must have been the wind. That must have been the sound you heard too."

"There's no wind today," Johnny said.

"Then it must have been the band," Lizzie said.

She saw Johnny watching her with those bright blue eyes and thought, He knows. He knows I'm lying. How can he? He's only six.

"Amelia says that the crystal speaks to her," Johnny said

seriously. "Maybe that's what you heard. She says it has healing powers."

"That's nice," Lizzie said, wondering how many more of Amelia's new age philosophies her little brother had absorbed. Not that she could criticise. She might not like possessing woo-woo powers but she could hardly deny they existed.

"Johnny?"

This time they both jumped. A man was crossing the hall towards them, young, tall, unmistakably related to Johnny with the same lean features and dark blue eyes. Where Johnny had ruffled blond hair, this man's hair, however, was black, and unlike Johnny he looked good in a morning suit. Lizzie thought he also looked familiar and wondered if they had met before. There had been such a crowd in the church, and she knew so many people, but she couldn't quite place him. Perhaps she'd seen him on a billboard; he looked like a model.

His gaze focused on her and Lizzie saw that he recognised her and, a second later, saw equally clearly, that he did not like her. It was a novel experience for her to be disliked. She worked hard to be sweet and appealing. There was no reason to *dis*like her.

"Hi, Arthur," Johnny said. "This is Lizzie."

"I know," Arthur said.

Arthur Robsart, Lizzie thought, of course. He was not a model but he did do something on TV, not that she ever had time to watch, and he had some impossibly glamorous fiancée who wasn't at the wedding because she was about to make it in Hollywood. He was also Amelia's older brother, or half-brother, she thought—Amelia's family was almost as complicated as hers—which, she supposed, explained his dislike for her. Her heart dropped a little. She'd tried to be nice to Amelia; after all, she was Dudley's oldest friend so she should be Amelia's friend too. But somehow it hadn't worked and evidently Arthur knew that and like some other mean people, thought she should get out of Dudley's life.

Johnny scrambled up from the step and held out his arms unselfconsciously to his brother, asking to be picked up. Arthur's face lightened into a transforming smile.

"Where have you been?" he asked, ruffling Johnny's hair. "Your mum's looking for you."

"I want to get out of this stupid outfit," Johnny grumbled, fretful as any ordinary six-year-old now.

"Come on then." Arthur swung him up onto his shoulders. "Let's go and get changed." He gave Lizzie a cool nod, nothing more. Her heart dropped a little further, which was weird since his dislike mattered not at all. She was seventeen years old and she'd already learned not to care about other people's opinions. She'd also learned not to get entangled with handsome men. Or any men, for that matter; the life lessons she'd already absorbed would probably make even a psychiatrist wince.

As Arthur's footsteps died away, silence washed back into the hall and with it the plaintive echo of the crystal's song. Unwilling but unable to resist, Lizzie moved back towards it. The glass had turned a pale violet colour now. It seemed too beautiful *not* to touch. And surely something so beautiful couldn't be dangerous.

Her fingertips brushed the surface of the ball. It felt cool and smooth, the drifts of mist within following the movement of her hand. Immediately Lizzie saw a vision of the crystal sitting in the window of a shop in Glastonbury surrounded by a whole variety of other bogus magical items from joss sticks to druids' robes. She could see Amelia exclaiming in delight, pointing it out to Dudley who had his habitual expression of bored amusement plastered across his face. Dudley shrugged:

"It's total rubbish but buy it if you want..."

Lizzie withdrew her hand. Psychometry gave her the ability to pry into other people's lives sometimes but she really didn't want to know what went on between Dudley and Amelia. She absent-mindedly rubbed her fingers over the lines of the stone angel's wings, tracing the intricate carving. It was a beautiful piece, the hands cupping the crystal ball, the head bent. As she touched it, she heard the thrum of the harp again but this time it wasn't sweet and plaintive. There was a cold edge to it like shards of ice that sent a shiver down her spine.

The world exploded suddenly around her. She felt a rush of movement and a blur of colour; she felt a hand in the small of her back, pushing hard, then she was falling, falling. There was a rush of air against her face and the lightness of empty space beneath her. There was fear screaming inside her head. Then, as quickly as they had arrived, the sensations passed. She was lying on the floor and people were buzzing around her like flies.

"What happened?"

"I heard her screaming..."

"Trust Lizzie Kingdom to try and steal the limelight today of all days..."

Lizzie sat up. Her head was woozy as though she had had too much champagne. Pieces of the crystal lay scattered about her in glittering shards, one of which had embedded itself in the palm of her right hand. It stung fiercely.

She could hear Amelia in the background, wailing that Lizzie had broken her gazing ball.

The stone angel lay next to her, unbroken. Lizzie felt dazed, her mind cloudy, sickness churning in her stomach. *What the hell had happened?* She knew she hadn't smashed the crystal.

People were still talking. No one seemed bothered about helping her up. She could hear Dudley's voice: "For fuck's sake, what's the matter? It was only some cheap ornament." Amelia's wails rose above the chatter. Lizzie focussed on keeping still and not throwing up. That would be the final humiliation. She felt like a pariah, abandoned in a sea of glass.

The crowd fell back a little, crunching the slivers of glass beneath their stilettos and hipster brogues. Arthur pushed through to her; he didn't say anything, simply held out a hand to help her to her feet. Lizzie grabbed it and scrambled up. She had no pride left. She followed him down what felt like an endless succession of dark corridors into what looked like an old scullery full of discarded wedding paraphernalia, piles of empty boxes and flower containers heaped up and left out of sight. This, Lizzie thought, was definitely the servants' quarters. She had been demoted from guest to unsightly wedding detritus along with all the rest of the rubbish.

Arthur was rummaging in a cupboard underneath a white ceramic sink. He emerged with a first aid kit in his hand. She turned her palm up so that he could clean the cut. The bleeding had stopped now but the wound throbbed, even more so when Arthur dabbed at it with antiseptic. Lizzie suppressed a wince as it stung. He was so dour and exasperated, and there was no way she was going to show any weakness.

"I'm sorry," she said, as the silence became blistering. "I really don't know what happened."

"Keep your hand still whilst I bandage it up," Arthur said. "It's Amelia you should be apologising to," he added. "It's her wedding you've ruined."

"Don't be ridiculous," Lizzie snapped. Her hand was smarting but not as much as her feelings. "If anyone has ruined the wedding it's Dudley, and that's not my fault."

"You think?" Arthur looked at her very directly and her heart did an odd sort of flip. He continued to wrap the bandage methodically around her hand and her wrist, as gently as before. Lizzie suddenly became acutely aware of his touch against her skin and by the time he had finished and tucked the end in she was squirming to escape.

"Thanks," she said, jumping up and heading for the door. "I'll just grab my bag and…"

Go. There was no way she was hanging around here any longer. She felt very odd.

Back in the grand hall, someone had swept up the glass and the place was empty. It was as though nothing had ever happened. Lizzie could hear the band playing and splashes and screams from the pool. The party had moved up a gear.

She called her driver, who was there in three minutes. She was in such a hurry to get away that she left her very expensive jacket behind. Days later, when she finally emptied the wedding favours, teabags and scented candle from her goody bag, she found that in the confusion someone must have accidently slipped the little stone angel in with all the other stuff. She meant to return it to Amelia but after all the fuss it never seemed like the right time. Then she saw Amelia wearing her jacket as though it were her own so she never mentioned it again but stowed the angel away in a cupboard. She knew it was petty but Amelia had started it and the jacket was probably worth more than the ornament anyway.

Over the years she forgot about the stone angel, but she never forgot Dudley and Amelia's wedding. She tried but there was no way she could ever forget a day that had ended with Amelia in hysterics and with blood on her hands. It felt ill-starred. It felt as though, sooner or later, something bad was going to happen.

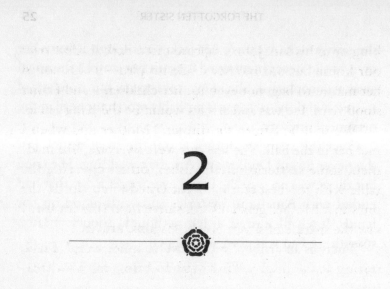

2

Amy: Stanfield Manor, Norfolk, August 1549

I MET ROBERT Dudley on a night of moonlight, fire and gunpowder.

The wind had a sharp edge to it that evening, summer already turning away towards the chill of autumn. It brought with it the scent of burning from the rebel camp twelve miles to the north. The sky burned too, in shades of red and orange below the dark clouds, so that it was impossible to tell what was fire and what was sunset. They said that there were more than twelve thousand men assembled on Mousehold Heath, more than in the whole of Norwich itself, and Norwich was a great city, second only to London. Among the rebels' prisoners was my half-brother John Appleyard, taken by our cousin Robert Kett, to help my father ponder whether his loyalty was to his

king or to his kin. John's capture cast a dark shadow over
our house but our mother made no plea—it was not in
her nature to beg, not even for her children—and Father
stood firm. He was and always would be the King's man.

"We will be fifteen for dinner," Mother said when I
met her in the hall. The servants were sweeping like mad-
men, some scattering fresh rushes, others covering the
table with the best diamond-patterned linen cloths, the
ones that Mother generally considered too fine for use. I
saw the sparkle of silver: bowls, flagons, knives.

"There is an army of rebels twelve miles away," I said,
staring at the display. "Is it wise to bring out your trea-
sure?"

She gave me the look that said I was pert. I waited for
the reproach that would accompany it, the claim that my
father had spoiled me, the youngest, his only daughter, and
that I would never get myself a husband if I was so forward.
Pots and kettles; I got three quarters of my nature from
my mother and well she knew it; from her I had inherited a quick mind and a quick tongue but also the knowledge of when I needed to guard it. Men say that women
chatter but they are the ones who so often lack discretion.
Women can be as close as the grave.

But Mother did not reproach me. Instead her gaze swept
over me from head to foot. There was a small frown between her brows; I thought it was because my hair was
untidy and put up a hand to smooth it. My appearance
was my vanity; I was fair and had no need of the dye. My
skin was pale rose and cream and my eyes were wide and
blue. I knew I was a beauty. I won't pretend.

"You are quite right," Mother said, after a moment's
scrutiny, with a wry twist of her lips. "You, of all our trea-

sures, should be kept safe at a time like this. Unfortunately, your father insists that you should attend dinner tonight."

I gaped at her, not understanding. I had only been referring to the plate and linens. Seeing my confusion, her smile grew, but it was a smile that chilled me in some manner I did not quite understand. It hinted at adult matters and I, for all my seventeen years, was still a child.

"Your presence has been requested," she said. "The Earl of Warwick comes at the head of the King's army. They march against the rebels. He is bringing his captains here to dine with us tonight and take counsel with your father. Two of his sons ride with him, Ambrose and Robert."

My heart gave a tiny leap of excitement which I quickly suppressed out of guilt. The Earl of Warwick was coming here, to my corner of Norfolk, bringing danger and excitement to a place that seldom saw either. It was a curious feeling that took me then, a sense of anticipation tinged with a sadness of something lost; peace, innocence almost. But the rebels had already shattered both peace and innocence when they had risen up against the King's laws.

"I'm sorry," I said. "About the King's army, I mean. It is hard for you, with John a prisoner and family loyalty split."

She looked startled for a moment and then smiled at me, a proper smile this time, one that lit her tired eyes. "You are a sweet child, Amy," she said, patting my cheek. Her smile died. "Except that you are not a child any longer, it seems."

She sighed. "Do you remember Robert Dudley?" She was watching me very closely. I was not sure what she was looking for. "He asked your father if you would be present at dinner tonight. No…" she corrected herself. "He requested that you *should* be present, which is a different matter entirely."

Her look made it clear what she thought of the sons of the nobility asking after a gentleman's daughter. I suppose she imagined that no good could come of it, despite my father's ambitions.

"I remember him," I said. I smiled a little at the memory for a picture had come into my mind, a small, obstinate boy, his black hair standing up on end like a cockerel's crest, a boy whom the other children had mocked because he was as dark as a Spaniard. More cruelly they had called him a traitor's grandson because the first Dudley of note had been a lawyer who had risen high in old King Henry's favour and had then fallen from grace when the new King Henry had wanted to sweep his father's stables clean. It had all happened before I was born, before Robert had been born too, but the ghost of the past had haunted him. People had long memories and cruel tongues, and as a result he was a child full of anger and fierce defiance, seeming all the more impotent because he had been so small and so young. I had secretly pitied Robert even whilst he had sworn he would be a knight one day and kill anyone who slighted his family name.

"When did you meet him?" Mother was like a terrier after a rat when she saw that smile.

"I met him years ago at Kenninghall," I said. "And once, I think, when the Duchess took us up to London."

My mother nodded. I felt the tension ease from her a little. Perhaps she believed that no harm could have come of a meeting between children under the auspices of the Duchess of Norfolk.

"You were very young then," she said. "I wonder why he remembers you."

"I was kind to him, I suppose," I said. "The other children were not." I remembered dancing with Robert at some childish party at court; Lady Anne Tilney had scorned his proffered hand for the galliard and so he had turned to me as second choice. We must have been all of twelve years old and he had spent the entire dance glaring at Lady Anne and stepping on my toes.

"They may be regretting that unkindness," my mother said, with another of her wry smiles, "now that his father rivals the Duke of Somerset for the King's favour."

A shiver tickled my spine like the ghosts of the past stirring again. I wondered whether Robert's father had learned nothing from his own father's fate. Why men chose to climb so high when the risk was so great was a matter on which I had no understanding. It was as though they enjoyed tempting the gods with their recklessness and re-peating history over and again.

Mother's mind had already moved on to more practical matters, however. "Wear your blue gown," she instructed, "the one that matches your eyes. Since you and I are to be present we shall at least make your father proud even if we will be bored to distraction by talk of military strategy."

"Yes, Mother," I said dutifully.

"I'll send Joan to you," Mother said. "And don't lean out of the window to see what goes on outside whilst you dress." Seeing my blank look, she said with a hint of ir-ritation: "Did I not mention but a moment ago that there is an army coming? There will be nigh on ten thousand men encamped in the fields beyond the orchard. I do not want you to become their entertainment."

"No, Mother," I said. I thought it would be easy enough to steal a look without being seen. The encampments, the fires, the horses, the food cooking, the scents and the noise… Stanfield Manor would be abuzz and it was impossible not to feel the expectancy in the air.

"Remember that soldiers are dangerous, Amy," Mother added sharply, "commoner or nobleman alike."

It seemed excessive to say "yes, Mother" again, so I nodded obediently and hurried away to the stairs, aware that her watchful gaze was pinned upon my back. There was nothing to dispute in what she had said, nor in those things that she had not put into words. I might be young but I knew what she meant about soldiers and the way in which they snatched at pleasure with both hands in case it was their last chance. I did not want to be that prize, seized for a moment's gratification then cast aside.

Even so, I thought about Robert Dudley whilst Joan helped me to dress and started to plait my long fair hair. She was slow and methodical, her tongue sticking from the corner of her mouth as her fingers worked. My thoughts, my dreams were the opposite of slow, skipping lightly from one place to the next. My memories of Robert were vague but that did not stop me from pinning my dreams on him. What sort of a man had he become? Was he handsome? Would he like me? Even as I counselled myself to hold fast to my common sense, I could feel excitement bubbling through me.

"Keep still, Mistress Amy," Joan tutted as the braids slid from her fingers. "You are hopping about like a hen on a thorn."

It seemed to take her an age of pinning and smoothing and straightening but finally she was done and I flew down the stairs. Yet when I reached the door of the hall I hesitated, stung by a sudden shyness at the sound of voices within. I smoothed my skirts, patted my coif, took a deep breath, but my feet seemed fixed to the flagstones. I could not move.

"Amy!" Mother appeared in the doorway, voice as sharp as a needle. "Why are you loitering there?" Her gaze darted past me, looking for trouble. When she found none, it did not seem to appease her.

"Come in." She flapped at me to go ahead of her.

The hall was hot. We did not need a fire in August but Father had ordered one lit anyway, all the better to show off the richness of his glass and silver. I wondered how the table bore the weight of so much food and spared a thought for the kitchen staff; Cook's sweat must have been liberally mixed in with the sauces. The servants were sweating too as they attended us, heat and nervousness making their faces redden and their hands shake. Father, never the most patient master, was snapping orders as though he were a general in the field.

"There is a space for you there, Amy—" Mother pushed me towards the centre of the table where there was an empty place laid. I sat. She sat opposite me, watching me like a cat with a mouse.

I felt like telling her that there was no need for her vigilance. On the one side of me was an old man who looked as though he had last ridden to war alongside the late King Henry at the Battle of the Spurs. On the other was a younger man who was so fat I wondered at the horse that had to bear his weight and whether he had to be winched into the saddle. A swift search of the room, conducted surreptitiously as I took my seat, had told me that neither

Robert Dudley nor his brother Ambrose was present. I felt disproportionately disappointed. The old soldier ignored me, sucking noisily on chicken bones and throwing the scraps to the dogs. The younger smiled shyly and poured wine for me.

At the head of the table Father was deep in discussion with Lord Warwick. The King's general was a fine-looking man, all the more so in his armour. He had presence and grace; I watched him as he talked, animated and at times fierce. I caught an echo of Robert in the proud lift of his head and directness of his gaze.

I picked at my food. The chicken was drenched in a sauce that was too rich and heavy. I wondered if Cook was a rebel sympathiser and wanted to give the King's men a stomach ache. Not that they were complaining. They looked half-starved and only the presence of ladies prevented them from falling on each dish like dogs as it came out.

There was little conversation. The weather, the poor quality of the roads, the availability of horses and the fine taste of Stanfield-grown apples sustained us through several courses whilst I sat and sweated and reflected bitterly that I had wasted my hopes and dreams on a fantasy.

I escaped to my chamber as soon as I was able. Mother had no need to chivvy me out whilst the men sat late over their wine and their strategy. I took off my pretty dress and released my hair and lay down but of course I could not sleep. I was too irritated; with Robert, who had asked for me and then forgotten me, with myself for building something out of nothing. Outside there was a cacophony of noise: shouting, hammering, horses, footsteps, sounds of urgency that now rather than exciting me only served to annoy me. After a while I realised that I was not going to sleep. That irritated me even more. I threw back the covers and strode to the window, pushing wide the leaded pane.

Outside there was full moonlight, bright as day and yet casting the world in only black and white. It was the moon that preceded the harvest, except that the rebellion had thrown the harvest into disarray this year. The crops lay trampled in the fields and there would be no festival of celebration though there could well be a reaping of souls if not of corn. Instead of mummers and music, shadow men walked amongst the trees of the orchard. Smoke rose white against the bleached night sky and the air was rich with the smell of cooking and dung, a curious combination that caught at my throat.

There was sudden movement below my window. A man swung down from his horse, tethered it to a tree. I saw him in flashes of silver and black; the moonlight on his armour, his long shadow. He took off his helmet and took a deep breath of air, head back, shaking himself like a dog coming out of water. He was dark; the moon lit shades of blue in his hair like a raven's wing. Then he looked up and the light fell full on his face.

I must have made some involuntary movement that caught his eye for he turned his head sharply to look at me. The gesture was so familiar even though I had not seen him for so many years. Recognition tugged deep within me. He raised a hand in greeting. I saw the flash of his smile. He knew me too.

I pushed the window frame wider. "Robert Dudley," I said. "You missed dinner."

He laughed. "I am here now." He set his foot to the climbing rose that grew beneath my window. The whole delicate structure shivered as he put his weight on it, the last petals of summer drifting down, and I leaned out further to stop him.

"You'll fall!" I had no care for propriety, only for his safety. I did not see the ranks of grinning soldiers pausing in their drinking and their gaming to watch us. I saw only him. Already I was swept away.

"Never," he said. "You won't lose me, Amy Robsart. I'll not fall."

A cloud passed over the moon, red like blood from the fire on the heath.

Despite the cumbersome weight of the armour he climbed fast, sure-footed, like a cat. He reached the window ledge and swung himself over and then he was in my room. A ragged cheer went up from the men below and he reached across me to close the window and banish them so that there was only the two of us there in the candlelight. He smelled of sweat and horses and smoke and the night air; it was exciting and my head swam.

We stood and stared at one another. His armour was dented and blackened by smoke. His face likewise was filthy with dirt and sweat. I put a hand up to touch his chest but could feel nothing but the coldness of hard steel beneath my palm so I raised it to his cheek and touched warm flesh. He was vital and vivid and all the things that my life lacked. His eyes blazed as he bent his head to kiss me.

That was how I met Robert Dudley again. By the morning we had pledged our troth and the seeds of our mutual destruction were already sown.

3

Lizzie: Present Day

THE CALL CAME through five minutes before Lizzie was due onstage. She was nervous which meant that she was also in a bad mood. She didn't *do* literary events; they really weren't her thing. Everyone knew that she hadn't written the book herself—she'd been quite open about that from the start—and she couldn't even remember much of what the story was about. What the hell was she going to talk about? What the hell were they going to ask her? She'd insisted on approval of all the interview questions and now she couldn't remember a single one of them or the answers she'd prepared.

She stood up and paced across the tiny space that the festival organisers had imaginatively called the green room. It *was* green because it was a corner of a marquee that had been cordoned off for her use. The carpet was actual grass. Lizzie could even see a ladybird crawling towards her. There was one lopsided mirror, an extension lead was the only source of power, and there was no proper lighting, which had made doing her hair and make-up a nightmare. It was so hot under the canvas that once her make-up was done it had all slid off her face anyway. The fruit juice was warm and the sandwiches had curled. Kat had reminded her that she couldn't expect the same VIP treatment at a literary event that she got at a film studio which had only made her more annoyed. It wasn't as though she was a diva. Everyone said she was lovely. But the whole thing was hideous and she was within an inch of walking out.

The other authors speaking at the symposium on Young Adult fiction, the real ones, were accommodated in the historic environs of Gloucester College but perhaps they hadn't thought that appropriate for her, the celebrity, the interloper. Here she was right next door to the main marquee where she would be doing her interview. She could hear the crowd arriving, hear the swell of sound and voices, and sense the pulse of excitement. Normally that would have excited her too with the buzz of a performance imminent, but that was when she was singing, or presenting, or performing on *Stars of the Dance*. She had spent most of her life in the spotlight. Tonight, though, was all about writing and she was so far beyond her comfort zone she couldn't even see it over the horizon.

She'd turned down the invitation to the event as soon as it had arrived but Bill had overruled her for once. He'd called her into his office in Bloomsbury, which was also unusual as he normally came to her. As her agent, he did work for her after all. It wasn't her job to go to him. And she was twenty-six now, not sixteen, as she had been when she had signed with him. She did not take well to being told off like a sulky child.

Thinking back, Lizzie remembered how distracted and irritable Bill had been that morning, even more than normal. She had hoped it was just his ulcer playing up but suspected that it was because of her. She knew Bill wanted her to change direction and move away from the kids' presenting into something more grown-up; he'd suggested a game show that was currently looking for a new host and she'd turned it down on the grounds that it would kill her brain cells faster than sniffing paint. Then he put forward a new show called *Celebrity Wrestling: The Hot Moves*. She'd told him it sounded like porn. Bill had slammed the flat of his hand down on his desk in exasperation.

"For fuck's sake!" he had shouted.

Lizzie hadn't jumped at the crack of Bill's hand on the wood. Her father had been given to sudden violent storms of temper and she was inured to it.

"Do you need a cup of tea, Bill?" she asked. "It might help you calm down."

"I need a client I can work with," Bill snapped. "It's time to grow up, Lizzie. You're too wholesome. It's infantilising. What are you now—twenty-seven?"

"I was twenty-six last month," Lizzie said coldly. Bill's secretary had sent flowers from him, a whole hothouse full of them. She'd known Bill had had nothing to do with it.

"Then act like it," Bill said sharply. "No more of this bubblegum pop and kids' shows. And get yourself a partner. I don't care what sex they are. This 'best friends forever' thing you have going on with Dudley Lester may have been cute when you were fifteen but it's cloying now."

Lizzie had known it wouldn't be long before her relationship with Dudley would be thrown at her. Dudley was her oldest friend—her rock—and she loved him as much as Bill hated him for the influence he had over her.

"You're well aware that I haven't written or performed any music for over a year," she said, ignoring Bill's comments about Dudley to focus on her other grudge against him. "*You* told me to stop and I did even though I loved it! I've been offered nothing but crappy kids' gigs ever since."

"Because you're such a princess," Bill said. "People still think of you as a teenager. Your reputation—"

"Is squeaky clean," Lizzie said. "And it stays that way. I'm not going to shag someone—of any sex—just to please you."

There was a long, dangerous silence. Lizzie could feel the tears stinging the backs of her eyes and blinked them away. She'd worked so damned hard for everything she had, distanced herself from the sleaze and scandal of her childhood, and she wasn't going to let Bill put any of that in jeopardy.

She saw his shoulders slump. "You're not just going to walk into *Newsnight* from the *Ninja Teatime Club*," he said. "You've got to put the graft in first." He tapped the papers in front of him. "Starting with the Oxford Symposium. I know you've refused the invite but if you want people to buy your books then you need to get out there and meet the readers."

"They're kids' books," Lizzie said. "I thought you said I should aim for a more mature audience."

"Writing adds gravitas," Bill said. "Loads of celebs write books for children."

"But it's Oxford," Lizzie objected. "They'll hate me. Everyone despises celebrity authors, especially the ones who don't even write their own books. We're the lowest of the low, taking huge advances we don't need and cheating ordinary writers out of a living."

"You've been reading *The Bookseller* magazine again," Bill said irritably. "I told you not to do that."

"You gave it to me so I could see how well my latest book was doing," Lizzie said. "Number one in the e-book charts for three weeks so far and in the top ten paperbacks—"

"Exactly." Bill cut her off with a snap of his fingers. "So get over to Oxford and keep it at number one."

"What do you think, Kat?" Lizzie said. She'd brought Kat Ashley with her even though Bill hadn't invited her, even though he barely tolerated her as a fixture in Lizzie's life. Nominally Kat was Lizzie's PA but she wasn't exactly efficient. Lizzie really needed a secretary to organise Kat but she was fiercely loyal to her because their relationship had nothing to do with work, not really. Kat was her godmother and had looked after Lizzie when her mother had died. She'd been in her life ever since, the only constant other than Dudley, and someone Lizzie clung to tenaciously because deep down she saw Kat as the last real connection to her mother.

"Don't ask Kat!" Bill exploded. "She'll only tell you what you want to hear."

Kat glared at him.

"She's my friend," Lizzie said. "Of course she's on my side."

"I'm on your side," Bill said bitterly, "if only you could see it."

"You should do it, honey," Kat said, surprising them both. "Bill's right. You want the books to do well; your fans love them…" She shrugged. "It's business, babes."

So here Lizzie was in Oxford on a wet September evening, about to be interviewed by some local journalist who probably couldn't believe his luck in getting to meet Lizzie Kingdom, one-time girl band member turned kids' TV presenter and now non-author of the *Celia Jones and Friends* books for pre-teen girls.

Her phone buzzed. She waved a hand at Kat, who was sitting on a hard wooden chair painting her nails turquoise, engrossed. Her tongue stuck out of the side of her mouth with the effort of concentration.

"Get that for me, would you, Kat?"

Kat looked pained but she stretched out her unvarnished hand for the phone without reproach. Lizzie felt a flash of guilt. She was behaving like a brat and had been doing so all day. It was the nerves. Nothing should make her nervous after all these years; she had been a child star at five and an adult one at twelve. Her father, a theatre impresario, had seen her potential as a performer when she was in nappies and had promptly signed her up to do baby commercials. After her mother had died, he had forever been taking her out of school for parts in various shows. It had all progressed from there. Tonight, though, was about literature, a subject on which she knew next to nothing. She didn't feel comfortable and she hated that sense of vulnerability.

"It's Dudley," Kat said, checking the caller ID. Her voice was expressionless in the way that could only imply disapproval. Kat was another one who heartily disliked Dudley Lester. Kat said that Dudley used Lizzie, that he lived off her success because he had never quite achieved the same level of fame himself and now that he had financial troubles he was even more of a leech. Lizzie knew there was a grain of truth in this. When Dudley's band had split four years before, he had wanted to move into presenting and Lizzie had helped, putting some work his way, suggesting joint projects. She didn't see the problem; that was what friends did for one another and Dudley had always been there for her. She could tell him anything and everything, and frequently did. He was the only person she loved and trusted completely. She knew Dudley could be petulant sometimes but he made her laugh. She didn't have many proper friends, people who understood what it was like to have a spectacularly messed-up childhood lived out under very bright public lights. Dudley genuinely appreciated that and had stood by her through it all. That counted for a lot.

Smiling, she took the phone from Kat's outstretched hand. It would be so good to talk to Dudley. He'd cajole her out of her nervousness. He could always make her feel better.

"Hi, Duds," she said. "Have you rung to wish me luck?"

"Lizzie." Dudley didn't wait for her to finish. "Thank God you're there. She's dead, Lizzie! I've only just heard. I don't know what to do…" He sounded dazed, his voice so broken and confused that Lizzie barely recognised it. She felt a lurch of fear. This did not sound like the Dudley she knew, the irreverent, impetuous, fun-loving companion who could tease her out of any bad mood.

"Dudley?" she said sharply. "What's happened? What do you mean? Who's dead?"

"Shit," Dudley said. "Haven't you seen it online? Are you locked in a cellar somewhere, for God's sake? I told you. It's Amelia. She's dead!"

Amelia. Lizzie's mind locked onto the name. Amelia was Dudley's soon-to-be-ex-wife, whose existence Lizzie so frequently—and so conveniently—forgot. The churning sickness in her stomach intensified. How could Amelia be dead? She was only twenty-eight years old. Had there been an accident, a car crash, like the one that had taken Lizzie's mother? For a terrifying second the present slipped away and Lizzie felt as though she was four years old again, watching through the bannisters as the police came to break the news to her father.

Sunlight, dust motes dancing in the air, the smell of whisky pervading the house, the radio chattering in the kitchen, the old battered panda clutched in her hand, her father, shielding his eyes so no one could read his expression, the ring of a lie in his voice as he expressed his grief...

"Lizzie?" Dudley's urgent voice broke through the memory.

Lizzie tried to pull her thoughts together, to focus. "What happened?" she repeated. "How... How did she die? Were you there?"

Dudley's voice was frayed, high-pitched. "No! It was nothing to do with me! I don't know anything about it." He stopped again. Lizzie waited, aware of the fear building inside her, of a sense of impending doom, of dark shadows gathering. For a moment all she could hear was the rising sound of the crowd in the marquee, all she could feel was the heat trapped beneath the canvas, pressing down on her, making her light-headed. She steadied herself with one hand on the back of Kat's chair and realised that she was shaking.

"Amelia's dead, Lizzie," Dudley repeated, and he sounded so lost that Lizzie felt the huge horrible weight of sickness settle hard in her stomach. "She fell down the stairs at Oakhangar Hall and broke her neck."

4

Amy: Stansfield Manor, Norfolk, April 1550

THROUGHOUT MY CHILDHOOD, whenever I had needed wise counsel, I had sought out my half-brother Arthur. He had always been the one to cajole me out of ill temper or soothe my tears when my mother and I disagreed. She and I were close; she taught me everything from how to run a large household to how to make herbal ointments, but she was brisk and too busy for my tantrums. My sister Anna and I scrapped like cats; John was a studious boy who grew into a distant young man. There was only Arthur who had the patience for me.

That day I found him in the stables. This was no surprise; he was seldom anywhere but on the farm. Our father had tried to educate him as a gentleman for he was his elder son, illegitimate or not, but whilst Arthur had done well enough at Oxford, he had shown no desire to enter either the law or the church. It seemed he had no ambition. Father did not understand that, though when Arthur expressed a wish to run Father's estates, he did not demur and respected Arthur for his skills, particularly with the animals.

I sat on a bale of straw, inhaling the scent of warm horses, hay and hot oil from the lantern, listening to the chink of the rope in the metal ring as the mare shifted beneath the curry comb. Arthur talked to her as he worked, soft words, affectionate, soothing, moving the comb in efficient circles over her coat. She seemed to like it, nudging him when he stopped for a moment. I knew better than to interrupt him and it was only when he laid the comb aside and picked up the dandy brush that he paused, shaking the hair out of his eyes, and looked at me.

"You will spoil your gown sitting there," he said. "The straw is still damp."

I shrugged. "It doesn't matter."

He raised his brows. "I thought there was something wrong. Now I know there must be. When were you so careless of your attire?"

"I am crossed in love," I said. "I care nothing for how I look."

His lips twitched into a smile at either the melodrama or the blatant lie or perhaps both. He and I both knew it would take more than a little heartache to reduce my vanity to ashes. Arthur was five years my senior, the result of a liaison between our father and a woman who had lived in a cottage on another of Father's estates at Syderstone. She had been widowed when she bore Arthur and died soon after of the flux. Arthur was taken into my father's household and there he remained. He had an uneasy relationship with my mother; they were always courteous to one another but I knew that his existence gave her pain, which was odd, I thought, since she had come to her marriage with two children of her own from her last husband. Perhaps it was the gossip that caused her grief, since it was still said in Syderstone, Stansfield and around, that Arthur's mother had been an exceptionally beautiful woman and that our father was utterly besotted with her. Certainly, Arthur had been blessed with good looks just as I had. We quite put John and Anna in the shade.

"Let me guess," Arthur said. He started to groom the mare again, long, firm strokes that brought up the shine of her coat to a rich chestnut gleam. "Our father is set on you marrying your fancy lord whilst your mother counsels against it. You must inevitably upset one or the other of them."

I stared at him. "How did you know?"

Arthur glanced up at me over his shoulder. "You need to ask? When the house has resounded to your parents' high words this week past? Everyone knows they are at odds, our father set on this ambitious plan and your mother arguing that his aims are too high."

"What shall I do?" I said plaintively.

Arthur straightened up, the brush still in his hand. "Why are you asking me? You will do exactly what you want to do, Amy. You want to marry Robert Dudley so you will have him regardless of any opposition."

Arthur knew me very well. I admitted, albeit to myself alone, that he was right. There was a whole host of reasons why I wished to marry Robert. Some were noble. We loved each other. Some were personal. He was hand-

some and charming. Others were less admirable. I wanted
to make a match that would have my half-sister gasping with envy. Anna had married a gentleman the previous year and gone to live at a fine manor house, but she
would never have dreamed of looking as high as I did for
a husband. She would be green with envy. Robert had no
money but he had connections, status and plans for greater
things. But this, it seemed, was my mother's objection.
Arthur was right, we had all heard the bitter words exchanged between our parents as day after day, night after
night they fought over my future.

"You are blinded by ambition," was Mother's refrain to
my father. "You overreach yourself in this alliance with
the Dudleys. Those who rise so high will surely fall and
take us all down with them."

Her protests, I knew, were prompted by fear. It was the
fear of a woman who had sat by on more than one occasion and seen how the grandiose plans of men could lead
to ruin. Our cousins Robert and William Kett had been
hanged at the end of the last year for their uprising against
the King. It was, she said, a woman's place to sit at home
and weep whilst their men threw away their lives.

I had happier hopes than that. I had no intention of
weeping. I would marry Robert and join him at the King's
court and my life would be a whirl of excitement. I saw no
further than that. I was young and in love; why would I?

"I sometimes think that Mother is a witch," I said,
standing up, shaking the straw from my skirts. "She fears
the future. Do you think that is because she has seen it?"

I half expected Arthur to make the sign of the cross at
my words, for he was a countryman at heart and as such
was full of superstition. He did not smile but nor did he

flinch from the question. "I think she has seen a semblance of the future," he said slowly. "We all have. We have all seen great men stumble and lose all they have worked to achieve. She does not want that for our father and least of all does she want it for you."

"I will do very well," I said. "I will be a great lady and live in a castle and have ten children. The Dudleys always have lots of children."

I liked that vision of my future. It would give me a place, a purpose. It pleased me very much to know that, for I was outgrowing my life at Stansfield. What was I to do if I stayed here, year after year, a spinster losing my bloom? I needed an establishment of my own and a place in the world.

"I do love Robert," I repeated, as though that was the charm that would ensure my future happiness. "We love each other."

Arthur did not reply and for a moment I thought I saw shadows gathering in his eyes. I wondered if he was thinking about the other sharp words that Mother had uttered in an unguarded moment; that Robert was infatuated with my beauty and wanted my body but that lust would never sustain a happy marriage. I had not really understood what she had meant. Robert made me feel desired and that pleased me as surely it would please any woman. Besides, I knew that the advantages were not all on my side. Father possessed influence in the county, which Lord Warwick intended to use to his benefit. Already there was talk of Robert serving as a member of the parliament for Norfolk and I knew that Father could make that happen. This was not such an unequal alliance.

So I told myself, but despite that reassurance I felt

somehow chilled. To comfort myself I reached up to kiss Arthur's cheek, resting one hand on the warm, smooth flank of the horse. It was peaceful here with them both in the stables but I was done with the peaceful life of a country maid. I had been fashioned for finer things.

"Thank you, Arthur," I said.

He gave me a hug, his arms strong and comforting about me. Even though I thought it would crease my gown, I returned the embrace. I would miss him when I went to London but I knew I would never tempt him to visit me in the city. He would have felt as out of place there as I now felt here in the country. Arthur belonged to the land. It would always call him home.

"Why do you thank me?" he said wryly. "All I have done is to tell you what you wanted to hear."

"I am thanking you for being the best of brothers," I said. "I know you will never fail me."

"That at least I can promise," Arthur said. He released me. He wasn't smiling. His eyes were grave. "If you need me, Amy," he said, "I will always be there for you."

"Of course you will," I said. I spoke carelessly, for why would I ever need him? On the contrary, I had already started to think of the favours I might gain for my family when I was a courtier's wife.

I went out into the stable yard. There had been a rain shower and the cobbles were glazed with water but the twilight sky had cleared to a pale blue. A sliver of moon climbed above the clouds. My natural good spirits had reasserted themselves and I felt excited and light of heart. I knew I would be able to persuade Mother to my point of view. She wanted to see me happy and Robert would make me happy. There would be no need for Father to overrule her. She would agree to the match and Robert and I would be wed.

Mother thought that she could see the future, but the one I was intent upon was quite different from her vision. Robert and I would grow together. I would impress on him my worth as more than just a beautiful wife and, God willing, a mother. His parents, like mine, had a strong mutual love and respect. The model was there for us to follow. He would quickly realise that a woman could not only be his sun and stars, the centre of his world, but his equal, his inspiration, his life.

There was no limit to my belief in him, and in myself. And of course I was right; Robert would indeed come to value one woman more highly than any other on Earth.

I had no idea that that woman would never be me.

5

Lizzie: Present Day

BILL HAD BARRELLED into the tent about a minute after Dudley's call came through, surrounded by a phalanx of security in dark suits. He'd cut Lizzie off in midcall and taken her phone away from her, saying that it was imperative that she didn't speak to Dudley or anyone else until they had spoken to the lawyers and come up with a story. Lizzie hadn't a clue what he meant but it felt bad. Bill had ushered her out of the back of the tent to where a car waited, anonymous with blacked-out windows. On the way out, Lizzie had caught a glimpse of the packed marquee; two hundred people, the girls all dressed up in red wigs with sparkles in their hair to look like Celia Jones, clutching books and silver pens. They looked so happy and excited that she had felt ashamed. In a moment some flunkey would get up on the stage and tell them that Lizzie Kingdom wasn't going to be able to come after all and there would be tears and complaints and none of it would touch her because she would be miles away by then, cocooned in the world that Bill had created for her, protected and adrift at the same time.

She wanted to talk to Dudley. She wanted it so badly she was on the edge of screaming at Bill to give her the phone back. She felt a brief, vicious flash of anger that Amelia had done this to him. Stupid cow, how could she be so careless as to fall downstairs? And how had she managed to kill herself? If she'd broken her arm, she could have done an interview for a magazine or two, all brave and smiling through the pain, and made herself some cash so that she wasn't always leeching off Dudley. As soon as the thought was formed, she felt ashamed all over again. Amelia was dead. It was horrific. She remembered Johnny in his pageboy's outfit ten years ago. He would be sixteen now and his sister was dead.

Lizzie dug in the pocket of her jacket and took out a bag of marzipan fruits. The rich smell mingled with that of Kat's nail varnish and filled the back of the car. Fortnum's had seen her snacking on some of their sweets during a documentary behind the scenes at *Stars of the Dance* and sent her a bag every week now. She'd never been able to resist sugar in whatever form it was presented, even though her dentist told her she would have false teeth by the time she was thirty. It was comfort eating, she supposed, and that meant extra time in the gym.

Amelia. Lizzie bit hard into the marzipan centre. She had always disliked Dudley's wife even though she hadn't met her often. Their paths crossed mainly at parties and premieres; Amelia had been a pretty, waiflike blonde who had never really found a role for herself. She'd tried modelling and had some auditions for TV, or so she had confided to Lizzie, and she had featured in a number of celebrity magazines. Periodically there were articles about her latest project, pictures of her posing at Oakhangar Hall, looking glamorous in the gardens or baking up a storm in the kitchen, but none of her plans seemed to come to anything. Lizzie, who could not remember a time when she had not been working, had always thought Amelia was lazy. Everyone else seemed to feel sorry for her. Even Bill, tougher than old boots, had once said he thought Amelia was as fragile as a butterfly. Lizzie had thought she was a different sort of insect, a parasitic one.

"Shit," Bill said suddenly. "This is just everywhere. The media are crucifying Dudley."

"Can I have my phone back, please?" Lizzie said. "I want to talk to Dudley. And I really need to tweet how sorry I am to hear about Amelia." She waited, but Bill was engrossed in scanning his own phone and didn't move. So was Kat; the brightness of the screens lit up the interior of the car and made Lizzie's eyes sting.

"I don't see what fault it is of Dudley's," Lizzie said, annoyed that they were both ignoring her. "I mean, he wasn't even at Oakhangar when it happened, was he? He told me he was going to see friends in Brighton—"

Bill interrupted her. "They're saying that Amelia may have taken her own life," he said. "That she threw herself down the stairs because Dudley had told her a couple of weeks ago he was divorcing her. Shit. Fuck. This is a mess." He shot Lizzie a quick look over his shoulder. "Did you know about the divorce? Did Dudley tell you?"

Lizzie wriggled on the sumptuous leather seat. She had the same feeling she had had on numerous occasions as a child, a sense that something very bad was about to happen and it wasn't her fault but that was beside the point and she would take the blame anyway.

"He might have mentioned it to me last month…" she muttered.

"Shit, Lizzie!" Bill exploded again. "He mentioned it to you before he told his *wife*? What is *wrong* with the pair of you?"

"We're *friends*," Lizzie said mutinously. "We've been friends since I was six years old, Bill, so it's no wonder we're close, is it? Dudley confides in me."

Bill muttered another expletive under his breath. "It's unhealthy, Lizzie," he said. "Frankly you both come across as weird and needy."

Lizzie ignored him and looked out of the window. It was dark outside the car now, the last vestiges of evening light fading from the sky. They were driving fast, on a motorway somewhere but she had no idea where they were or where they were going. No one had told her. Suddenly she felt so tired. They moved her around like a piece on a chessboard and never told her a damn thing.

Bill turned in his seat so that he could look at her properly. Lizzie felt a rush of irritation that another lecture would be forthcoming and kept her gaze firmly averted from his. "Did you also know that Amelia had been in hospital?" Bill asked, his voice deceptively soft. "Apparently she was suffering from depression and she'd become addicted to prescription painkillers. She was taking them for migraines or something, and seeing a whole raft of specialists." He shook his head irritably. "Whatever. Anyway,

Dudley had been paying for her rehab at Melton Abbey until last week when she went home to Oakhangar."

Lizzie hunched deeper into her jacket. She felt a coldness seeping through her body, a mind-numbing, bone-crunching chill like frost setting hard. She had had no idea that Amelia was ill. She thought about the paralysing sense of despair that depression brought with it, the flat darkness that stretched forever, the lack of any sense of joy and the hideous loneliness. She knew what it felt like to be on one side of that plate glass pane so that nothing, no sound, no sight, no love, could touch her. She'd lived with that, off and on, for so many years, ever since her mother's death. It seemed she had more in common with Amelia than she had known.

Lizzie shuddered. Desperately she rummaged in her pockets but the bag of marzipan, she was disappointed to find, was empty. Instead she let her fingers creep to her throat and the oak leaf necklace she always wore. It was a talisman; it grounded her.

"Where are you getting this stuff from?" she asked. "It sounds like tabloid rubbish to me. You know how they exaggerate." She tucked her chin into her collar, seeking warmth, but the car was stuffy and the coldness was within her not outside. "We've all been depressed," she said, hating herself even as she said the words. "It doesn't mean you throw yourself down the stairs."

"Jesus, Lizzie," Bill said. "We're talking clinical depression here, not feeling a bit low one day. Sometimes it's hard to like you, you know."

"Don't say that, Bill," Kat said, putting a comforting hand on Lizzie's arm. "Don't forget what Lizzie's been through herself. Can't you see she's hurting? She doesn't mean to sound callous."

Lizzie felt Kat's hand on her sleeve. Kat's touch was comforting; it said that she understood that Lizzie was miserable, lost in painful memories, and that she wanted to pretend she wasn't. In that moment Lizzie hated her for knowing. The trouble was that Kat had known her forever, since she had been a baby. Kat, her mother's best friend, had stepped in when a car crash had claimed Annie Kingdom at a shockingly young age. She'd taken Lizzie under her wing, attempting to soften the haphazard and destructive parenting methods of Lizzie's father. She'd been in Lizzie's life ever since. There could be no secrets from Kat.

She shook Kat's hand off. She wasn't going to show her that it mattered.

"I still don't see that it's Dudley's fault even if Amelia did kill herself," she argued. "They hadn't been close for years. They never saw each other; it was as though they were already separated really and Amelia must have known that Duds would want a divorce sooner or later."

"Amelia's friends are queuing up to say how unhappy she was." Bill was scrolling through his Twitter feed now. "Jeez, this is bad. They're saying she killed herself because Dudley spent all his time with you."

"It's nothing to do with me," Lizzie said, through her teeth. "And do they *know* it's suicide? It might just be an accident."

"Or murder," Kat said. "One of the gossip sites is insinuating Dudley might have arranged it." Her head was bent, long dark hair falling forward to hide her expression. Lizzie thought she sounded excited. "They say he wanted to save on the settlement so he bumped her off."

Lizzie felt a clutch of fear. "They're saying Dudley killed her? That's just…" She raised her hands in despair. "Please stop this, Kat. It's stupid and you're scaring me now."

Neither Bill nor Kat paid her the slightest notice. They were both too engrossed in the breaking news.

"Didn't they have a prenup agreement?" Bill was saying. "Christ! Doesn't everyone have one these days?"

"They married so young." Kat looked up from her phone. "Don't you remember, Bill? It was very romantic. Love at first sight. Amelia was only about seventeen and Dudley not much more. They married at Oakhangar and there were thrones and a crystal horse-drawn carriage, and they released rare butterflies—"

"Which all died because they couldn't cope with the British climate," Lizzie interrupted. "The RSPCA threatened to prosecute Dudley for cruelty." The scar in her palm itched sharply. She clenched her fingers over it. She hadn't thought about Dudley and Amelia's wedding for years. It hadn't been a favourite memory.

Bill made a huffing sound. "Cruelty, huh? That seems like a metaphor for the whole marriage." He shook his head. "Whether it's murder or suicide, this is a godawful mess."

"Hello?" Lizzie waved a hand. "Excuse me? Why can't it just be a simple accident? Horrible, I know—" she winced "—but it doesn't have to be either sinister or Dudley's fault."

"Quite right, babes," Kat said in the sort of absent-minded voice that Lizzie knew meant she was paying no attention at all. "Although the BBC is saying that the police are investigating."

"Good," Lizzie said. "Perhaps that will shut everyone

up." She sat forward. "I'd like my phone back now, please, Bill, and I'd also like to be taken to London. I don't know where we're going but I need to be back for rehearsals for *Stars of the Dance* next week."

"I think that would be a bad idea," Bill said slowly. "You'll come in for a lot of flak, especially as Dudley's taking part too. Perhaps you should lie low for a week or so."

Lizzie sat up straighter. "What? Why?"

"Dudley's dropped out of *Stars of the Dance*," Kat interrupted. "His people are making an announcement in fifteen minutes." She looked at Lizzie. "Do you think you should say something too?"

"No!" Lizzie said, before she could finish. "No way! This is absolutely nothing to do with me!"

"I agree," Bill said. "With any luck they'll pull this week's show anyway as a mark of respect since it's only two days away. A couple of the other contestants were Amelia's friends, weren't they?" He didn't wait for Lizzie to respond. "But then it's back to business. We don't want it to look like it was in any way Lizzie's fault no matter what social media is saying."

"Lulu Styles is giving a live interview on *AListed*," Kat reported. "She says that Amelia was depressed because she thought she could never compete with Lizzie." Kat turned up the volume and the tinny sound of Lulu's voice echoed around the car: "Amelia said Lizzie Kingdom already had it all but she wanted Dudley as well."

Lizzie shuddered to hear the naked excitement in the interviewer's voice: "You mean Amelia thought they were having an affair?"

"Oh God, no." Lulu sounded contemptuous. "Lizzie's kind of sexless, isn't she? But she and Dudley were so *cute* together, like they were still six years old. Amelia said she couldn't compete with that sort of friendship. She never got a look-in."

"Why are people making this story about me?" Lizzie locked her fingers together so tightly she heard her bones crack, heard too the thread of hysteria in her voice. "Amelia Lester falls down the stairs and I'm somehow to blame? It's horrible…" Her words caught on a sob.

"I did tell you," Bill said heavily. "I did tell you to keep the hell away from Dudley Lester but you wouldn't listen."

"Now isn't the time, Bill," Kat said sharply. Her voice became soothing as she turned back to Lizzie. "We all know it's not your fault, honey," she said. "But you know how it works; the media want to use your name for the publicity, that's all." She rummaged in her bag. "Here, have some of these." Lizzie heard the rattle of pills. "Just a little one. You'll feel much better."

"I don't want your fucking pills." Tears filled Lizzie's eyes. She despised herself. *Why am I such a child? Why can't I deal with this? Why did bloody Amelia Lester have to die?*

"I want to talk to Dudley," she said forlornly. "He needs me. There's no one else he can talk to."

"The less you have to do with this the better," Bill said. "Normally I'd be arguing for you to get all the publicity you can but this is toxic, Lizzie. You need to keep out of it for the sake of your career. Anyway, Dudley's got his family. Let him talk to them."

"Dudley and I *always* support each other," Lizzie said. "It's what we do."

"That's what I'm trying to tell you," Bill said grimly. "That's the problem."

"We're only trying to look after you, honey," Kat said.

"Really we are. Bill's right; this could ruin everything for you. It's got to be handled properly."

"I know," Lizzie said. Bill and Kat were right; this whole scandal could ruin her image and her career. She had to be careful. Suddenly she felt exhausted. The need to go to Dudley, to comfort him when so much horrible stuff was swirling around, was deep and instinctive. But it wasn't stronger than the survival instinct. That was the deepest and most visceral of all. She had worked so hard for everything she had, faced down the scandal of her parents' disastrous marriage and her sleazy father's endless affairs. A shiver racked her.

"Lizzie's kind of sexless, isn't she?"

She could still hear the bite in Lulu's tone. So what if it was true? If she controlled every detail of her life and her image it couldn't go wrong—or so she had thought until now.

She needed more than the necklace to ground her now that the world was swinging violently awry. She burrowed into the pocket of her coat again. Deep in the corner, next to the empty sweet wrappers, she found the little perfume bottle. The scent had been her mother's favourite, or so she'd been told, a classic of the nineties, smelling of summer flowers and vanilla. The bottle was long empty but the perfume lingered like the memory of a sweet dream and it was one of the few small mementoes she had.

She thought of the pitifully small collection of her mother's belongings that she had salvaged after she had died. She'd been like a child thief, surreptitiously gathering things up when her father's back was turned, a discarded book here, a T-shirt there, a cheap bracelet, even a battered phone card and a bus ticket. The housekeeper had bundled up all her mother's gorgeous clothes, bags and shoes and thrown them away in plastic bags; her books had been given to a charity shop. Her jewellery, Lizzie suspected, had been given to her father's new girlfriend. Harry Kingdom hadn't been the subtle type. They had only been married for a few years and Lizzie thought it had been easy for him to erase Annie Bowling from his life, burning the photographs, obliterating all evidence that she had existed. The one thing it hadn't been possible to obliterate was the four-year-old girl with his red hair but Annie's brown eyes and sharp, curious mind, although Lizzie sometimes thought that if her father could have got rid of her too, he would have done. Consigning her to Kat's care and then sending her to boarding school had been his way of dealing with her; until he had realised that he could profit from her talent.

Her fingers rubbed back and forth over the familiar shape of the perfume bottle. She knew all the lines and curves of it by touch alone and usually the contact with one of her mother's possessions brought her comfort and sometimes more—images of her mother, an echo of her emotions. Not tonight, though. Tonight she felt nothing. There was no comfort. She felt utterly alone. The old scar on the palm of her right hand itched viciously, a reminder of Amelia, and Oakhangar, and the nightmare of the wedding.

"I don't know where you're taking me," she said, "but I want to see Jules. She'll let me stay for a few days."

It was the place she always ran to when she was in trouble. Her cousin Juliet Carey was the only person who treated her as though she was normal. Not that Lizzie knew what normal was any more if she ever had, but Juliet's chaotic household was the closest to it that she could find.

She saw Bill and Kat exchange a look and then Kat gave a tiny nod and Bill dove in his pocket and extracted her phone. Lizzie saw him scroll through the numbers and punch in the one for Jules before he handed it to her.

The number rang and rang. Jules didn't believe in answering services.

"Didn't Jules say they were all going to France for a couple of weeks camping?" Kat said. Both her tone and her expression conveyed her utter bafflement at the thought of spending any time in a tent. For Kat, even the most luxurious glamping would be too primitive.

"Oh yeah…" With a sigh Lizzie ended the connection. She really was on her own then. Her only close friend was working abroad and there was no one else she would want to turn to at a time like this, no other friends, no family, only a raft of acquaintances who would sell her out to the press as soon as look at her.

Immediately her phone rang.

"Don't answer it," Bill said. "Turn it off."

Lizzie thought about ignoring him and calling Dudley but then Kat exclaimed: "Dudley's giving a press conference!"

Lizzie switched off the phone and stuffed it into her pocket. Kat glanced up at her then back at her screen. Once again, the tinny sound of voices filled the car:

"I'm distraught at the loss of my beautiful wife, Amelia." Dudley's voice sounded blurred by tears. "It was a terrible accident. I don't even want to address the other horrible rumours which have already sprung up and are nothing but hurtful lies. I only ask that my family and I are given respect whilst we grieve."

"Dear God," Bill said, "he looks terrible. And he sounds like one of those guys whose wife disappears, and he makes a public plea for her to come home knowing all along that he's murdered her and hidden the body. Jeez."

Kat's reply was overwhelmed by the cacophony from the phone as reporters scrambled to ask questions.

"Turn it off," Lizzie said irritably. "Please, Kat. I'm begging you." Tears stung her eyelids. She wanted to speak to Dudley, to comfort him and draw comfort from him just as she had when they were growing up together. She wanted to hug him and feel his arms about her. They made each other feel safe. Yet she had a horrible suspicion that everything had changed and they could never be so close, or so happy, ever again. It had all seemed so simple; the two of them against the world. Yet Amelia had always been there even when Lizzie had almost forgotten her. Her shadow had always been cast across them, the figure glimpsed out of the corner of her eye, the spectre.

Kat finally snapped off the sound on her phone just as Bill's mobile rang again. He listened in sharp silence.

"There's been a change of plan," he said, as he ended the call. "We will be going back to London after all. The police want to interview you tomorrow, Lizzie."

"Fine," Lizzie said sulkily. "Whatever. I don't know anything anyway."

"The lawyers will brief you first thing," Bill said.

"Fine," Lizzie said again with a half shrug.

"This is serious," Bill said with a warning note in his voice. "They haven't dismissed the possibility of murder."

Lizzie rolled her eyes. "Bill, this is ridiculous."

"Just do what the lawyers tell you," Bill said. He settled his shoulders back against the seat and fumbled for a cigar. "Must you smoke?" Lizzie said. "It's bad for your health." Bill swore but he put the cigar away. The car took the next motorway exit and headed back the way they had come. Soon there was nothing around Lizzie but the rustle and hum of the car as it sped through the dark, nothing but the endless photos on her phone screen showing her laughing with Dudley on the set of *Stars of the Dance*, juxtaposed with ones of Amelia looking frail and ill, nothing but the tumbling words of hate mail already flooding into her social media accounts. The images spun a pattern in Lizzie's head over and over, around and around until she finally slept.

6

Amy: Sheen Palace, June 1550

I MET HER first on my wedding day.

Robert's elder brother John had married the day before us, in a great ceremony of pomp and display. The boy King Edward had attended and had taken much pleasure at the masques and banqueting which had surprised me for I'd known him only as a studious youth not much given to laughter. Robert had presented me to him when first I had come to court. I had already divined that he was serious to the point of tedium, which I suppose was all very well for a king but made him a dull companion. Robert told me he was very clever but that did not impress me; intelligence without wit seemed dry to me. He had been flanked by his advisers, Robert's father Lord Warwick, all elegance and dark intensity, and the Duke of Somerset.

The two men seemed to tower over the boy king like tall trees above a sapling, blocking out the light.

John Dudley had married the eldest of Somerset's daughters, Anne Seymour, a pale and pious creature who was very aware of her own value. My marriage to Robert was an altogether smaller affair as befitted his status as a younger son and mine as a gentleman's daughter. There were sore heads and dull eyes from the previous night's revels but all the nobility was there for this pale echo of a Dudley marriage. It should have been the best day of my life.

Amongst that congregation of the nobility in St George's Chapel I saw her at once, the Princess Elizabeth. It was not that she was particularly animated, or brightly dressed or hung with jewels. She was quiet and pale and demure, her skin like fine Chinese porcelain, but her hair blazed like fire and the contrast of that red gold with the dark brown of her eyes was arresting, a physical shock. I knew her immediately: the Princess Elizabeth was half-sister to the King, daughter of the scandalous Queen Anne Boleyn, her life already mired in bloodshed and treason.

Robert had spoken of her a little, for they had shared a tutor when young. "She is clever," he had said. "As clever as any man, and witty and sharp as a needle."

He had not mentioned that she was beautiful and for some reason this disturbed rather than pleased me. Perhaps Elizabeth's looks were not of such conventional prettiness as mine but it was a woman's lot to be prized for her beauty and sweet nature rather than her wit. King Henry had worshipped Anne Boleyn for the quickness of her mind and that had not served her to any great purpose. Yet suddenly I was not so pleased with the portrait that

Robert had commissioned of me from the King's min-
iaturist as a wedding gift. It seemed that with me he saw
only the surface but with the Lady Elizabeth he saw and
valued what was beneath.

Telling myself that I was full of foolish imaginings, I
concentrated on the words of the marriage service and on
my new husband. He looked gravely handsome; although
he smiled at me, on one occasion I saw him glancing over
the heads of the congregation as his gaze sought her out.
Yet it was nothing, or so I told myself. There were many
women present and many of those smiled at Robert. I
could not be jealous of them all.

When the service was concluded my father swept me up
into his embrace, kissing me exuberantly on both cheeks.
He was pleased with me and very proud, and that warmed
me. My mother too; finally, she had relented and given
us her blessing although I sensed that beneath the good
wishes, she had not changed her opinion of Robert and
his reckless ambition. I did not ask her though. I did not
want to know the truth and damage the bond between us.

I was surrounded by friends and family congratulating
me; the faces spun about me like a whirling top and in
the mêlée I lost sight of Robert. It was odd how even at
my own wedding I seemed to get lost in the crowd, overlooked amongst the peacocking crowd of courtiers, and
without my husband I felt inconsequential and vulnerable. The King and his attendants swept out to attend the
feast. My new father-in-law strode away without a glance
in my direction whilst the Seymour girls looked down
their aristocratic noses and whispered behind their hands.

My mother was tugging on my arm. "Where is Robert?"
I did not know. "I'll find him," I said.

She matched my steps back down the empty aisle of the chapel. I wished she would not accompany me but did not feel I could dismiss her. Now that the church was no longer crammed with guests it looked huge and grand, a whispering gallery of all the moments in time and history the place had witnessed. Yet the whispering was real. I could hear it, soft but persistent.

"I will not fail you. I'll never fail you. I swear it."

I found them behind a pillar on the south side of the transept where the sunlight fell through the window glass to make distorted puddles of light on the stone. The light was also on her upturned face, for Robert was taller than she. Once again, I was struck by her pallor and delicacy, so much at odds with the fierce will that showed in her eyes. They were standing very close together and their hands were clasped. I saw a strand of her red gold hair brush against his cheek.

My mother gave a sharp gasp beside me. Robert straightened; turned. I could not understand the expression I saw on his face. It was too complex, too far from anything in my experience. There was love and protectiveness, but not the lust I had expected. Nor did he look guilty or ashamed. He let go of her hands so slowly and then he bowed to her with elaborate charm.

"I am sorry that you do not feel well enough to attend the wedding feast, madam," he said. "I will see you are escorted to your rooms."

Elizabeth nodded. "Thank you." Her golden-brown gaze dwelt on my face for a moment, mercilessly devoid of warmth. "I wish you joy on your marriage, Mistress Dudley," she said, then slipped past me and disappeared into the shadows of the church.

Mother opened her mouth to speak and I pinched her arm hard to quiet her.

"There you are, my dear," I said lightly to Robert, as though we had been married for years, as though there was nothing amiss at all. "Your father bids us to the feast. Once you have seen the Lady Elizabeth safely to her quarters, of course." And I stood aside to let him follow her down the nave and did not look at him at all.

7

Lizzie: Present Day

LIZZIE WOKE SUDDENLY. In her dream she had
been falling, the crystal gazing ball shattering in her hands,
spilling blood across the flagstones of the floor. She lay
still, gasping for breath, as her mind caught up with reality;
her sweat-drenched pyjamas, the pounding in her head.
She opened her eyes and saw the familiar outlines of her
bedroom in the half-light of an early autumn dawn. The
thundering of her heart settled a little. She was at home,
she was alone and she knew she ought to feel reassured
but the dregs of the dream still lingered and her mind was
shadowed with something formless and dark.

The day before had been vile. The lawyers had arrived
to brief her at eight for her interview at Blackfriars police
station at eleven. She'd only been listening to them with

half an ear because really, Amelia Lester's death had nothing to do with her and she was only helping police with their inquiries to build up a fuller picture of Dudley and Amelia's life, or so she had told herself. She had toyed with her fruit juice whilst a smooth corporate brief told her the facts of Amelia's death: that she had been found by one of the cleaners at the bottom of the stairs on the afternoon of 8th September. She had been alone in the house at the time except for a couple of members of staff who had been busy and had apparently heard nothing. Her neck had been broken and there were a couple of bruises on her face but she had no other injuries. That was as far as the facts went; the rest was just lurid speculation.

Lizzie had hidden her shock at hearing the stark details. It sounded a horrible way to die, so sudden and so lonely. She knew that the lawyers, like Bill, thought she was a cold bitch because she didn't cry for Amelia. They were as practised at hiding their emotions as she was but she could see the disgust in their eyes. She knew she had to be strong, though. With Dudley in pieces there was no one else. She didn't want Kat's gossipy sympathy; from the earliest age she was accustomed to dealing with crap all by herself. She just wanted to get on with it.

When Lizzie arrived at the police station it was clear someone had tipped off the press. They had to fight their way through the crowds just to get inside. The legal team stuck to her like limpets, often jumping in before she had the chance to answer any very simple questions which Lizzie thought made her look guilty and stupid. By the time she left two hours later she was in a foul mood and had a blinding headache. Outside, the crowd had doubled in size; Dudley had arrived, looking attractively haggard and rumpled. His tired face had lit up when he saw Lizzie but Bill wouldn't let her speak to him and shoved her into the waiting limo like a prison officer hustling away a convict.

Bill and Kat took her off to some sort of "safe house" after that, presumably a place Bill used for all the celebs he managed who blotted their careers with drink driving or drugs offences. Lizzie had never been there before and found it infinitely depressing. There was nothing to do except scroll through social media absorbing all the poison people were saying about her until she felt sick to the stomach. She didn't want to look at it yet somehow, she couldn't help herself. It was a compulsion. She tried to distract herself with music videos and films but she couldn't concentrate for more than a minute or two, jumping up, pacing the flat, whilst Bill was endlessly on the phone or flicking through news coverage and Kat chattered on her phone to family and friends about all kinds of inconsequential things. By the evening Lizzie was at screaming pitch. Then Dudley did another press conference and they all crowded around the screen.

"I'm innocent of any crime," Dudley said, so plaintive and puppyish with his sad face on. "The false accusations and fake news are truly hurtful at this difficult time. I can only hope that the police will swiftly exonerate me and I can be left to grieve in peace."

"I'm going home," Lizzie said, pushing aside the box of chicken tacos that Kat was offering her. "I've had enough." She wanted to see Dudley or at the very least, talk to him. She rang his number as soon as she got in the taxi but the call went to voicemail immediately. She felt annoyed that he was call-screening her along with everyone else.

"Dudley," she said, when the tape beeped at her to leave a message, "I'm thinking of you. Call me when you can." But he hadn't called back and when she rang again the line was dead.

Now she sat up in bed and reached automatically for the phone only to find that the battery was flat. Swearing under her breath she groped for the charger lead and plugged it in. In a minute she would try calling Dudley again.

The flat was quiet. That was unusual. In theory Lizzie lived alone but it never seemed to be like that. There was always someone hanging around; usually Kat or her family and friends, or Lizzie's ex-bandmates, or Dudley with or without one of his brothers, or other friends, people whose connection to her was so tenuous that sometimes she had no idea who they were. Today however, there was a stillness about the place that would have frightened her if she had allowed herself to think about it.

Lizzie stretched and, finding that she felt wide awake, got out of bed and wandered over to the huge windows that looked out across the river. She hadn't thought to draw the curtains the previous night and the whole panorama of London was spread out in front of her in the sullen grey of a Monday morning, the dome of St Paul's Cathedral piercing the sky just to the north-east. The river, greyest of all, shone like dull silk under the twinkle of a million lights from cranes, office buildings and vehicles. Although no sound penetrated the triple glazing up here, Lizzie knew she only needed to open the door and step onto the balcony to hear the roar of the city, to smell it and taste it. London was feral and she loved that about it. It helped her feel alive.

The TV remote was lying on the table by the window, next to her computer tablet. Lizzie felt her palms itch with the urge to pick up one or both. She wondered what people were saying about her this morning. None of it could be good, she was sure of that. The compulsion to read the whole, horrible, sickening onslaught of comments felt almost too strong to resist. She didn't know why she would want to torture herself with it knowing it would make her feel worse than she already did. For some reason she had become almost as much of a focus for public disapproval as Dudley had in the wake of Amelia's death. People were so fickle. She'd gone from being the sweetheart of children's TV to being a pariah.

When she gave in to temptation, opened her tablet and clicked on the news app, it was even worse than she had imagined. The story of Amelia's death and the fact that she and Dudley had been questioned by police led many of the reports. Rumours and conspiracy theories appeared to be rife, suggestions that Amelia had been pushed down the stairs, reports that witnesses had seen someone lurking around the house that afternoon. It was all very sensational and Dudley seemed to be making matters a great deal worse for himself, protesting his innocence of any crime, giving interviews, sounding like an aggrieved child.

Lizzie put the tablet down and turned away from the window. She had rehearsals for *Stars of the Dance* that morning. The show was going ahead and Lizzie was determined to be there. She was a professional and it was work, whatever Bill's advice. A car was coming for her at ten. She felt a pang of nerves at the thought of facing everyone. Not that it mattered; she had a horrible feeling that when the time came for the public vote, she would be sent home from the show. The cutesy little dance routines that had played up her fun and wholesome image suddenly seemed to jar horribly with the reality of Amelia's death.

The shower was hot, refreshing, and yet Lizzie's mind still felt fuzzy and disconnected in some way. The nightmare lingered, reminding her of Amelia and Dudley's wedding and the sense of terror as the crystal smashed and she'd felt as though she was falling. Was that how Amelia had felt in those brief few seconds before she broke her neck? Cold sweat broke out over Lizzie's body and she grabbed a towel and wrapped it tightly around her.

She gathered her stuff together automatically and shoved it into her bag. She needed something to help her focus this morning. She needed to ground herself. She glanced at the drawer in her bedside table but then she hesitated. When she had touched the perfume bottle two nights ago nothing had happened; she had been unable to connect to her mother's memory or derive any comfort or reassurance from the link to the past. Suppose that happened again? She used her gift of psychometry so rarely. It was secret and precious. If she reached out and failed, she knew she would feel even more empty and alone than she did now.

She slid the drawer open. It was full of a mixture of lip salve, earplugs, pens, crumpled tissues, a writing pad, headache pills… Her fingers touched a plastic wrapper and she pulled it out from beneath the pile of litter, a programme for an iconic rock concert in the 1980s. Really she should treat it better, but she needed it near her when she slept and somehow it felt appropriate for one of the few mementoes her mother had left her to be tangled up with lipstick and tissues and powder.

She took the programme out of the plastic bag, her fingers sliding over the smooth cover. For a moment nothing happened and the gap of time left a moment for her to worry that the gift—if that was what it was—really had left her. But then the sensations came to her. It was not simply a vision; it felt as though she was actually there. She could feel the sun on her, fiercely hot, and the spray of water that hit her bare arms like a cold shock. She heard the roar of the crowd and sensed the electric atmosphere about her. The world was alight. She felt excited, pulsing with adrenaline and intense pleasure.

She was Annie Bowling, twenty years old. There was so much she wanted to do, so much of life to explore. A boy was sitting beside her; she was holding his hand but they could not keep still; the music was around them and in them. It was a part of them and they were a part of the whole, and they leaped up and danced and kissed, and Lizzie could feel the tumble of emotion inside; the love, the happiness, the sweet sense of fun, a life that was simple and easy...

Lizzie opened her eyes. Her cheeks were wet with tears. The feeling of happiness was fading away now, leaving only an echo of emotion. She touched the programme one more time: LIVE AID, 13 JULY 1985. At the bottom, beneath a picture that was still crayon bright, were the words *This programme saves lives*. It had certainly saved hers on more than one occasion. Connecting to the mother she had never really known, knowing that there was a time when her mother had been happy, when her life had been uncomplicated and exciting, gave Lizzie strength.

Carefully she put the programme away in its bag and slipped it back into its place beneath the make-up and the pills. She felt bereft but steadier too. When she came out of the bedroom, Kat was in the living room, perched on the leather sofa, waiting to go to the dance studio with her. Kat had her own key to Lizzie's flat and came and went as she pleased. In the past Lizzie hadn't minded. Kat had been a part of her life forever and it seemed natural. Today, though, for the first time it irritated her that Kat would just walk in unannounced, essentially doing her job as she had done it for the past ten years or more.

I'm an ungrateful bitch, Lizzie thought, and gave Kat an extra-warm hug to make up for her thoughts.

"Are you ready to go, babes?" Kat was looking very smart, from which Lizzie judged that the press must be outside. She made no reference to Lizzie flouncing out on her and Bill the previous day, taking it in her stride the way she had dealt with so many other dramas in Lizzie's life.

"Sure." Lizzie picked up her gym bag. She still felt jittery and vulnerable, not wanting to face the waiting cameras. She straightened her shoulders. If Jules was here her cousin would tell her to get some steel in her backbone.

They went out into the foyer and Kat called the lift. It was so quiet in here, protected, soundless, a padded box. It was almost a shock when the lift doors opened and one of Lizzie's neighbours, a hedge fund manager called Natasha, stepped out and smiled at her.

"Hi, Lizzie," she said. "I guessed the paps were all here for you."

"Sorry," Lizzie said, cringing a little. "I seem to be bringing the place into disrepute."

Kat looked up from her phone in surprise as though anyone would find press interest a problem and Lizzie and Natasha exchanged another smile as they passed.

There was silence again as the lift descended. Kat seemed

engrossed in WhatsApp. Lizzie tapped her foot. The lift doors opened. Lizzie stepped forward.

"Whoa!" Kat caught her arm at the same moment that the noise and chaos hit like a tidal wave. Normally the security guards kept the press firmly outside the building but today the elegant marble-floored foyer was full of people. At least three uniformed security officers were struggling to restrain a slight blond youth in jeans and a grey hoodie who was fighting them off as though his life depended on it. Jason, the normally imperturbable duty manager, was shouting urgently down the phone whilst people flooded in from the street, taking pictures and videos.

"I want to see Lizzie Kingdom!" the boy was shouting. "I know she's here. Let me see her!"

"Sir—" one of the security guards was saying. "I'm asking you to stop fighting and lower your voice—"

"Shit," Kat said. She had frozen on the spot, her hand still resting on Lizzie's arm. "That's Johnny Robsart, Amelia's little brother." She hit the doors open button and tried to drag Lizzie back into the lift but it was too late; it had shot off back up to the top floor. "Shit," Kat said again, "this is a mess."

Johnny struggled out from beneath the weight of security and stared straight at Lizzie. She could see in the teenager the child she had met just the once, at Amelia and Dudley's wedding. The planes and angles of his face had sharpened and he was painfully thin. The wide blue eyes she had thought she remembered had darkened and reminded Lizzie of Amelia, although Amelia had always referred to her eye colour as lilac. Johnny's skin was so white it was almost translucent and there were purple smudges beneath his eyes. For one long moment they looked at each other and Lizzie felt the shock of his grief and anger like a physical blow. Then as he started forward towards her, one of the guards caught him in an arm lock and wrenched him backwards.

"For God's sake," Lizzie said, "let go of him—"

"Lizzie!" Johnny shouted. "Help me!" He started to cry. "I only want to talk. I need your help…" His voice broke on the words.

Lizzie flinched. She saw Johnny try to turn his head away to hide his tears but the way that the security guard was holding him made it impossible. His raw vulnerability was on show for all to see. He twisted from one side to the other, desperately trying to free himself. It was painful to witness so much distress and for one terrible moment it struck a chord deep inside Lizzie, drawing her back, reminding her of the dark suffocating press of her own grief when her mother had died, a grief she had pushed away for so many years until finally it had refused to be ignored. She swallowed hard and tore her gaze away from Johnny, stepping back, bumping into Kat in her eagerness to get away from the scene and the memories it brought with it.

"Let him go," she said. Her words came out hoarsely and she cleared her throat. "If he needs to talk to me then let him."

"I wouldn't advise it, Ms Kingdom." Jason had come to stand beside her. "Mr Robsart is disruptive and could be dangerous. The police are on their way."

"Lizzie!" Johnny yelled over his shoulder at her as they dragged him away from her. "Please! Let me talk to you."

"He needs help…" Kat said, putting an arm about Lizzie. "Come away, hon. Let the professionals deal with it. You need to get to the studio. We'll be late—"

"I don't care," Lizzie said. She shook off Kat's restraining arm and hurried across the concourse. Johnny was being manhandled towards the door and the crowd retreated before him with camera phones still flashing.

"Ms Kingdom—" Jason interposed his bulk between her and Johnny. "Wait—"

"Let go of my brother or I'll have you up on an assault charge."

Lizzie turned to find herself looking into the impossibly dark, impossibly angry eyes of Arthur Robsart. Even though she wasn't touching Johnny and Arthur's words weren't addressed to her, she found herself stepping back at the authority in his tone.

She hadn't seen Arthur since Amelia's wedding ten years before yet for a moment it felt as though no time had elapsed at all. She remembered the way he had bound up the cut on her hand with a dispassionate efficiency that hadn't hidden the fact he was exasperated with her. The look he was giving her now made his manner then seem positively warm.

The security guard dropped Johnny as though he'd been scalded. Johnny half stumbled, half fell into Lizzie's arms, only to be wrenched away from her by a blonde girl who had dashed inside in Arthur's wake. Lizzie vaguely recognised her as Anna, Amelia's younger sister. It had been a while since they'd met.

"Darling Johnny," Anna was saying. "Don't. Don't cry. It will all be all right." She glared at Lizzie like a tigress as she cradled Johnny close, stroking his hair. "Haven't you done enough harm, monopolising Dudley?" she demanded. "You're not getting your claws into Johnny as well."

Lizzie's mouth dropped open in shock. She knew it was unlikely that Anna would be her biggest fan, but the naked hostility took her aback.

"I was only trying to help," she said.

"Well, don't." Anna had an arm about her brother and was steering him towards the exit now. "Arthur—" She jerked her head towards the door. "We're leaving."

Arthur, who had been talking swiftly and quietly to Jason, broke off with a nod and followed his siblings out of the wide plate glass doors of the lobby and down the steps to a waiting taxi. Kat waited a discreet interval and then came steaming across to Lizzie's side, all outraged indignation now that Anna had gone.

"How dare she speak to you like that?" Kat fumed. "She's bloody rude!"

"She's upset," Lizzie said mechanically. She was staring after the family and caught one last glance of Johnny's pinched, unhappy face and those haunted blue eyes before he disappeared into the car. "Her sister's just died," she said. "Cut her some slack."

Kat shrugged, clearly unsympathetic. "I don't see why she's trying to blame you," she said. "That was totally uncalled for."

"Everyone is blaming me," Lizzie said tiredly. "It helps to have a target at a time like this."

"Then let them blame Dudley," Kat said. "It's his fault, not yours."

Lizzie pulled a face. The trouble was that she knew there had been some truth in Anna's words. She could shrug it off—if Dudley had preferred to spend time with her rather than with his wife, was that her fault?—but a small, nagging voice at the back of her mind said she could have behaved differently. She hadn't cared about Amelia's feelings. And now Amelia was dead.

"I didn't know Arthur was in London," Kat said, as though her celebrity radar had failed her badly. "He's practically a hermit these days." She opened her eyes wide. "He's a farmer, of all things. Can you believe it?"

"Sure," Lizzie said. "There are a lot of very good-looking farmers around."

"But he used to present all those nature and wildlife programmes with cute ducklings and baby birds," Kat protested. "He was on the TV, and he did some modelling, and then he gave it all up to go back to university. Beggars belief, doesn't it?" Her expression registered blank incomprehension. "One minute he's a celeb, and coining it in with sponsorship deals, and the next he's mucking out cows? Please! In what universe does that make any sense?"

"In one you don't inhabit," Lizzie said. She shrugged. "Not everyone wants to be a celebrity, Kat."

Kat was scrolling through her Facebook feed, talking at the same time as she tapped out messages. "Did you see that the press are linking all the recent deaths in Amelia's family?" she asked. "They've raked up the story of Amelia's mother *and* Arthur's fiancée. They're calling them the cursed celebrity family."

"That's not very catchy," Lizzie said. Even so, she shuddered. Press stories could be crass and intrusive at the best of times; introducing some sort of horror story element into a tragedy was unpleasantly sensationalist.

Kat, however, seemed hooked. "Oh. My. God," she said. "I'd forgotten how terrible Jenna looked by the end." She glanced at Lizzie. "Did you ever meet her? Jenna Gascoyne? She was in a few high-profile films but her career

tanked when she started to suffer from anorexia." Kat
paused. "Poor Jenna, she looks like a ghost in this photo.
They say she was living on tissues and laxatives. Arthur
did his best but she was beyond help. He—"

"—is coming back inside," Lizzie said. "So you'd better
stop talking about him." Her chest tightened with something akin to panic. There was no chance of getting into
the car and heading to the studio until the scrum of reporters had eased a little and the last thing she wanted
was Arthur coming in and taking up where Anna had
left off. He was crossing the foyer towards them now. Kat
smoothed her skirt and stood up a little straighter, smiling as he approached. "Wow," she breathed in Lizzie's ear.
"He is so hot."

Lizzie didn't reply. She would have categorised Arthur
as very hot indeed were it not for the fact that he was
looking at her with absolute disdain which prejudiced her
against him quite strongly. The scar on her palm where
the crystal had cut her tingled suddenly. She pressed her
hands together.

"Hi," Kat said, before Arthur could speak.

Arthur gave her a cool nod. His gaze was fixed on Lizzie
and again she felt the depth of his disapproval, all the more
powerful for not being articulated.

"Miss Kingdom," he said formally. "I'm Arthur Robsart,
Johnny's half-brother. We met once before?" he continued
as though indifferent as to whether or not she remembered.
"I wanted to apologise on Johnny's behalf. He shouldn't
have accosted you like that."

"He's upset," Lizzie said. She felt simultaneously relieved
that Arthur wasn't going to have a go at her and protective

of Johnny. "I understand how he feels," she said. "He—you—must all be going through a horrible time."

Arthur Robsart's mouth flattened with dislike. Evidently she wasn't entitled to offer sympathy to Amelia's family. "Nevertheless," he said, "Johnny won't trouble you again."

"He only wanted to talk to me," Lizzie said. "I'm sorry we didn't get the chance…" She waved a vague hand around. Under Arthur's objective scrutiny she felt embarrassed. The security guards were still standing nearby in a watchful silence, arms crossed. They were paid to protect her and they had been doing their job but it didn't feel like a good excuse.

"As I said," Arthur repeated, "he won't trouble you again." His expression was cold. He turned to go.

"Wait." Lizzie caught his sleeve.

She felt a burn of sensation against her fingers immediately. It was exactly like the feeling she had when she touched her mother's possessions, or read other objects, and yet at the same time it was completely different. She had never experienced any sort of telepathic response when touching people before. Yet now it was as though she had stepped directly into Arthur Robsart's mind.

The emotional connection was sharp, immediate and shocking. There was a buzzing in her ears like static and her mind was flooded with Arthur's feelings. She sensed his fierce love and concern for Johnny and beneath that a welter of other emotions: impatience, anger, determination and dislike, all directed towards her, alongside a strong attraction, all the more disturbing for being twinned with such animosity.

Lizzie looked up at him and saw the flare of disbelief in

his eyes before he shut all emotion down. The connection between them died abruptly like a slammed door cutting off sound. She knew Arthur had felt it too, though. She would have known even if she hadn't seen his reaction.

She felt completely shaken. She hadn't even realised she *could* read people's thoughts. It had never happened before. It wasn't the same as reading objects; that was crazy enough and she kept it to herself like a guilty secret, half believing, half fearing that it was a phenomenon conjured up by her imagination from a desperate desire to connect to her past. She had always assumed, or tried to tell herself, that it only happened because of her sense of closeness to some members of her family which meant that she associated strong memories or emotions with them. This experience with Arthur Robsart was a whole different thing. She didn't want to go there. She wasn't flaky or into spiritual stuff; she'd never wanted to contact her mother's spirit through a medium or anything like that. The thought made her shudder.

"Lizzie?" Kat prompted her, and she realised she was still holding Arthur's sleeve. "Are you OK, babes?"

Lizzie let go. "Sorry," she said, a little weakly, not daring to look at Arthur again. "I... I only wanted to say..." She risked a quick glance up at him. "I mean... Johnny will get help, won't he? He seemed so upset—"

"We'll look after him," Arthur said. Without another word he turned and walked away.

"Well!" Kat said, staring after him. "That was..."

"Weird," Lizzie said, "totally weird." She realised that she was physically shaking.

"You seemed..." Kat paused delicately. "Smitten?"

"Not exactly," Lizzie said. "I don't think he likes me much."

"Well," Kat said vaguely, "he probably thinks that you spent too much time with Dudley—"

"Whatever," Lizzie cut her off. She made a show of checking her watch. She didn't want to talk about it. "We'd better go," she said. "I've wasted enough time." She set off across the foyer to the door. Her car was waiting. The press and the crowds of onlookers turned back towards her, pushing phones and microphones close.

"Lizzie, any comment?"

"What is your connection to Johnny Robsart?"

"Have you been interviewed by the police about Amelia's death?"

Questions, questions, over and over, a cacophony beating down on her, and Lizzie, like the professional she had been from the age of five, with a smile fixed on her lips:

"Excuse me. I'm going to work. I have no comment to make at all."

8

❀

Amy: Castle Rising, Norfolk, Summer 1551

ROBERT AND I were happy that summer of 1551, or at least that is how I remember it now. Perhaps time has sweetened my recollection of those days and nights. To begin with we lodged at Ely Place in Holborn, the old bishop's palace, where the gardens reminded me a little of the country with their tumbledown walls and secretive orchards and the nightingales singing. On the hot nights of June we would run barefoot over the dew-drenched grass and make love beneath the shadows of the trees. I loved Robert so dearly then. His blatant desire for me was the balm I needed to convince me that his love for the Princess Elizabeth was no more than the courtly devotion of an old friend.

We journeyed into Norfolk too later that year. Both

my father and Lord Warwick were anxious to establish
Robert as one of the most influential landowners in the
region. He became Constable of Castle Rising, which
was no great privilege since the medieval walls were in
great decay and overrun with rabbits. We lodged in the
new buildings, which were already more than fifty years
old and leaked whenever the wind drove the rain in from
the east. Robert spoke of repairing the ruins but I knew
it would not happen. We had so little money and though
Robert was already gathering other estates and offices, I
knew that our future lay in London rather than the flat-
lands of my birth. Arthur came to see us, however, and
was his usual easy company. I had not expected him to
like Robert but they shared a passion for horses and for
riding. Robert recognised Arthur's skill with animals and
respected it. Their friendship made me happy.

My mother and my sister Anna also visited one day in
August when the fields baked in the hot sun, clattering
over the stone bridge and through the gatehouse to where
I waited in the inner bailey. I was poised to apologise for
the meanness of receiving them in such a tumbledown ruin
and then I saw Anna's face as she looked up at the soaring
towers and stone buttresses. She was completely overawed
and the sensation of triumph I felt was sweet. Her mouth
pinched, her brow furrowed and she greeted me with a
kiss that was cold as a noblewoman's charity.

"Sister…" Anna said coolly. Her awe had already
changed into resentment.

I saw Mother give her a meaningful look and then Anna
smiled at me although the smile did not reach her eyes. "It
is so good to see you again, Amy," she said, and I thought:
She wants something from me.

We went into the solar and the servants brought us ale and cold pigeon pie. We spoke of Stansfield and the harvest and our great brood of family. Mother asked after life in London, grasping eagerly for details of the court and the latest gossip. Then I saw her kick Anna under the table; an awkward silence fell, which Anna broke by clearing her throat.

"Amy," she said, "out of the love you bear me—"

Which is small, I thought.

"I would beg a small favour from you." Anna stopped. Mother was staring at her fixedly. I tried not to appear too impatient.

"As you know, my husband Antony Huddleston is not in favour with the King," Anna blurted out. Colour had come into her face now, the red of anger and embarrassment at having to ask for goodwill from the little sister she had once patronised. "It is to our eternal grief that he is overlooked, for he could offer great service to the crown."

I did not know Antony Huddleston well. He had a manor house at Sawston in Cambridgeshire and before Robert had sued for my hand in marriage he had seemed a good enough catch for Anna, the modestly dowried stepdaughter of a knight. I wondered if she ever wished I had wed first so that she could have gone to court and found herself a lord.

"Antony's Catholic sympathies make that impossible," I said coldly. "Surely you understand that? The King is not sympathetic towards papists."

Anna cast her eyes down. "Antony has recanted," she said. "He realises that the path he chose was the wrong one. I have helped him to see—"

"That Robert's position could gain him preferment," I finished for her, "as it has for our brothers."

"Amy!" Mother exclaimed. "Shame on you for playing out your childhood grudges now. You are not yet too fine a lady to escape *my* censure."

Now it was my turn to blush, with mortification. Mother was right to reprove me. It had been childish of me to take impulsive revenge and I was ashamed.

"I'm sorry," I said reluctantly, "I'll speak to Robert but I can promise nothing."

Anna looked at me with her pale blue eyes. There was something disturbing in their very blankness. I knew then that she had hated asking me for anything and that having heard my response she hated me all the more. The air in the solar suddenly felt stiflingly humid, as though her dislike was a palpable thing, smothering me. I stood up abruptly.

"Let us walk," I said. "We have no flower gardens here but the herb beds are pretty at this time of year."

Mother was all eagerness, shepherding Anna out ahead of her, chattering about the demands of running a household. There was little I could contribute to the conversation; I had always intended to take up the reins of household management but I had servants to organise everything for me now and whenever I told Robert I felt I should do more, he just laughed indulgently. "Why would you wish to dirty your hands in the pantry or make tinctures in the still room?" he would say. "You are a fine lady now."

I might have said that I wished it because I was bored, because I wanted to have a purpose and to be more than merely Mistress Dudley but I never did. How could I complain of my lot when so much good fortune was mine? Besides, things would be different when I had a child.

"It is good to have you close by, Amy," Mother said, squeezing my hand. She waited for Anna to echo the sentiment but my sister stopped instead to breathe in the scent of a briar rose growing against the barn wall, and pretended not to hear. Mother sighed.

"I hope," she continued, "that we will see you at Stansfield Manor—and perhaps even at Sawston?"

I doubted that Robert would ever consent to visit Antony and Anna, and given that she had not invited us—anyway I thought it wise to give a politician's answer and a polite smile.

"Perhaps," I said.

"Anna is expecting a child," Mother said, almost desperately. "Perhaps you will stand sponsor to it?"

My eyes met Anna's in a moment of surprising unity. Both of us deplored Mother's attempts to make us like each other more than we were able. At a distance it was entirely possible; we wrote politely to one another but had no desire to be more intimate. Thus it was sometimes with siblings. I loved Arthur but I could not love Anna.

"I congratulate you," I said to my sister, suppressing a stab of envy. Robert and I had been wed a year now and I had not yet conceived.

Anna cast down her gaze. "It is early days yet. I pray this one will go full term."

"Amen to that." On such a subject we could be in easy agreement, knowing how infinitely dangerous and difficult such matters could be.

"You should not ride back," I said impulsively. "It cannot be good for you. Take our carriage."

Mother looked gratified but Anna shook her head. "The roads are too bad," she said. "I'd rather ride."

I was still feeling affronted that night as Robert and I lay in bed together. I told him of the visit and complained how little Anna liked me. "Darling Amy," Robert said, pulling the neck of my nightgown down, kissing my bare shoulder, "how could anyone dislike you? Your sister is but sour and ugly and envious. Pay no heed."

I giggled. "Robert," I said, playfully pushing away his hands to encourage him all the more, "Anna is with child. Now for that I do envy her."

Robert laughed. "There's an easy remedy for that, sweetheart," he said. He rolled me beneath him. "We try..." His lips brushed my ear, then moved down the line of my throat, "and if at first we do not succeed, we keep trying. How does that suit you?"

"It suits me well," I admitted.

Robert's hands were moving over my body now and my skin was damp and my heart was pounding with the pleasure of it. I forgot everything. I forgot about Anna. I forgot to ask for the favour for Antony Huddleston. I never thought on it again.

9

Lizzie: Present Day

LIZZIE WORKED HERSELF hard in rehearsal that day. Partly it was to distract herself from thinking about Johnny Robsart—and Arthur. She still couldn't get hold of Dudley and felt as though she was letting him down, but what could she do if he didn't answer his phone? She could hardly go around to his flat, not without sparking a whole load more speculation. But the anxiety gnawed away at her so she focussed it all into the practice. Even Alessandro, her professional dance partner, who was a perfectionist, brought her a bottle of water and an energy bar after she had spent nine hours and skipped lunch to practise her steps for the jive.

"Take some rest, Lizzie," he said, "go home." He smiled at her. Alessandro was ridiculously handsome, almost stereotypically so with his dark puppy eyes and curling lashes. Whenever he smouldered at her during their live performances Lizzie wanted to burst out laughing. "It won't make any difference how much you practise," he said. "You dance like an angel, but…" he gave an expressive shrug, "but they will vote us off anyway when they get the chance."

"I know," Lizzie said. She snapped the top off the water bottle and took a deep gulp. "I want to do my very best all the same," she said fiercely. "I want to show everyone what a farce it is." To her horror her eyes filled with hot tears. "I'm so sorry, Al," she said. "We were good. We could have won and now it will all go wrong. It's so unfair."

Alessandro gave another very expressive shrug. "It's life, Lizzie. It's show business. You know that."

"It's still wrong," Lizzie said. "It's not your fault, is it?" Alessandro had been one of the professionals on *Stars* for four years now and had never been in the final. This time she knew he had thought he had won the jackpot and it was going to be snatched away from him because of her.

"I'm not sure it's your fault either," Alessandro said. "People say you broke up Dudley's marriage and caused his wife to kill herself." He made a scornful sound. "This is rubbish. He did that all by himself." He wrapped her in a very muscular hug. He smelled outrageously of a mixture of citrus and jasmine and something Lizzie thought was black pepper. She tried not to sneeze. It was very comforting though. She snuggled closer.

"Thanks, Al," she said. "I really need a friend at the moment."

"Hey." Alessandro released her gently and kissed her on both cheeks. "You've got plenty of friends. Come around

for supper with Christy and me sometime soon. I will cook
you proper spaghetti."

"I'd like that," Lizzie said. "As long as Christy doesn't
think I'm trying to break you up. I do seem to have a reputation as a homewrecker at the moment."

Alessandro rolled his eyes exaggeratedly. "Listen to me,
Lizzie. Dudley and Amelia got married too young. They
were infatuated with each other and when that went—"
he snapped his fingers, "there was nothing left. You are
not to blame. You are just friends, no?"

"Yes." Lizzie's head ached suddenly and she rubbed a
hand across her eyes. "We've been friends since we were
kids," she said, "but no one seems to get that. They treat
it as though it's weird."

Alessandro smiled. "It's tricky, you know? The two of
you seem very close. People are either going to think that
you're secretly having an affair, or—how you say it?—you're
kind of dependent on each other and it's a bit childish and
inappropriate?"

Lizzie pulled a face at him. "Thanks!" she said. It was
hurtful to have an outsider's view of her friendship with
Dudley spelled out in those terms even though that was
only what Kat and Bill had been trying to tell her, in
their different ways. Move on, grow up, get yourself a
boyfriend…

It wasn't that she hadn't had relationships. She'd gone out
with one of her co-presenters on *Saturday Survival School*
for six months, but somehow, he hadn't been as much fun
to hang out with as Dudley was. And there had been a
fling with a backing singer she had met on tour, and a few
other dates that hadn't amounted to much, but she worked
too hard to bother with casual relationships and spent too

much time away for serious ones, and anyway, why would she want to when she was the poster child for dysfunctional families? She knew that her parents' marriage had been a disaster area. She had stored away the fragments of memory, the tactless comments people had sometimes made, and most of all the vicious headlines from the newspapers. Harry Kingdom had been fodder for gossip and scandal long before the internet age. It was not the sort of thing Lizzie wanted to read and it had left her with the fierce belief that it was easier, safer, to be self-reliant and keep away from complications.

Alessandro shrugged. "It's true. You and Dudley, you want different things. It's not a good combination and it means you are bad for each other." He looked away as though weighing whether or not to say anything else; then he sighed. "Dudley does care for you, I think. It's sweet, but he also wants to use you. You're more successful than he is, on the way up…" He shrugged again. "You know how ambitious Dudley is. Whereas you…" He took her by the shoulders, his gaze searching her face. "I'm not sure what you want from him, Lizzie," he said slowly. "You care for him too. I realise that, and you're very loyal to him. But you're too good for him. He doesn't deserve you." His hands fell to his side. "*Cazzo!* This is none of my business. I should just shut up."

Lizzie's lips twitched. "I'm not sure what *cazzo* means, Al, but I get the general gist." She gave him a quick kiss on the cheek. "Thank you. I know you mean well. You're such a good friend."

Alessandro shook his head, said something else in Italian that she didn't understand, and wandered off to pick up his bag, giving her a casual wave as he went out. Lizzie felt bad, as though she had trivialised his kindness to her.

"Lizzie." Kat, as ever, was at her elbow. "The car's waiting."

"Thank you, Kat." Lizzie tried to shake off her dark mood but she could feel it dogging her steps as she went outside. So many people disliked Dudley. They didn't understand. It felt as though her friendship with him was always under siege. She knew that Dudley had ruffled some feathers in the carving out of his career, but so had most people. It was part of the business. There were journalists he had insulted and paparazzi whose cameras he had broken. There was a long line of bar and hotel staff across London and the world who had had to clear up after his excesses. He could be short-tempered and impatient to the point of rudeness. He made fun of people he didn't like and because he was clever, he could also be cruel. It was no wonder that some parts of the media were taking this opportunity to crucify him. She didn't like it but she could understand it. She wasn't blind to Dudley's faults. She knew he could be selfish and self-seeking. In a tiny corner of her heart she was almost prepared to admit that perhaps Bill and Alessandro were right and Dudley did use their friendship for his own advancement.

She stared unseeingly at the London landmarks as they sped past. To her, Dudley was also the boy of eight who had been the first, the only person, to speak to Lizzie when she had arrived, grief-stricken and alone, at her new school. Her mother had died, she had hated the world and been horribly rude and prickly, but somehow Dudley had understood that and had tolerated her. He had helped her with her homework until she caught up with the rest of the class and then she helped him because she was as clever if not cleverer than he was. He was interested in mathematics; Lizzie had preferred languages. They had been friends ever since. How long ago it all seemed now. She remembered how she had felt when Dudley had met Amelia. They had had a whirlwind romance and married and Lizzie had been riven with jealousy and fear to start with: fear that she would lose one of the few lasting relationships of her life. But as it had turned out, nothing had really changed. Dudley still hung out with her. They still talked about anything and everything. Soon Amelia had moved to Oakhangar Hall whilst Dudley lived most of the time in London. It had felt almost as though Amelia did not exist.

Lizzie shifted uncomfortably on the seat. The feelings she had for Dudley were deep-rooted and important to her but they were completely devoid of sexual desire. Not once in their long, intimate friendship had she felt the same shock of connection she had experienced that morning with Arthur Robsart. She had never felt such awareness, such a sense of recognition, with anyone else. In fact, now she thought about it, she had seldom been strongly attracted to anyone. It wasn't just the wariness engendered by her childhood; it had been lack of interest, almost to the point where she had wondered if there was something wrong with her.

And then she had touched Arthur and the world had exploded into sensation.

I know you.

It was stupid. It was mad. In some way it had to be connected with her gift of psychometry but she had no idea how. Yet it felt as though there was an affinity, an instinct as old as time, that drew them together. Lizzie felt the goosebumps rise over her skin. She did not want that connection to Arthur and she was certain he didn't want it either. She curled her fingers over the scar on her palm and squeezed tightly as though she could eradicate it. She told herself it didn't matter anyway. Very probably she wouldn't see Arthur again—it was hardly likely she'd be invited to Amelia's funeral—and even if she did see him, she'd make sure never, ever to touch him.

She felt restless, thoughts of Dudley, Johnny and Arthur turning over and over in her mind. As soon as she got home, she went down to the swimming pool in the basement. To her relief, it was empty. It lay flat and turquoise blue as a summer sky, the underwater lights throwing ripples and shadows upward to reflect against the white arch of the roof. There was a strong smell of chlorine and the hum of machinery, and beyond the huge glass windows the river Thames ran dark grey, another world.

Lizzie swam lengths for as long as she had the energy, counting her strokes, feeling the resistance as she carved through the water, emptying her mind of thought and focussing only on sensation, sound, light and touch. She was exhausted when she climbed out but infuriatingly, as soon as she stepped from the water, the thoughts she had kept at bay for the past hour and a half rushed back clamouring for space and attention. She wondered what Johnny had wanted to talk to her about. She wished he had had the chance to speak to her, wished she had insisted on it. Remembering the solemn child she had met at the wedding and seeing him as this damaged teenager was deeply painful. His situation resonated deeply with her. She wanted to help him and was furious with herself for standing back.

Not getting involved, avoiding emotional engagement of any sort had become something of a habit with her. She wondered whether that was why she relied so heavily on the people she had known right from the start, because she was afraid to make new connections...

She sent out for sushi and tempura scallops and settled on the balcony in her bathrobe, her laptop on her knee, watching dusk sink over the river.

Once the food had arrived, she put the boxes on the wooden table next to her, dipping into her favourite Albacore Truffle Ponzu whilst she typed Amelia Lester's name into the search box. She forced herself to scroll past all the recent lurid stuff about Amelia's death and the headlines from that morning describing her showdown with Johnny. It seemed like an age ago. Out of sheer curiosity she clicked on the Wikipedia entry that gave Amelia's family background and found that it was almost as dysfunctional as her own. Half- and step-relations littered the page; it seemed that Arthur Robsart was the eldest, the son of Amelia's father Terry and a supermodel called Layla El Ansari who originally came from Dubai but now lived in America. Terry Robsart had been a fashion photographer in the eighties and his affair with Layla had been as tempestuous as it was short. He had cheated on her with another model, Jessica Scott, whom he had gone on to marry. This second relationship had produced Amelia, Anna and Johnny before Terry was caught *in flagrante* again and Jessica walked out on him. After their divorce, Jessica had married an academic called Sam Appleyard, who worked for the British Antarctic Survey.

Lizzie scrolled through various images of the family. Terry Robsart looked startlingly like her own father, not in looks but in the fleshy, *bon viveur* style of a man who had enjoyed the finer things in life and taken them to excess. He had been a very well-known and successful photographer until he'd drunk himself into an early grave. Jessica, Amelia's mother, had also died relatively young, from cancer, a few years ago. Lizzie grimaced. Johnny could only have been about fourteen at the time and his siblings not much older. Their mother's death must have devastated their lives and now they had lost Amelia too. She pushed the hair back from her face with hands that shook a little. What utter crap people had to deal with sometimes.

A buzzing on the entry phone disturbed her. She didn't really want to see anyone this evening. She was bone-tired and wanted to sleep.

"Lizzie." It was Dudley's voice. "Let me in."

Lizzie's heart leaped with a mixture of relief and anxiety. She'd kept trying to ring Dudley and had sent him a load of texts but he hadn't replied to any of them. She jumped up, pressing the button to let him in and rushing across the flat to the door. She grabbed him as soon as he came in, wrapping her arms about him, holding him close. He felt warm and reassuring and smelled of his citrus cologne, and she almost cried at the familiarity of it.

"Dudley," she said, muffled against his shirt. "Thank God. Oh, I'm so glad to see you." She hugged him tighter. "I'm so sorry, so very sorry about everything."

It took her a moment to realise that Dudley wasn't returning the hug. He stood limp within her grasp, and when she drew back to scan his face, he looked down at her with an expression she recognised from childhood. Lizzie's heart sank. Dudley was sulking. Next would be the recriminations.

Dudley pulled away and strode across the room with restless energy to throw himself into one of the low armchairs by the window. His fair, open face was marred by a ferocious scowl.

"What the fuck?" he said, running a hand through the hair that flopped over his brow. "Where have you been when I needed you?"

"That's not fair." Lizzie felt awful, hot, guilty and miserable. "I've been working all day today. It's not as though I didn't get in touch. I tried ringing but you were always engaged or your phone was switched off. I texted you as soon as I could and I've lost count of the messages I've sent you since. I've been worried sick about you!"

Dudley stared at her, his dark eyes full of bafflement and anger. "Why didn't you come to find me?" he asked. "Oh wait—I totally get it. You're cutting me loose like everyone else. I'm toxic now. My career's over."

"What are you talking about?" Lizzie stared at him. She'd expected Dudley to be devastated; she'd imagined that he must be experiencing a whole cocktail of complex emotions about Amelia's death and the police investigation, but she hadn't expected his prime concern to be his career.

"Bill told my agent today that they've offered the co-host role on *Musical World* to Damon Wood," Dudley said. He sat forward, his gaze accusing. "I thought you and I were doing that show together?"

Lizzie spread her hands wide. "I don't know anything about it." She shook her head. "I'm sorry, that was really insensitive of Bill to do that now—"

Dudley interrupted her. "Don't give me that bullshit," he said. "Bill doesn't breathe without your permission. Of course he would have told you."

He stood up and strode across the room as though he couldn't keep still. Lizzie could feel the air crackling with his anger and frustration. "Have you any idea how crap all this is for me?" he burst out. "Dina practically forced me to withdraw from *Stars of the Dance* even though I didn't see why I should. Now I've lost this show too, and another three jobs I thought were in the bag. Everything's falling apart around me and you don't give a shit."

"That's not true," Lizzie said, trying to hold onto her temper. "Of course I care! But you know what this business is like, Dudley. It can be brutal. You just need to give everything time to settle down. It's hardly surprising people are jittery. You've just lost your wife and there are a lot of rumours going around…" She thought of Johnny and his vivid despair, and the contrast with Dudley and his self-pitying interviews online and in the news. She rubbed her forehead. She wanted to tell him that he needed to show some humility and preferably some genuine grief if he wanted to get people on his side, but she knew that would only make him angrier.

"That stupid cow," Dudley said, with a savagery that shocked her. "I swear she did this on purpose to ruin everything for me. The police have interviewed me twice now and the press are crucifying me and it's *all her fault*."

"Dudley!" Lizzie shook her head. "I know you're upset that Amelia's dead—"

"I don't give a shit about Amelia," Dudley said with brutal frankness. "She was like a fucking leech, living off my money and my name. We were separated. I'd told her I wanted a divorce, so why does everyone expect me to be sorry she's dead?" He looked genuinely baffled.

Lizzie took a deep breath. "I think you must be very

upset to be talking like this, Duds," she said carefully. "You know you can say anything to me and I'll never repeat it, but…" She went over to him and took his hands in hers. "Even if you didn't love Amelia any more it's still a tragedy that she died so horribly. People will expect you at least to express sincere regret over that—"

Dudley shook off her touch. "All I know is I'm losing everything," he said. "Everything! And you're just like everyone else—you won't help me." He threw himself back down on the sofa and looked at her with dark, pleading eyes. "Please, Lizzie. Help me."

"I *am* trying to help you." Lizzie sat down beside him. "I'm always here for you if you need to talk, Dudley, but…" She hesitated. She didn't want to be too harsh in case she sent Dudley spinning off into another rant. He had always been mercurial but his self-absorption was truly shocking.

"Sorry." Dudley dropped his head into his hands. When he looked up Lizzie saw tears in his eyes. "I'm so sorry, Lizzie. I didn't mean it. I'm not myself. That little shit Johnny Robsart came looking for me last night, making threats, saying all kinds of things. I had to report him to the police. This whole business has been awful for me—"

"Wait…" Lizzie raised a hand to stem the flow of words. "You reported Amelia's little brother to the police?"

"He was off his head," Dudley said plaintively. "He accused me of wanting her dead, of pushing her down the stairs. I thought he might be dangerous so I called the police."

"He's seventeen years old, Dudley," Lizzie said furiously, "and his sister's just died. Couldn't you have been a bit more sensitive?"

Dudley shrugged. "They should lock him into the loony bin," he said. "Best place for him. He's such an emo kid, totally out of it. He's always been like that, ever since I've known him, always talking weird stuff and appearing and disappearing like a ghost. I remember once at Oakhangar he and Amelia were playing some trick where he vanished like it was magic. So childish but they thought it was funny. She was as bad as he was." He caught Lizzie's eye and spread his hands wide in a gesture of innocence. "What are you looking at me like that for? If they section him, he'll get help there, won't he?"

Lizzie shook her head and turned away. She felt so tired; tired of Dudley's volatility and self-obsession, tired in an odd way that she had stuck by him because she had known all along that he could be shallow but she had hoped he was better than this. She had believed he was. This self-pity had to be a reaction to grief.

"Dudley," she said. "Go home. Go to sleep. This isn't you talking. You need to calm down, give yourself time to grieve—"

"I'm not sitting at home on my own," Dudley said. "It's the pits. Come out with me, Lizzie." With the mercurial suddenness of which he was capable Dudley was smiling, exuding charm again. He leaped up to grab her hands and pulled her towards the door. "Let's go to a club, somewhere private, quiet. Hell, I could do with drowning my sorrows." He looked hopeful, boyish.

Lizzie hung back. "Duds, is that really a good idea? Amelia only died two days ago. Like it or not you're under police investigation. You can't—" She stopped, seeing the frown descend on his brow again. "People would find out," she said, "even if we went somewhere quiet. And if I came with you there would be even more talk."

"Like I give a shit," Dudley said. He tugged on her hands again. He'd stopped smiling. "They're going to have to get used to it, aren't they? We can be together now."

It took Lizzie a moment to realise what he meant and when she did, she felt as though she had stepped off a cliff edge into the dark.

"What? No!" She freed herself from Dudley's grip, taking such a hurried step back that she almost tripped over the table leg. "We're friends, Dudley, nothing more! I mean—" Shock and panic raced through her. "We've been friends forever and it's great but I don't want..." She gulped. "Surely you knew, I mean, I thought you felt the same..." She stopped. Dudley was wearing what she privately thought of as his winsome look, the one that told interviewers and fans that he knew he was irresistible but he was going to pretend to be modest about it.

"It's OK, Lizzie," he said. "I understand. I know it's too soon. I guess I've had time to think about it because Amelia and I were divorcing, but I guess you'd prefer to wait a while before we get together—"

Lizzie threw up her hands. "No," she said. "Stop." She looked at him, saw the self-satisfaction on his face, and realised afresh what she already knew. No one had ever turned Dudley Lester down. He simply could not believe it would happen.

"I thought that what we had was different," she said slowly. "We're childhood friends, Duds. I think of you like a brother, like you're my best friend, and that's special. But it's not..." She struggled. "It's not romantic. It was never like that. It was *better* than that. To change it would spoil everything—" She rubbed a hand across her forehead. "Oh God, I'm doing this all wrong! I know I am. I really like you, Dudley. You're incredibly important to me. But—"

Dudley's face had darkened as she was speaking. She knew she was making a terrible mess of everything. She'd never expected to be in this situation with Dudley of all people. She thought they understood each other. She felt disoriented and shocked to have got it so wrong. "This isn't the time to talk about it," she said quickly. "It's late and I've got to work tomorrow. I'm doing an orienteering event with kids from St Giles School. I need an early night."

"Orienteering?" Dudley looked at her, brows arched. "Because you're, like, really interested in the outdoors?"

"It's a charity thing for Life Changers," Lizzie said defensively. "I'm an ambassador for them—"

"Yeah, that figures," Dudley said. "Because you're a perpetual child yourself." He grabbed his jacket from the back of the chair. "I'm going to Mackenzie's. Perhaps I'll see you around. If not…" He shrugged.

The door slammed behind him. Shit. Lizzie resisted the urge to call him back or grab a quick change of outfit and head out after him. It was habit, ingrained in her, to look out for him. Even now, when she was reeling at how badly she had misread their relationship, she was still taking responsibility for him.

She scrubbed her hands through her hair in exasperation. She knew exactly what would happen if she did go after him. Dudley would be thrilled to see her, as though their quarrel had never happened. Perhaps he'd interpret it as her changing her mind, succumbing to his irresistible charm. She pulled a face. On the other hand, if she didn't go, he would get drunk and get himself into deeper trouble, generate more headlines, probably end up in jail.

Lizzie walked through to her bedroom. The flat, so spacious and open in design, suddenly seemed claustrophobic, almost like a prison. She needed to get away. She was gripped by something almost like desperation. She needed to make a break from Dudley and from the life that he represented; the shallow, high-profile celebrity-driven world that she'd inhabited for as long as she could remember. She had no idea where she could go, though, or what she might do. It was a terrifying thought, as though she wanted to throw away the compass of her life and start over—and she wasn't sure she was brave enough to do that. For a moment she was tempted to reach for the concert programme as she had done that morning, and conjure up memories of her mother to soothe and comfort her, but that felt wrong, as though she were overusing the gift. Instead she lay down on the bed listening to the traffic and the sirens, and thinking about Dudley reporting Johnny to the police for harassment. It must have been directly after that that Johnny had come looking for her. No wonder Arthur had been so protective of his little brother; he must have been afraid she would complain too and that they would take Johnny away.

With a muttered curse she sat up again. She needed to find Dudley and try and talk some sense into him before he did something even more stupid or hurtful.

She threw on some clothes, took the first jacket that was hanging in the closet, picked up her bag, checked her purse and keys and went out. Down in the foyer, Jason looked up from the desk with a frown between his brows.

"I'm going out," Lizzie said, then felt annoyed with herself. Since when had she had to explain herself to everyone? Was that another habit she had somehow got into, accounting to Bill and Kat and everyone else for her life, ostensibly the one in control, definitely the one earning the money, and yet dancing to their tune?

"You're a perpetual child…"

She knew that Dudley's words had been intended to sting because she had rejected him and wounded his pride. She wondered if he really cared for her or whether his suggestion that they should be together was just another way for him to use her. Suddenly nothing seemed certain any more. When had her judgement become so faulty?

The taxi dropped her directly outside the discreet members' entrance of Mackenzie's Bar and a doorman came forward to meet her. It was raining now, the London lights reflected in streaky patterns on the wet roads and pavements. Music pulsed from the building. As she ducked under the proffered umbrella and reached the slightly damp red carpet, she saw Arthur Robsart was in the doorway. Great, his massive disapproval was all she needed to make the evening even worse.

"I'd be grateful if you could let me in," he was saying. "It's an emergency. I need to find my brother-in-law urgently—"

Arthur was looking for Dudley? Lizzie felt a trickle of anxiety down her back. Dudley had said that he'd reported Johnny to the police only the day before. She couldn't imagine that Arthur would be looking for him to thank him.

She realised there was a way to find out.

She touched Arthur's arm very lightly. This time she

was braced for the shock but she wasn't sure Arthur was. He spun around as though he'd been burned.

"I'm sorry, sir." The doorman was deferential even when he was refusing entry. "Members only—"

"He's with me," Lizzie said. She steered Arthur inside and after a second felt the rigid tension in his arm relax a little. The door closed behind them, cocooning them in the warm opulence of the hall. Arthur leaned close to her. His breath stirred the tendrils of hair against her cheek.

"You've got to stop doing that," he said.

"I was trying to help," Lizzie said. "You said it was an emergency."

Arthur's gaze searched her face. It was odd; when she wasn't touching him she couldn't read his thoughts at all. He had inscrutability down to a fine art. The contrast between the intimacy of reading him and the true distance between them was deeply disconcerting.

"What did you see?" Arthur said. "What did you see when you touched me?" Lizzie couldn't read his tone either but his words alone made her shiver.

"There's no point pretending it doesn't happen," Arthur said, when she didn't immediately reply. "We both know it does."

"OK," Lizzie said. She cleared her throat. "It's just so… weird."

"Granted," Arthur said drily. "Perhaps we can have a chat about it sometime. For now, though, what did you see?"

Lizzie paused for a moment, analysing the emotions she had sensed in him and trying to form them into words. "You're looking for Johnny," she said. "He's…disappeared. You think he might be trying to find Dudley. You're afraid for him." She could feel that fear, visceral and raw. Arthur knew exactly how vulnerable and alone his brother was feeling and he wanted desperately to protect him. Lizzie understood that urgency and envied the closeness of the bond that had produced it. "You're hoping Dudley might know where he is," she added. "That's why you're here."

Arthur nodded slowly. "Spot on," he said. "That really is uncanny."

A waiter brushed past them, looking curiously at the two of them. "Come on," Lizzie said. "Dudley's probably in the VIP bar downstairs. It's where he tends to hang out. Though I doubt he'll be of much help," she added, remembering what Dudley had said about Johnny earlier. "He and Johnny don't exactly get on, do they?"

"I've checked everywhere else I can think of," Arthur said grimly, and again Lizzie felt the razor-sharp edge of anxiety beneath his words. "Dudley's my last hope. Not that I expected to have to accost him in a club. Not two days after Amelia died." Once again, Lizzie could sense the anger and disgust in him, held under tight control. "I had to search the celebrity gossip online to find out where he was likely to be. Can you believe that?" He broke off. "Yes, of course you can." He shook his head sharply. "You probably came here to spend the evening with him."

"Less of the judging please," Lizzie said. "I'm helping you, remember?" She didn't even bother trying to explain to Arthur why she was looking for Dudley herself. "Let's hope he knows something," she said. "And that you won't end up punching him."

She saw Arthur smile. "I have more self-control than that, and certainly more than Dudley has."

Lizzie didn't doubt it. "You really don't like Dudley,

do you?" she said. "By which I mean you hate him." The power of the antagonism she sensed in him shocked her. She knew Dudley would hardly be Arthur's favourite person but it felt as though there was something very dark and complicated here.

Arthur raised his brows. "You don't need to be a mind reader to know that," he said curtly.

They went down the white staircase, past the twirling statue of a mermaid on a unicorn, into the aquatic-themed cellar bar. A few people nodded and called out a greeting to Lizzie. People were looking at Arthur as they passed, probably because he was so good-looking but also, Lizzie suspected, because they were wondering where they had seen him before. Most of them wouldn't remember. The world of celebrity had a high turnover.

The bar was only half full and a quick check proved that Dudley wasn't there. Lizzie followed the insistent thud of the beat towards the dance floor but couldn't see him there either.

"The guy behind the bar says Dudley hasn't been in tonight," Arthur said, joining her, his gaze fixed on the swaying dancers. His shoulder brushed Lizzie's. She felt acutely aware of him and wasn't sure whether it was the intimate darkness or the pulse of the music that was influencing her.

"I'm sorry," she said, as they made their way back through the bar. "It was a long shot."

"Dudley told you he'd be here, though," Arthur said, and it wasn't a question. "You expected to find him."

Lizzie stopped. They looked at one another. "OK," she said after a moment, "evidently I'm not the only one who can read minds."

She thought Arthur almost smiled. "It was an educated guess," he said, "no more. I don't share your gift."

"All right," Lizzie said, sighing. "I didn't want to tell you because I thought you'd make another of your judgemental comments, that's all. Dudley was round at my flat earlier and he mentioned he was coming on here. I guess he changed his mind. I didn't come here to party with him," she added, hating that she was explaining herself. "I just thought… I thought he wasn't doing himself any favours by being so crassly insensitive at a time like this and I wanted to try and persuade him to go home."

"That's hardly your responsibility," Arthur said, holding the door open for her as they exited the bar and started back up the stairs.

"No," Lizzie admitted.

"I'm looking out for Johnny because he's my brother, he's seventeen and I've looked out for him all my life," Arthur said. "Whereas you and Dudley—"

"There is no me and Dudley," Lizzie snapped. "I was trying to be a friend, that's all."

Arthur was silent.

"Look," Lizzie said, as they reached the top of the steps and were standing once again under the huge central chandelier in the hall. She fumbled for her phone, pulling it out of her pocket. "I know this is important so I'll give Dudley a call—"

Arthur's hand closed over hers on the phone. "Why?" he said. "Why would you care?"

"God, you make things difficult," Lizzie said. She stared up defiantly into his eyes. "I care about Johnny because it's clear he's desperately unhappy," she said, "and I understand how horrible it feels to lose someone close to you, especially when you're so young and you've already gone through so much—" She stopped dead, aware that she was revealing far too much about herself to someone who was practically a stranger, and an unsympathetic one at that.

Arthur let go of her hand. Still holding his gaze very deliberately, Lizzie flipped open the phone and dialled Dudley's number. There was no reply.

"He's probably blocking me," she said, after she'd let it ring twenty times. "Dudley and I aren't exactly on good terms at the moment." She shrugged, sliding the phone back into her pocket. Dudley's tantrums were only an irritant compared to what Johnny might do in the extremity of his misery. "I'm sorry I couldn't help," she added. "I don't really know what else to suggest."

"Thank you anyway," Arthur said. He looked suddenly tired. Lizzie had to repress the urge to reach out and offer comfort. Hell, she was in a mess.

"Would you let me know when you find Johnny?" she asked, a little awkwardly. "I'd like to know he's safe."

"Yes, of course," Arthur said quietly. They stood for a moment longer in silence whilst the distant thud of the music made the floor vibrate and nearer at hand a drunken couple fell out of a doorway amidst shrieks of laughter.

"Time to go," Lizzie said.

They went out into the London night. The rain had grown heavier, streaking the pavements and reflecting the streetlights in flat black puddles. It was almost two o'clock.

"Can I give you a lift?" Arthur asked.

"That's OK, thanks." Lizzie smiled at him, feeling less vulnerable now they were saying goodbye. "The doorman will call a taxi for me. Anyway, I imagine you're keen to head off and look for Johnny, so…"

Arthur didn't move. "One day soon," he said, "we'll need to talk about this gift of yours and what it means for us."

"We could just ignore it," Lizzie said lightly.

"I doubt very much that will happen," Arthur said. He raised a hand and she thought that for a fleeting moment he brushed the raindrops from her cheek, but perhaps she had imagined that. "Goodnight, Lizzie Kingdom," he said.

Lizzie watched him walk away, disregarding the water that was now running in rivulets down her neck. He didn't turn to look back at her. The most disturbing thing was that when he vanished from sight down a side street, she felt bereft.

The ringing of her phone was a welcome distraction.

"Lizzie." It was Dudley. He sounded as though he was crying again. There was noise in the background, the chink of glasses and a roar of voices. Not Mackenzie's, then, but another nightclub somewhere nearby.

"Lizzie, help me," Dudley said. "I can't do this without you… I need you."

"Where are you?" Lizzie said. She looked along the empty street; Arthur had gone. Nor, she realised, did she have his number. "Dudley," she said again, "where are you?" Her first thought, her only thought, was to find him so she could ask him about Johnny.

"I'm at the Lizard Lounge," Dudley said. "I need you to come and get me. Please Lizzie…" His voice broke.

"All right," Lizzie said. "I'm on my way."

10

Amy: Whitehall Palace, Summer 1552

ROBERT WAS INSANELY ambitious. I had always known it but never was it more apparent than in those summer days of 1552. The serious boy king had been ill that spring; he was a sickly youth whose permanently pallid air gave the impression that all life and vitality had long since drained from him and he was no more than a husk. He spent all his time at his books and writing his letters but it scarcely mattered. My father-in-law was the Duke of Northumberland now and he ruled the Kingdom. The Duke of Somerset had been executed for treason and the Dudleys had climbed so high it felt as though we were touching the stars.

That day there was to be a joust, one in a long procession of masques and tourneys I remember that year. The

flower-bedecked pavilions, the ladies fluttering and gos-
siping, the press of the spectators, the blaze of heraldry, the
stir of trumpets... I hated every last moment of it. Robert and his brothers were like so many flaunting peacocks
amongst the crowd and I was supposed to smile until my
face ached and applaud until my palms were sore.

"How fine your husband looks!" Lady Margaret Palmer
gave me a sideways glance and an arch little smile. "All the
women are hot for him." She leaned further out over the
balcony, crushing the sweet-smelling roses that garlanded
the stands in attempt to catch Robert's eye. In contrast I
tried to draw back a little. I hated the dust and the heat
and the blood of the tourney. My head was already aching and I put up a hand to rub my brow.

"Amy?"

My sharp-eyed mother-in-law had noticed my with-
drawal. She was a kind woman, the Duchess, in a brisk
manner that still intimidated me after two years of marriage. Weakness was not something that she either understood or tolerated. Generous to me though she was, I
knew that she, along with the rest, had thought Robert
should look higher for a bride. It was a long time since his
love for me had seemed sufficient to protect me from those
slights either real or imagined. Now our desire seemed an
ephemeral thing; it was no longer so heady as in the early
days of our marriage and it was all too quickly satisfied.
Often it left nothing but emptiness between us in its wake.

I needed a child. Without one, I was nothing, less than
a wife. The knowledge that a son would transform my
status was becoming an obsession with me. Anna had lost
her babe the previous year and yet still, ashamed as I was
of it, I envied her. I had not even conceived yet.

"Do you feel the heat?" her grace enquired. "Is it the sun?" She drew me beneath one of the fluttering canopies. "Sit, my dear. Take some rest." Her gaze flickered to my stomach. "You look very pale. I wonder... Do you think you may be with child?" She looked at me with her kind, hopeful eyes.

I could have told her no. I should have done. I was hot and sick because my flux was coming, as regularly as it always did. But I was tired of disappointing them, of the monthly letters to my mother that were full of inconsequential chatter and no news of a babe. Pain gripped me and a desire to be of consequence for once. It was pleasant to be approved of, to be ushered to a seat in the shade, to sit quietly whilst the Duchess sent a servant scurrying for a glass of wine to revive me. I lowered my gaze and pretended that I did not see the glances of surprise and hear the whispers that had already started:

"Can it be true? Amy Dudley is enceinte?" Then a voice, quickly hushed: "I thought she was barren."

Ah, my sister-in-law Anne Seymour, so loud and tactless, articulating what everyone else was thinking. Anne had grown sourer still with the death of her father and I supposed that was no surprise, for who would wish to be trapped in a marriage to the son of their father's murderer? It was a harsh world we inhabited for all that it was dressed up in silks and gaudy colours.

I swallowed the bitterness of Anne's words. She had no children herself so perhaps like me she was driven by envy. Yet how little time it had taken the whole court to condemn me because I had failed to perform a woman's natural function, a woman's only important function, and fall pregnant. Robert, even now demonstrating his virility in the lists, was surely as fecund as the stallion he was riding. Thus ran the logic. If there was no child then it must be my fault.

Even as I rested my hands demurely over my stomach, I knew this could only end in more disappointment, more disapproval. Yet still I said nothing, sitting in the dusty June heat, dreaming, as though that would make it true.

It was not long, of course, before everyone knew there could be no child. The year slid into autumn and then into winter and I did not increase. I felt a curious sense of disappointment and loss, as though I had almost convinced myself of the lie along with everyone else. I grieved for the child I was not carrying and the canker of doubt, of a belief in my barrenness burrowed a little deeper into my heart.

Nobody mentioned that there was no babe. Indeed, I think perhaps that Robert barely noted it. He was too occupied with other matters, not that he ever discussed them with me. I had tried to talk to Robert about affairs of state, of the court business, of politics when he attended the parliament, but he had no interest in my opinions. I quickly came to realise that he humoured me. He never sought my advice, perhaps because he was so certain of his own mind. Robert was now a gentleman of the King's Privy Chamber and his father had granted him more estates in Norfolk. This made me happy, though less so when I discovered we were not to go there. I missed the landscape of my childhood and I missed Arthur very much too, but Robert shook his head when I bearded him in his study and begged to go home again.

"It is more important to be at court now than buried

away in the country," he said. "All the things that matter happen here."

"Then what are our manors *for*?" I felt frustrated. "If not to be lived in?"

Robert laughed though I glimpsed irritation in his eyes. "You are such an innocent, Amy," he said. "Owning land is always about power and money."

I could see that, but to me it was also about building a home, a place to raise the family I was still so hopeful we would have. It was about belonging. I was only just starting to learn that I needed to have a settled home, now that I felt so rootless.

"My father wishes to increase his authority in Norfolk," Robert said, "Suffolk too. They are…unruly places, dangerous to the stability of the realm. So he grants me land and authority there to keep that danger in check."

I was not so naïve that I did not know what he meant. There were festering resentments in the east of the country; people did not like the imposition of the new religion and held fast to older loyalties. There was always the possibility of insurrection.

"Was that why you married me," I asked suddenly, "to buy my father's loyalty and increase your influence?"

I wished the words unsaid as soon as they were out of my mouth. I knew Robert well enough by now to know that he admired independence of spirit and could not bear what he saw as a mawkish need for reassurance. Even so, if he had denied it immediately, all might have been well. If he had kissed me and told me fondly that I was foolish to doubt him, I would have pushed those fears back into the dark recesses of my mind. He did neither. He stood gazing out of the window for a moment and he seemed lost in thought, as though he had not heard me. Then:

"Your father's loyalty was never in doubt," he said.

He went back to his desk, picked up his pen and resumed the writing I had interrupted. I felt hot and furious. I clenched my fists by my side.

"I shall go alone then," I said. "My mother would welcome a visit, I know. She has been ailing of late."

"A wife's place is with her husband," Robert said, without looking up this time. "You will stay here at court with me."

"But I have nothing to do!" I burst out. "I cannot be forever at my needlework or reading…"

The quill snapped between Robert's fingers. "Why are you troubling me with this, Amy?" he said. "Surely after three years you can find your own amusement? Go and visit your aunt in Camberwell or—"

I did not hear what other suggestions he might have for my entertainment for I had left the room. I did not wish to be amused; I wanted to have something to do. Later though, when we supped at court with the King, and the Duke and Duchess of Northumberland, we behaved with complete composure as though nothing were amiss between us. I had learned that to dissemble one's feelings was the aristocratic way.

The Duke, my father-in-law, was, as always, at pains to compliment me on how well I looked, reminding me that my role was as an enhancement to my husband. The Duchess drew me to her side with her usual kindness.

"I fear you must give up Somerset Place soon and return to Ely Palace," she confided in me later in the evening. "The King is minded to send the Lady Elizabeth to live there."

The Lady Elizabeth. It was not the first time in my married life that the Princess's name had been mentioned but it was the first time in years that I felt such a strong prick of jealousy. Perhaps it was because Robert and I had quarrelled. Perhaps, that had made me realise how far apart we had already drifted and how his history with her lent their relationship deeper roots than we could ever achieve.

I glanced down the table to the empty stool that was the Princess's place. When they were at court both Elizabeth and her half-sister Mary were denied the right to sit with the King beneath the canopy of state. Both were obliged to kneel to him and fulfil all the intricate rituals of royal ceremony. I could not blame them for so frequently sending their excuses in order to be free of his company. It was one of the things I disliked most about the King; to my mind Edward was fortunate to have his family about him yet he did not value his sisters. Instead he demeaned them in ways great and small through his arrogance. I had little liking for Elizabeth, of course, but it made me wince that Edward made no secret of the fact that he believed his sister a bastard. I wished the King would marry her off to some foreign prince in a miserable political bargain and put an end to both her humiliation and my jealousy.

"I will not regret a move from Somerset House," I said. The new palace was half built and draughty and uncomfortable. "I shall look forward to summer back at Ely Place. The strawberries in the garden are the best in London."

Her grace smiled but it did not reach her eyes. "Summer is far away," she said. "Who knows where we shall all be then?"

I did not much care. The news that we were to leave
Somerset House had heartened me even though I wished
Robert had been the one to tell me. It had been unpleas-
ant living in a house designed for the Duke of Somerset,
not only stepping into a dead man's shoes but occupy-
ing the chamber he had planned for himself. The place
was haunted by the ghost of his ambition. It mocked me
at every turn, showing me what happened to those who
rose too high. Robert laughed at me when I shivered and
told him how much I hated living there. He did not understand, even when I tried to explain. I remembered
one morning lying in the huge oaken four-poster in our
chamber. The window was open and the breeze blew in
from the river. I could hear the cries of the boatmen and
the splash of the waves. There was a scent too, of fresh air
and dank water mingled with thyme and lavender from
the gardens, an odd mixture of sweetness underpinned
with something less pleasant. I looked up at the rich red
velvet folds of the bed hangings and felt smothered by how
opulent our life was. No, I should not be sorry to go even
if it meant that the Lady Elizabeth was once more casting
her shadow over my life.

In the event, our remove was short-lived. The King
developed a fever during that winter and was often struggling for breath. He rallied but then he would fail again.
He started to cough up blood and bile. The doctors, at
first hopeful of a recovery, started to despair as gradually
Edward grew wasted and weak. In the end he wanted to
die. I could see it in his face. He wanted the peace of it.
Yet with each step closer, the Duke too came closer to disaster. I knew that he and Robert and other members of
the Privy Chamber plotted like thieves through the spring

and Robert grew ever more distant and did not confide in me. Perhaps I should have been glad of it for had I known what was to come I do not know how I would have borne it. It is not good to know the future.

I should perhaps have guessed at the wedding in May. It was a ridiculously ornate affair, a triple union of powerful families, with Robert's younger brother Guildford marrying Jane Grey, the King's cousin, whilst two other cousins were also parcelled off to tie the bonds of alliance tighter. The King presided over it looking sick in heart and spirit, and despite the celebrations there was about it an air of conspiracy and hurry that felt ill-wished. Two months later Edward was dead and Jane, as bookish and quiet as he, was the new Queen.

"You are crazed," I said to Robert when I discovered it. Even though a part of me had not wanted to know the treason they plotted, I was still furious he had not told me his father's plan. I could not hold my tongue. "The people will never accept Jane over Mary. You live in a fool's paradise." I had not been there when Jane was proclaimed Queen but I had heard that the news was received by Londoners in silence but for one poor man who shouted out for Mary and was fiercely punished for it.

Robert and I were in the old solar and there were servants all around, their ears out on stalks, but I was too fearful and too angry to care. Robert, who had an equally hot temper, caught me by the arm in a grip that made me wince and hustled me behind an arras. In the enclosed space of the alcove behind I was suddenly overwhelmed by his physical presence and the sheer force of his anger.

"Hold your tongue, Amy," he said bitingly. He gave my arm a little shake before he let me go. "Why do you think I did not trust you with the truth ahead of time?" His eyes were narrowed, his face set hard. "I do not wish to hear your gloomy counsel. Jane was the choice of the King himself. We do but enact his will."

"You may dress it up however you please," I said, "but this is your father's work."

Robert's gaze scanned my face for one impossibly angry moment. Then he shrugged, some of the tension going out of him. "What if it is?" he said. "Someone must steer the Kingdom."

"Don't you see?" I burst out. "I am afraid for you! I am afraid for *us*! I am your wife, Robert. I do not want to lose you."

It was, by good fortune, the best thing I could have said. His face cleared miraculously and he pulled me close and wrapped his arms about me. "Sweetheart," he said, against my hair, "you will never lose me. I swear it."

He tilted up my chin and kissed me. There was some of the old fervour in that embrace; I could see he was lit with excitement just as he had been that night we had met at Stansfield. For Robert the game was all and the riskier the better. "This is for us," he whispered, as he let me go. "There is no limit to how high we can climb, Amy, with a Dudley Queen on the throne."

I did not think that the Lady Elizabeth would wish to bend the knee to a Dudley Queen and I wondered how this ambition squared with Robert's loyalty to her. However, I had the sense to say no more for those sweet moments were increasingly rare between us even if to me they secretly felt poisoned. Robert's fingers were entangled with mine and he kissed my hand as he released me, and then he was gone, his mind already on the weightier matters of treason, and I was left in the window embrasure, staring after him.

That same day Robert left for Cambridgeshire, tasked with hunting down Princess Mary and her supporters. Knowing Robert, I imagine he had no fear of failure. His father was busy trying to buy the support of the privy council and I clung to the Duchess and my sisters-in-law, an unhappy little assemblage of Dudley wives who tried to put on a brave face whilst we waited endlessly for news.

It came that evening, when the window embrasures were thrown wide to try to draw in the slightest breath of coolness in a London summer that felt as overheated as a powder keg. We had abandoned any attempt to play at cards and were conversing in low voices whilst our ears strained for any sound that a messenger might have arrived. It was a terrible, nervous time; I had not eaten for several days, picking anxiously over my food, staying within doors because it was too dangerous to venture out. We all knew that Queen Jane could not command the support of the people and dreaded what was to come.

Even so, the messenger took us by surprise for it was the Duke himself. He swept into the room and we scattered like chaff; he went straight to his wife and took her hands in his.

"Forgive me, Jane," he said, and afterwards I wondered whether he was apologising for the entire, ill-founded disaster. "I have to leave. Robert pursued the Princess Mary as far as Sawston, but he was too late. The east is rising to support her now; I must take an army."

I gasped, loud enough to catch his attention. He turned to me. "Rest easy, Amy," he said, with a tired smile, "for Robert is quite well."

He had assumed, unsurprisingly, that my concern had been for my husband. I caught his sleeve. "Your grace—"

He was anxious to be gone like all men are when they have resolved upon war, but he turned back to me courteously enough. "You mentioned Sawston?" I said.

"Yes," the Duke said. "The Princess had taken refuge at Sawston Hall but she was long gone when Robert arrived." His expression hardened slightly. "It seems Huddleston got her away to safety." I saw something change in his eyes as he remembered my connection to the place. There was pity in them now. "I have no news of your family," he said quietly. "I am sorry." Then: "Robert ransacked the hall and burned it to the ground."

I do not know how long I stood there staring at him, then I ran from the room, regardless of all those watching eyes, and just managed to stumble into the privy before I was sick with the little that was left in my stomach.

Lizzie: Present Day

"WHAT WERE YOU THINKING?" Bill froze the frame on the picture of Lizzie supporting Dudley out of the nightclub, stumbling into a taxi together like a couple of drunks. "Talk me through it," he added, his tone deceptively soft. "Talk me through your thought processes here so that I can understand why it was a good idea for you and Dudley to be seen out in the early hours going home together from a club two days after his wife had died?"

Lizzie didn't say anything. She hated it when Bill was in one of his viciously sarcastic moods. It didn't happen often; usually Bill was too aware of her value to him to let rip at her but she had seen the way he treated other people and had cringed. Today, though, she was his target and Kat wasn't helping her at all, her face turned away from Lizzie as she scrolled through her phone messages, making the point that Lizzie had let them both down.

"Well?" Bill snapped. He had summoned her to his office that afternoon rather than come to her. Her career was definitely on the slide.

"Dudley was upset," she said expressionlessly. "He rang me in tears and I went to fetch him home. He's all over the place at the moment and needs a friend. Besides, I wanted to ask him something urgently—"

Bill interrupted her before she had a chance to finish. "You know what the news sites are saying?" He waved a hand towards the screen again. "That you comforted him with a night of torrid passion." He glared at her. "For fuck's sake, Lizzie—"

"He slept on the sofa," Lizzie said. "Not that it's your business—"

"It *is* my business," Bill corrected her, "because I look after your business, Lizzie. You won't be surprised to hear that Life Changers have cancelled today's event and dropped you from their campaign. You don't fit the sort of image they want to project anymore. And I had a couple of other charity events lined up for you but they've fallen through as well."

"It's not my fault that people see scandal where none exists," Lizzie argued hotly. Her overriding emotion was hurt that people were so quick to think badly of her, but she knew that in the hothouse of celebrity, public opinion and mood could turn so quickly. There had always been people who hadn't believed she and Dudley were just friends and now they had fuel for their fire. And it hadn't even been worth it; Dudley had been as drunk as a skunk and when she'd finally got through to him that Johnny had disappeared he'd mumbled something rude and gone back to sleep. Only a very late message from Arthur via the front desk had reassured her that Johnny was finally home and safe. Arthur had left his number and she had immediately programmed it into her phone, feeling a bit like a teenager with a crush.

"I've pulled you out of *Stars of the Dance*," Bill said now. "There was enough shit flying around before this happened, but now—"

"You've done *what?*" Lizzie sat bolt upright on the slippery leather sofa. "You had no right!"

"They would have booed you off the floor," Bill said brutally, "and I doubt you could have taken that. You need to be loved, Lizzie. You can't cope with rejection. Don't worry—I've talked to Alessandro, told him it was for your own good. He understands."

Lizzie gaped at him like a stranded fish. There was so much in what Bill had just said, some of it too accurate for comfort, some of it breathtakingly arrogant, all of it objectionable, that she didn't know where to start. On one point Bill was absolutely right, though. Three days had been all it had taken to transform her from celebrity sweetheart into toxic property and some of that was her own fault. If only she hadn't gone to rescue Dudley.

"You don't want to look at Twitter, Lizzie," Kat said, not looking up from the screen herself. "Some of these comments are vicious."

"You're your own worst enemy, Lizzie," Bill said heavily. "I don't understand you." He brought his fist crashing down on the desk, making Kat drop her phone. "You're headstrong, just like your father. Or perhaps it's bad judgement. I don't know. But you go too far and you don't seem to care."

There was a long, appalled silence. Lizzie could feel the colour draining from her face and the angry tears burning her eyes.

"Bill," Kat whispered. She was staring from one of them to the other, making no effort to retrieve her phone.

"Never," Lizzie said, her voice shaking, "ever, compare me to my father, Bill."

Bill, apparently tone-deaf to the atmosphere, merely shrugged. "OK," he said, "so I suppose you're not a drunk or a druggie—"

"Nor do I treat people like shit or send my young child away to school until I decide I want to exploit her as a child star," Lizzie said.

Bill's laptop pinged with a notification, breaking the tense silence. "Dodo Strange has landed the role of Elle in *Legally Blonde* for the new tour," he said.

"Hooray for Dodo," Lizzie said. She'd really wanted that part. It was over a year since she'd done any singing because Bill had pushed her presenting career so hard. She missed the music.

"Don't be downcast, babes." Kat hurried into the breach. "You know how things go around. Everyone will have forgotten Amelia Lester in a few weeks' time once the funeral is over. Besides, you're a grafter; people know that and they love you for it. Throw yourself into your work and forget about everything else. You've still got *Musical World* and the travel dating show coming up in a few months—"

"*Musical World* has been postponed," Bill said heavily.

"I'd rather change direction anyway," Lizzie said. "I'm

sick of all this presenting stuff. I want to write and record some music of my own like I used to do."

That was if she could remember how to play the piano. It was so long since she had touched it, she wouldn't have been surprised if the lid had sealed shut. But the idea had already taken strong root; she wanted desperately to escape the life that had been carved out for her. When she had wrested control of her career back from her father it had all been about the music, the singing and the songwriting. It had been fun. That was before Bill had told her that TV was the way to go and she'd allowed him to guide her. She felt a sudden, huge nostalgia for the way life had been, the way it was surely meant to be.

"You can't go and hide away, hon," Kat objected. "People will believe you really are guilty if you do that! Besides, if you write and record you could be gone for over a year. Everyone will forget about you!"

"That," Lizzie said, "sounds idyllic." She jumped up, suddenly energised. "I'm going home."

"Bill!" Kat appealed to him. She struggled to her feet, knocking her phone to the floor in her agitation. "Say something! Stop her!"

But Bill wasn't saying anything. He had a thoughtful look in his eyes, the sort of expression that Lizzie knew from long experience meant that he was planning something.

"It might be a good idea," he said slowly. "Put it about that Lizzie has gone into a sort of exile, that she's writing a collection of songs about love, loss and heartbreak, inspired by everything that's happened. It would make her appear penitent…"

"If you do that, I'll deny it," Lizzie said flatly. "I've

nothing to be penitent about. I'm going away because I want to write music and for no other reason."

Bill ran an exasperated hand through his hair. "How about you take a holiday instead? A couple of weeks in the Seychelles, some photo opportunities of you alone, reading, walking on the beach, looking sad and soulful. Hell, you could even pretend to be composing on the hotel piano—"

Lizzie felt a hot rush of fury. "I *am* going to compose," she said.

"You haven't written anything for over three years," Bill said. "Your future doesn't lie in that direction, Lizzie. We agreed."

"No." Lizzie was astonished to realise that she was so outraged she couldn't catch her breath. "We didn't agree. I don't remember anyone asking me what I thought. You *told* me that TV and presenting was the way to go and for a while I did agree with you, but now—"

"What?" Bill roared, making them both jump. "Now you've fucked it all up through your own stupidity so you've decided you're a singer/songwriter after all? Lizzie, you've got a nice enough voice but you were in a second-rate girl band and your songwriting will never amount to much. You're about as good a pianist as someone down the pub. You had a lucky break, that's all, because your father had some influence in show business and was able to give you a start. But don't think you got this far through talent and don't throw the TV stuff away because you're pissed off with everyone hating you! Kat's right—they'll forget about it soon. You just have to play the game. Hell, the celebrity magazines will all be calling for you and Dudley to get together in a few months, as though none of this had ever happened."

"That's not why I'm doing it," Lizzie said, trying to keep a grip on her temper. Bill always exaggerated when he was angry; she was used to it although it always stung. "I want to write music, Bill. I want to do something different. And," she added, "I don't want to get together with Dudley so don't even think about lining that up as a publicity stunt for the future. It makes me feel sick."

Bill strode across the room—sending the papers fluttering from his desk with the violence of his passing—and came to stand in front of her, arms crossed, legs braced apart, intimidation in every line of his body.

"You're such a princess, Lizzie," he said. "You have no idea how hard I work to line up all this stuff for you and now you're talking about throwing it all in. And the idea of you going off on your own somewhere to write is insane. You wouldn't last a moment. You can't cook. You haven't driven for years. I don't know where you're planning to go but there probably won't even be a mobile signal. You can't organise yourself out of a paper bag and you'll come running back begging for help."

Lizzie heard Kat give a little gasp. She was shocked too, completely taken aback by Bill's harshness. He was often irritable and on a short fuse but he had seldom tried to bully her in so transparent a manner and she hadn't realised that he held her in quite such contempt. There was a very long silence.

"Well," Lizzie said, meeting his eyes, "thank you for making your opinion so clear, Bill."

Bill's gaze fell first. "I apologise if I sounded unsympathetic—"

Lizzie brushed the pseudo-apology aside. "It's been a stressful time," she said. She took a deliberate step back and watched as he unfolded his arms and softened his stance. "We'll all benefit from a break from each other," she added pleasantly. "And thank you for your concern, but I'm sure I'll cope fine, wherever I go. I hate all this metropolitan shit about everywhere but London being stuck in the dark ages."

"But everywhere outside London is so boring," Kat wailed. "I'll hate it! Can't we go abroad? Or—" she spun round, gesturing to Bill, trying to draw him in to support her "—let Bill find you a house in the country with staff, so you can concentrate on the music. Somewhere other celebs hang out, like the Cotswolds, where we won't feel too isolated and there'll still be plenty of stuff to put on social media."

Lizzie felt a flash of irritation at Kat's assumption she would come too. How had she failed to notice before how tightly the tentacles of Kat and Bill's control had wrapped about her life? Yet she knew she had been happy enough to go along with their ideas when it suited her and to let Kat organise everything. She had been very self-absorbed.

"I don't want to hang out with celebrities," she said firmly. "I want a change. You don't need to come with me, Kat," she added. "It's about time you took a break too, isn't it? You've been working so hard. We're all exhausted, as this morning proves."

There was a silence. Kat was looking hurt; she hadn't been taken in by Lizzie's attempt to parcel her dismissal as concern. Bill was uncharacteristically quiet too, simmering, Lizzie thought, but for once keeping his temper.

"Well," he said, after a strained moment, "if that's what you want. Keep in touch, wherever you go, and good luck with the songwriting. Let me know if the police call and you need the lawyers again."

Lizzie ignored the heavy sarcasm and gave him a polite smile. "Thanks, Bill."

"Call me, sweetie." Kat had evidently decided to forgive her too. Neither she nor Bill moved. It was as though they were daring her to walk out on them, Lizzie thought, as though they were certain she couldn't do it. For one long, terrified moment she wasn't sure she could. She'd relied on them for so long. The silence stretched and then she heard the sound of voices and the clatter of a door in the office outside and it broke the spell. She walked over to the door and went out, closing it softly behind her.

There was a taxi waiting outside; there was always a taxi waiting at Bill's offices. The driver recognised her and greeted her with a smile which warmed Lizzie's bruised heart a little.

"You all right, Miss Kingdom?" he asked, looking at her in the mirror as he pulled out into the traffic. "You look a bit pale."

"I'm good thanks, Gary," Lizzie lied. "How are you? Did you and your wife enjoy the long weekend in France?"

"It rained all the time," Gary said without a hint of regret. "It was great to get away, though." He looked at her again. "You should try it. Looks like you could do with a holiday. I'm sorry about all the stuff they're saying about you at the moment. They haven't a clue."

"Thanks, Gary," Lizzie said again. She looked out of the window. London in October matched her mood, at least on this particular day. The pavements were wind-scoured and the trees looked bare and fading. The sky was pewter grey. Dull.

Depressing. She felt the dark shadow breathing down her neck like a stalker.

She wondered what Bill and Kat were saying about her. It was almost as though she could hear them: she would change her mind because she was so flighty, she wasn't strong enough to go it alone, it would all come to nothing and tomorrow they could go back to how things had been and pretend this tantrum of hers had never happened...

Or perhaps they weren't talking about her at all. Perhaps she had become so self-obsessed in her celebrity bubble that she assumed she was more important than she really was.

The taxi stopped at traffic lights and someone thrust a camera phone towards the window. The flash went off, making Lizzie blink, waking her from her absorption. A family was crossing the road ahead all wrapped up against the chill in woolly hats and padded jackets, the children's gloved hands clutching those of their parents. They were laughing as the leaves tumbled about them and a fine drizzle of rain started to fall.

The taxi pulled up outside her flat and Lizzie paid it off with thanks and went inside, from one protected cocoon to another. There was no one in the foyer and no one in the lift. The quiet seemed deathly, the flat a tomb. With a sigh Lizzie went through to her bedroom and started to pull a suitcase out of her wardrobe. It was one of the heavy-duty ones that she used for overseas trips and it caught on the corner of her shoe rack and tumbled half a dozen pairs to the floor. The scent of her favourite perfume caught at her senses as the racks of clothes shifted and whispered together. There would be no need of those gala and premiere dresses for a while.

It was like sloughing off an identity. She picked up a

random pile of T-shirts and jeans and threw them into the case. Then the enormity of what she was doing hit her like a blow and she crumpled to sit down rather heavily on the floor. Where the hell was she going to go? She knew loads of people and she was sure most of them would welcome her with open arms but they weren't *proper* friends, they were business acquaintances or other celebs or just people she knew… She didn't trust any of them not to run to the press with the sort of story Bill had talked about: Lizzie Kingdom running away, Lizzie Kingdom having a breakdown, Lizzie Kingdom stricken with remorse… She felt like crying. Her mood teetered on the edge of self-pity and she wanted to give up the whole stupid plan and go back to all the things that were easy and familiar. Bill had been right. She had no grit, no sticking power.

She opened the wardrobe and groped through all the party dresses for the one that hung at the back, a nineteen fifties dress in cream, splashed with a pattern of red roses. It had belonged to her grandmother, Jocelyn; Lizzie had seen a photograph of her wearing it to her graduation, smiling proudly as she was introduced to the Queen Mother. She had looked like a film star.

Lizzie's fingers brushed the stiff cotton of the dress. Now, more than ever, she needed the comfort these familiar objects could give her. She closed her eyes. The images came: Her grandmother with her college friends, their excitement and pride as fizzy as the champagne in the glasses in their hands. Jocelyn's emotions were hers too, the dizzy sense of achievement and the idea of limitless possibilities for the future.

Lizzie felt the customary warmth and reassurance of the emotional connection but this time it was tinged with sadness as well because she also knew the future. She knew her grandmother had given up a promising career as a research scientist to marry and have a family, just as she knew that Jocelyn's daughter, her mother Annie, had made a terrible, fatal choice in her marriage and had died horribly as a result, running out on a row and crashing her car moments later.

Lizzie put her face in her hands. This gift of hers really was a double-edged sword. She should not depend upon it for it hurt her almost as much as it comforted her. From the present she could look back to a point in the past that was full of bright hope and promise. She could experience the unvarnished happiness of the people she had once known but she also knew what happened next, how those hopes were crushed and joy extinguished.

Tears blocked her throat and she gulped in a breath. She stumbled backwards. Depression unrolled inside her; she was on a knife's edge, before the plunge. Then, suddenly, she caught sight of herself in the huge, long mirrors inside the wardrobe doors, spotlit by the special bright bulbs she had had installed to illuminate her reflection as though she were onstage. The whole set-up struck her so hard then, the vanity and the superficiality, that she started to laugh instead of crying, slightly hysterically, rolling over on the floor as the tears stung her eyes. She was twenty-six years old and she had people to do everything for her: food, laundry, cleaning… She'd have to learn how to look after herself all over again. But she was resourceful and now that she had her world back in perspective, she was determined. And of course she knew exactly where she could go. The gorgeous cream and red dress had reminded her. She could go to Burford, to the house that had been in her mother's family for generations and which she had inherited from her mother. Years before, Bill had arranged for the house to be let but Lizzie thought she remembered him complaining a few months back that he hadn't been able to find new tenants for a while. Probably, she thought, because he would be charging a fortune for the kudos of renting Lizzie Kingdom's house.

She thought about the house, of the pink roses against the mellow golden Cotswold stone wall, the big old-fashioned kitchen and the rambling bedrooms with their diamond-paned windows. Usually she felt conflicted about The High; there were too many childhood memories of her father there, the faintest of happy memories from a time *before*, those brief few years when her parents had been to-gether, but so many memories from *after* of the escalating rows between them and the terrible moment when they came to tell her that her mother had been killed...

She found she was gripping the bedcovers as tightly now as she had gripped the bannisters then, a four-year-old child trying to steady herself in a vicious adult world that gave no quarter. It would be a challenge to go back to The High but perhaps that was something else it would be good for her to face. It was time she allowed herself to change.

Her mobile rang. For a moment she was confused since she thought she had turned it off, then she realised it was the private one, close family and friends only. Wiping away the tears from her face, she checked the caller display. It was her cousin Juliet.

"Hi, Jules!" She hoped she didn't sound as hysterical as she felt.

"Lizzie!" For her part, Juliet sounded breathless or down the end of a distant and very crackly line, or possibly both.

Lizzie felt warmth slide through her as she visualised her cousin; Jules would be wearing her old hiking boots and a battered waterproof coat, her hair would be in a messy blonde bun beneath an old velvet hat and she would be holding the mobile away from her ear as though it was some sort of alien object. Jules and her siblings had grown up on a farm surrounded by animals, two loving parents and lots of happiness. Her upbringing was about as far away from Lizzie's as could be imagined. She was also a partner in a legal firm with chambers in Clerkenwell and was a razor-sharp lawyer.

"We've only just got back to Arreau and heard that you were in trouble!" Jules bellowed. "What the hell's going on? Why didn't you tell me? I looked at the internet, well, as much as you can get it up here with no signal, and I saw the stories about that wife of Dudley's and how he's supposed to have murdered her and how you're to blame. Absolute tosh! About you, I mean, not Dudley. He's definitely a candidate for arrest, if you ask me! I've always said—"

"How was the camping?" Lizzie interrupted, anticipating a diatribe. Dudley and Juliet had never got on.

"Yeah, great," Jules said, "except for the rain and the insects. The kids loved it. They want to go on to the Sierra Nevada now for a couple of weeks but I've said we're coming home to see you. You *need* us."

Lizzie felt a rush of affection. "That's so kind," she said. "I'm really lucky to have such a great cousin."

"Well, we don't have much family left," Jules said, "so we have to stick together. No word from your ghastly father, I suppose," she added. "Is he still living in California?"

"As far as I know," Lizzie said. "I don't want him popping up now," she added with feeling. "That really would be the last straw."

"Bastard," Jules said. "Anyway, we were talking about you. What's going on?"

"Nothing much," Lizzie said. "Things are dying down now. Don't put off your holidays on my account, although aren't the kids due back at school soon anyway?"

"Probably," Jules sounded vague. She sighed. "Damn. They'll send us to jail this time if Kit and Olivia take any more unapproved absence. That old buzzard of a head-mistress insists they should get a full-time education."

"She has a point," Lizzie said drily. "And someone in your position should really be seen to uphold the law."

"But they learn so much when we're travelling," Jules argued, revisiting a topic that the two of them had talked about a number of times. Lizzie, the product of boarding school, had appreciated the structure and discipline it had given her when her life was in shreds even though she had been miserable at first. Jules had argued that structure and discipline was death to the imagination.

"Look," Jules said, "what I really rang for was to check if Bill has got the whole legal aspect of this case covered for you? He may be a leech but he's always got good law-yers on retainer."

"I'd rather have you," Lizzie said involuntarily, "but yes, he has. They're rather too aggressive for my liking. I mean, I haven't *done* anything and paying a bunch of sharks makes me look guilty."

"You know I'd act for you if I could," Jules said, "but I could be legitimately accused of being prejudiced. Look, Lizzie, brace up. I'll come back anyway, just in case I can help."

"That's really sweet of you, Jules," Lizzie said, "but only if you're sure. It would be good to see you, but like I said, it's all dying down now. The police probably won't want to interview me again. I mean, why would they?" She paused. "I'm going away for a while," she added, "but you should be able to get me on my mobile."

"Did you say you're going away?" Jules bellowed. "This line is terrible. Where are you going? You should carry on as normal, you know. Otherwise you make the police suspicious."

"I can't carry on as normal," Lizzie said. "I've got no work. Everything's fallen through because of this thing with Dudley and Amelia. I've been totally contaminated and until Dudley is exonerated, I'm a pariah."

"Bloody unfair," Jules said. "Look, you know we'd ask you to stay with us except that the kitchen's being redone and all the stuff is in storage, and the place is a total mess."

"I think it's about time I looked after myself," Lizzie said drily, "but thank you for the thought." She paused. "I'm going to The High."

"I thought you didn't like that house because it reminds you of your father," Jules said. "Still, it's not a bad idea. At least it would be a bolthole and Avery would keep an eye on you. She may be ninety but she would see the paps off with a pitchfork."

Lizzie smiled. She'd forgotten about Avery, her grandmother's oldest friend. Avery could be quite terrifying.

"Are you taking anyone with you?" Jules demanded. "Bill? Kat Ashley? I thought they were always hanging around?"

"I think we're all a bit tired of each other," Lizzie said carefully. "We need some time out."

"Well," Jules said, with her customary forthrightness, "I've thought for years that it was all rather unhealthy. But you're a celebrity, Lizzie. They're not like other people, or so I'm told. Apparently, you need people to smooth your path through life and protect you."

"That's rubbish made up by celebrities to justify being spoiled," Lizzie said, laughing. "It's infantilising and it's about time I got real."

"Good for you," Jules said warmly. Her voice changed. "You're not taking Dudley with you either, I hope?"

"No Dudley," Lizzie said firmly.

"Good," Jules said. "There's no one else, I suppose?"

Lizzie thought involuntarily of Arthur and forced herself to stop thinking about him immediately.

"Jules," she said. "Stop trying to marry me off."

"You don't have to *marry* anyone!" Jules stopped and for a moment Lizzie thought she was in for another diatribe, but instead her cousin's tone softened a little. "This self-imposed celibacy is ridiculous, Lizzie," Jules said. "We all have *needs*, for God's sake. It's perfectly normal. You'll turn into a sexless, dried-up old prune at this rate."

"Oh God," Lizzie said. "How did we come to be talking about my sex life now? Jules, I do appreciate your concern, but it's hardly that extreme. I just haven't found anyone I like yet, that's all."

Jules ploughed on. "You're surrounded by users. You need someone on your side! Dudley's a rotter, Bill's a snake and Kat's a hanger-on. Get rid of them all and find someone who cares about *you* like we all do."

"Thank you, Jules," Lizzie said, a lump in her throat. "I love you all too."

"Got to go," Jules said. "The twins are fighting. See you soon, darling!"

Lizzie was smiling as she ended the call. She glanced around the room at the piles of clothes and half-filled suit-case. It would be good to see Juliet and her family again and spend some time with them.

Her phone rang again, startling her. In the past few days it had barely rung at all. None of her so-called friends had wanted to be associated with the toxic mess that was her life at the moment.

She didn't recognise the number and was tempted to allow it to go to voicemail but something prompted her to answer.

"Lizzie?" She recognised the voice at once, young, breathless, desperate. "It's Johnny Robsart."

"Johnny?" Lizzie almost dropped the phone. "Where are you?"

"I'm outside," Johnny said. "I need to see you."

"Come up," Lizzie said at once. "Top floor, take the lift. I'll be waiting."

"I'm out in the street," Johnny said. She could hear the quiver in his voice. "They wouldn't let me into the foyer. They threatened to call the police. Can you come down and meet me?"

"Sure," Lizzie said. She was already halfway to the door. "I'm on my way down. Don't move. I'll be right there."

12

Amy: The Tower of London, March 1554

"MIND YOUR STEP," the warder said, steadying me with a hand under my elbow as I slipped on the worn stone in the half dark. I could hear the drip of water and feel the moisture and the despair that permeated the air. My head spun and my ears rang with noise, the screams and shouts of the demented, the lost, those abandoned to death and darkness.

I will be strong.

I had told myself this every day for the past six months as the sickly, humid days of summer had given way to the damp misery of a grey autumn and finally the cold desolation of winter. Living on the charity of my mother's relatives had not been easy. The ties that bound our family were strong but it felt all wrong that I had slipped from benefactress to pensioner.

The memory of court, of golden sunshine and masques, mocked me as each dreary day passed. To have fallen so far, so fast, to have known the riches of ambition and success and now to be *"poor, dear Amy,"* an object of pity, curiosity and malice, left a bitter taste. I could blame my father-in-law for overreaching himself and trying to set the usurper Jane Grey on the throne of England, I could blame King Edward for dying so inconveniently, but in truth I mostly blamed Robert. I tried to love him still but it was hard. I was angry and alone. The man I had entrusted with my future had led us all to destruction.

Robert had failed. All the work that he and my father and the Duke of Northumberland had done to build their power and authority in East Anglia lay in the ashes of Sawston Hall and from that had flowed all else: Mary's escape, her proclamation as Queen, the Duke's downfall and the shocking executions of Jane Grey and Guildford Dudley.

My mother had written to me from Norfolk, reminding me—as though I required it—that the destruction of Sawston at Robert's hands had brought even greater hardship to my sister Anna. Perhaps being a helpless witness to so much pain and bloodshed had hardened me. I told her nothing of my sickness on hearing the news but wrote back saying that now Mary was Queen, Antony Huddleston would be well rewarded for the loyalty he had shown to her. Such were the murky waters in which I now swam, my loyalties divided between the old and the new, between family and politics just as my mother's had been at the time of Kett's rebellion. Now I was the supplicant; I could have asked Anna for help when, just as I predicted, Antony was raised high in the new Queen's favour whilst I was married to a traitor who was condemned to execution, but I would not demean myself. I know it would have given her pleasure to refuse to help me.

I heard Robert's voice and his raucous laughter before we reached the door of his cell. He shared quarters with his brothers; not for them the putrid air of the dungeons below but apartments in the Beauchamp Tower with high arched ceilings and light from outside. Though the family was disgraced, the Duchess still retained sufficient funds to keep her surviving sons in comfort.

The laughter shut off abruptly as the gaoler opened the door and ushered me into the room. They were all there: Robert, John, Ambrose and Henry, gathered around a table that was littered with playing cards, tankards and empty wine flagons. The fifth place, where until recently their brother Guildford would have sat, was empty testament to his death on the scaffold.

"Praise be, a visit from my lovely wife!" Robert staggered to his feet, wiping the back of his hand across his mouth. "How do you fare, sweeting?" He kissed me clumsily. His breath stank of wine and there were stains on his doublet. I could smell stale sweat on him and tried not to flinch away. Imprisonment, boredom and drink had coarsened these men, or perhaps I was simply seeing what had previously been hidden beneath the silks and courtly manners.

Henry stood up too. "I need some fresh air," he said, "or I will run mad." His gaze dwelt on me. "I do not want to have to hear the sounds of your swiving, brother. It makes me envious."

"Send out for a trull then," Robert said crudely. He kissed me again, long, lingering, making a point. I stood stiff beneath the embrace, if that was what it was.

"I have news," I told Robert, when he finally released me. "Your mother works hard to plead your cause with the Queen, as does your brother-in-law Sidney." I thought that the mention of the Duchess might steady him, that it might restore them all to some semblance of sobriety, but they did not care. Henry paused a moment before ostentatiously turning his back and rapping on the door for the gaoler to escort him up to the roof leads. Ambrose and John turned their attention back to the game of tables. Robert caught my wrist and pulled me through to the inner chamber where, without further words he tumbled me amongst his frowsty blankets like a common whore. I could hear the shouts of his brothers at their game just beyond the door and feel the cold air on my bare thighs and Robert's clumsy hands on me and smell his wine-laden breath. It was all over in moments.

I had enjoyed the intimacy of marriage in the early days, or perhaps I had enjoyed the fact that Robert so transparently desired me. At least then he had made some effort to please me as well as himself. Now he made no attempt and I was shaking as he rolled off me and I tidied my clothes and smoothed my hair. I felt used and drab. My mind spun as I tried to find some way to anchor myself and restore some semblance of self-respect. This was not a man I could easily continue to love.

"Your mother works hard to plead your cause with the Queen, as does your brother-in-law Sidney," I repeated, as though our conversation had not been interrupted. "He speaks of travelling to Spain to seek King Philip's support since it seems he will soon be our King too."

Robert threw himself back on the bed. He made no response and there was blankness in his eyes. Something had happened to Robert since his brother's execution, something dark and painful. The young man I had known, with his unshakeable confidence and over-vaulting ambition, had turned inward and become haggard and dead inside. Perhaps it was because Guildford had been the baby of the family and so his sacrifice seemed all the more heinous when the older brothers lived. Perhaps it was the shadow of the raised axe on the wall. None of us knew when it might fall and we lived under its threat each and every day. I told myself this, and tried to forgive him his callousness.

"Robert?" I tried a third time. "Her grace has petitioned the Queen that you and your brothers be permitted to take Mass."

Robert threw back his head and laughed then. There was a wild quality to it that chilled me.

"My mother seeks to oblige us to take that papist abomination?" He wiped the tears from his eyes.

"She does it to secure your release," I said and he cast me a look of such contempt I felt whatever love and loyalty I still had towards him wither within me.

"I know that, Amy," he said, as though explaining to an idiot, "and in truth I would sup with the devil himself if it bought us all our freedom." He sighed; stretched. "If only I might do the special pleading myself," he said. "I would win over that dried-up old spinster in a moment."

I felt a rush of hatred for him then, for his patronising dismissal of me, his contempt for Queen Mary and his arrogant belief in his own attractions. When Robert had been captured and taken to Framlingham Castle, he had thrown himself at Mary's feet and begged for forgiveness. The fact that he was still alive now, he had attributed to his powers of persuasion. It had not occurred to him that Mary might have made a decision to spare him based upon statecraft.

A silence fell between us. I felt a sense of hopelessness fill me that we had so little to say to one another. The links that bound us were proving too flimsy to survive this pressure.

"Well," I said tartly, after a moment, "if you have no further use for me, I will leave you to your prayers. Be sure to pay your gaoler to tell the Queen how many hours you spend at your devotions. I am sure that *that* will impress her."

Robert stood up with all his former, lithe grace, stretching again. "I shall take your advice, wife," he said. "But before you leave, I do have one more *use* for you."

Dislike and disquiet prickled along my skin at his tone. There was mockery in his voice, and something else that felt more threatening and roused an instinct deep inside me. I braced myself to run from him, though I have no idea where I might have gone. But all he did was cross to the battered desk that stood in the corner of the chamber; there was a letter there, folded and sealed. He picked it up and weighed it in his hand.

"You will deliver this to the Lady Elizabeth," he said. "She walks in the palace privy gardens each day; you will wait for her and hand it over in person." He looked half ashamed, half defiant, but wholly determined. His voice had softened when he spoke her name.

I gaped at him. To be directed like a servant was insult

indeed, and to be asked to run errands to the Lady Eliza-beth… Leaving aside my personal dislike of her, this was madness. A moment before, Robert had been speaking of currying favour with the Queen. Now he was planning recklessly to consort with her most dangerous enemy.

"Robert," I said, trying to sound calm, "is that wise?"

It was fortunate that I said no more. I saw again that un-governable black fury rise in his eyes and I shrank from it.

"It rains," I said petulantly. "The Lady Elizabeth will not be walking out of doors today."

"Then you will wait until the rain stops," my husband said.

We stared at one another for a long moment and then I snatched the letter from his hand, stowed it in my bod-ice, and went out of the room, rapping imperiously on the cell door to be let out.

"Can't wait to escape your husband, eh, Mistress?" The warder leered as I pushed past him to run down the stair. The parchment of the letter pricked my skin. I could thrust it down a drain; I could tear it into a thousand little pieces; I could burn it in the fire; anything rather than conform to Robert's assumption that he could ask his wife to deliver messages to the woman he… I paused under the lintel of the Beauchamp Tower. Did Robert love the Lady Eliza-beth? Certainly he admired her and his loyalty to her was absolute. It must be to take such a risk as this.

The rain had stopped. I crossed the inner ward, skirting the Queen's lodgings. This, I knew, was where the Lady Elizabeth was housed as her mother had been before her. I felt a sharp spurt of spiteful pleasure to think of her re-siding in such ill-fated luxury. I hoped she dwelt on her mother's fate each and every day as she waited to follow her to the block. It was bitter of me, and shameful, but I could not pity her. I blamed her for driving a wedge between Robert and me even when I knew that their friendship had begun long before he had met me. He had been tainted before ever I had him; we had been doomed from the start because of her.

The privy gardens were to the east of the Queen's gallery, the grass gleaming with droplets of water in the pale March sun. It was cold in the shadow of the high walls and there was something daunting about the austere formality of the paths and the statuary. It seemed I was alone, yet after a moment I caught my breath at the sight of a slender figure, cloaked and hooded, lingering by the sundial where two of the paths crossed.

She did not move as I approached. Her very stillness captivated me for her fingers were tracing the surface of the sundial as though she were trying to capture time itself. She must have heard my steps on the path yet it was only when I was close that she turned.

We looked at one another, the Princess Elizabeth and I. Her eyes contained the same sort of distant, bruised expression I had seen in Robert's, the face of a person who had withdrawn into themselves for very survival. I waited to hate her but the sensation did not come. She looked lost and young; it was like looking at a mirror image of myself. Then she seemed to come awake and those brown eyes sharpened on me and I dropped a curtsey, demure as you please.

"My Lord asked me to deliver this to you," I said, reaching into my bodice for the letter. The breeze caught it and tried to snatch it from my fingers. Already it had lost the heat of my body.

"Thank you," she said.

That was all. I met Elizabeth only thrice in my life and we exchanged so few words but in that small time I knew there was a bond between us. Neither love nor hatred, it was both lesser and greater than that.

As I walked away she made no move to open Robert's letter and when I passed through the gateway into the inner ward I turned to look back at her. She was watching me too and the letter was still in her hand.

13

Lizzie: Present Day

"THIS IS VERY kind of you," Johnny Robsart said. "I'm so sorry to trouble you." He sounded like a very well brought-up schoolboy, Lizzie thought, but he looked like a spectre, translucently pale, shivering, bruised blue shadows beneath his eyes. "I do hope you don't mind that I called," he added. "Millie had your number on her phone and I realise it was probably a private one but I really needed to talk to you."

Lizzie nodded. She took his elbow and gently guided him through to her kitchen. He felt thin, and brittle; though he was tall he had no bulk. His wrists stuck out from the ends of his sleeves as though he was growing out of his clothes as soon as he put them on. He was half man, half frightened boy and Lizzie, who had never in her life felt maternal before, wanted to give him a hug and a square meal.

"Please don't apologise," she said, as she gestured him to the big basket chair in the corner by the window. "Would you like something to drink?" She wondered what to offer him. He was still shivering although it was warm in the flat. "Coffee?" she suggested. "Or hot chocolate?"

Johnny smiled and his face became boyish, transformed. "You have hot chocolate? The proper stuff? With whipped cream and marshmallows and sprinkles? That would be awesome."

Lizzie laughed, opening the cupboard to get out the hot chocolate maker. It was one of the few gadgets she actually used. Her cupboards were bursting with shiny expensive stuff she'd never touched, but since she loved chocolate, she had made an effort to learn how to do this.

"I'm very sorry we didn't get the chance to talk last time," she said, over her shoulder. "I've been wondering how you were. Things must be so awful for you—" She stopped, not wanting to sound trite or even to imply that she knew how he must feel with his grief so new and so raw. Bereavement was a uniquely horrible and lonely experience. She had recognised Johnny's misery and wanted to offer comfort but she knew he might not want it.

Johnny was watching her and though his long, lanky body was now slumped wearily in the chair, his blue gaze was alert and sharp. Yet she sensed no animosity in him, not like she had with Arthur. Her reaction to Arthur had been so vivid and complex but she didn't need any psychic powers to read Johnny. He was a boy pushed to the limit of his endurance.

"They won't let us bury Amelia," Johnny said abruptly,

"not whilst the police investigation is going on. She's lying in cold storage somewhere. And they've rehashed all the stories about Mum's death, and even dragged Jenna into it. They say we're cursed." His mouth twisted. "I'm not sure I can bear it." He shifted uncomfortably as though his bones were too sharp. "I mean, I know I have to, somehow... But I don't know how I will."

Lizzie put the chocolate maker carefully on the worktop and turned to look at him.

"No," she said. "Sometimes it can seem impossible to believe that you will ever be able to cope or that you will ever feel any better."

Johnny smiled faintly. "Most people tell me that I'll be fine," he said. "That doesn't help."

"Most people don't know what to say at times like this," Lizzie said. "They're doing their best but they're out of their depth."

Johnny's mouth twisted. "I suppose it's better than the people who say nothing at all and ignore me because they feel awkward," he said. He shrugged. "The whole thing is a hideous media circus anyway, thanks to Dudley—" He stopped; looked awkward. "Sorry, can we talk about him?"

"Sure," Lizzie said, "we can talk about whatever you like." She poured milk into the machine and added the chocolate syrup. The hot chocolate maker hummed into life.

"Dudley's a selfish bastard," Johnny said, with feeling. "It's always all about him, isn't it? His wife dies so he uses it to self-promote. He makes me so angry." He looked up suddenly. "I'm sorry he's dragged you into all this too," he added. "I know all the stuff they're saying about the two of you getting together isn't true."

Lizzie raised her brows. "How could you possibly know that?" she said. For the first time she acknowledged her culpability. "Those photographs from last night looked pretty bad," she said. "I mean, it wasn't how it seemed, but even so…"

"I know," Johnny said. "But pap photos are never really what they seem, are they? Actually, I think Dudley may have set them up." His eyes met Lizzie's very directly. "Dudley's been having an affair with Letty Knollys," he said, with devastating simplicity. "I think he's using you to deflect attention."

Lizzie stared at Johnny incredulously. "What? But… Letty Knollys? Are you sure?" She groped for a chair and sat down. "Letty's married to Walt, one of Dudley's band-mates in Call Back Summer," she said. "I mean, surely even Dudley wouldn't…" She stopped, frowning. "How do you know this?"

"Millie hired a private detective to follow him," Johnny said. He caught Lizzie's expression. "I know. Trust is dead in a celebrity marriage, right? But she thought as they were divorcing, she might get more cash out of him if she could prove he was being unfaithful." He shook his head. "None of this is pretty."

"No," Lizzie said, "it isn't." She realised that she was feeling genuine shock at Dudley's behaviour for the first time in a very long while. "God, I had no idea."

"I hope you don't mind too much," Johnny said politely.

"Not in the least," Lizzie said, realising as she said the words that they were absolutely true. "Not for myself. Dudley isn't my property and he never was. But," she pulled a face, "I do mind him betraying Walt. Walt's a good guy and friend and I bet he has no idea. That's really uncool; a horrible way to behave." She sighed. "Look, Johnny, whilst we're on the topic of bad behaviour I should get this off my chest. I may not have been involved with Dudley in that sense but I monopolised far too much of his time. It was selfish and needy of me. I know I should be apologising to Amelia for that," she added, with an awkward shrug, "but for what it's worth…"

Johnny avoided her gaze, fiddling with the button on his jacket. "It's OK," he mumbled, "I understand the two of you have been friends for years." He looked up suddenly. "But he's taking you in too, Lizzie. He's using you."

Lizzie rubbed a hand across her eyes. It felt as though she was looking into a hall of mirrors. Dudley, who had been one of the few constants in her tumultuous life, was a cheat and a liar. She knew he had used her before and she'd chosen to ignore it because she'd felt a residual loyalty to him. She had thought that no matter how badly he treated other people, she was special to him. Now, though, she felt like a fool, remembering Dudley's weird declaration of love and how bad she had felt upsetting him with her rejection. If Johnny was right—he had no reason to lie—then Dudley only really loved himself and used everyone else to his advantage. She felt a pang of real regret as she remembered how close they had been as children and how uncomplicated things had been then. She'd been lonely and miserable and Dudley had stood up for her. But times have changed, people change, and perhaps all the fame and acclaim at a young age had soured Dudley beyond saving. He'd always been ambitious; now it seemed he was just a sleaze.

"I never got what Millie saw in Dudley," Johnny said after a moment. His face was pale and pinched, his eyes tired. "He dazzled her, I suppose. I mean, even I can see that he is very good-looking. But it wasn't long before it all went wrong. I don't know how she put up with it for as long as she did; ten years married to Dudley is a hell of a long time. Anyway," his shoulders lifted, "we were all glad when she said they were divorcing. She was packing to leave when…" his breath caught "…when it happened."

"It sounds as though the two of you were very close," Lizzie said, "if Amelia confided so much in you." She wondered whether it had been such a good idea for Amelia to expose Johnny to the ugly underbelly of her marriage. It seemed a bit selfish.

Johnny nodded. "Yeah, we were very close. We talked every day. Dudley is," he corrected himself meticulously, "*was* the worst thing that ever happened to her. Right from the start he sort of sapped all her self-confidence and her spirit."

The chocolate maker gurgled to an end and Lizzie poured the drink into two mugs, reaching into the fridge for the whipped cream and lavishly adding marshmallows and chocolate to the top. "Enjoy," she said, pushing one of the mugs towards Johnny and giving him a long spoon to go with it. "You deserve it."

"Thanks," Johnny said. He took an indulgent spoonful of cream and marshmallow and closed his eyes. "Awesome," he mumbled.

"Thank you," Lizzie said, feeling ridiculously proud. "Where were we? Oh yes, Dudley… Yeah, I can see you wouldn't be very fond of him but I hope you don't think he had anything to do with Amelia's death. I mean, I know he's got a lot of faults but I don't think he'd murder anyone."

"What? Oh…" Johnny waved a hand around a little self–consciously. "No, of course not, that's stupid." He blushed. "In the beginning I blamed Dudley. I was upset." He shrugged uncomfortably. "I suppose I do feel that he contributed in a way because he made Millie so unhappy, but…I'm sure it was an accident."

Lizzie wondered if he meant it. There was something in Johnny's voice that struck a false note, but she didn't want to press him. If he thought that Amelia might have taken her own life it would be unbearable to make him talk about that unless he wanted to.

"Millie was my best mate," Johnny said now. "After our mum died—" Lizzie saw a tremor go through him. "Well, Millie understood what I was going through and she was always there for me. It was horrible, Mum dying of cancer so young. We were all totally devastated. Sam—my stepdad—was away a lot. He works for the Antarctic Survey. He's a great guy but I think taking himself away from things was his way of coping. But without Millie and Arthur…" He stopped; looked at her. "I had depression really badly, and they helped me through the worst times."

"I'm very sorry," Lizzie said. Her heart turned over for him. "Depression is such a horrible thing."

"I was terrified," Johnny said, and Lizzie was struck by the starkness of his words. "I felt as though I was trapped somewhere that was completely barren. I knew people cared about me but I couldn't *feel* it, I couldn't connect emotionally with them. It was like I was on one side of a glass wall and they were reaching out to me but nothing could get through to me." He shook his head. "I guess it's hard to understand if you haven't experienced it for yourself."

"Even if you have," Lizzie said, "it can still be hard because it's not the same for everyone. To understand you need to listen and be tolerant and not judge..." she smiled faintly "...all the things that a lot of us aren't great at doing."

"You seem pretty good at listening," Johnny said, taking one of the shortbread biscuits Lizzie had set out on a plate. "I would never have guessed." He turned scarlet. "God, I'm sorry, I didn't mean—"

"It's OK." Lizzie was laughing. "I know a lot of people think I'm pretty self-absorbed. And maybe I am," she added ruefully. "But I've also had depression myself—and some counselling—so I try to be...aware." She pushed the chocolate pot towards him. "Would you like some more?"

"Thanks," Johnny said, topping up lavishly and adding a spoonful of sugar for good measure. "It's easy to talk to you, actually," he added. "Not just because you're a good listener but also because you're almost a stranger." His bright blue gaze fixed on her in a way that made her heart clench with pity for him. "The others are all so *careful* around me. I know they're trying to protect me but it can be stifling. I think they think I might kill myself."

Lizzie flinched inside. Most people were not so blunt about suicide, preferring to talk in code about their thoughts and feelings. Johnny was looking it straight in the eye. She admired him for that whilst finding Arthur's concern for his younger brother all the more agonising. No wonder Arthur had been so terrified of the consequences when Johnny had gone missing.

"Have you thought about that?" she asked.

Johnny shook his head. "No. Oh, don't get me wrong— Millie's death hurts like hell on Earth, but..." He stopped.

"I don't want to die too. It's the opposite. In fact, I'd do anything to bring her back," Johnny said suddenly, fiercely, "anything I could. If only I'd realised in time—" He stopped again, abruptly, and Lizzie waited but he didn't complete the sentence. Once again, he looked lost in his thoughts.

"It might help to talk to someone," she said, after a moment. "I was very closed off after my mum died. I was shipped around various people for a few years and went to boarding school so I just sort of bottled things up. That's when I met Dudley and actually, I have to give credit to him—he was a good friend to me, when I had so few people to talk to. Anyway," she took a breath, "when I finally started to talk about it with a professional, it was really helpful."

"I did see a counsellor after Mum died," Johnny said. "He was great but I just don't… The time isn't right yet."

"Well, you're the one who can judge that best," Lizzie said.

Johnny smiled at her, vivid and warm. "You're quite something, Lizzie Kingdom, you know that?"

"Thanks." Lizzie almost blushed. "At the risk of ruining my credibility," she added, "have you told your family where you are now? Only I bumped into Arthur last night when he was looking for you and I got the impression he'd just like to know you're safe."

"Yeah." Johnny nodded vigorously. "I'm sorry I took off like that yesterday. I needed time to think. I thought Arthur would be mad at me but actually—" his grin was wicked, surprising her "—he didn't seem to mind that much, which was all to do with meeting you again, I think."

Lizzie raised her brows. "Arthur's hardly my greatest fan," she said.

"Arthur," Johnny said, "doesn't know what to think of you and that's quite unusual, I can tell you. I love seeing Arthur confused. Normally he's really together. Then you did your weird mind meld thing on him—"

"Hold on a minute," Lizzie said involuntarily. "My *what?*"

"Mind meld," Johnny said. "Like Spock in *Star Trek,*" he added helpfully. "You touch someone and read their thoughts. It's very cool."

"Did Arthur tell you about that?" Lizzie asked.

Johnny shook his head. "Arthur doesn't talk much about the supernatural stuff. He's not like Millie and me. We were both totally cool with it but Arthur always was the down-to-earth one." He took another shortcake biscuit. "No, Arthur didn't say anything, but I saw the two of you together the other day. I was watching through the taxi window when he came back to speak to you. You touched his arm and he looked at you, and I could tell you were reading his thoughts." He looked at her. "Have you always been psychic?"

Lizzie opened her mouth to deny that she was and then shut it again. "I'm not sure I am psychic really," she said slowly. "I've never done that before—read people's thoughts, I mean. Sometimes I read objects. It started with possessions that belonged to people I loved, people like my mum and my gran. Maybe I wanted to feel a sense of connection with them. I don't know. But it kind of went on from there."

Johnny nodded. "I can understand why your family link might trigger that," he said, "but your gift is bigger than just psychometry. It must be if you can read Arthur's mind as well. It's really cool you have these gifts," he added. "You shouldn't be afraid of them." He paused, wiping some stray chocolate from his chin. "Can you travel in time as well?"

"*What?*" Lizzie stared at him. "Now come on, that's a whole different thing. I mean..." She gulped. "No. Stop. That's not possible."

Johnny shrugged, grinning. He didn't seem remotely fazed. "Psychometry and telepathy are possible but time travel is impossible? OK."

Lizzie shook her head. "You sound a lot more comfortable with all this stuff than I am," she said. "But seriously, I don't really like feeling different, so I tend to push it aside and try to ignore it. It's a bit of a guilty secret. Or it was," she amended, "before Arthur and I had our moment. Now I guess it's not secret anymore."

Johnny was smiling too. "Don't worry about Arthur," he said. "He's totally fascinated by you even if he'd like to deny it." He stretched. "Besides, there's no need to be uncomfortable about supernatural stuff. It's a bit weird but then so is dark matter or string theory or whatever."

"I suppose," Lizzie said, wondering what string theory was. "How did you get to be so wise so young?" she added.

"I must have been born that way." Johnny shrugged, looking a little uncomfortable. "Anyway, I'm weird too. Millie and I were psychic."

"You and Amelia had a psychic connection?" Lizzie felt surprised then wondered why she would be. Perhaps it was because Amelia's interest in the supernatural had always seemed fake. But then, she supposed she had rather unfairly dismissed Amelia as fake in every respect. She should try to be less judgemental, especially since she hated people judging her.

"Yeah," Johnny said. "Millie and I had a gift. We could talk to each other in our heads. We'd always done it, right from as early as I can remember." He shifted in his seat, clasping his hands together around the mug of chocolate. "Mum was totally into paranormal stuff so it never seemed strange to me, just natural, you know?"

Lizzie didn't really know. Her experience had been very different, hiding her gift of psychometry from her father, from Kat, especially from Bill, who would probably have tried to turn her into a stage psychic if he had known about it. She had pushed it aside and kept it as a secret thing; she had been confused and almost ashamed of something that seemed so bizarre. She was already different; the child from the outrageously dysfunctional family. She didn't want anything else marking her out.

"It was just Millie and me, though," Johnny went on. "The other sibs couldn't do it—Anna and Arthur, I mean. Millie and I were the only ones who could read each other's minds. Anna was really cross that she wasn't tele-pathic too." He was hunched forward now and the line of his shoulders was thin and tense. "I guess that was why Millie and I were the closest," he said, "although I love Arthur dearly. He's the best." He said it quite unselfcon-sciously and Lizzie's heart clenched.

He loves you too, she thought, but she didn't say.

"Shall we go through into the other room?" she asked. "It's more comfortable there."

Johnny got up and followed her through to the living room. Like most people he was drawn to the huge floor-to-ceiling windows like a moth to a flame. It was night outside now and the pinprick lights of London together made a tapestry of dazzling hues.

"Wow," he said. "This is an amazing place."

"It's pretty cool, isn't it?" Lizzie smiled. "I could sit looking at the view for hours."

"This was once the site of a royal palace, you know," Johnny said. "It was called Baynard's Castle. The foundations are right under this building. Henry VII rebuilt it and apparently it was very beautiful. Great view of the river too; the nobility grabbed all the best locations."

"That figures," Lizzie said. These days it was the rich who could afford prime real estate in London, celebrities, bankers, power brokers, the aristocrats of their day.

"I could show you a picture of it," Johnny said. "It's amazing when you imagine what all the old palaces along the river must have looked like." He patted his pockets. "Damn, I must have dropped my phone in the car."

"Some other time, then," Lizzie said. "History isn't really my thing but I'd be interested to see it." She sat down and after a moment Johnny did the same, taking the chair opposite her, leaning forward again, clearly unable to relax.

"This wasn't really how I thought it would be," he said, after a moment. He looked up at her, half rueful, half laughing. "You being so nice, I mean. It makes it more difficult…" His voice faded away. "Sorry," he said. "It's just that I have something I need to ask you, and…" He stopped again, frowning.

"Why don't you tell me what prompted you to come to find me the other day?" Lizzie said. "You said you needed my help then. We could start there."

Johnny's face cleared. "Yes, OK. Thanks." He looked down at his clasped hands; he was gripping them together so tightly that the knuckles showed white. "This might sound odd," he said slowly, "but I wanted to ask you about what happened at Millie and Dudley's wedding."

"Oh." Lizzie was taken aback. She wasn't sure what she had been expecting but it hadn't been this. "Well," she said, "I remember that you were six years old and you didn't like your pageboy outfit."

"It was gross." Johnny shuddered. "But that wasn't what I meant. I wondered—" He looked at her. "I know it's a bit weird to be asking now but what did you see in the crystal that day?"

Lizzie wasn't going to pretend that she couldn't remember what he was talking about, especially now he knew she had the gift of psychometry. She thought of the crystal ball clasped in the hands of the angel and the plaintive notes of the harp she had thought she heard.

"You asked me that at the time," she said slowly. "It was an odd question from such a young child."

"I knew even then that you had some sort of psychic gift," Johnny said. "I could sense it, maybe because I was psychic too."

Lizzie shifted, thinking back, feeling the uncomfortable memories crowd back in. "I told you the truth," she said. "I didn't see anything in it at all. It was beautiful; I wanted to touch it, it called to me, but I resisted." She hesitated. "Like I say, I'm not always comfortable with my gift, and I was even less so in those days. And the crystal felt dangerous in some way, as though there was something malignant about it." She shivered suddenly, though the flat was warm.

Johnny was watching her closely. "It broke in your hand," he said. "You must have touched it."

"You weren't there when that happened," Lizzie said. "How did you know?" The scar on her palm itched suddenly, fiercely.

"I heard about it," Johnny said with a grimace. "The whole house heard. Amelia was screaming loudly that you'd deliberately broken her gazing ball."

"It wasn't deliberate," Lizzie said. "OK, yes I did touch it, later, after Arthur had taken you away. I couldn't help myself. I reached out and just touched it lightly with my fingertips. I didn't pick it up. And I did see something: I saw Amelia buying it in a shop in Glastonbury. That's all." She stopped. She could feel Johnny's gaze on her as though he was trying to gauge if she was telling the truth. She could also feel the insistent throb of the scar, like a heartbeat.

Johnny was frowning. "I thought you must have seen something frightening and accidentally cracked the glass," he said.

Lizzie shook her head. "I'd have been a lot more badly injured if I had," she said. "As it was there was only a little cut where some of the splinters caught me." She curled her fingers unconsciously over her palm. "I think I must have knocked the stone angel somehow, and the ball was dislodged," she said. "Why do you ask? It was a long time ago."

Johnny didn't answer directly. "That carved angel was very old," he said. "Unlike the ball it was a genuine antique. It had been in the family for years and there have always been stories about, how it was unlucky, or cursed." He hesitated. "Millie didn't believe them, obviously. She adored it. But I always wondered—" he looked at Lizzie very directly "—whether it was the angel that had sent you a dark vision rather than the gazing ball."

Johnny's words seemed to shiver in the air just like the cascade of notes Lizzie had heard when the crystal had called to her. Or she had thought it was the crystal. Perhaps Johnny was right. She shuddered convulsively. The memories repeated, the sense of falling, tumbling through space, plummeting into the void, terrified... She remembered the nightmare she had had only a few nights before and how she had wondered whether Amelia had also experienced that sense of terror when she had fallen to her death. She told herself fiercely that it had been a coincidence. Her gift of psychometry enabled her sometimes to look back to the past. She had never had the gift of foresight. Yet if Johnny was right and her psychic powers were greater than she had thought, perhaps she had underestimated what she could do.

She pushed the idea away. She could not accept that she had foreseen Amelia's death on her wedding day. The idea was unbearable. The horror and panic suddenly clogged her throat. She could not tell Johnny that he might be right, that she had experienced a falling sensation akin to what his sister would go through ten years later, a vision of death. What good would that do?

She shook her head vigorously. "Like I said, all I saw when I touched the crystal was an image of Amelia buying it. It was after that I must have knocked the stone angel by accident and that was how the ball was dislodged and smashed."

The lie hung in the silence between them. It sounded loud. Lizzie could feel guilt flooding her face and jumped up. "Really, I should..." She waved a vague hand around.

"I'm supposed to be heading off tomorrow and I haven't finished my packing."

"Yes, of course." Johnny accepted his dismissal like the well-mannered child he was. "I'd better be going too. I'm sorry to have bothered you. I… I guess I just needed to talk to someone."

"No problem," Lizzie said. "I'm here if you need me."

"If I might just use your bathroom before I go…" Johnny sounded awkward. He blushed.

"No problem," Lizzie said again.

Whilst he was gone, she collected up the mugs and took them through to the kitchen. She was still thinking about the stone angel. Should she give it back to Johnny? It felt so awkward now, after all these years, especially with the family stories of how it bore a curse. It probably wasn't the right time.

When Johnny reappeared he had his jacket on and his rucksack slung over one shoulder.

"Would you mind walking with me as far as the Tube station?" he asked diffidently. "I could show you the plaque marking the spot of Baynard's Castle on the way."

"Sure," Lizzie said. "I'll get my coat." The last thing she really wanted to do was to go looking at historic monuments in the dark but it would be good to see Johnny safely on his way home.

The foyer was as empty as when Johnny had come in. Jason glanced up incuriously from the desk and then went back to his computer screen. The phone rang; he took the call quietly, discreetly. Lizzie wondered suddenly how she had come to live in such a hermetically sealed bubble. Sometimes it felt as though her life wasn't real at all.

Out on the street it was completely different. The air

was warm and loud, alive with noise, thick with the scent
of fat, spices and fumes. It was a shock, like a slap across
the face. Lizzie dug her hands into the pockets of her coat
and followed Johnny's long, loping stride down the alley
at the side of the block of flats. It was full of rubbish and
the smell of decaying food, as unlike the polished front-
age as it would be possible to find.

"I guess you never see this stuff," Johnny said, catch-
ing her expression in the dim cast of the street lights. He
grinned. "It's taxis, limos, penthouses, and five-star ho-
tels all the way."

"I don't walk much," Lizzie admitted, "at least not in
London." And these days, she thought, she seldom went
anywhere else except for when she was filming. It was
weird to realise all of a sudden how much her life, on the
face of it so privileged and glittering, had shrunk to fit
such small parameters.

After the closeness of the streets above, the air off the
river felt cold and dank, little eddies of mist blowing across
the surface. The water shifted in a ceaseless pattern of light
and dark, so much more real and immediate than the view
from her flat high above. Lizzie felt odd, and small, to be
out here instead of locked inside behind the glass walls of
her flat or floating in the infinity pool.

Johnny was leaning against the Embankment wall, looking out across the wide stretch of the water. His shoulders
were hunched, his face in shadow. "London's extraordi-
nary, isn't it," he said, "so magical and so humdrum at the
same time, thousands of years of history layered on top of
each other." He turned to face her. "I promised I'd show
you the plaque," he said. "It's over here."

He caught her hand, pulling her over to the wall behind them, high, brick-built, rising to Lizzie's apartment building above.

"Look… Here…" Johnny sounded breathless all of a sudden. He pushed back the brittle fronds of dying ivy to reveal a plaque, white letters on a dark background, bright in the pale orange light from the street lamps:

NEAR THIS SITE STOOD BAYNARD'S CASTLE, 1428–1666.

"I told you your penthouse was built on the site of a palace," Johnny said. "It's amazing, isn't it?"

"Wow," Lizzie said blankly. "That is amazing. I had no idea that was even here." She stretched out a hand towards the wall. The brick was clearly modern, neat courses with tidy mortar sandwiched between. Her fingers slid across the smooth, cool surface, feeling the dampness of the mist like grease on its face. The smell of the river was stronger now; fish and decay, brine and damp basements. It seemed to catch at her throat, smothering her. The wind off the water was growing stronger too, tugging at her hair, a cold rain chill on her face. She touched the blue plaque and suddenly everything changed. The wall vanished and she could see cobblestones beneath her feet and the remains of brick and chalk and mortar, a jumble of stone and rubble that would once have been a building. She had the dizzy sensation that she could see the high walls and tall towers of Baynard's Castle rising above her like a cliff, a pennant blowing against a bright blue sky. She could hear the lap of the river at the water gate and the gulls calling. The stench of mud filled her nostrils. There was sun on her face now

instead of rain and sufficient heat was blazing down that
she felt the sweat spring to her forehead. Voices sounded
close by and the clatter of hooves on cobbles.

Lizzie withdrew her hand from the stone as though she
had been burned. She turned to look for Johnny but she
could see nothing other than his shadow, a bar of darkness falling across the blinding sunlight. The sense of seeing into the past was more powerful even than when she
touched familiar objects. She had stepped into the past instead of simply viewing it, and it was immediate and terrifying, all the more so because she had not anticipated it.
She had not for one moment expected this.

She felt sick. The world spun like a loose wheel. Darkness pressed close and with it a sense of time spiralling
away. She thought she must have fainted even if only for
a moment because she came around to the feeling of water
on her face—either rain or tears, she was not sure—and
the coldness of the London night. People were talking over
her head, a jumble of voices, curious and eager:

"I'm calling an ambulance—"

"It's Lizzie Kingdom—"

"What's happened to her?"

Hard wood scored her cheek and she realised that she
was slumped on one of the benches along the edge of the
river embankment. People were crowding around her. She
felt confused and disoriented.

"Johnny?" she said, remembering. She tried to raise her
head. It felt weighted with lead. There was a bitter taste
in her mouth as though she had swallowed dust and ashes.
"What happened? Where's Johnny?"

"…An ambulance…" someone repeated. "The police—"

"I'm fine," Lizzie said. "Really, there's no need for an ambulance."

A flash went off, adding to the sense of unreality, and then another. Lizzie wondered how long she had been unconscious. She had absolutely no idea but she had the oddest feeling that time had skipped a beat, that it was dislocated, that the moment she had thought no more than a second had somehow stretched into an hour, or even an infinity.

She levered herself up onto her elbows and then to a sitting position, looking around. All she could discern were strange faces, crowded close, giving her a momentary sense of panic and claustrophobia.

"Where's Johnny?" she repeated. "He was here a moment ago..."

Another flash from a phone exploded in her face. The crowd seemed to be growing exponentially, like sharks drawn to blood. It was frightening when Lizzie felt so off-balance and so ill-equipped to deal with it. If this had happened a few weeks ago she would have chatted to everyone and made light of it all as she hurried back to the flat but that had been in the days when everyone liked her. Now there was an edge to the crowd. She could sense their mood.

"Johnny?" She craned her head, searching the dark sea of faces, but he was nowhere to be seen. A chill crawled over her skin. Johnny had been right beside her when she had reached out to touch the plaque. She'd seen his shadow against the light. She remembered the vivid kaleidoscope of images before the dizzying spiral down into darkness...

"Who's Johnny?" someone asked. No one was offering

any practical help; they were jostling to take pictures and viewing her like a zoo animal.

"Excuse me." She stood up and immediately felt horribly sick. Her stomach lurched. She had to find a way through the crush of people. "I need to go home—" she said. "Excuse me."

Her phone was still in her pocket. She felt a clench of relief as her hand closed about it. She could call Bill. He'd get someone to help her within five minutes. There was no need to panic. She felt shaky and light-headed as she dialled his number.

Suddenly the crush of people moved, falling back. Lizzie could see flashing blue lights at the top of the alleyway and several dark figures running towards her. There were voices calling out. She was blinded by the glare of torches. She pressed the button to end the call just as Bill's answering message cut in.

"Someone reported that Lizzie Kingdom had fallen in the river." A policewoman had come to a halt in front of her. Lizzie recognised her from the Blackfriars station. She was breathing heavily, resting her hands on her thighs, as though she'd run a marathon. "Does anyone know what happened..."

"Nothing happened," Lizzie said. She was desperate to get away before this became any more of a circus. Panic clawed at her. "I'm fine," she said. "I'm sorry for the false alarm."

The policewoman straightened up and swung her torch around to Lizzie's face. "Oh. It's you, Ms Kingdom. You haven't drowned." She sounded disappointed.

"I'm fine," Lizzie repeated. She smiled weakly, trying to force a way through the press of people that had closed about them again. "I'm sorry for all the fuss. I felt a bit faint but I'm all right now."

"Take it easy, Ms Kingdom." A paramedic and another police officer had joined them now. The paramedic caught her elbow as she stumbled. "We should get you to hospital, check you over—"

"Definitely not." Lizzie tried to sound authoritative. "Thank you so much for coming out but really, I'll be OK now. My flat's just around the corner. I'll head back for a cup of tea."

"We found her slumped on the bench," a man in a striped sweatshirt and matching baseball cap pushed forward. "I thought she was drunk—"

"Which I'm not," Lizzie put in hastily.

"She was asking for someone called Johnny," the man said, as though she hadn't even spoken. "Said he'd gone— disappeared. Into thin air, she said—"

"I don't think I did," Lizzie said. "I'm sure I didn't say that."

"Well," the policewoman said as she and her colleague started to herd Lizzie through the crowd. "Let's get you back home and we can talk about it."

Lizzie swallowed her irritation at being treated like a child. Perhaps this was standard operating procedure. Anything that would get her away from this rather volatile crowd had to be good anyway. Once she was home, she could ring Johnny and see what had happened to him. It would all be fine. Perhaps he'd been scared and run away when the psychometry had grabbed her so violently and so suddenly. That would hardly be surprising even though he already knew she possessed the gift. He'd said he was fine with paranormal stuff but that was in theory. Seeing it in practice was a different matter.

A light rain settled against her skin and made her shiver again. The paramedic placed a foil blanket around her shoulders.

"Thanks," Lizzie said, teeth chattering.

The cobbles were slippery beneath her feet as they climbed back up to the main road, a rat slinking across their path and away behind the overflowing wheelie bins. Predictably there were paparazzi outside the flat. Flashbulbs went off, all the more so when the photographers saw she was being escorted by the police. It was starting to feel ridiculously like a premiere, except that Lizzie suspected she looked far from red carpet ready.

The foyer of the flats felt too bright. Lizzie blinked, disoriented all over again. What time was it? How long had it been since she and Johnny had gone out? She wanted to ask Jason but there was no way she was going to do that in front of the police.

"Ms Kingdom—" The paramedic was touching her arm. He was tall, lanky and laidback with a strong Liverpudlian accent. "It really would be a good idea to check your blood pressure and a few other things just to make sure you're OK." He glanced over his shoulder at the crowds outside. "I think mine would be sky-high if I had to cope with that lot," he added with a grin.

"Thanks," Lizzie said, "but I'm fine. I don't want to waste any more of your time but thank you so much for coming out."

"Well, if you're sure…" He shrugged. "Can I have your autograph for my daughter? She loves your books." He fished a dog-eared receipt out of one pocket and a biro out of the other, holding them out to her.

"Of course," Lizzie said, taking them and scribbling "Lots of love from Lizzie Kingdom" on the crumpled paper. The weird disconnect between reality and what had happened down on the Embankment seemed to deepen. She couldn't relate to either.

"Cheers for that," the paramedic said, pocketing it deftly. With a wave he disappeared out into the street, shrugging off the eager questions and camera flashes.

"Thank you." Lizzie turned her best smile on the police-women, hoping they would follow suit. "I really appreciate your help and I'm sorry to have called you away from more important business."

The police were not so easily dismissed. One rummaged in her pocket and snapped open a notebook whilst the other gestured Lizzie to a seat.

"Could we ask you a few questions, Ms Kingdom?"

"Of course." Lizzie looked around. The reception was brightly lit; she felt as though she was in a goldfish bowl. "Would you like to come up to the flat? It's a bit exposed here."

"It's fine." The PCs directed her towards some chairs in a corner by the lifts. "We'll only be a moment."

Even sitting with her back to the window Lizzie thought she would be lit up like a Christmas tree. She could just imagine the pictures already circulating on Twitter.

"Would you tell us exactly what happened, please?" The first policewoman, PC Morgan, according to her badge, leaned in whilst the other sat with her pen poised. "Just for our report, so it's clear."

"Of course," Lizzie said again. "I was with Johnny Robsart. He came to see me earlier for a chat. We walked down to the river together for a breath of fresh air on his way to Blackfriars Tube. I felt a bit faint so I sat down on the bench. I must have lost consciousness for a moment. Like I said, I'm sorry to have caused a fuss about nothing."

She could hear the whisper of the pencil on paper as the other PC recorded her words. It made her feel nervous. PC Morgan simply looked at her. That too was unnerving.

"Would that be Johnny Robsart who is the brother of Amelia Lester?" PC Morgan asked after what felt like several minutes.

"Yes," Lizzie said. She felt panic tighten its claws in her chest again. She wanted to blurt out all the stuff she had already told the police; that she knew nothing about Amelia and Dudley's quarrels, that she had had nothing to do with Amelia's death, that it was all just a coincidence and an ongoing nightmare… She kept her lips tightly pressed together.

"Are you a friend of Mr Robsart?" PC Morgan asked. "Only he was here a couple of days ago, wasn't he, demanding to see you, and you had him thrown out."

"No, I didn't!" Lizzie moderated her tone at once when PC Morgan raised her brows. "I mean, yes, he did ask to see me and there was some trouble with the security people here but I didn't tell them to eject him… It wasn't my fault—" She stopped. "Johnny's brother came and took him away," she said. "I would have been happy to talk to Johnny then just as I was tonight."

"Did you contact him to invite him here?" PC Morgan asked sharply.

"No," Lizzie said. "He contacted me."

PC Morgan nodded as though Lizzie had just said exactly what she expected her to say. "Our colleagues are checking whether Johnny has been in touch with his family since he left you," she said. "Hopefully he will have arrived safely home…" She let the phrase hang. Lizzie resolutely held her gaze and said nothing.

"Did you also see Dudley Lester this evening?" PC Morgan said after a moment.

The hairs on the back of Lizzie's neck prickled. When the police had interviewed her in the aftermath of Amelia's death they had focussed heavily on her relationship with Dudley and it was impossible to escape the feeling that they thought she and Dudley had cooked up an accident for Amelia so they could be together. Lizzie had told herself at the time that she was being paranoid but now she felt anxious all over again. Was PC Morgan implying that she and Dudley had conspired to get rid of Johnny too because he knew something that incriminated them both in the death of his sister? Lizzie told herself to get a grip. Her imagination was running away with her.

"No," she said. "I haven't seen Dudley Lester today."

"We'll check the CCTV," PC Morgan said, and it sounded like a threat.

"Of course," Lizzie said. She wondered whether there was also CCTV footage from down on the Embankment and if so, what it would show. She was aware she had been somewhat economical with her description of what had happened with Johnny, but talk of psychic powers and psychometry was unlikely to help the police view her any less suspiciously.

"The gentleman we spoke to down by the river said that you told him Johnny had disappeared," PC Morgan reminded her. "He said that you seemed distressed and confused."

"I don't remember talking to him at all," Lizzie said. "I suspect he was making it up."

The officers exchanged a look before PC Morgan nodded and they both stood up. "That'll be all for now, Ms Kingdom," PC Morgan said. "Thank you. Please don't go anywhere without informing your local police station. We may have some more questions for you, given that the investigation into Mrs Lester's death is still ongoing and Mr Robsart's whereabouts are currently unknown."

"Of course," Lizzie said numbly. "I understand. Please do let me know if there is any news of Johnny," she added, and saw suspicion deepen in PC Morgan's eyes. She wondered why on earth she felt so guilty when she hadn't done anything wrong. It didn't help that she felt so oddly out of it, so disconnected. The whole experience of reading the history of the old palace had been weird. She hadn't thought twice about touching the plaque because it had looked modern but perhaps it had been mounted on one of the old stones that had made up the Tudor walls. Even if she had known that, though, she wouldn't have hesitated because she had never had a vision involving a place before rather than a person. But then she had never connected directly to a person before she had met Arthur again… She frowned. It seemed her gift was a great deal more complex than she had thought and she didn't really like that. Regardless of what Johnny had said about not being afraid of her paranormal abilities she still felt spooked by them.

She watched the police head off down the road towards Blackfriars then pushed the button for the lift. It purred up to the penthouse. Lizzie's steps made no sound on the thick carpet of the corridor. It felt almost as though she was not there. The flat was equally quiet, as though Johnny's presence had left an indelible imprint and now there was a vacuum where he had been. She took out her phone and automatically checked for calls. There was nothing from Johnny so she texted him:

Good to see you this evening. Hope you are OK. Let me know when you're home.

She hoped she didn't come across like a fussy older sister. Johnny had given the impression he had enough of those. Perhaps that was why he dropped out of his life every so often; she could imagine the pressure he must feel with Arthur and Anna and the others trying to look after him. It would be their anxiety and their attention that would push him further away. Yet they had every reason to worry. Hell, in their place she would have worried too. She was worried anyway; everything seemed so bizarre, and Johnny wasn't the sort of person she could imagine walking out on someone who was ill or in trouble. He seemed too responsible for that. She rubbed her forehead again. If only she could remember what had happened but there was nothing; the vision of the palace, the sensations of sound, smell and touch so vivid and real, and then the fall into darkness, just like when she had touched the stone angel...

Seeking a bit of normality, she checked her phone messages. Alessandro had called to invite her to have dinner with him and Christy. "Keep the faith, Lizzie," he had said. "We know you haven't done anything wrong." Lizzie felt the tears spring into her eyes and rubbed them away with an impatient hand.

There were no voicemails from either Bill or Kat. It was unprecedented. She thought they must both be really angry with her. Or more likely they were waiting for her to admit she couldn't manage on her own and beg for help. She felt relieved she hadn't succumbed to the temptation of asking Bill for help when she had been down by the river—although if the police came back again, she supposed she would have to call the lawyers. She had no clue how to do that without his help.

She felt a sudden sharp ache of loneliness. She wished Jules was there. How long would it take her to get back from France? She needed someone she could trust. She'd been lonely all her life in the deepest sense of the word, and she was used to it now, but sometimes it was hard.

She wandered into the living room. The chair where Johnny had sat still retained the dent of his weight. Lizzie sat down opposite, as she had done earlier in the evening. The silence of the flat pressed closer on her. She could hear it, actively, as though it were breathing. It felt oppressive, smothering. She needed something to steady her and help her fight off the irrational waves of fear and reaction that were starting to swamp her. She needed to ground herself. She reached for the golden oak leaf-shaped necklace but it wasn't around her neck. She knew she had been wearing it earlier when she had been packing her bags. The links were very old and worn; perhaps she had dropped it in her bedroom. Jumping up, she hurried down the corridor.

The blank panels of the bedroom door confronted her. That was odd. She knew she had left it open. She hesitated, feeling fear tiptoe up her spine. Had someone broken in to the flat whilst she and Johnny were out? But that was impossible; the flat was like a fortress. No one could get in.

She threw the door open. The room was in darkness. She'd left it with all the lights on. The snap of the switch sounded loud in the quiet and when the light flooded the room again it seemed brighter than ever. Nothing was different. Nothing had changed. Lizzie thought she must have turned out the lights and closed the door after all, and that she was losing her mind. She'd been sure…

Then she saw the jewel box. It was a big old bronze box that was another vintage piece she had inherited from her grandmother. She'd left it on her dressing-table whilst she'd been packing, intent on selecting a few bits and pieces to take with her when she'd finished choosing her clothes. Now, though, it was lying on its side on the bed, the contents scattered across the duvet. Lizzie stared. Her first thought, that it had been a burglary after all, was almost immediately followed by the realisation that nothing was missing. All her really valuable stuff was in the safe anyway, and she could see the diamond earrings she'd bought in Hong Kong and the gold bracelet she'd picked up in a souk in Dubai…

She started to gather up the box and put all the bits and pieces back. Perhaps she'd moved it over to the bed and had simply forgotten. She was so tired and her head still hurt. Then she noticed. The stone angel, the one she had accidentally taken from Oakhangar Hall on Amelia and Dudley's wedding day, which she had shoved into the bottom section of the box years ago and forgotten, was not there.

She sat down on the edge of the bed.

Johnny.

The closed door, the lights extinguished… She hadn't been imagining things. Johnny had been in here and since he had not bothered to cover his tracks, he obviously did not mind her knowing it.

She had no idea why Johnny had taken the stone angel; she didn't even know how he had come to realise she had it in her possession. The only thing that seemed clear was that he had planned it all. The thought hurt her. She'd thought that Johnny liked her. She'd felt empathy for him because she had seen something of her own situation in his and now it felt as though he had lied to her and screwed her over. Worse, though, was the fear of what he had really been feeling and thinking. Johnny was obviously even more disturbed and unbalanced than she had feared. He needed help. She hoped desperately that he was home and safe.

She flopped down on the bed in the middle of the sprawl of clothes and half-filled bags. What a mess. Johnny had stolen from her something she should have given back years ago. Somehow, he had known she had the stone angel, and where to find it. And why had he then asked her to go down to the Embankment with him to look at the remains of Baynard's Castle? She had thought at the time that it was odd but now she wondered whether in fact it had been random or if it was all part of a plan. She had touched the stone, she had seen the vision, and Johnny had gone, leaving her sick and alone... None of it made any sense to her but the more she thought about it the more disturbing it became.

Scrubbing her palms over her eyes, she blinked and sat up. It was then that she saw the notebook, or a corner of it, poking out from beneath the end of the bed. She leaned over the edge and snatched it up. It was a small dark green rectangle, lined inside, the pages ruffled as though well used and with a thin darker green ribbon sticking out of the bottom. Lizzie opened it. It was full of endless notes, diagrams and drawings, sprawling charts that looked like family trees, dates with more scribbles written over the top, crossings out and different colours, chaotic and rambling.

She had never seen Johnny's writing but she knew this must be his. She wondered whether he had dropped it, or left it on purpose for her to find. She wondered if he was messing with her mind. Was this payback for Amelia? Suddenly she didn't know anything anymore.

Lizzie took a deep breath. The notebook might be able to tell her something if she was willing to use her gift. It might give a clue to Johnny's feelings when he wrote in it and that in turn might help work out where he was and what was going on.

She felt a ripple of apprehension at what might happen if she employed the psychometry but Johnny—and Arthur—were more important than her fears. Very deliberately she pressed one palm to the cover of the book, the palm that so long ago had been cut by the shards of glass when the crystal smashed. She kept her mind light and empty; open to images, thoughts and emotions. She felt the cool smoothness of the paper against her fingers, the slight creases and the rough edges of the pages. She waited.

The images, when they came, were overpowering. Lizzie felt Johnny's emotions like a blow to her stomach. It was such a complicated mixture, his eagerness and determination, desperation and terror, all connected in some way to the notes he had made in the book. She could sense that there was something that Johnny wanted so badly that it literally made him feel sick with longing and fear, and yet the desire for it drove him onward.

The sensations shifted and Lizzie saw her own past then,

saw the gazing ball and the carved stone angel in the hall at Oakhangar on the day of the wedding. She saw the moment she touched the angel's wing and the crystal ball exploded into shards. The images were like a film running through her head on a loop. And then she saw something else: six-year-old Johnny on the staircase at Oakhangar as he peered through the bannisters, watching her.

She came back to herself, and the flat was warm and bright with lamplight yet the shudders still racked her. The notebook had slid unnoticed from her lap and was lying on the bedcover once again, the pages fanned out. Lizzie stared at it, trying to make sense of the images she had witnessed and the feelings she had experienced. It seemed clear that Johnny had seen what had happened that day. He'd seen her touch the stone angel and he'd seen the crystal ball shatter. Perhaps he'd also witnessed someone putting the stone angel in her bag later in the general fuss and confusion, and that was how he had known she had it. He'd asked her about it to get her version of the story and perhaps to see if she would own up to having it.

What she couldn't understand was how the stone angel connected to the emotions she had experienced in the vision, Johnny's emotions. The sense of desperation and longing had been so acute. She could not begin to unravel them. Perhaps the clues to that lay in the book itself but she didn't want to touch it again just yet. She felt completely exhausted, as though the psychometry had drained her of all energy.

She wished, suddenly and fiercely, that she could talk to Arthur. She reached for her phone and called up his number. Then she stopped, cancelling the call. It had been a totally instinctive reaction but she realised how stupid and potentially dangerous it would be. She barely knew Arthur, no matter the strange connection there was between them. After the police had interviewed her about Amelia's death, the lawyers had told her to have nothing to do with the Robsart family at all. She'd already broken that commitment several times. Ringing Arthur up and pouring out a weird story about how his brother had been to see her, stolen an ornament that wasn't hers in the first place and had then vanished was asking for trouble.

She walked over to the window. The view of the river was different from here; she could see the Shard and the News Building on the southern bank, and Blackfriars Bridge lit up in pink and gold above the inky black water. Often the view over London excited her, sometimes it soothed her, but tonight she felt impossibly restless and hemmed in.

Her phone rang in her hand. She did not need to look at the screen to see the caller ID. She instinctively knew exactly who it was.

"You wanted to talk to me," Arthur said, without preamble.

"Yes." Lizzie took a deep breath. "Yes, I did."

14

Amy: Baynard's Castle, London, Spring 1557

I FIRST SAW the ghost boy on the day I had the news that my mother had died. She had been living at Stansfield Manor still, and had been ailing for a while. When he had died, my father had left the manor to her for her lifetime with the stipulation that it would pass to me on her death along with a number of his other estates. I was his heir; he had left nothing to Arthur, yet it was Arthur who had continued to care for my mother in her sickness and it was Arthur whose writing I recognised now on the letter.

I remember everything about that day so clearly. It was very early spring still with more than an edge of winter. The first leaves were starting to tinge the trees with green but the winds were cold. We were at Baynard's Castle, one of Queen Mary's favourite palaces. Robert was once

more a courtier but our lives had changed out of all recognition. Gone were the estates, the grand style of living,
the power, the royal favour. Robert had his freedom but
precious little else. The Queen had no fondness for him.
How could she, when he had been the man sent to take
her captive only five years before? In her eyes he was a
traitor and never to be trusted.

Mary's spies watched us constantly. The Queen was no
fool; men spoke disparagingly of her blind stubbornness,
that she baulked like a donkey when thwarted, but she
knew her false friends and she knew Robert's loyalty lay
with her sister Elizabeth and not with her. No, it was her
husband Philip, the Spanish King, who had taken Robert
into his retinue and sometimes I thought he had done it
deliberately to spite Queen Mary. He had no affection for
her though she mooned after him like a young lovestruck
maid. Philip disliked her and he hated England and he
showed it in many small and petty ways. One of the tools
he used to taunt her was his friendship with Robert.

Life at court was expensive, especially in the retinue of
Philip of Spain. Robert's brother had made over to him
an estate in Hales Owen, somewhere in Worcestershire,
in order to give him an income, but one small plot of land
was nothing to a man who had once held so many manors.
We never went there though Robert ran it dry.

"Ambrose has so much," Robert grumbled one night,
"and I so little. He could give me more and it would not
harm him."

I could have told him that more would never be enough
for him but I held my peace. Robert did not tell me things
in order to gain my opinion. He had no interest in my
views. Something had broken between us that day in the

Tower of London, a trust, a loyalty. Or perhaps it had only ever existed in my imagination or my dreams. I did not know. What I did know was that whatever emotion held Robert and I together, it was a shallow thing, a shadow of the feeling he had for the Lady Elizabeth. We were wed and so my fortunes were tied to his but there was nothing else to bind us. I mourned the love I believed I had once had for him now it was gone.

On that spring morning, Robert, King Philip, a number of the other Spanish gentlemen and a few of the English were down in the tiltyard, practising the joust. With Arthur's letter clutched to my chest I made my way down there, pushing through the crowds of pages and esquires, the throng who would turn out to see the King and his courtiers at play, hoping for a word or a favour. There were few women there. I hated the coarseness of the tiltyard, the rough masculinity. It was in the air, the pounding of the horses' hooves, the smell of hay and sweat and dung. It was in the shouts of the men. It felt dangerous.

Outside the sunlight blinded me and I realised that it was because my eyes were full of tears. There was a pressure in my chest with the weight of my grief. It was so long since I had seen my mother and although we had written frequently the sudden realisation that I would never see her again hit me hard. My half-siblings and I were scattered, Arthur in Norfolk, John at college in Oxford and Anna in Cambridgeshire where her husband was rebuilding a grand house in place of the one that Robert had destroyed. The Queen had compensated them well for their loyalty to her and although I had seen both Anna and Antony in London when he came to sit in the parliament, we were not reconciled. I knew she would be unlikely to write to me to share our grief over Mother's death and that hurt to my soul.

A raucous cheer went around the tiltyard when some of the men saw me. Robert had just finished a bout against Philip himself, which he had cleverly let Philip win, but not too easily. He slid down from the horse, patted its sweating neck, and strode across to where I was standing. He was frowning and for one horrible moment I thought he was about to upbraid me for seeking him out, here in front of all the men. But I had misread him. Instead he swept me up into his arms, the letter crumpled between us, and kissed me hard. I stiffened to pull away but he was already releasing me, his point made, his virility emphasised by the joust and the embrace of a pretty girl. I suppose I should have been glad that the pretty girl had been me.

"My mother is dead," I blurted out, too overset for any finesse.

Robert was still breathing hard and I could see the excitement of the joust was still in his blood. He was very still for a moment and I wondered if he had not heard me, but then his eyes blazed and he reached for me, and with horror I thought he was about to kiss me again.

"Robert!" I said. I knew exactly what he had been thinking and it was not of my mother's death or my grief; it was of my father's will and the money and the estates, and the fact that we could sell the land now and not be forever in debt or pinching and scraping to survive. I saw it all in his face before he said a word; he had spent my inheritance before he even offered his condolences.

Then the light went out of his face and he stepped back.

"I am very sorry," he said formally. "You will wish to

be chief mourner, of course. I will ask Hyde to arrange
your journey to Norfolk."

William Hyde was the weasel who managed our financial affairs, one of a group of unsavoury characters whom
Robert seemed to collect around him like maggots to a
carcass. I did not know the work they did for him and I
took care not to enquire too closely but when there was a
tavern brawl or a knifing down a dark alley it seemed one
or other of them were often involved.

I stared at him. "Will you not accompany me?"

"I am to go abroad with His Majesty very soon." Robert
glanced across to where Philip was talking to one of his
knights. "It is all agreed. There is talk of war with France."

"You did not tell me." Grief was making me stupid
and slow.

He did not look at me. "It was only recently that His
Majesty discussed it with me."

I knew this meant that everyone else was aware of the
plan and that as usual I had not been deemed important
enough for Robert to tell me. I felt a huge surge of anger;
I was aware that I was making a public scene, that men
were watching us out of the corners of their eyes and some
more openly, and that Philip himself was tapping his foot
impatiently as he waited for Robert to rejoin him. The
King had no time for awkward, clinging wives. He was
cruel enough to his own and did not tolerate anyone else's.

"And what will become of me?" I said. My voice shook.
"Where am I to go whilst you play at heroics with His
Majesty?"

"I have made provision for you," Robert said. "You will
be staying at a fine manor in the country, with goodly
company."

This evidence that he had planned my future as well as his own without any word to me knocked the breath out of me for a moment.

"I am to be sent away?" My voice rose dangerously now. "You must reconsider now that I have come into my inheritance. I shall go to Norfolk and take up the running of the estates." Suddenly I wanted it more than anything else in the world, wanted a place to belong, a path of my own to follow that was not tied to Robert. Arthur would be there; he would help me. I could learn all about the land and the seasons, the animals, the crops, the estate business. The idea intoxicated me.

Yet Robert was shaking his head.

"That would not be seemly, wife," he said. "We have people to run our affairs for us, men whose knowledge of business is far superior to your own." He looked down his aristocratic nose at me, the provincial daughter of a gentleman whose lineage went back a great deal further than his own.

"I see," I said. "You will allow me no say in the running of *my* estates. Have you already borrowed against them to fund your extravagances?" My contemptuous gesture encompassed the tiltyard, the preening peacocks of the court. "I see you have. My land is already as good as sold and the money already spent—"

His hand closed warningly about my arm. "Amy. We'll speak of this later."

"Very well." I took a deep breath and grasped for the ragged edges of composure. "Just tell me where you had planned for me to go."

"Later," Robert said, with a swift glance, a nod over his shoulder to the King.

"*Now,*" I said.

He grimaced but he conceded this one, small point. "William Hyde has generously offered his manor at Throcking in Hertfordshire," he said. "It is conveniently placed between London and Norfolk—"

It was, I realised, also very conveniently placed for Hatfield Palace, where the Lady Elizabeth currently languished in exile from her sister's court. If Robert were to visit her, I would be the pretext.

"Convenient indeed," I said cuttingly, "to be able to visit your wife and your mistress within easy distance of each other."

Fury darkened his eyes, violent and terrifying. His previous irritation had been no more than a shadow of this. "Do *not* speak thus of the Lady Elizabeth," he said, very softly.

I knew it was indiscreet of me but by now I was drunk with grief and anger, all the more so because I knew that his concern for her sprang from a love I simply could not understand. All the misery and neglect I had fostered within me unknowingly over the past years seemed to well up.

"Why should I not?" I was shaking. "I know your regard for her far outweighs your love for me."

"Amy," Robert said again and this time his tone shrivelled what was left of me. His hand tightened on my arm. I winced at the pain. "You are distraught," he said smoothly. "You there—" A scurrying servant slid over to us. "Take my lady back to her chambers. She is in grief." His lips touched my cheek in a kiss as cold as snow. "I will come to you soon—"

"Leave me alone!" I wrenched myself away from his grip and ran, slipping on the cobbles and the manure, dirty water splashing my skirts from the gutters. I blundered into the palace, momentarily blinded by the darkness after the bright light outside, aware of nothing but the gaping faces around me as I clutched Arthur's letter in one shaking hand. The sobs tore at my chest and I was obliged to stop to steady myself, one hand against the wall, my breath coming in pants.

"Mistress… Dudley, is it not?"

I dashed the tears from my eyes. There was an unnatural stillness around me all of a sudden. The crowds had fallen back, waiting.

It was the Queen. I had not seen her approach. She peered at me, head poking forward like a myopic tortoise.

"I beg your pardon, Your Majesty." I dropped the best curtsey I could manage under the circumstances, wiping my eyes and, surreptitiously, my nose. "Please excuse me. I did not realise…"

"A moment—" She touched my sleeve, staying me. "Walk with me. Tell me what ails you."

I would much have preferred not to but I had no choice. It was a royal command. Reluctantly I fell into step beside her.

"I have but this moment received the news of my mother's death," I said, carefully. "I fear my grief has overset me."

"I am very sorry." Her faded, dark eyes appraised me sadly. "I still recall the deep sorrow of losing a parent."

I could only imagine that she was speaking of her mother, Catherine of Aragon, to whom she had been inordinately loyal and whose memory she still honoured. The death of her father, the late King Henry, who had been such a tyrant towards her could not have been the cause for much regret.

"Thank you, Your Majesty," I said.

"You were coming from the tiltyard." The impression of a weary, ageing woman was misleading; she was sharp. "You were apprising your husband of the news?"

"Yes, Your Majesty."

"I see." I thought she probably did. "Did he tell you that he is to accompany the King to Picardy?"

"Yes, madam, he did."

"You had not known?" She was a shrewd reader of tone and expression. "Ah." Her shoulders slumped. "It is a difficult matter to be a neglected wife, Mistress Dudley, is it not? It is even more difficult to be a childless one." Her eyes met mine and I felt a ripple of shock at the pain and disillusionment I saw there. This woman and I were not so dissimilar though she was Queen of England in her own right and surrounded by all the trappings of majesty. She could not command a man's good opinion or his loyalty, nor could she, apparently, bear his child. Since the supposed false pregnancy she had experienced eighteen months before there had been nothing.

Something snapped in me then at the accumulated weight of grief and frustration. I grasped her sleeve, pulling her back when she would have walked on, careless of convention.

"Can you help me, Majesty? Please—I beg you. My husband wishes to sell the estates I have inherited from my mother, whilst I wish to run them myself. Would you rule that they should be mine alone? It would give me so much more purpose—" My voice broke.

I heard the gasp as people fell silent, some shocked, some prurient, to witness my distress. I did not care. I was looking at the Queen and at her alone, the material of her sleeve scoring my fingers because I gripped so tightly. "Majesty—" I said desperately, but I knew it was too late. The expression in her eyes had hardened into ice. I had misread her; we had little in common after all. She had given King Philip an equal share in her kingdom no matter how little he deserved it. She would not take away my husband's right to my inheritance. She might despise him but she would not use me to revenge herself against him as I had hoped.

"Good day, Mistress Dudley," she said, quite as though I had not spoken, and she withdrew her sleeve from my grasp with unhurried lack of concern and walked away.

It was then that I saw the ghost boy, across the heads of the crowd. I noticed him because he was standing very still in the shifting throng and he was staring directly at me. He could not have been much above sixteen years, maybe a little more or a little less. He was tall and thin as a rake, dressed like a street player or a beggar, with a short black cloak and cowl, ripped hose and muddy boots. Beneath the edge of his hood his face was pale and his eyes frightened. We stared at one another for what felt like a very long time and it seemed to me as though the flagstones tilted beneath my feet and the earth spun around me.

"Who are you?" I said. "What are you doing here?"

I doubt he heard my words for the passageway was still full of chattering courtiers. None of them seemed to have seen him, or if they had, they paid him no notice. He opened his mouth to speak. I saw his lips move and tried to listen, tried to hear his words.

Someone jostled me and did not trouble to apologise, and when I had regained my balance and looked again, the ghost boy had gone.

15

Lizzie: Present Day

"THANK YOU FOR SEEING US," Arthur said, very formally. "We're grateful."

"It's the least she could do." Anna contradicted him almost immediately. She shot Lizzie a distinctly unfriendly glance as she pushed past them both into Lizzie's flat.

"Do come in," Lizzie said politely. It was the morning after Johnny had disappeared and she had arranged to meet Arthur at ten. She hadn't expected him to bring Anna with him, though. It wrong-footed her and she was angry for reading more intimacy into their interactions than existed, and for assuming Arthur would come alone. In the dark reaches of the night, lying awake for hour after hour, it had comforted her to think there was some sort of bond between them. Now in cold daylight she realised that she had been naïve. Johnny had never arrived home the previous night. Arthur wanted to find him. She was the last person who had seen him so she might be able to help. That was all there was to it.

Lizzie felt tired and slow. She'd waited and waited for either the police or Arthur to call to confirm that Johnny had finally turned up. She had kept her light on for hours to ward off a darkness that felt as though it was inside her as well as outside. Finally, she had turned out the light and had lain quietly listening to the sound of the rubbish being collected out in the street, the rolling of empty barrels, the shouts of drunks, all the noises that filled a London night. The city was never silent and at least she did not feel entirely alone.

Arthur, she thought, didn't look as though he had slept any better than she had. Stubble darkened his jaw and his eyes were tired. Lizzie couldn't read his emotions other than the obvious exhaustion and concern for his brother. It felt as though he was deliberately shutting her out, which was an odd, disconnected feeling, as though instinct and reason were at war with one another, a deeply uncomfortable sensation. She tried to see things from Arthur's point of view and then wished she hadn't. She could see he had every reason to be wary of her. Johnny had come to see her and now Johnny was missing.

"Is there any news?" she said, and felt hope drain away when Arthur shook his head.

"Johnny still hasn't turned up," he said. "We've spoken to everyone now, and checked all the places we can think of."

"You look as though you need coffee," Lizzie said involuntarily. "Have you been out all night looking for him?"

"Yeah." Arthur gave her a brief smile. It didn't reach his eyes. "At least the last time he disappeared he turned up of his own accord, but this time there's been nothing. Not even a text. I don't suppose you've heard from him either?"

"I would have told you if I had," Lizzie said, and Arthur nodded, grimacing.

"Sorry," he said. "I'm sure you would. I was just hoping…" He shrugged.

"He's not here," Anna called, from the living room. Lizzie raised her brows at Arthur, who had the grace to look embarrassed.

"I apologise for Anna," he said. "We're all a bit on edge."

"It's OK," Lizzie said. "Come through." She caught the corner of his thoughts then; the fact that he too was feeling the conflict between intuition and logic, between affinity and wariness. She sensed he liked it as little as she did.

Anna was standing in the middle of the living room, hands on hips, looking to Lizzie like a smaller, more self-assured version of Amelia. Physically they shared the blonde hair and blue eyes that had given Amelia her waif-like quality but Lizzie thought that if Amelia had had an ounce of Anna's toughness, she wouldn't have tolerated Dudley's behaviour for a moment. She wondered if Anna's truculence came naturally but then she remembered how gentle she had been with Johnny that time in the foyer and thought she should cut the younger girl some slack. It was a sentiment she retracted almost immediately.

"You were the last person to see Johnny," Anna said. "Did you push him into the river?"

"Don't be ridiculous, Anna," Arthur said. Anna flushed but there was defiance in her eyes.

"What?" she said. "I'm only trying to find out what happened."

"No, I didn't," Lizzie said. There was a silence. Anna waited for her to say more. Lizzie tacitly refused. Out of the corner of her eye, she saw Arthur bite back a smile as he watched them.

"I don't understand why Johnny came to see you in the first place." Anna couldn't hold back any longer. She eyed Lizzie belligerently. "What did he want?"

"He wanted to talk about stuff," Lizzie said. "About Amelia and Dudley and how he was feeling." It wasn't exactly true; she wasn't sure whether everything Johnny had done had just been an attempt to get into her confidence and her flat and to take the stone angel. She might tell Arthur that but she wasn't going to tell Anna.

Anna gave a dismissive snort. "I still don't get it. Millie's body is in cold storage, Dudley is being investigated, you're an accessory after the fact, whatever that is, and Johnny thought it would help to talk to *you*? Doesn't he realise how toxic you are? What planet is he on?"

Lizzie took a deep breath. "I'm not an accessory after anything," she said, "and maybe Johnny recognised that and isn't as prejudiced as you are. Look," she tried to sound conciliatory, "would you both like some coffee—or something else to drink? We can have a chat, try and work out what might have happened—"

"I'm not stopping, thanks." Anna didn't let her finish. "I only came along to make sure you weren't hiding Johnny's body."

"*Anna*," Arthur said.

"Feel free to search," Lizzie said mildly.

Anna just glared at her. "Arthur said Johnny told him

that he *likes* you. He said you were kind to him when he was a kid at Amelia's wedding. I mean—really? I'm sorry, but he's totally lost it this time."

"For God's sake, Anna," Arthur said. "Stop this."

Anna shrugged. "You said so yourself," she said. "You said you thought Johnny was nuts to trust her."

"I'm not sure I put it quite like that," Arthur said. There was a hint of colour on his high cheekbones. Lizzie wondered how much of their conversation the previous night he had relayed to Anna. She was glad now that she hadn't said much beyond the fact that Johnny had been to see her and that she was worried for his state of mind.

"I'm walking over to Dudley's place now," Anna said. She jerked her head towards the Millennium Bridge. "If Johnny turns up there again and threatens him, Dudley will have him arrested." She came closer and Lizzie saw the sheen of tears in her eyes, the despair behind the anger. "Did you know Dudley has hired a posse of heavies for protection? It's in the papers this morning. He claims Johnny might attack him! As though Johnny would hurt anyone." A tear escaped from the corner of her eye and she scrubbed it away impatiently. "I fucking *hate* Dudley. This is his fault—Millie's death, Johnny disappearing… His fault and yours," she glared at Lizzie again, "behaving as though Millie just didn't exist, flaunting yourselves all over London—"

"Anna." Arthur sounded really angry this time.

"It's OK," Lizzie said again. She met Anna's angry blue gaze very directly. "You're right," she said. "I was selfish. I didn't care about Amelia's feelings and I'm very sorry about that. I said as much to Johnny last night. But I know nothing about Amelia's death, Dudley and I have never been romantically involved, and I certainly wouldn't *ever* do anything to hurt Johnny. I only want to help him."

"I don't see why." Anna was relishing the argument as a release of pent-up energy.

"Because," Lizzie snapped, "Johnny is struggling to deal with depression and I've some insight into how that feels. It's a horrible, horrible thing and Johnny is beyond brave, and if you think I would hurt him in any way then you're the one who's lost it."

For a moment Anna looked nonplussed then she shrugged. "Whatever," she said ungraciously. She nodded to Arthur. "I'll call you if I hear anything." She marched off down the hall and the door slammed behind her. The air seemed to quiver before settling into quiet again.

"Well," Arthur said into the silence, "that was interesting."

Lizzie took a deep breath to try and regain her self-control. "I shouldn't have snapped at her," she said wearily. "I'm sorry."

"She asked for it," Arthur said. "Anna always pushes to get a reaction. Sometimes she goes way too far." He shifted a little. "I'm sorry for all the stuff she said. She's upset and worried—we all are—but it's no excuse."

"I understand," Lizzie said. She folded her arms and rubbed them although she wasn't cold. "I know it's hard to believe I might want to help Johnny," she said, "but I do." She spread her hands in appeal. "I helped you the other night, didn't I?"

Arthur drove his hands into his pockets. "Yes, you did," he said slowly, "but I still don't really know if I can trust you. Hell, Lizzie—" he ran a hand through his hair "—no matter what I *feel*, I don't know you. It's entirely possible that you and Dudley might be in cahoots and have cooked up this whole business between you to get rid of Amelia and now to silence Johnny."

"That's exactly what the police were getting at when they interviewed me last night," Lizzie agreed pleasantly. She took a deep breath. "Everyone's watched too many box sets, I think. But let's indulge your theory for a moment." She caught the glint of amusement in Arthur's eyes and carried on doggedly: "Leaving aside the fact that I'm not a psychopath, I've also no motive to kill Amelia. It's not as though we're in the Middle Ages, is it? Dudley and Amelia were getting divorced. If he and I *had* wanted to get together—which we don't—there wasn't anything stopping us."

"Bumping off Amelia would save Dudley having to pay alimony," Arthur said, "but actually it's more likely that Dudley's motive would be financial gain in a different way. Dudley's lost—or rather, he's spent—almost all he ever earned. He's close to bankruptcy. Whereas Amelia was a very rich woman. Perhaps you didn't know, but our father left her a fortune. She inherited just about everything from him."

Lizzie was taken aback. "No, I didn't know that," she admitted. "Dudley never mentioned it."

"Well," Arthur said, "I don't suppose he would. Amelia was always portrayed as the clinging one, wasn't she, living off Dudley's money and success. It was far from the truth."

Lizzie felt a judder of remorse. That was exactly how she had viewed Amelia. She'd made assumptions because Dudley was so brash and full of his own importance. Suddenly she didn't feel as confident that Dudley had no motive. She'd viewed any involvement on his part in Amelia's death as fantasy, but if he was going to inherit a fortune from her that didn't look good at all. She could see why the police would be suspicious.

"Inheritance is a minefield, isn't it?" she said with feeling. "Didn't you mind being cut out of the will? And what about Anna and Johnny?"

Arthur laughed. "I'm not big into inherited wealth, to be honest. I wanted to make my own way. I talked about it with Dad. He left Anna and Johnny a trust fund each for school and university fees but we felt Millie was the vulnerable one who might need it one day."

"Because of Dudley," Lizzie said bluntly.

Arthur didn't deny it. "We all thought the marriage wouldn't last long," he said. "They were very young, Dudley has a short attention span, and Millie never really found anything she was good at. Dad gave her the money to buy Oakhangar Hall and left her his investments to give her an income. It's all Johnny's now," he added. "He was the sole beneficiary of Millie's will. She rewrote it to cut Dudley out when he asked for a divorce. He gets nothing."

"Whoa," Lizzie said. "Does Dudley know that?"

"He'll know now," Arthur said drily.

"And Johnny?" Lizzie asked. "Not that he'd care. I imagine he'd return it all in a heartbeat if he could have Amelia back."

Arthur gave her a curious look. "Did Johnny tell you that last night?"

"Yes," Lizzie said. "He said he'd do anything to have Amelia back again." She sighed. "OK, well I get that you don't like Dudley and that you might even believe he would want to get rid of Amelia somehow but do you seriously believe that *I* would be capable of murdering her, never mind harming Johnny?"

Arthur's mouth twisted. "I don't think you would murder someone; not unless they threatened you or something or someone for whom you cared deeply." He paused. "But you might cover up a crime for someone you loved, or even connive in it. I don't know. I don't know you well enough to say."

Lizzie was startled to realise that she felt angry. She wanted Arthur to think better of her than that and it annoyed her that it mattered so much to her. Arthur, she realised with a pang, was trying to ignore any intuitive link between them and rely on logic, which was completely understandable but hurt her more than she cared to analyse.

"So, your theory is that I helped Dudley kill his wife because I was madly in love with him," she said coldly. "And that Johnny knew something to incriminate us so we dealt with him too?"

"I didn't say that," Arthur said, "but even if it's true that you don't love Dudley in that way you have always cared about him. You said so yourself. You might misguidedly try to help or protect him."

Lizzie absorbed this. She didn't want to admit it, but Arthur's words did make sense. The thought that he would ever believe her complicit in such a crime was hard to hear but she could see that from his point of view she couldn't be trusted. If she was going to convince him she would need to be completely honest about everything that had happened with Johnny and even then, there would be no guarantee he would accept it.

"Well," she said, on another sigh, "trust me far enough

to let me make you that coffee and then we can talk about Johnny and you can judge for yourself."

"Thanks," Arthur said. He gave her a tired smile. "And thank you for seeing my point of view."

Their eyes met and for a moment Lizzie thought he was going to say something else, something about the affinity they shared, but the moment passed.

"What a nice flat," Arthur said as he followed her into the kitchen. "I was expecting—" He stopped.

"You were expecting marble floors and gold leaf," Lizzie finished for him. "Each to their own, although bling isn't really my thing." The tension inside her eased a little at his evident embarrassment. There was something so self-contained, so controlled about Arthur that it was actually a relief to discover that he was as prone to a gaffe as the next person. But perhaps he was nervous too. It was such an odd situation they found themselves in.

"I'm sorry," Arthur said. He rubbed the back of his neck. "That was rude of me."

Lizzie smiled. "You made assumptions. People do." She took a deep breath. "Look, shall we try and start again—with as few prejudices as we can manage?"

Arthur's answering smile made her heart miss a beat. "That would probably be for the best," he said.

"Do sit down." Lizzie gestured him to the chair by the window where Johnny had sat the night before. "How do you take your coffee?"

"Strong, please." She could feel Arthur watching her as she filled the cafetière. She felt strangely self-conscious. Arthur felt simultaneously like a stranger and someone she knew very well. It was beyond disconcerting.

"Where did you leave your car?" she asked. "The parking's non-existent around here."

"I left it outside," Arthur said. He smiled faintly. "The guy from the private parking company promised to keep an eye on it for me. I don't think he'd seen a car like mine before."

"It takes a lot to impress them round here," Lizzie said. "What do you drive?"

"An original Land Rover Defender," Arthur said. "Held together by mud and rust. He would probably have towed it away but he was afraid it would fall apart."

"You're a farmer." Lizzie remembered Kat's breathless disclosures about him.

Arthur nodded. "It's a busy time of year for me," he said. "I should be back in Norfolk really. Luckily I have a very efficient and long-suffering farm manager." He took the mug from her with a word of thanks and took a deep, appreciative swallow. "Ah, that's good. I thought you'd have a coffee machine."

"I do," Lizzie said. "But if you need proper, strong coffee, the cafetière is best." She poured for herself and added a generous mixture of sugar.

"When we met at Dudley and Amelia's wedding you were on TV, weren't you?" she asked. "What made you give all that up to farm?"

Arthur gave her a direct look. "That's a very personal question."

"Sorry." Lizzie shrugged. "It's part of my stock in trade, I suppose, interviewing and presenting. I was interested, that's all."

Arthur didn't reply immediately and she thought he wasn't going to answer at all but then he did.

"It felt very glamorous when I started out." He spoke slowly, thoughtfully, as though he was thinking back over something he hadn't talked about in a long time. "I was only nineteen—they signed me up for the TV show after I'd just gone to college. Mum was furious when I dropped out; she'd walked away from the whole modelling thing because she said celebrity was corrupt but I just thought she was spoiling my fun." He shrugged, a little awkwardly. "She said fame bred insecurity and unhappiness. I told her not to be stupid. I'd had my head properly turned."

"You wouldn't be the first," Lizzie said. "And you were very young." She was surprised all the same. Arthur seemed so grounded but perhaps he had learned the hard way what was real and worthwhile and what was not.

"Yeah, well…" Arthur shifted a little. "It was all new and exciting for me, and after a couple of years I met Jenna, my fiancée, and she was a model and an actress and it was very glamorous… It felt as though we were really *living*, if you know what I mean." He looked at her. "It's as though all the special treatment and first-class travel and people fawning over you validates you in some way, but I guess you've experienced that for yourself."

"Yeah," Lizzie said. "It's easy to believe in your own legend. You need to be very sure of who you are before fame happens if you're not going to get spoilt."

A smile touched Arthur's lips. "Who knew you were so wise?" he said.

"Bitter experience," Lizzie said lightly. "I was very young when I started and it did spoil me. I can't deny that. I do try to be aware of it now but a sense of entitlement can be a hard habit to break."

Arthur's smile lingered. "You don't do a bad job," he said, and she felt as though he'd given her a present.

Arthur broke the moment. "I think I must have been unbearable," he said. "Jenna and I were so full of ourselves." He pulled a face. "But underneath it… Jenna was totally messed up. I tried to help but it wasn't enough."

"I'm very sorry," Lizzie said. She remembered Kat saying that Jenna had died of anorexia. She wondered whether that was where Arthur's tendency to try to save people stemmed from. It must have been appalling to lose his fiancée like that and to feel so helpless.

"Was that why you turned your back on it all?" she asked. "A change of direction?"

"It wasn't really that different," Arthur said. "I've always loved the countryside and I was making shows that focussed on animals and nature—you know the sort of thing. Farming is just a different emphasis, really. I went to the US to study agriculture. My mother lives in the States these days and it's a kind of second home to me. I studied at Cornell and then went to Uppsala in Sweden for my postgraduate degree." He didn't make any reference to how Jenna's death had made him feel and Lizzie didn't push. The fact he'd told her it was a very personal question showed how significant it still must be to him.

"I'm thinking of doing something different," Lizzie said. "Well, not different exactly, but more writing and composing. I was the songwriter for my band back in the day and I really enjoyed it." She caught herself up in time before she told him more. It was easy to talk to Arthur because she felt close to him and difficult to remember that there was more that divided them than brought them together.

"Anyway, come back through," she said awkwardly.

She was very aware of Arthur following her through to the living room. He went over to the seat by the window, sparing one long, appreciative glance for her bookshelves and a second one for the view before turning his attention back to her.

"I'd forgotten that you lost your mother when you were even younger than Johnny," he said unexpectedly. "That must have been very painful. No wonder you have such an affinity with him."

He caught Lizzie off guard. Grief ambushed her, visceral and raw. She swallowed hard. "I don't remember my mother very well," she said, trying to sound as though it didn't matter. "I was too young."

"Earlier on I brushed you off when you asked something that was still very personal to me," Arthur said wryly. "Now you've done the same." There was tension in the line of his shoulders. "I guess that until this issue with Johnny is resolved we'd better just stick to the straightforward stuff."

"There's not much of that around," Lizzie said, with feeling.

"No," Arthur said. "I suppose not. OK, let's just go for it. Last night when we spoke you said that you'd got something you wanted to tell me in person, something to do with Johnny's visit."

"Yes." Lizzie realised that her fingers were knotted together tightly with tension. She sat forward, deliberately unlocking them and wrapping her hands about her own coffee mug. The heat of it was soothing.

"Johnny and I talked about lots of things last night," she said slowly. "How he was feeling about Amelia's death, his parents, Dudley…" She rubbed her eyes. They felt gritty and sore this morning, as though she had spent the night in a smoky room. "I thought he just wanted to talk to someone who was a step removed from everything, you know?" She looked at Arthur. "You're all dealing with the grief as well, and you in particular are trying to hold everything together and you're worried about Johnny..." She smiled at him. "I thought perhaps Johnny needed a break from all that and space to talk." She took a breath. "Well, I suppose he did, but that wasn't all."

Arthur was watching her, his gaze steady and perceptive. "What happened?"

"For a start, Johnny told me that he and Amelia had been telepathic," Lizzie said bluntly. She looked at Arthur, waiting for a reaction, but he said nothing. She could see what Johnny had meant about him being the strong and silent type; he had such a good poker face.

Arthur stirred at last. "You did cover a lot of ground," he said.

"You think?" Lizzie said sarcastically.

Arthur laughed. "Sorry," he said. "I didn't mean to be unforthcoming."

"Yeah, you did," Lizzie said and Arthur spread his hands in a gesture of surrender.

"All right," he said. "I only hesitated because..." He stopped, shrugged. "I guess I always feel wrong-footed with you because we have this strange psychic thing going on and I'm just not really comfortable with any of that stuff..." He made a slight, dismissive gesture. "Anyway, it's true about the telepathy in the sense that Johnny and Millie always seemed to know what the other was thinking or where the other one was. They would do some curious sort of party trick where one of them would think of a word and they would both write it down and it would be the same. It was uncanny."

"OK," Lizzie said, "that's interesting. I thought it must be true but I wanted to be sure."

"I didn't want to believe it at first," Arthur admitted, "because I couldn't understand it." He sat back in the big chair, stretching his long legs out in front of him. "After a while, though, I got used to it. It was just Millie and Johnny—just the way they were, like Anna gets belligerent when she's unhappy. It was a part of their characters and their relationship." His gaze came up to hers, suddenly very direct. "I'd never experienced telepathy myself, though, until you touched me. I don't like feeling you can read my mind whenever you choose."

Lizzie's heart jumped in her chest. "I thought we weren't going to talk about us?" she said. "But since you brought it up, I don't like it any more than you do. It's never happened to me before. I usually read objects, not people, and I don't even enjoy doing that." She could feel herself becoming hot and bothered under Arthur's steady dark stare.

"It seems I've met someone even less comfortable with the fey stuff than I am myself," he said. He sounded grimly amused. "How inconvenient it must be for you to possess that gift when you don't want it."

"It's not funny," Lizzie said crossly. "And anyway, I thought you just said you didn't believe in it?"

"I didn't say I didn't believe in it," Arthur said, "just that I wasn't comfortable with it. There's no point in denying something that is patently obvious even if both of us would prefer it not to exist."

"Yeah, we're stuck with it," Lizzie said. "I promise not

to invade your privacy with my mind tricks. It'll be fine as long as we don't touch each other."

"Right," Arthur said, with a scrupulous courtesy that for some reason made her feel even more hot and bothered.

"Returning to Johnny," she said frostily. She couldn't immediately see how Johnny's gift of telepathic communication with Amelia was relevant to what had happened the previous night. It had certainly given him a greater understanding and acceptance of her own gift of psychometry, and yet Lizzie felt that there had to be more to it than that. She knew there was. She just couldn't see the connection yet...

"When Johnny left last night, he took with him a stone carving that had originally come from Oakhangar Hall," she said. She shifted uncomfortably. "You may remember at Amelia and Dudley's wedding... There was an angel holding a crystal gazing ball. It smashed and cut my hand—the glass ball, I mean. You patched me up." She tried to sound as casual as she could. "Someone must have slipped the angel into my bag thinking it was mine because I found it much later and never got around to handing it back." Embarrassed, she avoided Arthur's gaze. "Anyway, like I said, Johnny took it last night."

"Sure, I remember," Arthur said. "Do you mean you gave the carving back to Johnny last night—or he took it?"

"He took it," Lizzie said bluntly. "Technically, of course, it wasn't mine in the first place. But I didn't realise until later that he had stolen it back. I thought I should tell you in case it had any significance." She waited, hopeful, but after a second Arthur shook his head.

"I don't know why he would do that," he said. He met

her eyes. "Presumably you didn't tell the police that bit because…"

"Because I didn't think it would help the situation to suggest that your brother was a thief," Lizzie said, "for a number of reasons."

"I guess that's true," Arthur conceded. "Well, there must be a good reason he wanted it, but—" He stopped, frowning.

"He knew where it came from," Lizzie said, "and he knew I had it. The more I think about it, the more I think the whole evening—the whole 'I want to talk to Lizzie Kingdom' thing—was all about getting it back." She leaned forward, eager to try to explain. "At one point in the conversation Johnny said that the evening wasn't really how he'd imagined it would be. He said I was being so nice, which made it more difficult. But he didn't say *what* was difficult. At the time I assumed it was because he wanted to hate me for monopolising Dudley and upsetting Amelia in the process, but now I wonder… I wonder if all along he was planning to steal the stone angel and he felt bad about it."

Arthur's frowned deepened. "I don't get why it was so important to him," he said.

Lizzie sighed. She felt deflated. "No," she said. "Maybe I'm wrong then. It just seemed significant, and I thought I should tell you."

Arthur's phone pinged. "Sorry," he said, reaching into his pocket. "I should probably take this." He scrolled through the message quickly. "It's Anna," he said. "She says Dudley's place is like a fortress. The paparazzi are out in force. Apparently, there's been some story leaked to the press that Dudley is the father of Letty Knollys's baby." He looked at Lizzie, brows raised. "Did you know about this?" Lizzie shook her head. "I've no idea if it's true or not about the baby but apparently they were having an affair. Johnny told me last night that Amelia had hired a PI to follow Dudley and that was how she found out."

"What a sleaze." Arthur looked disgusted. "This will make the story of Millie's death and Johnny's disappearance even more of a circus." He put the phone away. "God, I knew Dudley was a self-absorbed shit but really?" He shot Lizzie a sharp glance. "You're upset," he said, and it sounded almost like an accusation.

"I'm sad," Lizzie corrected him. "I'm sad for everyone whose lives Dudley has buggered up so carelessly and I'm sad that I stood by him for so long. I've been pretty blind and now I feel stupid."

"Don't beat yourself up." Arthur's tone had softened. "Dudley's fooled a lot of people."

"He was so cute as a kid," Lizzie said sadly, "and so loyal. But I guess people change." She drained her coffee mug. "There's something else," she said. "Johnny also left this behind, either deliberately or by accident, when he took the stone angel." She reached up to the bookshelf, where she had left Johnny's little green notebook. She handled it gingerly but there were no repercussions, no echo of the emotions she had experienced the previous night when she had held it. It was as though its potency had vanished. She passed it to Arthur, making sure their fingers didn't touch. "I might as well tell you I did try to do a reading on it. I wanted to see if I could find out where Johnny had gone and what was going on with him."

"And what did you see?" Arthur asked.

"It felt full of energy," Lizzie said slowly. "Anger and fear and determination. Whatever Johnny wants, wherever he's gone, he's desperate. I don't mean—" She put out a quick hand towards Arthur in reassurance then withdrew it equally quickly. "I don't mean he planned to take his own life," she said. "Quite the reverse. There's something he's desperate to achieve. It consumes him. But I don't know what it is."

Arthur said nothing. His gaze was dark and inward-looking. Lizzie had the impression he was thinking very hard and very quickly, sifting information, considering and rejecting what to tell her. There was something there, a deeply held secret, but she shied away from reading his mind. She had promised she wouldn't and she wasn't going to break that promise and undermine the fragile trust they were building.

"I would have thought," Arthur said slowly, "that the thing Johnny wants more than anything in the world is to have Amelia back again. That's what he told you. That's what we all know. But as that isn't possible..." He shrugged. "I really don't know what else he might be planning."

Lizzie shivered, remembering Johnny's words the previous night, his fierce protestation that he would do anything he could to bring Amelia back. She could hear the echo of his voice:

"If only I'd realised in time—"

Realised what? she wondered. He had not said.

"Have you read the book?" Arthur flicked through the notebook. "Do you know what's in it?"

"No," Lizzie said. "I couldn't. It was too..." She hesitated. "The emotions it stirred up were too powerful," she said, and was glad when Arthur merely nodded. He might not be comfortable with the paranormal stuff, she thought, but at least he was accepting.

"I'll take a look," he said. "It might help." He slid the book into his pocket; sighed. "Before I go," he said, "would you mind telling me exactly what happened when Johnny disappeared?" He spread his hands. "I know you told me—and the police—that you fainted and when you came around Johnny had gone, but how did that all come about?"

"We walked down to the river," Lizzie said. "Johnny asked if I'd mind going with him to the Tube. He wanted to show me the plaque that commemorated the fact that this was once the site of a palace called Baynard's Castle. He'd mentioned it earlier in the evening and seemed really into the idea that these flats were built on the site of an old palace."

"That's Johnny," Arthur said ruefully. "He's hooked on history."

"Yeah, the notebook is full of dates and stuff," Lizzie said. "That much I did notice. Anyway, we went down to the Embankment and Johnny showed me the plaque and stupidly I touched it." She stopped. "It's weird," she said slowly, "but normally the psychometry only works when I want it to. I mean, I have to deliberately open my mind up to the possibility of reading an object. I touched the plaque without really thinking. I wasn't expecting anything to happen."

"And something did," Arthur said.

"There was nothing, at first," Lizzie said. "Then everything changed and it felt as though I was actually there in the past, and I could see the castle, and smell the river and feel the sun on me as though it was real…" She gave a convulsive shudder. "Then I blacked out."

"And came around to find that Johnny had done a runner and you'd drawn a crowd," Arthur finished drily.

"That's about right," Lizzie said slowly. "I don't know when Johnny left me, or why. Perhaps he was scared by what happened."

"I doubt it," Arthur said. "We both know Johnny is much more comfortable with this paranormal stuff than either of us."

"That's true." Lizzie was remembering Johnny telling her how cool it was that she had psychometric powers and that she shouldn't be afraid of them. "Perhaps I was right then to think that he'd been playing me all evening," she said, "and he was just waiting for a chance to slip away."

"He'd hardly ask you to go with him then, would he?" Arthur pointed out. He sighed. "I feel as though we're missing something here."

The insistent buzz of a text interrupted them again and with a muffled curse Arthur reached for his phone. "Anna's managed to see Dudley," he said. "She says Dudley denies seeing Johnny for several days." He scrubbed a hand through his hair. "Shit," he said. He looked up at Lizzie. "Apparently the police are on their way over here to see you. Anna says they've hinted at new evidence but won't say what it is."

Lizzie's stomach dropped. Memories rose of the last time she'd been questioned, the doubts, suspicions and endless questions, the sense of isolation and fear. She'd done nothing wrong and yet she already felt guilty, off-balance and scared. She could feel herself shaking, shrinking in on herself as she had as a child for protection and self-reliance.

Trust no one. Rely on no one. Once upon a time she had thought she could trust Dudley but that had been an illusion. She'd just started to forge some trust with Arthur and this had blown it apart already.

Her own phone pinged with a text—Bill, telling her that he was sending the same legal team over to Blackfriars that she'd used before. It seemed everyone knew before she did that she was about to be arrested.

"The police will be here soon then," she said, as steadily as she could. "Good luck, Arthur. I hope you find Johnny soon." She smiled. "Not just for my sake."

The entry phone buzzed sharply, several times, and Lizzie went to answer. She just wanted to get this over with.

The hall was awash with people: two women in suits with briefcases, several bodyguards, uniformed police officers, Kat, wearing Chanel and a distraught expression, and Bill, talking urgently on his mobile, apparently to a national newspaper. "Dudley Lester has already been taken in for questioning," Lizzie heard him say. "Bishopsgate police station…"

PC Morgan stepped forward and started to speak. There was a buzzing in Lizzie's ears; she felt time slow down.

"Ms Kingdom, we would like to ask you some more questions in connection with the death of Mrs Lester and the disappearance of John Robsart. I'm asking you to accompany us to the police station."

"Are you arresting me?" Lizzie asked.

"Not unless you refuse to come with us." PC Morgan smiled thinly.

"Dudley's under arrest," Kat said, helpfully. "He refused to go."

That didn't surprise Lizzie at all. Trust Dudley to turn the whole thing into a drama. Not that Bill was any better. She could see he was still on his phone.

"We'd like to search your flat as well," PC Morgan said.

"Be my guest," Lizzie said. "I just need to get my bag." She turned to Kat. "It's really kind of you, Kat," she said, "but I don't need either Bill or you to come with me."

"Sweetie!" Kat's face crumpled. She smoothed the Chanel skirt. "Of *course* you need us. I know we had a tiff but this is really *important*."

"I know it is," Lizzie said. "That's why I'll manage on my own. But thank you anyway."

There was a movement behind her. She spun around.

"Lizzie," Arthur said.

She turned to look at him. "I'd never do anything to hurt Johnny," she said, and despite the crowd of people around them she spoke to him alone and let the defences in her mind fall, hoping that somehow, he could read through to her heart the way she could read him.

"I know," Arthur said.

And then they took her away.

16

Amy: Hatfield, Hertfordshire, Summer 1557

I HAD GROWN up in the country and learned to ride as a child, but it was typical of Robert's attitude towards me that whenever we had travelled, I had either been transported by litter or been given the least challenging of horses to ride. Indeed, some of them had seemed so docile that it was difficult to encourage them to move at all. Robert loved to hunt but had seldom encouraged me to accompany him. In the beginning I had fondly interpreted this as a sign of his care for me; I felt like a china doll, so proud to be cosseted. Later I came to realise that it was merely another sign of Robert's contempt for me. He had never asked if I could ride well and assumed that I could not.

William Hyde, whose care I had been consigned to

whilst Robert was out of the country with King Philip, had evidently been given the same instruction for he wrapped me about with so much caution and coddling that a vain woman would believe herself highly prized.

"We must take care of you as well as Sir Robert would do," he would declare roguishly when I expressed a desire to take the air and he refused to allow it. "You cannot go out at present, there is too chill a wind." In such small ways he made my life a misery.

Today was different, however. Today I had been allowed out—under the strict supervision of Mr Hyde's grooms—because Robert had an important commission for me to fulfil, and as I reined in my horse on the rising land above Hatfield House, I felt the smallest frisson of pleasure to be out in the world.

The Princess Elizabeth's house was considered a palace but even I could see the irony in that. She might have been happy there as a child, sharing her brother's education, but now the brick walls were her prison. Queen Mary knew that her sister was as unscrupulous as a usurer and as sly as a fox. The Queen had set her under lock and key here, and I admired her for it.

My move from the court in London to Throcking in Hertfordshire now made a great deal of sense. As I had thought, it was nothing to do with me, and all to do with the Princess Elizabeth. Robert wanted me to be close by her so I could run the errands to her that he could not. Had he shown me but an ounce of the unswerving devotion he had for her I would have laid down my life for him. Yet that was as nothing to him. He could not even see me when Elizabeth was in his mind, for she eclipsed all else as the sun eclipses the moon. Robert was dazzled, blinded. He had to be to take such risks when his position under Queen Mary was so precarious.

The groom knocked vigorously at the door and I shivered for we were deep in shadow here. The tall brick gables of the hall loomed high over us. A black-clad servant showed me into the hall and left me for an age seated on a horribly uncomfortable wooden chair; I believe they wanted me gone. However, I had a commission and I was engaged upon it. I waited.

Eventually one of Elizabeth's ladies, also in black, swept me up and carried me away to a little panelled antechamber. She was impatient. She had no time for this.

"You can give Sir Robert's message to me," she said to me, holding out her hand imperatively. "I will see that it reaches the Lady Elizabeth."

I had been expecting this. "I beg your pardon, ma'am," I said, with a respectful curtsey to soften the refusal, "but Sir Robert insisted I hand it to none other than her highness herself."

My choice of address for the Princess did not go unnoticed, just as I had intended. Here in this house, loyalties were split like shards of glass. Some of the Princess's ladies spied for the Queen. Others were dedicated to her service. This woman, Lady Vane, I knew to be one of the latter for her mother had been a friend to Queen Anne Boleyn.

I saw the expression shift in Lady Vane's eyes and her manner thawed a very little.

"Sir Robert's devotion to Her Highness has always been appreciated," she said.

"He is indeed most devoted," I agreed smoothly. "No one could be more loyal to her."

The truth of my words mocked me. What other man

would send his wife with a message to the woman he loved?

I waited. After a moment Lady Vane had come to her decision. She nodded. "Follow me," she said.

I had travelled over twenty miles from Throcking to Hatfield in order to deliver Robert's gift to the Lady Elizabeth but those last few steps through the shabby old house were the most difficult for I hated her so much. In my imagination I had turned her into a monster. My heart was thumping so hard I thought my steps would falter. Yet when I walked into the library and saw her sitting at the octagonal table, her head bent over her book in the prettiest pose imaginable, my first sensation was disappointment rather than anything else.

She is but a woman like me.

I had seen her before, of course, but I realised that in my jealousy I had built her up to be more than she truly was. After all, she was my own age, and less beautiful than I, and her history was mired in scandal. What was there here to fear? What was there to hate?

A moment later I knew the answer, for she looked up, haloed in a sunlight that turned her hair to spun copper and gold. She was dazzling, radiant, not simply to my eyes but somehow to my soul as well. I saw her and recognised her worth. Robert had been right; Elizabeth *was* special. She burned with a spark few could ever match, certainly not the Queen, her embittered husk of a sister. Elizabeth was everything that Mary was not, charming, clever as a scholar, demure as a milkmaid, cunning as a thief. Had she not been all of those things and more she would have been dead before now.

As she put the book aside and stood to greet me, I felt

the same frisson of antagonism that always stung me in
her presence. I felt at a disadvantage in so many ways. I
might be beautiful but she was dazzling, faceted like a
jewel where I was dull and simple. The hanging cupboards
of books that surrounded us only served to emphasise my
own lack of learning and made me feel slow and stupid.

"Your Highness." I inclined my head in the briefest of
acknowledgements.

"Lady Dudley." I could read nothing from her tone.
She did not ask how I was. She said nothing to ease my
discomfort.

"I bring a gift from my lord, madam," I said. I opened
my leather satchel and took out a book, the cover finely
tooled in deep red leather, lettered in gold. It was a gift
that typified Robert, extravagant, showy, proclaiming a
wealth and importance he longed for but did not possess. I
placed the book on the table next to the one she had been
reading and as I did so we all heard the clink of coin from
the hollowed-out compartment within. Lady Vane's eyes
widened but Elizabeth showed no surprise.

"Robert assures you of his steadfast loyalty," I said.

Elizabeth nodded slowly. Her gaze was on the book,
not on me. She ran her fingers gently over its smooth surface. "Thank you. Sir Robert is a dear friend and generous when he has so little himself."

I swallowed the retort that Robert—and I—would have
a great deal more if he were not given to such extravagant gestures. Bitterness consumed me as I remembered
the hopes I had nourished when the money and Robert's
letter had first arrived. Mr Hyde had called me into his
study and I had seen the gold and thought for one brief

dizzy moment that it might be for me, that I might buy myself a new gown, or indeed several.

"Does Sir Robert plan to visit us?" I had asked Hyde, hating myself for the pleading tone in my voice. But he had shaken his head and looked at me pityingly and then I had realised that I was the one who was giving away my inheritance to the Princess Elizabeth for this money had surely come from the sale of some of my Norfolk estates.

"Has Sir Robert returned from Picardy now?" The Princess was addressing me directly. She did not invite me to sit, or offer refreshment. This, then, would be a very brief exchange.

"Yes, Your Highness," I said.

I saw the glimmer of amusement in her eyes as she waited for me to elaborate and I stolidly refused. I might have appeared churlish but in truth I knew very little news to pass on to her. After a cursory enquiry into my health, Robert's letter had told me only that his brother Henry had been killed in battle, blown to bits by a cannonball before his very eyes. He and King Philip had returned to court and he would be lodged for a time in London. He made no suggestion that I should join him. Instead he had gone on to exhort me to deliver the coin to Elizabeth at Hatfield with all protestations of his love and loyalty. That had been the sum total of his correspondence.

"Please convey my thanks to Sir Robert," Elizabeth said and my mind jerked away from Robert's neglect and the new blue gown that was not to be mine and I looked up to meet her mocking brown eyes. "And thank you, Lady Dudley," she added. "I admire your obedience to your husband in what I imagine to be an onerous duty."

My temper caught at that. It was mean-spirited of her

to make fun of me simply because she could. There was a moment when I tried to hold my tongue, but my outburst had been a long time building and now it was unstoppable.

"Why?" I burst out. "Why must you have Robert, of all men? You, who could have any man!"

She did not answer immediately. Instead she ran her hands over the book's cover again, like a lover's caress.

"I love Robert," she said simply, after a moment. "I always have."

Rage caught in my throat. "You will never have him," I said. "I shall make sure of that."

I heard the lady-in-waiting gasp at my words but Elizabeth did not look shocked. She stood illuminated by the sun, cloaked by books and learning, so far above me in so many ways.

"You mistake me, Lady Dudley," she said, "I have far grander plans than to be any man's *wife*." She said the word as though it had a bitter taste. "Even less," she added disdainfully, "would I be a mistress."

I saw my mistake. I had judged her according to the conventional fate of women down the ages, defined as I was, as even the Queen was, by men: daughter, wife, mother. Yet that was to underestimate her. The Princess Elizabeth valued herself high. She would not wed if it meant her life would be dictated by a husband. One day, if she continued to be clever and lucky and walked the tightrope and did not fall, she might be Queen of England and I could not imagine this imperious creature sharing her power with any man. I saw her ambition and I marvelled at it.

Queen Elizabeth. She would stand alone, above them all. There was many a slip in the world of politics and high treason but somehow, I knew she would achieve it.

It was then that I foresaw Robert's downfall too with
the certainty that comes from knowing someone inside and
out. Robert was ruthlessly ambitious. When Elizabeth's
star rose, he would want his to rise too, higher and ever
higher, the equal of hers. Yet that would never happen.
Her ambition would always outstrip his, her life would always run ahead of his, and though he would try, he would
never be able to catch her.

Robert Dudley and Elizabeth Tudor… Yes, they did
love one another. I could see that. They needed the other
to exist. Yet they were also the other's torment.

If I wanted to profit from that I needed to play them
at their own games. I had been too small in my thinking,
too unambitious. I needed to take Robert's vaulting ambition and use it to my own ends.

I laughed aloud, for the revelation filled me with a lightness of spirit. It was so long since I had felt joy but now it
bubbled up in me like water from a fountain. I swept the
Princess Elizabeth a low curtsey.

"Thank you, Your Highness," I said. "I am indebted
to you. I do believe you have shown me the road ahead."

It was the first and only time I saw Elizabeth discom-
fited. Her gaze narrowed on me as though she was afraid
that she had somehow given away more than she had intended, and for a brief second I saw that this girl, so well
defended, so drilled to carefulness by a lifetime of danger,
existed on the knife's edge of fear the entire time. That
was sweet revenge.

"Good day, Your Highness," I said. "Fare you well."
And I left her in her prison with the money and Robert's
promise of devotion.

It was hot outside. The sun beat down from a relentlessly blue sky. My docile mare had no desire to work and picked her way with agonising slowness along the track toward Throcking, her ears flicking irritably to ward off the flies. Mr Hyde's grooms took out their frustrations at being obliged to nursemaid me by knocking the heads of the tall-growing dandelions beside our path. I was the only one who was wholly content that afternoon. I rode in a daze, my mind far away as I thought and planned.

To begin with all I had wanted was to be a good wife to Robert, the mother of a growing family, the chatelaine of a home. That would have been sufficient for me—a grand scheme indeed—but it had been denied to me. Since then I had been railing against a fate that had thwarted me and against a husband who had scorned me, palming me off onto one of his servants like some unwanted chattel. That resentment ate away at me; it did no harm to Robert or indeed to the Princess Elizabeth. I was the only one who suffered for it.

It was time to seize my own future. I could see a glimmer of light to guide me on the path ahead. It was time to take back what was mine; my life, my freedom. I dug my heels into the mare's side and she was so startled that she leaped into a canter, leaving the grooms with their mouths open and far behind.

17

Lizzie: Present Day

IT WAS A strange, suspended existence in police custody. Time ceased to have much meaning and Lizzie quickly lost track of the hours. The world outside the one small interview room seemed an irrelevance. There was no light and dark, no peace, no sleep, nothing but endless questions, about her relationship with Dudley, about Johnny, where he was, when she had last seen him, what had happened between them on the Embankment. Lizzie felt sick and confused and she had seldom been so frightened.

Eventually they told her that there was CCTV footage of her with Johnny the previous night. They showed it to her and Lizzie, tired and emotional, almost cried when she saw the fuzzy images of herself and Johnny emerging from the flats and taking the alleyway down to the river.

The film switched to another camera and then another. The quality was grainy but she recognised their two figures walking along the Embankment, chatting, stopping to look out across the river.

"The second camera on Paul's Walk wasn't working," one of the police officers said. Cook was a gaunt detective inspector who looked as though he spent too much time indoors staring at computer screens or possibly cadavers. He treated Lizzie with respect and utter courtesy which somehow scared her all the more. "However, there's another one here—" he stopped the tape and pointed to the screen "—which picked up some images. They aren't as clear as we would like but they're interesting." He pressed play again. "Could you tell us what you were doing here?"

Lizzie watched her own image as she and Johnny stopped in front of the blue plaque that marked the site of Baynard's Castle.

"I've already told you about this," she said, as patiently as she was able. "Johnny had told me that my flats were built on the site of a medieval palace. He wanted to show me where it had been."

"It looks as though you're reaching out for something," DI Cook said.

"I was touching the plaque that commemorates the site," Lizzie said.

She leaned in closer, her heart suddenly beating hard in her throat. She had no idea what the camera was going to show. Both she and Johnny were in the frame, their figures close together, blurry but distinct enough to see.

The jerky black-and-white images seemed to freeze for a moment and then there was a flash of bright white light with a darker tinge around the edges, like a firework exploding. Lizzie caught her breath.

DI Cook froze the image. "What happened there?" he said, with deceptive quietness.

Lizzie shook her head. "I don't know. I don't remember anything—" She stopped as she caught sight of the fleeting expression of scepticism on DI Cook's face.

"You hadn't fainted at this point," he said, pointing to her figure on the screen, "yet you don't remember?"

"No," Lizzie said.

"If my client says she doesn't remember," the lawyer put in, "then she doesn't."

For a moment Lizzie met DI Cook's eyes and they were both united in a shared exasperation. He restarted the film. The bright white light expanded, blanking out everything else in the image for a few seconds, and then it died away. Neither Lizzie nor Johnny were visible in the picture anymore. The frame was empty.

Without commenting, DI Cook changed screens to another camera. "This is from the corner of White Lion Hill, where you were found. It's about twenty yards away and this is just over three minutes later."

Lizzie could see herself lying on the bench. People started to come towards her. She sat up. The tape stopped.

"Three minutes," she repeated. She looked at him. "And Johnny?"

DI Cook looked at her for the longest time. "There is no further footage of him," he said. "Not on the Embankment, not at Blackfriars station, not anywhere else we have found." He waited, and when Lizzie said nothing, he sighed.

"The footage of the explosion—if that is what it was—

has been analysed," DI Cook said. "They think it was a type of calcium and strontium."

"I'm sorry," Lizzie said. "I never studied chemistry."

"Simply put," DI Cook said, "they use it in fireworks. It's very volatile." He got up and stretched. "There was no firework residue found at the scene, however, and none of the witnesses reported a smell of sulphur or anything else unusual." He leaned on the desk close to Lizzie. "It's a mystery, isn't it?" he said pleasantly. "An explosion you say you have no memory of, with a substance that seems untraceable and a companion who's missing." He glanced across at the lawyer. "We've got some further questions but I'd like Ms Kingdom to have a bit of time to think about this first."

"You have to tell me what's going on," the lawyer, who was called Rebecca, hissed at Lizzie as they stood in front of the sink in the ladies' room. Lizzie caught sight of her reflection in the harshly lit mirror and winced.

"I can't do anything if you don't tell me," Rebecca went on. "All this silence isn't helpful."

"I'm silent because I can't explain," Lizzie said. "I've told everything I know."

The lawyer looked baffled and angry. "That can't be true. None of this makes any sense."

"Tell me about it," Lizzie said tiredly.

It all began again. They told her that they had found Johnny's phone in her flat. Lizzie couldn't understand how it had got there. Johnny had told her he must have dropped the phone in the car on his way to see her. She told the police this; they asked her whose car he had been in. Lizzie could not answer, did not know. Johnny had not said. She puzzled over it for hours; the only people who had been in

the flat after Johnny were Arthur and Anna. Had one of
them deliberately planted the phone there and if so why?
Did either—or both—of them hate her so much because
of Amelia that they would want to deliberately throw suspicion on her? Anna barely knew her. Could she really be
motivated by such hatred for someone she had met only
once, as a child? Lizzie supposed it was possible if Anna
had been as protective of Amelia as she seemed to be of
Johnny. It was Arthur, though, who troubled her more.
He's tricked you, said the traitorous voice at the back of her
mind, the demon that so often planted its barbs when she
felt at her most vulnerable. She knew Arthur hated Dudley. She had felt the depth of that visceral hatred. She also
knew Arthur's feelings towards her were equivocal at best.
When it came to a war between logic and instinct was it
foolish of her to trust in an affinity she had never sought?
She didn't know. It felt as though there wasn't much that
she did know any more and it was easy to become paranoid in those long, lonely hours.

She dismissed the lawyers that Bill had engaged for her
after they advised her to leave and she was promptly arrested in the full glare of publicity.

"Bill engineered that," she said furiously. "For fuck's
sake, you're supposed to give me good legal advice not
conspire with him to plaster me all over the papers."

The police were appalled and refused to interview her
further without legal representation present so she told
them they should send for her cousin Juliet Carey. She
had no idea whether anyone would act on the suggestion.
She waited.

Then, at some point, the door opened and Jules was

there. Lizzie, who had held it all together the whole time, promptly burst into tears.

"Hey." Jules grabbed her and gave her a fierce hug, sharp suit notwithstanding. "You're released on bail pending further inquiries," she said grimly, adding, "Come on, we're leaving. Don't say anything until we're out of here."

"I owe you," Lizzie said, impatiently brushing her tears away as her cousin marched her down the brightly lit corridor towards the reception. "How on earth did you swing that?"

"I'll tell you in the car," Jules said. She stopped and gave Lizzie another hug. "Get a grip, Lizzie," she added, not unkindly. "We'll be out of here soon."

"Sorry," Lizzie sniffed. "It's just... I felt pretty lonely, you know?"

"Yeah." Jules's mouth twisted. "You've had a crap time. But you're not alone. You've got me now." She gave Lizzie a grin. "You do know how expensive my legal fees are? I'm right out of your league."

"I'll take out another mortgage," Lizzie said, smiling back, her spirits lifting. "Who put up the bail money? Bill, I suppose." She sighed. "I hate feeling indebted to him."

"You suppose wrong," Jules said. She signed for Lizzie's belongings at the front desk and pushed a pair of dark glasses onto her nose. "Arthur Robsart posted bail for you," she said. "You can imagine what the press made of that, and the police, for that matter. It was Arthur who contacted me to let me know what was going on. Keep moving," she added, as Lizzie stopped dead, staring at her. "We've got to get you out of here without too much hoopla."

There was an enormous crowd of people outside. "Shit,"

Jules grumbled, "how do the press always find out about these things? The car's over here—" She steered Lizzie over to the kerb and flicked the automatic locks. "Hop in. You don't get a limo anymore."

Jules slid into the driver's seat next to her and drew out into the traffic, scattering onlookers like pigeons. "Here's the plan," she said, checking the mirrors to make sure they were clear of the crowds. "You need a bath," her nose wrinkled delicately, "but you're going to have to wait until you get to The High. I don't want to take you back to the flat. I've packed up all your stuff—" She gestured at the overflowing rear seat. "Didn't know what you wanted so I brought everything. God, you have a lot of stuff."

Lizzie turned up the heating. She wasn't sure how cold the day actually was but she was racked by little shivers. "Is there any news of Johnny?" she asked. She'd wanted to know from the moment Jules had stepped into her cell. "They wouldn't tell me anything in there. I spent hours wondering whether he had been found or—"

"Johnny's still missing," Jules said. "That's why they arrested you when those useless lawyers told you to walk out." She shot Lizzie a look. "They are trying to connect Johnny's disappearance to Amelia's death. You were the last person to see him, and with the CCTV footage, it looks pretty bad for you. In the end, though, they had to agree to bail because there was nothing—nothing forensic, any-way—that suggested that a crime had been committed."

Lizzie's shudders were increasing. Whether it was re-lief or shock or some sort of fear, she wasn't sure. Fear for Johnny, fear for herself…

"I don't understand what's going on," she said. "I can't explain any of it."

Jules didn't answer immediately and Lizzie sensed there was a lot more she hadn't told her. "They're planning to dredge the river," Jules said. "They think that there was an argument between you and Johnny, and that you attacked him with something and then pushed him over the Embankment. That explosion—" She glanced at Lizzie again, her face troubled. "What the *hell* was that? Do you really not remember?"

"No," Lizzie said. "I don't remember that and I don't remember what happened in the three minutes before the CCTV picked me up on the bench." She knew she would need to tell Jules about the psychometry at some point but now wasn't the time. She was so tired she could hardly think straight and she wanted to get clear in her own mind first what part the psychometry might have played.

She looked out of the window. The crawl of traffic out of the city had been slow. Now they were passing endless rows of suburban houses and grey acres of concrete and tarmac in the equally grey afternoon. She was still feeling a sense of disconnection from normality. "I certainly didn't attack Johnny or push him into the river," she said. "I know that. And I don't think he's dead. In fact, I'm certain of it. I have a sense…"

"Arthur doesn't think so either." Jules still looked troubled. "I don't know how you guys can be so sure. I'm all for optimism but you have to face the fact that you might just be hoping for the best. I suppose he could have run away—" She sighed. "But Arthur said he wouldn't vanish without getting in touch."

"I wish I knew who the other person was who saw Johnny that night," Lizzie said.

"What?" Jules frowned at her.

"Someone else saw Johnny that night," Lizzie said. "Someone gave him a lift to my flat. He said he had dropped his phone in their car. I know they found the phone in my flat," she ignored Jules's attempt to interrupt, "so either Johnny was lying to me, or he left the phone there deliberately, or someone else put it there later."

"You mean Arthur?" Jules said. She frowned. "That doesn't seem likely. Arthur got in touch with me as soon as you were arrested. He's withholding stuff from the police for your sake, you know." At Lizzie's sharp sideways glance, she smiled. "Yeah, he told me all about the notebook and about your weird psychic visions. I wish you'd told me yourself, Lizzie. I can't help if I don't know everything, you know."

"OK," Lizzie said after a moment. "I'm sorry. I just haven't had a chance to think everything through and I didn't want you to decide I was mad."

Jules laughed. "I've known about it for years," she said. "I've known you were psychic since we were kids."

"What?" Lizzie was so surprised she sat bolt upright. "How?"

Jules shot her an exasperated look. "Oh God, Lizzie, don't you remember my costumed doll, the one from Italy? You picked it up and started to tell me all about how Grandad had found it on a market stall in Sorrento and how he'd haggled over the price with the stallholder. You described it all so vividly and there was no way you could have known all that stuff. There were other things too…" The car increased speed as they joined the M40 slipping into the traffic. "I've always known," Jules finished with a shrug.

"You never said." Lizzie stared at her.

"Well, you never gave the impression you wanted to talk about it," Jules said. "So I respected that. Anyway, Arthur told me everything—or I assume it was everything." She glanced at Lizzie. "Plus, whilst we're on the subject of you and Arthur," she said, "don't forget he posted bail for you. That's a huge amount of money, Lizzie, so don't go running off or you'll ruin him. But I reckon that suggests he trusts you." She gave Lizzie a sly smile. "Kind of against his better judgement, but still…"

"That just about sums up our relationship," Lizzie said. She felt too tired to process anything and Jules could clearly see that because she touched her hand.

"Don't worry about any of this now," she said. "I'll get you to The High and you can have a bath and a sleep, then we'll talk properly. Arthur's going to call you tomorrow and arrange to come to see you when you've had a bit of time to settle in."

"Well, I certainly wouldn't want anyone to see me like this." Lizzie had caught a waft of the unpleasantly fusty smell of her clothes and Jules smiled.

"That's more like it," she said. She squeezed Lizzie's hand. "Please don't worry, Lizzie," she repeated. "They can't pin Amelia's murder on you anyway, or even that you conspired with Dudley to murder her, because there's no strong evidence that it *was* murder. In the same way they can't find any proof that anything suspicious has happened to Johnny. We'll find out what happened."

Lizzie nodded. She closed her eyes as Jules pulled out to overtake a lorry and dozed as the countryside flashed past like speeded-up film. When she woke up, they were turning off the A40, down Burford Hill. The old houses lined the street, mellow even in the dull afternoon. It felt surprisingly familiar and reassuring given that she hadn't been there for years. Another right turn and then a left, bumping along tiny narrow roads now, and suddenly the traffic and noise was left behind and there were the gates to The High standing open and Jules swung the car onto the drive and came to a halt. Lizzie scrambled out, looking up at the house.

"Oh my God," she said blankly.

Virginia creeper cloaked the entire building, choking the stone, smothering the windows. The drive was thick with dandelion and rosebay willowherb, poppies, convolvulus and ground elder, rioting in violent triumph. The lawn evidently hadn't seen a mower in years.

"I didn't have the chance to check it out before we came," Jules said, scrambling out after her. She was looking shocked. "Bill said it was empty, which I took to mean the most recent tenant had vacated it rather than that it was actually derelict. Look, let's find you a hotel instead."

"No," Lizzie said. The thought of checking in to a hotel, of having to speak to people, to have so little privacy, was impossible just now. She needed some quiet time. She started to laugh. If ever there was a metaphor for the state of her life, it was standing right in front of her in dire need of some attention.

"No," she repeated. "It's about time I sorted myself out and I can start here. The High is my home. I'm staying."

18

Amy: Throcking Manor, November 1558

SO EMPTY HAD my life become in the autumn of 1558 that I lived for the letters I received all too rarely. Most highly prized were those from my brother Arthur in Norfolk, where he had bought a number of estates and turned a tidy profit from the wool revenues. Not even William Hyde had the temerity to open and read my correspondence from Arthur even though he reported to Robert on all my activities. Arthur was generous with both news and gifts although when I asked for money, he did reprove me.

I dislike this secrecy, Arthur wrote to me sternly. *If you require additional funds you should ask your husband for money. It is his responsibility to provide for you.* Nevertheless, his parcel to me also contained a bag of gold, hidden within a beautifully woven shawl.

You may tell Robert if the secrecy disturbs you, I wrote back airily, knowing he would not betray me. *I require the money only so I may buy my husband a Christmas gift.* Oh, my duplicity knew no bounds that autumn.

With Robert I was all docile and mild. I visited him in London; he came to see me in Hertfordshire. We were the very ideal of domestic bliss, if the ideal is a smooth surface with nothing but emptiness beneath. Robert had no suspicions of me. He did not realise that after I had visited the Princess Elizabeth, I had already started to hatch a plan for my own independence.

Robert was increasingly frustrated that year, chafing at his situation. It was a pleasure to see how he squirmed. He was not welcome at court when King Philip was absent and as Philip had no desire to be long in England, Robert's ambitions were stymied. He talked of buying a house in Norfolk but I knew he would not. Being a country gentleman was not to Robert's taste. It was nowhere near grand enough.

There had been rumours that Queen Mary was pregnant again and for a little while it seemed England might yet have a Catholic heir. I saw how that infuriated Robert and I enjoyed his displeasure, knowing it was prompted by fear and thwarted ambition. But there was no child. Instead the rumours changed to ones of the Queen's ill health. Robert, I knew, was waiting for her to die but in death as well as in life, Mary was stubborn. She would not end her life to suit Robert Dudley.

I wanted her to live forever.

Meanwhile, whilst Robert simmered, I was frequently

left at Throcking to kick my heels in idleness. I had no household to run and precious little business to deal with although Robert did allow me to conduct the smaller matters of his Norfolk estates in his absence. I think it made him feel generous to concede to me a little of the running of my inheritance. No doubt he felt I should be grateful, and I was. The business gave me the opportunity to take a little, just a very little, of the income each time, small enough that Robert would not notice, monies that could get lost in the larger whole, but for me added up to freedom.

Throcking was a beautiful place, but so lonely. There was no society beyond Mr Hyde's household. It felt like a closed world. The house too should have been delightful, a manor of mellow brick with a pretty little moat. But in the summer the moat stagnated and smelled and the water was dark and impenetrable. I was as much a prisoner as the Princess Elizabeth in my own way.

I well remember that day in November when we heard the news of Queen Mary's death. How could I ever forget? The house was still asleep when there was a clatter of hooves over the bridge and Mr Hyde's voice rose above the hubbub, shouting for the grooms. We tumbled from our beds; I grabbed my shawl over my nightgown for the autumn air was chill and laden with the scent of wood smoke and cold ash, the fire dead in the grate and too early for a maid to have come in to build it anew. I winced as my feet touched the cold floor.

I ran to the window. The first light of a grey dawn was creeping across the flat lands about Throcking, a mist floating above the moat, and below in the courtyard I could see William Hyde and Robert and a whole army of men in the Dudley livery. Steam rose from the sweating horses, urgency in every breath.

"The Queen is dead!" I heard the words pass from man to man, running like lightning through the crowd of servants now thronging the courtyard.

My heart gave a strange, sickening lurch and I thought I might fall. I opened the casement to call down to Robert, to ask if it were true, but then I saw that he was leaving already. They were leading out another horse for him, a showy white stallion that disliked the morning chill as much as I did and was sidestepping and trying to rear. Robert brought him under control with a ruthless hand, turning once more for the bridge over the moat.

He paused, looked up and caught my eye. He said nothing, made no gesture, hesitated for less than a breath. I knew where he was going. Robert was ever the showman, even at a time like this, on his white charger as he rode to the Princess Elizabeth's side. This was his moment, his time at last. Now his ambition would be unleashed.

I closed the casement silently and sat down.

Let it begin.

19

Lizzie: Present Day

THE HOUSE LOOKED even worse in the daylight, like a nightmare version of Dickens crossed with an explosion in an upmarket hotel. Every surface was thick with dust. Ivy and Virginia creeper clawed at the windows, cutting out what natural daylight there was. Cobwebs hung as thick as curtains from the chandeliers. Lizzie groaned and stuffed her head under the pillow. Then she realised that the reason she had woken in the first place was because she could hear someone knocking at the door.

Jules had gone home the previous night when Lizzie had insisted she didn't need anyone to babysit her. She was desperate to have her own space, which was odd when she had been isolated for so long, but it was how she felt. Jules had grumbled that she needed someone to keep an eye on her but to Lizzie this felt like a watershed. She'd come back to The High to make a fresh start and she was doing that on her own. She'd had a hot shower, drunk some tea and eaten some toast that Jules had whisked up and had fallen into a deep and dreamless sleep, much to her own surprise.

She struggled out from underneath what appeared to be an ancient eiderdown. She vaguely remembered Jules putting her to bed in her grandmother's room and assuring her that the sheets at least were clean. She wasn't complaining; she would have slept on a clothesline if needs be. The air was cold and smelled stale; reaching for the huge fur-lined coat she had found in the wardrobe the night before, she dragged it on over her pyjamas and stumbled downstairs.

The knocking sounded again. Lizzie felt disoriented. There couldn't be anyone at the door because they couldn't get past the huge gates and even if they had, she shouldn't open up because it was probably some paps who had discovered where she was—she didn't want a photograph taken with her hair as tangled as the cobwebs and her make-up all over her face. LIZZIE KINGDOM IN MELTDOWN would be the inevitable headline.

The knocking was coming from the kitchen. She peered around the open door and saw a face staring back at her through the window. It was an old lady, a very old lady with curly white hair and sharp, bright eyes, her head tilted like an inquisitive blackbird. When she saw Lizzie, she smiled and knocked even more vigorously. Lizzie felt a huge rush of warmth and affection.

She struggled across the kitchen, stubbing her toe on the table leg and repressing a curse. The woman at the window was gesturing and pointing, by which Lizzie, who couldn't hear her through the triple glazing, assumed she meant she would go to the back door. This led to another confusing five minutes whilst she tried to find which door led out to the porch and where the keys might be.

"Aunt Avery!" she said as the door finally creaked open, freeing a spider to bolt for freedom. "It's so wonderful to see you again!"

The *Aunt* was an honorific title. Avery Basing had been her grandmother's oldest and closest friend, and godmother to Lizzie's own mother, Annie.

"Elizabeth!" The old lady enveloped her in a hug. She was warm and smelled of a very expensive perfume. Her marketing basket bumped Lizzie's hip, making her wince. "It's lovely to see you too! You've grown!" She let Lizzie go and swept past her, small but stately, into the kitchen, where she put the basket down on the worktop. "My, you've some cleaning up to do here. It's a good job you've come home at last."

Lizzie laughed. "Neither the house nor I are fit to be seen."

"Juliet rang me just now to ask me to look in on you," Avery said. "I didn't want to intrude earlier, but really, Elizabeth—" she glanced at the clock "—it's about time you were getting dressed, isn't it?"

Lizzie laughed. She had always liked Avery's no-nonsense style. "Absolutely," she said. "Excuse me and I'll go and do that at once."

She was away up the stairs and into the shower before Avery could say another word. By the time she came back down, feeling clean and warm in a variety of outlandish outfits from the wardrobe including two pairs of her grandfather's knitted wool socks, a polo neck jumper and an old tweed jacket, Avery had put the kettle on and there was a delicious smell of warm croissants filling the kitchen. It was a start, Lizzie thought, although the house was still chilly and smelled of damp. The ancient wiring was buzzing threateningly. Lizzie wondered if it would blow all the fuses in the house. Bill, it seemed, had done a cosmetic refurbishment of the place to make it look nice to let, but had cut corners on costs, which was exactly what she would have expected of him.

"Juliet's told me what's been going on." Avery was ensconced at the big farmhouse table. "I hear the police are barking up the wrong tree and the press are behaving as badly as they usually do." She shook her head. "Really, Elizabeth, this celebrity business isn't good for you, you know. You need a break from it all."

"Well, I—" Lizzie started to say but Avery was still talking.

"We're all so pleased to have you home." She beamed at Lizzie, her bright blue eyes the most vivid thing in a face deeply lined with age. "You can help with the choir and join the new bowls club, and at last I can get someone in to cut down those dreadful Leylandii trees that are knocking my wall over. That awful caretaker you employ—what's his name—Ben, Barry, Bob?—Well, I'm sorry to tell tales, dear, but he's never here and when he is, he's so rude! I've asked him time and time again to get the Virginia creeper cut back because it threatens all the brick work and he told me that if I organised anything myself that affected your house or garden, he would sue me. I'm afraid he's a bad lot, dear."

Lizzie realised Avery was referring to Bill. "Yes," she said. "I'm afraid he is. I'm very sorry I didn't realise. I've been a bit too wrapped up in things."

"Not to worry." Avery was bracing. "You'll have it sorted in no time, I'm sure."

"I'll add it to the list of things to do," Lizzie promised, "along with calling in the tree surgeons and a gardener and a cleaning company."

Avery looked horrified. "My dear, you cannot employ a cleaning company! They will take pictures and sell them to the newspapers and then everyone will know where you are. Surely you know that? We thought—" she shot Lizzie a sharp look "—that you came here for some privacy?"

"Well, yes," Lizzie said, "but I can't tackle the whole house myself. It's too much of a mess. I really have let Bill get away with so much because I couldn't be bothered." She pulled a face. "I'm sorry I've neglected The High so badly. I feel as though I've let the family down in some way."

Avery patted her hand. "You're a busy girl. We all understand, and I know it's never been a favourite place of yours."

"No," Lizzie admitted. "After my mother died, I came to hate the place, but I think that was more to do with Dad than anything else. Now it feels much more like home again."

"Oh well, your father…" Avery's shrug encompassed everything there was to say about Harry Kingdom. "Such a vulgar man! I'm sorry to say it, Elizabeth, but it's true. When he changed the name of The High to The High Kingdom, I thought that summed him up." She cocked her head. "Is he still alive? I don't recall seeing an obituary."

"Just about," Lizzie said. "We haven't spoken for years. He's with his fifth wife now and runs a nightclub in California."

"Each to their own, I suppose," Avery said, with a sniff that indicated just how much she disapproved of Harry Kingdom.

Lizzie smothered a smile. "I promise I won't let the place go again," she said. "And I need a piano tuner for the baby grand," she added. "I'd like to write some songs."

"I know someone," Avery said. "He tends to my Bechstein. He's very discreet. I don't believe he even owns a mobile phone so there's no likelihood that he would think of posting pictures of your house online."

"That would be wonderful, thank you," Lizzie said.

"The croissants will be ready in a minute," Avery said. "Would you be a dear and make the tea? I'll go and fix the heating. I'm a hardy creature, Elizabeth, but it is Arctic in here." She looked Lizzie up and down. "No wonder you're wearing such practical attire."

"Jules and I did try to get the heating going." Lizzie immediately felt defensive. "We tried to turn it on last night when we arrived but we couldn't get it working."

"I'll have it on in a jiffy." Avery was already heading towards the door of the utility room. "I have the same system; I'll just press random buttons until something happens."

Lizzie found a teapot, warmed it and added three bags. She imagined Avery wouldn't approve of weak tea. The croissants were crispy and she found the butter and milk Jules had stocked up with.

"Heavenly," she said, as the heating hummed into life and Avery re-entered the kitchen, dusting her palms. "Thank you so much."

"They aren't homemade croissants," Avery said. "I am terrible at cooking and I hate baking with a passion but we do have a couple of excellent delicatessens in town that stock wonderful bread." She was rummaging in the cupboard. "Here we are; your grandmother's last batch of whisky marmalade. It will have matured nicely with all that alcohol in it. Ah, how we used to enjoy our nightcap of single malt together."

"I don't remember her very well," Lizzie said regretfully. "I only have impressions of her really—that she was very tall, that she had hair almost the same colour as mine and that she smelled of one of those famous 1990s perfumes. Was it Coty? I remember the bottles. They were so elegant! I wanted to be like her when I grew up."

"Vanilla Fields." Avery smiled. "Yes, she was a very elegant woman. You have a great look of her. I often think—" She stopped.

"What is it?" Lizzie had a mouth full of delicious croissant; not very elegant at all. Her grandmother would not have been proud of her.

Avery shook her head. "Oh, just what a terrible tragedy it all was," she said. The light had gone out of her eyes. "Like some sort of appalling play, with everyone dying in a uniquely horrible way, first your grandparents, and then your mother. She should never have married Harry Kingdom." She shook her head. "I'm sorry if I offend you, dear, but he was never going to be a faithful husband. To have multiple wives or partners plus all those other women; it has to be a sign of a very unsteady temperament!"

"He used to claim it was the triumph of hope over experience," Lizzie said, "but basically that was just an excuse for his womanising. He's not a very nice person." She picked up another croissant. This one had chocolate sprinkles on the top.

"For a while I was afraid you might follow in your mother's footsteps and fall for that squalid fellow the papers are so fascinated with!" Avery declared. She poured another cup of tea for both of them. "Oh, don't misunderstand me. He is terribly good-looking and I can quite see why women adore him—after all, poor Amelia Robsart was dotty about him for a while—but they had a name for his sort in my mother's day, you know, dear. He would have been spoken of as a *cad*."

"You're talking about Dudley," Lizzie said, her lips twitching.

"Well, of course! Dudley Lester!" Avery shook her head in disgust. "He's a dreadful lothario. I know you've been friends forever, dear, but don't step over that line. Not that we think you have," she added. "We *all* know it's complete nonsense. *We* weren't surprised to hear about Lettice Knollys." She fixed Lizzie with her very clear blue gaze. "You need to find yourself a nice beau, my dear. Would you like another croissant?"

"I couldn't squeeze any more in, thank you," Lizzie said. She was simultaneously distracted by Avery's use of the word "beau" and the fact that she was as on top of all the gossip as any celebrity reporter. "I didn't realise you knew Amelia," she said. "How was that?"

"I know everyone, dear," Avery said benignly. "Amelia's mother Jessica Scott was a client of mine in London in the nineteen eighties. I was a fashion designer," she added, seeing Lizzie's look of bemusement. "I'm *very* disappointed you haven't heard of me. I designed the dress Jessica wore for the premiere of *Chariots of Fire*. It was known as the naked dress ever after and quite stole the show!"

"I'm so sorry," Lizzie said. "I'd have liked to see that."

"I'll show you the photographs," Avery said with a smile. "Celebrity is very fleeting, Elizabeth dear. None of us are immortal, as you'll discover."

Lizzie laughed. "I think I've already learned that," she said. "Do you know Amelia's brothers and sisters as well?"

"Not the younger ones," Avery said, "not the poor boy that's disappeared." Her expression lightened a little. "I know Arthur. I knew his fiancée Mia too."

"I thought she was called Jenna," Lizzie said.

"Jenna," Avery said vaguely. "Of course. Yes, she was a sweet girl but so frail. In spirit, I mean. For a while they were all so close, Arthur and Jenna and Dudley and Amelia, before it all turned sour. Amelia bought Oakhangar Hall from me, you know. It had been in my family for centuries. And then she did all those appalling alterations," she added thoughtfully, "as though it didn't look like a dog's breakfast already."

"I hadn't realised," Lizzie said slowly. "That Oakhangar had belonged to your family, I mean. I've only been there the once, when Dudley and Amelia got married."

"Don't go back," Avery said, and suddenly her voice was devoid of all warmth. "It's not a *good* place, Elizabeth. There's something wrong with it. My ancestor built it from the stones of Cumnor Place." She spread her hands expressively. "What can you expect if you build the memory of a tragedy into the very fabric of a new building? Nothing happy will come of it, that's for sure. And so it proved, with Amelia falling down the stairs..." She shuddered. "Just like poor Amy Robsart."

Lizzie felt the light brush of something along her spine like feathers, or cobwebs. She shivered convulsively. "Who?" she said.

"Amy Robsart," Avery repeated. "She was the wife of Robert Dudley, later Earl of Leicester. He was the favourite of Queen Elizabeth I. Such a demeaning word, *favourite*," she added. "It makes him sound like a gigolo. Still," she shrugged, "women have been demeaned as royal mistresses for centuries and I don't suppose we should feel sorry for Robert. He did very well for himself."

"You said Amy was called Robsart," Lizzie said. "Was Amelia descended from her?"

"Amy had no children," Avery said, "but yes, it's the same family as Arthur and Amelia. They originated in Norfolk in the fifteenth century, I think, but Amy lived— and died—at Cumnor in Oxfordshire, which is only a few miles from here. So is Oakhangar Hall, of course. I did wonder..." She looked troubled for a moment. "When I heard about Amelia's death I wondered if the curse of Oakhangar had struck again," she said slowly. "It sounds fanciful, but it has happened a number of times before and the circumstances were so similar I could not help but think on it. My son tells me I'm a silly old woman, but he is a quantity surveyor and has very little imagination."

"I don't think it's silly," Lizzie said. She was thinking of her own gift of psychometry. "There are plenty of things that are impossible to explain rationally," she said, "but that doesn't mean we should assume they are fantasy."

Avery's bright blue eyes considered her. "That's very sensible, Elizabeth," she said, after a moment. "It would be arrogance to think we can explain everything away logi- cally." She sighed. "When I first set foot in Oakhangar Hall I knew there was something wrong about it; some- thing awry. It was all the fault of the Third Earl Basing. When Cumnor Hall fell into disrepair in the early nineteenth century, he took the stone to build his new manor at Oakhangar and to repair the church there. Not that he was particularly mean with money," she added, with a twinkle in her eye. "The Basings were extravagant to a fault, but it was a common practice in the past to reuse the materials from old buildings. All those monasteries that Henry VIII destroyed! There are pieces of them in buildings all over the country, and bits of Roman villas too. We're a magpie breed; we take what we want but sometimes, perhaps, we take more than we imagine."

"You mean that the stone retains a memory of the past in some way," Lizzie said hesitantly, "that certain buildings can contain the memory of events that happened hundreds of years ago?"

Avery's gaze was very direct and very clear. "I think that's true," she said quietly. "A physical place can hold an emotional memory."

Lizzie wondered why she hadn't thought of it before. It was such a close match with psychometry; reading objects that had emotional memories attached was akin to reading the history of a place through its fabric. Perhaps she could do that too. She hadn't made a habit of going around touching the walls of old buildings... A flash of memory came to her and she saw herself standing on the Thames Embankment, touching the blue plaque that marked the site of Baynard's Castle. The vision she had seen then had not been an emotional memory, though. With the heat of the sun and the scent of the river, it had felt as though she was actually there.

She blinked, coming back to the sunlit kitchen and the bright chirruping of the birds outside. Avery was watching her and it felt as though she saw so much, knew so much, of what Lizzie was only starting to work out...

"Be careful, Elizabeth dear," she said. "I know you are curious, but there has been enough hurt."

She reached for her basket and unpacked more milk, butter, eggs, cheese, ham, lemonade, a loaf of granary bread, a sausage roll and three other brown paper bags. Her busy movements and averted gaze indicated that the subject had been very firmly changed. "These are just a few things to keep you going," she said. "Your grandmother would have wanted me to look after you, I'm sure." She passed Lizzie a copy of a magazine. "This is the local paper. It's got a list of all the events and societies in Burford at the back so you can join in. This is a community," she added. "You're one of us now."

"Thank you," Lizzie said, overwhelmed. She turned to the back of the magazine. A bewildering array of activities met her eye: badminton, crafting, horticulture, knitting, the soup and pudding club... There was yoga, but probably not the type of class she was accustomed to doing at the World's End Studio in Camden, which was generally accepted to be London's premier urban yoga experience.

"Perhaps I could try something new," she said weakly. "The art society? I'm very poor at drawing."

"What an excellent idea." Avery smiled warmly. "Everyone wants to be a celebrity these days so it's refreshing to meet a celebrity who wants to learn a new skill."

"I expect there's a reality TV show already showing celebrities doing that," Lizzie said. "And if there isn't, there soon will be."

Avery kissed her cheek, gathered up the empty basket

and gave her a little wave. "I'll see you soon, my dear. Just call around if you need me."

The air seemed to buzz and quiver before settling after her departure. In the sudden silence, Lizzie's phone rang. When she saw that it was Bill her heart sank.

"Lizzie! Where the hell are you?" Bill sounded exactly the same, as though they had never had an almighty row, as though she hadn't ever been arrested, as though she hadn't dismissed the lawyers he'd sent. "You disappeared from London before I could get hold of you."

"Hello, Bill," Lizzie said. "I'm so glad you called. I wanted to ask you—"

"Look, Lizzie, I've had *The James Gordon Show* on," Bill interrupted. "They want you for an interview tonight. It's a special feature on public shaming; from golden girl to enemy of the people sort of thing. There'll be you, and that politician who faked his expenses and was sent to jail, and a kid who was a chess champion until they worked out he'd been cheating—"

"Bill." It was Lizzie's turn to interrupt. "No. Just—no."

"I know it's short notice," Bill continued, "and that you won't be able to talk about the legal case since it's ongoing, but you can drop a few hints, I'll get the lawyers to brief you. I'll send a car if you tell me where you are. And the producers of *Famous and Frozen* have been in touch. You know, it's the show where celebrities are abandoned in the Arctic for weeks with just a tent and a few tins of food. They thought the public might like to see you tackling something like that as a kind of punishment—"

"Again," Lizzie said. "No. Thank you. But as you're on the line, can I ask you why you let The High get so run-down when I was paying for a caretaker and a gardener?"

"Where?" Bill said. "Look, where are you?"

"At The High," Lizzie said, "hence the question."

"Right," Bill said, "right." He sounded slightly more cautious now, as though the penny had finally dropped. "You're in Burford. Of course—that's where you said you'd go. I didn't really think you'd do it."

"Clearly not," Lizzie said warmly. "Whilst Jules helps me sort out this legal mess I'm going to be writing some music, just like I mentioned. Or I will be when I get the house cleaned and the garden cleared and the piano tuned and all the other stuff done that I was paying you to sort out."

"Look, Lizzie," Bill said, "there was no point throwing money away on that place. I...ah...I invested it for you instead. I'll give Francis a call; ask him to send you the financial details..."

Bill, Lizzie thought, had never been so keen to involve her in discussions with her accountants before.

"Please do call Francis," she said. "Tell him I'm moving my business to Carpenter's. Oh, and Bill—you're fired." She pressed the button to end the call. It felt good. She felt free.

Humming a few lines of music under her breath, she went into the library. The heating had not yet started to make an impression on the room. It felt cold and unwelcoming and the shelves were thick with dust. In her grandparents' time the books had all been catalogued and sorted by topic like in a proper library system. Her grandfather had been a keen antiquarian collector with a particular interest in local history. Lizzie's father had let all of that go; in fact, she thought he had probably only kept such an esoteric collection of books to give the impression that he was cultured. Plenty of the stacks had drinks stains and cigarette burns on them.

She found what was left of the history section. Roman Britain mingled on the shelves with the history of the Habsburg Empire and Fatimid Egypt. She searched in vain for something on the Tudor period, resolving to go down to the Burford library as soon as she could to find a book about Elizabeth I and Robert Dudley. Then she saw a slim volume with a worn red leather cover and rough-cut pages. On the spine, in gold lettering it read: *An Historical Account of Cumnor—with some particulars of the Death of the Countess of Leicester* by Hugh Usher Tighe. The date at the bottom was 1821. Lizzie wrapped her grandfather's big thick jumper more closely around her and settled down in the leather armchair to read.

Hugh Tighe, she quickly discovered, had been a huge fan of Sir Walter Scott. Scott had based his book *Kenilworth* on the story of Amy Robsart and this had heavily influenced Tighe who saw Amy as a tragic and ill-treated heroine, the victim of a ruthless and ambitious man. For all Lizzie knew this could well have been the case but she thought Amy sounded rather feeble. Whilst Robert Dudley was living it up at the court of Queen Elizabeth I, Amy pined away, neglected and alone in the Oxfordshire countryside. Eventually Robert, keen to be rid of his inconvenient wife in order to marry the Queen, had allegedly arranged Amy's murder. "*The corpse of their wretched victim was precipitated down a flight of stone stairs, which led from the long gallery to the hall below, under the hope that it might give a plausibility to a tale by which they intended to conceal their crime,*" Lizzie read in Tighe's lurid prose. "*From this time the vengeance of heaven appears to have fallen, not only on the perpetrators of this atrocious murder, but also on the house in which it was committed."*

Lizzie shivered violently. This was close to the story that Avery had told of an emotional memory being held captive in the very fabric of Cumnor Hall and subsequently transferred to Oakhangar, where the curse had repeated itself with Amelia falling down the stairs and breaking her neck in precisely the same way that Amy had. Except that Amy's death had apparently been murder... She wondered if that was true. She wondered if Johnny knew the story and if so, what he had thought of it. Parallels, echoes of history, memories captured in stone...

She could hear Johnny's voice: *"This was once the site of a royal palace, you know. It was called Baynard's Castle. The foundations are right under this building."* Down by the river he had caught her hand and pulled her over to the wall to show her the plaque. When she had touched it, Johnny had been right beside her. She had seen his shadow in the vision, cutting across the sun...

She thought about the CCTV footage and the explosion of white light. Perhaps that had been a manifestation of the psychometry that couldn't be caught by the naked eye, in the way that spirit orbs were apparently captured on camera. She knew very little about that sort of thing but it might explain the lack of any physical evidence at the scene. Nothing, though, could explain why Johnny had been there one moment—caught in the frame—and the next, he had gone. Unless... She could see him sitting in the kitchen that night, the chocolate cup in front of him, spoon in hand, and he had asked her if she had the gift of time travel as well as the gift of psychometry.

And she had laughed it off because of course time travel was a fantasy, wasn't it?

Johnny the fey one, the one with the telepathic gift. He had seemed so much more at ease with the psychic stuff than she was. He knew she possessed the gift of psychometry. He'd seen her read the stone angel when he had only been six years old. He'd seen her read Arthur's mind that day at the flat. He knew she could read objects and people, and he had suggested that her gift was a great one and that she shouldn't be afraid of it. Perhaps he had already suspected that she could connect to the memories captured in buildings as well as in objects. Perhaps he had wanted to test that theory by taking her down to the remains of Baynard's Castle and seeing if she could call a memory from the stone. It would explain why he had asked her to go with him that night.

The book clattered to the floor as Lizzie jumped to her feet. She didn't notice. She walked over to the window, touching the cold, cobwebbed panes, trying to clear her mind. Johnny understood her psychic powers so much better than she knew them herself. There could be a number of explanations for that but given that he had admitted to being telepathic himself, one reason might be that he was a great deal more gifted than she was. She had assumed that his talent for telepathy worked only with Amelia—it certainly hadn't existed with her, and Arthur had referred to it as Johnny and Amelia's party trick. She hadn't imagined that Johnny might have other paranormal abilities as he hadn't mentioned them to her at all. But perhaps that had been deliberate. Perhaps he had not wanted her to know. He had told her enough so that she had thought they were kindred spirits but not so much that he would scare her.

She saw again the picture from the Embankment. Johnny had been beside her. She had touched the stone and inadvertently called up the vision of the old palace, and then Johnny was gone. She could hear Arthur telling her that his brother had a habit of disappearing, and behind that was the memory of something that Dudley had said; something about Johnny vanishing practically in front of his eyes. She'd assumed it was a figure of speech—but perhaps it was not.

Lizzie pressed her forehead to the glass and closed her eyes. She remembered Johnny talking about Amelia's death, the desperation in his voice and the pain:

"Millie's death hurts like hell on Earth. I'd do anything to bring her back, anything I could."

When she'd picked up Johnny's green notebook, she had felt the echo of those same emotions from him. She closed her eyes, trying to conjure once more the sense she had when she had held the notebook in her hand. She needed to speak to Arthur, needed the notebook back. All the clues would be in there, she was sure, and if she held it again, she would know.

She bent to pick up the book about Amy Robsart. She thought about Avery telling her that there was a curse on the Robsart family that had repeated down the years for centuries, a curse that had now claimed Amelia. If Johnny wanted to break that curse would he stop at nothing to do it? Would he go back in time to try to save Amelia? Or would he need to go back further still, to a palace that had been built hundreds of years before, to find Amy Robsart and save her in order to stop the whole pattern from repeating down through time?

Lizzie turned the idea over in her mind very carefully,

half afraid that she was losing her own sanity. No one could ever believe such an irrational theory. She acknowledged it. If psychometry sounded fanciful, time travel was surely impossible, utter madness. Yet Johnny had vanished without trace; Johnny, who was psychic, who had a habit of disappearing at will, who wanted to save his sister's life.

Lizzie knew she was right. She sensed it.

She also had no idea how to find Johnny and she knew she had even less chance of bringing him back.

20

Amy: Melford Hall, Suffolk, May 1559

IT WAS A long journey from Throcking into Suffolk, further than I had gone to carry Robert's messages to the Princess Elizabeth in Hatfield, further than I had travelled alone before. I say alone, but of course I was not; I had a maid with me and a groom and I had the escort of William Hyde himself. He had little choice but to fall in with my plans, not when I had told him that I knew he was robbing my lord of sums of money considerably larger than those I stole myself.

William had been quite unable to believe me when I had told him that if he did not accommodate my plans, I would tell Robert about his dealings. He had goggled at me as though the curtains themselves had spoken, so accustomed was he to thinking I was of no account. Although at first, he had laughed.

"He will not believe you," he said contemptuously. "Sir Robert knows that I am his loyal servant."

"I have copies of the accounts, Mr Hyde," I said sweetly. "Did you think I could not read, could not count? What did you think I did with all my time here in the back of nowhere? Oh, of course, you never considered it. Well, now you *know*."

He had goggled at me some more. He had blustered. But when I asked him to apprise me of Robert's exact whereabouts—for naturally Robert had not seen fit to tell me himself—he gave in.

"Sir Robert is in Suffolk," he said sulkily. "He has business there."

"The Queen's business?" I asked, and saw by the way his gaze slid from mine that my guess was correct. He had gone to meet with Elizabeth in secret. This interested me, for the past six months had been full of nothing but gossip of how he was forever in her company at court. They danced together, rode together, dined together. Whilst I was left to rot in the country, they made Elizabeth's new kingdom their playground. They made no secret of their preference for each other's company, so whatever had taken Robert on this clandestine journey had to be very important.

"You will escort me into Suffolk then," I said. "For I too have business with him."

William had looked properly appalled but I was insistent and he seemed so stunned at the change in me that he agreed.

"Sir Robert stays at Melford Hall," he informed me sullenly, and now, as he raised his hand to knock at the door of this fine manor, I thought what a very beautiful place Robert had chosen for his tryst with the Queen. No back stairs tumble for her.

The appalled expression on the face of the steward when William Hyde introduced me was a mirror for Hyde's own a few days past. I walked straight inside.

"Pray do not trouble to announce me to my lord," I said airily. "I will announce myself."

"Madam—" The steward was ashen. "I do not believe Sir Robert is expecting you…"

"No," I said. "That is rather the point."

Though the steward was struck dumb and Hyde was watching, grim-faced and silent, it was not difficult to work out where Robert was housed. I simply followed a servant carrying wine. He knocked at a chamber door and having been given the word to enter, I followed him in.

Robert was sprawled in a chair before the fire. He was alone. I had guessed he would be as had the Queen been present Hyde and the steward between them would have made more effort to detain me. As it was, perhaps they wanted to witness what would happen when Robert's docile wife turned.

"I thought I would find you here, Robert," I said. I stripped off my gloves and threw them down on the chest. I realised that I was enjoying this. I felt a rush of power and excitement. "I see you were expecting company," I added, glancing at the table set for two, the silver plate and the fine crystal, the flagon of wine. "I am sure she would not begrudge me refreshment. I have travelled a long way to see you."

Robert leaped to his feet. It was the first time in all our

acquaintance that I had been able to surprise him. It was most gratifying. He ran a hand through his hair, ruffling it like a nervous schoolboy. "How did you know where I was?"

"Oh…" I glanced over my shoulder towards the passage. "William told me. He escorted me here." I raised a brow. "Surely you did not think I came alone?"

"William Hyde?" He looked confused. "But—"

"I know," I said. "He is supposed to be your loyal man but I found a way to persuade him."

I saw Robert absorb the news of William's betrayal. His mouth set grimly. He did not care for disloyalty.

"How?" he said.

"That need not concern you," I said. "You cannot dismiss him," I added gently. "We need him."

His dark gaze snapped up to mine. "What do you mean?"

I poured for myself, since surprise seemed to have robbed him of his manners. I noted that my hand was quite steady. Robert was not so in command of himself. His gaze darted repeatedly to the open door so I walked over and closed it.

"Pray, sit down," I said. "Do not agitate yourself. If the Queen comes…" I smiled. "Well, for once she will have to concede her place to your wife."

He shot me a look of pure hatred. "Her Majesty does not care to be kept waiting."

I shrugged. "I can only imagine how difficult your life must be in that case." I raised my glass in a mocking toast. "To your future happiness."

Robert poured a glass too, slopping the red wine onto

the cloth where it spread like a bloodstain. He drank it down in one gulp.

"Why are you here?" he asked.

"To negotiate a truce," I said, "to suggest a solution." I sat, arranging my skirts carefully. "You want to marry the Queen," I said. "I want to be free. There is a way for us both to get what we want."

He stared at me. I waited to see if he would insult me with some sort of conventional denial, an expression of shock or a false vow of affection. To his credit he did none of those. That time was past and we both knew it.

"The Queen would never marry me," he said, "even if I were free."

I thought this was probably true. From the moment I had seen Elizabeth at Hatfield I had doubted that she would marry anyone, no matter how her advisers urged her to make a foreign alliance. Danger and experience had taught her to be wary. She would never risk compromising her power as her sister had done, never risk putting herself and her country in any man's hands. She loved Robert. She had said so. I thought she loved him a great deal, but not quite enough to put him above all else. And being Elizabeth, she probably thought she could demand his love, his adoration, his attention, his devotion and everything else she wanted without giving him the ultimate prize.

My aim, however, was to convince Robert of the opposite because only if he believed he had a chance to wed her would he agree to my plan. I did not think this would be too difficult. Robert's weakness had always been his arrogance and ambition. He would want to believe he could change Elizabeth's mind and persuade her to marry him. If the path were clear...

"She would change her mind," I said, "if you were free. She loves you. She told me so herself."

I saw a spark leap in his eyes, then it dulled almost immediately. His mouth turned down at the corners. "Do you think I have not considered all possible ways to achieve it?" he said. He looked at me, his gaze shadowed now. The subject wearied him. I could see it was a familiar trap, an unbearable frustration. "There can be neither annulment nor divorce for us. This leaves only…"

"Death," I said.

The word dropped into the silence of the room like a stone in a deep pool.

"Do not tell me," I said, "that you have not considered it."

"Amy." He looked uncomfortable, sheepish, too committed to lie yet too much of a coward to admit it.

"Of course you have," I said. "How could you not wish it? I die and the path is clear."

He frowned fiercely. "I would never hasten your end, if that is what you fear."

I was not sure whether I believed him or not. In the whispering hall of mirrors I was imprisoned in it was all too easy to believe rumour and gossip. I did not know whether they were true or falsehood. Reason was slippery but I grasped after it.

"I do believe you," I said, "because to kill me would be a foolish thing to do and though you may be a desperate man, I do not think you are a stupid one."

I had his full attention now. "What do you mean?"

"If there was even the slightest suspicion that you had sought my death," I said carefully, "your enemies would seize upon it. They would never let it be forgotten. The

Queen cannot allow any rumour of foul play to besmirch her reputation. She would send you away and your chance of marrying her would be gone forever."

I saw the expression in his eyes and knew in that moment that he *had* considered it. Perhaps he had even started to plan my murder. Desperate times bred desperate remedies and if Robert had thought for even one second that he might get away with it, he would act.

I should have felt afraid then, when I saw the depths to which he would go, but I did not. I sat back in my chair, stretching my aching limbs towards the fire, seeking the warmth and relaxation. It was pleasant in that little chamber, oddly comfortable and comforting as though we were a long-married couple supping together.

"Think about it," I said. "Don't be a fool, Robert."

He had turned away from me so that I could not read his expression. Not that I needed to see it to know. I had guessed and guessed aright but he did not want me to think he would have had me killed. He wanted me to believe that even with the stakes so high he would have remained loyal to me.

I knew better.

"It does not matter anyway," I said, as though he had spoken to deny his guilt, "for there is another way."

He looked at me as though he were seeing me for the first time, as though the assumptions he had made about me for all of our married life were dropping away at last.

"Tell me," he said. He refilled my glass. This time his hand was completely steady.

"I can disappear," I said. "To all intents and purposes, I would be dead. Only you and I and whichever is the most trustworthy of your men—Anthony Forster, perhaps—would know the truth."

He waited.

"First we must spend some time together in London," I said, "to allay suspicion. We want people to think that we are reconciled."

"The Queen," he said, at once. "She will not like it."

I felt a pang of irritation that when I was offering him all he ever wanted, still he was subject to her whims.

"You cannot tell her the truth," I said sharply. "You will have to manage the situation. I will come to visit you." I smiled at his expression. He looked as though he had the toothache. "It will not be so bad," I said, "a few weeks only."

He nodded. I could see he was eager to hear the meat of my suggestion to work out whether it was worth the pain of Elizabeth making his life a misery for a while. "When I leave," I said, "I will go somewhere remote, somewhere even more isolated than Throcking." I waited for the barb to bite. "It was unkind of you to send me there, Robert, and simply forget about me."

"I know." He looked ashamed. "I was so angry with you, so angry with *us*." He made a gesture of resignation. "I hated the situation I found myself in. I wanted so much to be free; I thought it would drive me insane with wanting."

"That is why the knot must be cut," I said. "I too wish to be free."

He nodded again, so eager now, malleable in my hands. "How is it to be done?"

"Anthony Forster has a house at Cumnor in Oxfordshire, does he not," I said. "I will go to stay there for a few months. He is the most well-respected of your men. People believe him honest." I smiled. "That will be important."

"Forster is a sound man," Robert agreed.

"He is your paid flunkey like the rest of them," I said cuttingly, "but he is better at hiding his corruption." I had had years and years in which to observe Robert's retinue and my observation was that men took their lead from their master. Just as Robert could be brutal and none too scrupulous in pursuit of what he wanted, so did they echo him in their different ways.

"Whilst I am at Cumnor," I continued, "you will send me money and will arrange safe passage for me to Holland. I want false papers and a place to live."

I saw Robert's eyes widen. His Adam's apple jumped as he swallowed.

"I know it can be done," I said calmly. "Anything is possible if you wish it enough and can afford the price."

"Yes…" I could see he was thinking hard, and quickly. "It is possible. But…"

"I don't want to know the difficulties," I said. "I want you to arrange it. You owe me that." I took a breath. "And of course, you will need to procure a body."

Now he stared at me as though I were indeed insane. "Come, Robert," I said. "Do you think I do not know how your retainers are little better than a band of thugs? How they brawl and maim and even kill, and you spend a fortune to buy them out of gaol and bribe judges and settle their affairs to avoid difficult questions asked? It would not be hard for Richard Varney or John Butler or any number of them to provide you with the body of a woman of the right age, height and colouring to match mine."

Robert was looking a little sick. I was not sure whether

he was repulsed at the thought that I knew all about his sins or that I had the indelicacy to mention them.

"I do not scruple to talk of it," I said cheerfully, "since both you and I know they are varlets and murderers."

He ran an agitated hand through his hair. "Even if they were," he said, "we cannot pass off some pox-ridden trull from the back streets of London as Lady Dudley. You think that if we dress her in your clothes and claim she died of a fever, people will be taken in?" He shook his head. "You are dreaming."

"Not so." I sat forward, eager to make him see how it could be achieved. "I have it all planned," I said. "Of course, we will need some help, but not much. The fewer people who know the better it will be. We can choose a day when the whole household is away—at a market or a fair, perhaps. I could feign illness but insist they go without me." I dismissed the detail with a wave of my hand. "Your man brings the body in secret. That is why I think Cumnor Place serves us best. It is remote and lonely. Even better, I have learned that there is an outer stair to the tower there that is perfect for our purpose. A man could enter and leave the building unseen."

"It is utter madness." Robert spoke violently. "I should not encourage you in such intemperate ideas!"

"If you do not have the stomach for it," I said, "I will achieve it alone. This is my future we speak of, as well as yours. How do you think it feels to be locked away in idleness day after day whilst my husband dances attendance on the Queen? When men speak of him as her *favourite*?" I said the word as though it were poisoned. "I have pride, Robert, and I have a desire to live the life I want as much as you do. I wish to be rid of you as much as you wish to be rid of me!"

He stood up. I could see that my words had stung him and wondered if he had really thought that being Lady Dudley should have been enough for me regardless of the price I paid.

"How?" he demanded. "How will you achieve it? Will you persuade Forster as you persuaded Hyde? How did you do that? With your body?"

"That is none of your affair," I said coldly, "when the entire world gossips of your exploits with Her Majesty."

Robert made a sound remarkably like a growl but he subsided into his chair and glared at me from beneath low-ered brows. "Go on," he said curtly. "Finish your fairy tale. Tell me what happens next."

"We place the body at the base of the stair," I said, "face down, so it looks like a fall. I am spirited away to my new life. Anthony calls a couple of servants who recognise my clothing and will testify that I have had an accident. He then carries the woman to my chamber and locks the door. He formally identifies the body as mine and sends to tell you I have met with an untimely, tragic, but entirely in-nocent end."

"And what will happen when the household returns and sees the corpse?" Robert spoke with heavy sarcasm. "Do I have to pay them all off or are you expecting they will suffer from a collective blindness that will prevent them from noticing this woman is not you?"

"Neither," I said. I tried not to sound too pleased with myself. "They will not see the body," I said simply. "It will already have been identified by someone who knew me. Why distress them with the sight of their dead mistress?"

Robert rolled his eyes. "There would have to be an in-quest."

"Of course," I said. "But the jurors need not be known to me." I paused a moment to allow him to digest that. "Why should they recognise my likeness?" I pressed the point. "A woman is dead. Anthony Forster tells them it is Lady Dudley. Why would they question?"

Robert was very still.

"To make all safe," I finished, softly, "you could choose a man to be foreman of the jury. A stranger to me," I added, "but one who is beholden to you—or to the Queen. There must be many such men anxious to oblige her..."

"A queen's man..." Robert whispered the words. I thought he looked a little dazed.

"He would know nothing," I said, "other than that it was in his interests to make sure all went smoothly with the inquest."

He nodded. I could see that the flame of the idea had caught hold. All I had to do now was fan it into belief but I needed to tread carefully. Too much fire and I might scare him away from the idea. In my favour was the fact that he *wanted* to believe the plan would work because it could grant him his heart's desire.

"It has the merit of being quite simple," I said, "when you consider it. A woman is dead, identified as Lady Dudley. I will be gone to a new life, and will never trouble you again."

He stared at me for what seemed like the longest time and then he raised his goblet to touch mine. Gold met gold with the softest kiss. Looking into his eyes I saw how it might have been for us in a different place, a different time; an ambitious man with a clever, beautiful and ambitious wife at his side. We might have risen high together, instead of which for him to rise, I had to fall.

"This way we can both gain all we desire," I said, and after a moment he smiled at me and I almost fell in love with him all over again until I remembered that *she* was coming, the Queen of England, and that if anyone was the Queen's true man then it was he.

"So be it," he said, and our pact was made.

21

Lizzie: Present Day

LIZZIE HAD ARRANGED to meet Arthur in one of the tea shops in Burford High Street. It was busy, full of shoppers and tourists, and it felt impersonal enough to give her confidence. Even so, she was edgy as she waited for him, checking the door every few seconds, aware that she didn't really know how to feel or how it would be to see him again, let alone how to broach the subject of Johnny. Another night of broken sleep had done nothing other than give her a headache and convince her that her thoughts about Johnny's paranormal powers were the result of stress and tiredness, but even so, at the back of her mind, a stubborn instinct lingered that she was right.

"Is this neutral territory?" Arthur enquired as he slid into the seat opposite her. She had been distracted by the appearance of tea in a big pot shaped like a thatched cottage and had missed his arrival after all. He bent to brush her cheek with a light kiss and the touch ran through her and made her disturbingly aware of him even though it was all over in a second.

"I thought it would be easier to meet here," Lizzie admitted. "I feel kind of nervous. I'm not sure why." She fidgeted with the teaspoon, looking up to see Arthur watching her with a smile in his eyes. Her stomach swooped.

"Me too," he said.

"You?" Lizzie stared at him. "Nervous of me?"

"Not exactly of you," Arthur said, "more of us." He shrugged slightly uncomfortably. "Nothing about our relationship seems normal, you know?"

Lizzie did know. She nodded. "How are you?" she asked.

"I'm doing all right." Arthur's quiet words were belied by the deep lines of tiredness she could see in his face. She imagined that the constant worry of Johnny's disappearance must be endlessly stressful.

"I guess the first thing I should say is thank you for calling Jules, and for standing bail for me," she said. "So, thank you."

Arthur gave her a proper smile and her heart turned over. "You're welcome," he said. "I trust you not to abscond." He took off his jacket and sat back, looking around. "They do great fruit cake here," he said. "Would you like some?"

"I've already ordered a chocolate cupcake," Lizzie admitted. "I have a very sweet tooth."

The cake arrived, and with it a latte for Arthur. He sat back in his chair and took a long, heartfelt swallow of the coffee whilst Lizzie took the thatched roof lid off the teapot, stirred its contents and poured. She thought of all the things she needed to talk to him about and tried to work out how to start.

"Why did you do it?" she blurted out. "Why did you put up the bail money?"

Arthur laughed. "That's direct. Has no one ever done you a favour before?"

"Not on this scale," Lizzie said, "and not without wanting something in return."

Arthur raised his brows. "And that's cynical."

"You didn't tell the police about Johnny's notebook either," Lizzie said bluntly. "Why not?"

"Is this an interrogation?" Arthur looked to be enjoying himself.

"If you like," Lizzie said. "Why didn't you tell them?"

Reaching into his pocket, Arthur tossed the green notebook down onto the table between them. "I didn't think it would do you any favours if they knew it had been found in your flat."

"That's true," Lizzie said. "Especially since Johnny's phone was apparently found there. Did you plant it on me?"

"I'd hardly plant one piece of incriminating evidence and remove another, would I?" Arthur said.

"You might," Lizzie said, "if it was a double bluff."

"I don't even begin to understand that," Arthur said. He leaned forward. "Look, Lizzie, I'm a pretty straightforward sort of person. I don't play games. You'll just have to take my word for it that I didn't plant the phone on you. Anna says she didn't put it there either, so Johnny must have dropped it and you simply didn't notice sooner."

"I don't think so," Lizzie said, frowning. "Johnny told me he had left his phone in the car. Unfortunately, he didn't say who had given him a lift the night he came to find me. It was just a casual remark at the time and I didn't think to ask."

"Well, it wasn't me," Arthur said, "and Anna doesn't have a car."

"OK." Lizzie's shoulders slumped. "I suppose it's just another thing that doesn't make sense, then."

There was quiet for a moment. The waitress brought Arthur a piece of fruit cake and another chocolate cupcake for Lizzie. All around them the shop hummed with visitors and chatter, it felt warm and the air was scented with freshly baked cakes, but Lizzie still felt edgy. She thought about letting the whole time travel thing go, ignoring her instincts and not saying anything to Arthur. Then she wondered if that made her sensible or just a coward.

"I had something else to ask you," she said in a rush. Her palm itched and she closed her fingers tightly over it. "This is going to sound weird," she said, "but bear with me."

Arthur looked amused. "Is it weirder than all the other stuff that's already happened?"

"Yes," Lizzie said, "much." She took a deep breath. "OK. I'm just going to go for it. You mentioned in passing that Johnny has a bit of a habit of disappearing. Dudley said the same thing. I wondered whether you meant he would just wander off somewhere to be on his own and then come back when he felt like it, or whether there was more to it than that." She saw Arthur's frown and hurried on. "I mean, has he vanished for long periods of time before? Or has he—I don't know—just seemed to be there one moment and be gone the next?" She thought she was probably expressing herself very badly but couldn't see how to put it any better. She wasn't ready to blurt out that she thought Johnny travelled in time and she didn't think Arthur would be ready to hear that either.

Arthur started to speak then checked himself. "Why do you ask?" he said quietly.

Lizzie looked him in the eye. "I can't tell you that right now. Please, Arthur, believe me, this is very important."

"All right," Arthur said. "But tell me first what Dudley said."

"Not much," Lizzie said. "It was whilst he was telling me about how he'd reported Johnny for threatening him. I'm afraid I jumped down his throat. I wish I hadn't now, but at the time I didn't realise how important it might be." She closed her eyes for a second, trying to remember Dudley's precise words. "He said that Johnny was always saying weird stuff and appearing and disappearing like a ghost and that once, at Oakhangar, Johnny and Amelia were playing some childish trick where he vanished like it was magic."

Arthur had turned very pale and his mouth was set in a grim line. "It's odd you should mention that," he said slowly, "because my immediate reaction to what you asked was that yes, Johnny would sometimes wander off on his own but there was no more to it than that. Then I remembered something."

Lizzie's heart sped up. She found that she desperately wanted to eat another cupcake, as was so often the case when she felt stressed, but this wasn't the moment to order a third so she sat on her hands.

"It was when Johnny was a kid," Arthur said, "about seven or eight, I suppose. We were at our dad's place in

Norfolk, and Johnny just disappeared, literally seemed to vanish into thin air. He was gone for hours. Jess, Johnny's mum, was frantic. We searched everywhere and then he just popped up again as though nothing had happened. He said he'd been playing with Amy. We assumed he meant Amelia and that made Jess even angrier because Amelia wasn't even there that day so he had to be lying."

Lizzie's mouth was dry. "Perhaps he wasn't lying," she said. "After all, that's pretty much what he's done now."

There was a very long silence. She let it spin out.

"Jules told me about the CCTV," Arthur said at last. "I haven't seen it but I have to admit that was what it sounded like." He met her gaze. "You do know what you're suggesting?" He sounded almost angry. "You're implying that Johnny has the ability to travel to a different dimension of time, which is a physical impossibility."

"By all conventional measures," Lizzie said steadily, "all of the things we've been talking about are impossible: psychometry, telepathy…" She shrugged. "If you believe that there are things we can neither explain nor understand scientifically, and manifestly there are, then this is only one other thing on the list."

Arthur was silent again. His head was bent and there was a heavy frown on his brow. Lizzie could sense his emotions even though she wasn't touching him: there was anger and conflict in him, but she knew it was because he was very close to believing her—and he did not want to acknowledge that. It was way too much, too soon. She could understand that. She surreptitiously gestured to the waitress to bring her another cake.

"Johnny could be in Scotland, or Peru, or…or on a

beach in Bali," Arthur said. "All of those are far more likely scenarios than that he's somehow gone back in time."

"I agree," Lizzie said steadily, "and if Johnny pops up having spent a fortnight in Bali I'll be delighted. But I don't think he will." She leaned forward. "You don't really think he will either, do you, Arthur?"

Arthur scrubbed an exasperated hand through his hair. "It's insane. Even if it were a physical possibility, why would he want to go back? *Where* would he go? What is he trying to achieve?"

"I think I know the answer to that," Lizzie said. "I think Johnny believes that if he can change the past, he will be able to prevent Amelia's death."

"The past can't be altered to change the present," Arthur argued. "I'm not even going to start on the butterfly effect or parallel universes or all those theories—" He stopped. "Are you eating *cake* at a time like this?"

"I can't help it," Lizzie said, her mouth full of icing. "I have a sweet tooth and stress gives me a sugar craving." She swallowed. "Arthur, the point is not what *we* believe but what Johnny believes. To stand any chance of finding him, we need to think like he did."

Arthur swore. "You really believe this, don't you?" His dark gaze fastened on her. "*Shit.*" He shook his head. "I can't believe we're even talking about this and at the same time I can—because of this." He touched Johnny's green notebook. "I think you said you didn't ever get the chance to look through it properly?"

Lizzie shook her head. "After I'd tried to use it to connect to Johnny that first time, I was too exhausted and disturbed to touch it again," she said.

"It makes for interesting reading," Arthur said, "especially in view of your theory about Johnny. I thought at first that it was notes for a history project—Johnny's studying history along with maths and design at school in Oxford. Then I realised it was much more than that." He gave the book a little push towards Lizzie. "Take a look," he said. "I don't think it will hurt you now. It feels...it feels as though its power is spent somehow, if that makes sense."

Lizzie touched the cover gingerly. Arthur was right; there was no flash of sensation this time, no visions, no sense of Johnny's emotions when he had written his notes. It was as though he had somehow severed his connection to it and it was now nothing more than a pile of pages. Curious, though, she opened it.

Just as she remembered, there were endless scribbles, diagrams and drawings, sprawling charts that looked like family trees, dates with more jottings written over the top, crossings out and different colours, chaotic and rambling. She found the Robsart family tree and started to read.

"Sir John Robsart," she said, "born circa 1480, son of Terrence and Lucy Robsart, married Elizabeth Scott, one child, Amy born 1532, died 1560..." Lizzie noticed that Amy had been twenty-eight when she had died, just like Amelia.

She read the next line of Johnny's notes: "Amy had one elder half-brother, Arthur Robsart, son of Sir John Robsart and an unnamed mother, illegitimate but accepted into the family, and a number of other half-siblings..."

She looked up and met Arthur's unreadable dark gaze.

"The similarities are uncanny, aren't they?" he said evenly.

"I was reading about Amy Robsart last night," Lizzie said. "This was exactly what set me thinking about Johnny's

reasons for disappearing. Avery mentioned Amy to me—
you remember Avery Basing? She sold Oakhangar Hall
to Amelia." Then, when Arthur nodded, she went on: "I
don't know much about Amy—I haven't had the chance
yet to find out about her—but Avery drew my attention
to the parallels between Amelia's death and Amy's." She
glanced back down at Johnny's notes. "It seems that Johnny
had worked all that out for himself."

"Yeah," Arthur said, "that and much more." He shifted
in his seat. "Johnny's notes suggest that Amelia's death was
part of a replicating pattern that has played out a number
of times down the centuries. It hasn't just happened once
and all the deaths are connected in some way to Amy
Robsart, or Cumnor Hall or later, Oakhangar."

Lizzie was silent. Around her she was aware of the chink
of china and the hum of voices, the repeated ring of the
bell as the shop door opened, the scent of cinnamon and
chocolate. It felt reassuring and distant at the same time.

"Avery suggested much the same thing," she said. "She
thinks there is something evil trapped in the fabric of
Oakhangar Hall and that it draws on the original tragedy
of Amy Robsart's death." Despite the scented warmth of
the shop she shuddered. Her tea had gone cold. She looked
around for a waitress to request a refill.

"That sounds like stone tape theory," Arthur said, then
at her blank look explained. "It was a Victorian pseudo-
science and became fashionable all over again in the nineteen seventies when someone made a movie about it."

"Stone tape theory..." Lizzie picked up the notebook
again. "Isn't there something about that in here..." She
flicked through the pages. "Yes, here—" She read aloud
from Johnny's notes: "The Stone Tape Theory speculates

that inanimate materials can absorb energy from living beings. A 'recording' is laid down during moments of high tension or emotion. This stored energy can then be released, resulting in a display of the recorded activity. In some cases, place memories can be replayed by gifted individuals who claim to be able to interact with the events that are released." She looked up. "I guess that individual would be me," she said bleakly. "That's what happened at Baynard's Castle, except that I was the one who released the memory and Johnny was the one who interacted with it. It was just like reading an object only more intense."

"It's hard to believe that Johnny set all this up," Arthur said. "Would he really stitch you up like this? He seemed to quite like you."

"I think he felt bad about it," Lizzie said, "but yeah, I do believe that he was so fixated on saving Amelia that he would have done just about anything to achieve that."

"I guess so," Arthur said. "You know, you're the Queen Elizabeth I equivalent in this version of the story, if Johnny's theory is to be believed."

"Which has to be one of the most bizarre aspects of this apparent repeating pattern," Lizzie said. "I'm nothing like her."

"There are similarities." For the first time in a long while, Arthur smiled. "The red hair, the…ah…strong personality and—" he nodded at the crumbs on her plate "—the sweet tooth."

"You mean I'm a diva," Lizzie said. She sighed. "Well, you could be right." She looked round. The tea shop had emptied whilst they were sitting there and the staff were rather ostentatiously polishing the tables and looking at them sideways. "I think we've outstayed our welcome," she said. "They want to clean up. We'd better go."

They paid the bill and went out onto the high street. Daylight was fading; the church clock chimed five. The stream of cars up the hill seemed relentless.

"It's an odd mix, isn't it," Lizzie said, "all this noise and modernity in a place that looks like a costume drama film set."

"It's managed to keep its character, though, despite everything," Arthur said. "Burford's a beautiful place. I'll drive you back," he added. "Protect you from the paparazzi."

"Thanks," Lizzie said. She pulled on a felt hat of her grandmother's that was adorned with an outsized flower.

"That hat totally works," Arthur said, straight-faced. "No one will recognise you at all."

"I'm sure no one cares really," Lizzie said, sliding into the passenger seat of the Land Rover. "It's refreshing. Actually, I could walk," she added, as the vehicle roared into life, setting the little phoenix charm above the dashboard swinging and making a number of tourists jump. "It's only two minutes away."

"It's no problem," Arthur said. He pulled out into the traffic and waved his thanks. "I'd like to see The High. It's supposed to be a nice example of Georgian architecture."

"It's not a good example of anything at the moment," Lizzie said, "apart from what can happen when nature takes over. Renovating is on my list of things to do," she added, "along with trying to decide what I want to do next with my life."

"Any thoughts?" Arthur gave her a sideways glance. "I know you said you were planning on writing music again, but you could do anything else you want to. Travel, go to university, set up a charity…"

"Or all of those," Lizzie said. "I'll let you know. The High is here on the left," she added, gesturing to him to go through the wrought iron gates. "I told you it was close."

The Land Rover roared over the gravel and drew to a stop at the front door.

"The High is an interesting name," Arthur said, "considering it's halfway down the hill. Where did it come from?"

"I've no idea," Lizzie said. "I'll ask Avery. She's bound to know. Before I forget, there was one other thing I wanted to tell you."

"Only the one?" Arthur said.

"It's the stone angel," Lizzie said. "The one that Johnny took the night he disappeared. That day at Amelia's wedding when I cut my hand on the gazing ball and you bandaged me up—"

"Yes?" Arthur was smiling at the memory. "You were a sulky teen in those days."

Lizzie pulled a face. "Please don't remind me." She sighed. "When I touched the stone angel that afternoon, I saw a vision. Or more accurately, I experienced one." She swallowed hard, holding Arthur's gaze. "Arthur, I felt as though I was falling. I could feel the air rushing past and I felt utterly terrified." She broke off. "I think… I'm scared that I foresaw Amelia's death."

"Or had a flashback to Amy's," Arthur said grimly. He put his hand over hers. "God, Lizzie, how horrible." His grip was warm and strong. Lizzie had the sense of him drawing comfort from her touch as much as giving it.

"I know," Lizzie said miserably. "I wish none of this

had ever happened. I wish I'd never met Dudley and I wish I didn't have this gift and that I didn't think Johnny was lost—"

"Hey," Arthur said. He put his arms around her and drew her closer. It was awkward trying to hug in the Land Rover but she really didn't mind because it was lovely. "We're all tired and emotional," Arthur said, against her hair. "Don't think about it for now."

Lizzie tilted her face up to look at him. She could smell the scent of his skin and feel the warmth of him. She swallowed hard, her throat suddenly dry. "I sometimes wonder what it would be like if we..." She stopped.

"I wonder about that too," Arthur said. His gaze held hers.

Lizzie took his face in her hands and kissed him before she could change her mind. For a second he didn't respond and terrifyingly, she could read nothing of his emotions, and then everything changed. He slid a hand behind her head and the kiss became hotter and more urgent, and Lizzie felt the emotion explode, fusing his feelings with her own, and leaving her in free fall.

"I have a sense," Arthur said, as they finally broke apart, "that we've just made everything a whole lot more complicated."

"Well, at least now we know," Lizzie said. "We'd better avoid doing that again. It could ruin the experience with anyone else."

She saw Arthur smile. "Tell me again that you've never had this sort of connection with anyone before."

Lizzie couldn't begin to deal with how she was feeling. "It happens to me with everyone I kiss," she said shakily. "It's very commonplace. I'd be lying if I said otherwise."

"I don't believe you." Arthur put his arms around her and kissed her again. She could feel him smiling against her mouth. This time there was no hesitancy, simply a rush of physical sensation that almost swept her away.

"Lizzie Kingdom," Arthur said, his lips an inch away from hers. "Who would have thought?" Then: "I should go. I really should."

Lizzie hesitated for a split second. She was aware of the conflict inside her, the old fear of intimacy, the need for emotional safety versus an excitement so vivid it lit her up. She'd never felt like this before. She had had no idea. All the times she had thought that there was something wrong with her because she didn't want a relationship, she just wasn't that into someone...

"Stay with me," she said, "Arthur. Stay with me. Please."

22

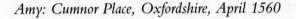

Amy: Cumnor Place, Oxfordshire, April 1560

IT HAD BEEN a day of sharp little gusts of wind that raised the tapestries from the wall at Cumnor Place and squally showers that shattered on the diamond window-panes. By four of the clock evening was already drawing in and the promise of spring that had set the daffodils dancing only the day before had vanished. The day was dark but my mood was fair. Revenge on Robert for all the neglect and injustices and humiliation he had piled upon me was a wonderful tonic. I sat before the mirror in my grand chamber, brushing my hair slowly, dreamily, as I imagined what my life might be in the future. In the chest beside me, hidden beneath the folded clothes, the gloves, shawls, petticoats and gowns of a quality appropriate to the wife of the Queen's favourite, was the money I had accumulated.

Since coming to Cumnor I had been performing the most elaborate show. My entire life was now a play; a performance of devotion to my absent husband, of mute acceptance of his neglect, a display of sweet nature and pliability. Occasionally I would allow my sadness to show, as I had the previous day when Sir Anthony Forster had invited our neighbours to dine and I had mournfully pushed my food about my plate, rousing myself to smile and make conversation before sinking into reverie again. It was this pretty display of patience that had prompted my friends to visit me that afternoon—to cheer my mood or perhaps to feed on my misery. I did not care either way. They too were unwitting actors in my play.

They had clattered into the parlour:

"Dearest Amy, we are here to lift your spirits!"

Lady Pollard had brought me sweetmeats and was sympathetic: "Our poor, *dear* Amy! What a cross you have to bear."

Mrs Wayneman was soothing and gave me a vial of sweet wine to help me sleep. "I am sure Sir Robert will send for you to join him at court soon," she said, her gaze darting away from mine as she spoke. We both knew she lied.

Mrs Mutlowe was bracing and as usual she had brought nothing but trenchant advice: "Perhaps if you were to take the air more you would find that your humour improved," she said. Mrs Mutlowe, so conscious that she was lower born than the rest of us, made a virtue of plain speaking. "I'm a plain woman and I speak as I find," she would say.

In truth I knew that they were all gleeful to discover me still so downcast. Misery loves company; their lives were almost as tedious as mine and it comforted them to see that for all my name and my status, I had a worse time of it than they. I was very glad of their spite. From the moment I had come to Cumnor Place I had used them to spread the rumours I wanted told against Robert:

"Poor Amy Dudley is ailing again..."

"She is so neglected she is in a despair."

"She has a malady of the breast..."

"She fears poison..."

For the past six months I had watched and listened as the stories of my unhappy life rippled outward like water from a tainted pool. I had followed their journey in my mind as they flowed from neighbour to neighbour, through ale-houses and inns. I knew that they would run like a plague of rats through the villages and towns as far as all the great houses of England, for that was what gossip and scandal did. In time the tide of it would reach London and the court of Queen Elizabeth herself where my husband basked in her laughter and occupied her virgin's bed.

"The wife of the Queen's favourite is such a sweet-natured, beautiful lady... She has been shamefully abandoned and is in fear of her life..."

I had even greater ambitions for those stories. I wanted them to take sail across the sea to the courts of Europe, travelling through ambassadors' quills and merchants' talk, until they returned to England much embroidered. I wanted the whole country, the whole of Europe, to hate my husband.

Robert, of course, had no notion how I stoked that fire of scandal. He wrote to me complaining that men spoke against him and that it would ruin all our plans. I wrote back soothingly, telling him I did all that I could to stem the flow of malice. *My friends know how content I am,* I wrote, *and will spread the word to counter these vicious slanders.*

Alas for Robert, he believed me. The hope that he would soon be free to court the Queen dazzled him even more than before. He was drunk on her presence, on her very being. I hated that she possessed the power to entrance him so but I could see its uses. She kept him occupied. His obsession addled his brain and he had no more idea that I was deceiving him than that he could fly to the moon.

Poor Robert, he never divined my plan, that I would take his money and his papers and begin my new life whilst he was perpetually locked into the old one. I knew that no matter how or why I "died" Robert's enemies would use it against him. He would never be able to escape the shadow of suspicion. It was a nightmare malady, incurable. The Queen would not marry him. He would never attain his heart's desire. Cruel revenge, perhaps, but he had stolen my life. I could have been a wife and mother, the mistress of a fine house and a great estate, not some wraith passing from place to place.

"You will be properly mourned," he had promised me on the last occasion we had met in London. "The whole court will observe it and I will give you a grand funeral to match your state." Perhaps he thought I would thank him, this man who was already thinking of me as dead.

The only pang of sorrow I felt was for my brother Arthur. I had no wish to cause him pain. Anna, I thought, would not miss me but Arthur had been a true and steadfast friend to me through all, and it gave me some guilt to think that I was deliberately deceiving him. I entertained the idle idea that one day I might write to him from my new life. Yet I knew I could not.

That afternoon, when Lady Pollard and Mrs Wayneman and Mrs Mutlowe had gone, I sat alone in the parlour
for a little. My hands were idle but my mind was busy.
The rumours were sown now and it was time to begin
the next part of my plan. It was time to give my lord's letter of instruction to Sir Anthony Forster. I stood up and
smoothed the skirts of my gown. It was a new one, satin
trimmed, with lace and ribbons tied in true lovers' knots.
I loved the deep indigo blue of it; it spoke of innocence
and heavenly grace.

Down in the cross passage I met one of the maids.

"Is Sir Anthony in his study?" I enquired. "I have a
commission for him."

I need him to arrange my death.

She dropped a curtsey and murmured her assent. I felt
her gaze on my back as I walked away; I knew there would
be pity in it. She, like all the others, believed me to be
ill used.

My hand was raised to knock on the study door. I felt
the rush of cold air as the main door creaked open. I
turned. The maid had gone and there was no one in the
passage. The shadows shifted; cobwebs scuttered across the
flagstones of the floor. It felt as though the world paused
for a moment in its turning.

I saw the boy standing beneath the arch of the tower
door, the same boy I had seen at Baynard's Castle, and had
thought a ghost. As before, he was dressed in a hooded
cape of black with boots and hose, and he looked young
and gaunt. In his eyes was a desperation that clutched at
my heart.

"Amy!" he said. "Oh, dear God, I have found you!"

He spoke as though he knew me, but then over the

years I had found that many people pretended to an acquaintance they did not possess. Usually it was because they hoped I had influence with Robert, although that had not happened recently, of course. I thought him a beggar boy, down on his luck. He certainly looked thin and threadbare enough.

"If you go around to the kitchens," I said, "they will feed you—"

I recoiled as he stepped forward and grabbed my arm. "No," he said. "Listen to me." He fumbled in the leather satchel that he wore across one shoulder. "Remember this," he said. "You gave it to me when I was a child."

He held out to me a little ornament; an angel carved from stone. It was a pretty piece, head bent, wings folded, hands outstretched as though in supplication. It did look familiar to me but I could not place it. I looked at him in bafflement. Poor boy, not only was he a beggar but surely his mind was turned. The thought prompted me to speak gently to him.

"I'm sorry," I said. "I don't remember. But tell me how I can help you."

He laughed a little wildly at that. "It is I who have come to help you," he said. He stepped so close I felt his breath on my cheek. He smelled of sweat and chalk dust from the roads, and I tried not to shrink from him.

"Your husband plans to murder you in secret," he whispered. "He will send a man to push you down the stairs, here at Cumnor Hall. You are to fall and break your neck. You must save yourself! Get away from this place!"

The shock was absolute. This time I was the one who grabbed him, my nails digging into his arm.

"Do not speak of this," I hissed. I could see at once

what had happened: one of Robert's retainers had spoken loosely during a drunken night in the brothels or stews, and this foolish boy thought to profit by it. Or perhaps he truly believed he could help me. I knew not. All I knew was that if a word of the plan, garbled or not, was to escape ahead of time, everything would be ruined.

"Go!" I said. I pushed him towards the door. "Go and never mention a word of this again or I will see to it that my husband's retainers will hunt you down and kill you."

He scrambled back from me, his white face a mask of horror.

"You do not understand——" he started to say, but I gave him no time. The wind caught the oaken door again and it yawned wide, and I pushed him hard, out into the porch. He fell sprawling on the cobbles. He was there one moment—I saw the shock and despair in his face—and then, what seemed like a mere second later, he had vanished.

23

❀

Lizzie: Present Day

LIZZIE SAT IN the garden at The High, her tablet in her hand. The afternoon was mildly melancholy; there was the imprint of autumn in the way that the bars of low sun striped the grass and in the little breeze that chased the already fallen leaves. She was wearing a pair of her grandmother's trousers and a big wool jumper that had belonged to her grandfather. Her own bags, which Jules had so kindly dragged all the way from London, remained largely unopened. Over the crumbling drystone wall, she could hear Avery exhorting her gardener to chop down the Leylandii hedge "because dearest Elizabeth would never sue us." It was odd but comfortable to be in a place where she could hear the lives of other people unfolding around her, the sounds from the high street, the church bells and the snatches of conversation. She realised that everything about her flat had been designed to cut out this sort of interaction. It was isolation masquerading as privacy and luxury. She had appreciated that sometimes when life had been so manic but now, she realised how apart she had become, how divorced from reality. Her life was opening up again and it felt good.

Arthur had left for Oakhangar Hall that morning and had rung her to say that Sam Appleyard, Johnny's step-father, had finally got back from the Antarctic and that the police were coming over to brief him on the investi-gation. Lizzie had felt a huge burst of joy just to hear Ar-thur's voice and then she had felt horribly guilty that in the middle of so much grief and uncertainty she felt so happy.

She took a deep breath of the wood smoke–scented air, wrapped an old tartan rug more closely around her legs and opened up her tablet, typing in the name Amy Rob-sart. She'd had some vague idea that in the absence of any other clues to Johnny's disappearance, the more she could learn about Amy, the more it might help. First, she looked for a portrait, and found some suitably melodramatic ones painted by the Pre-Raphaelites that showed Amy's prone body tumbled at the bottom of the Cumnor stair. That was not what she wanted, though. Searching again she found a little miniature that historians had identified as possibly Amy Robsart. It was pretty and innocent-looking with the sitter recorded as aged eighteen years, her bodice adorned with a brooch that combined a spray of oak leaves and some yellow flowers.

Lizzie's first thought was that she looked remarkably like Amelia had done when they'd all attended a medieval banquet as part of some event organised by Dudley's management years ago. It was uncanny.

She turned to the written articles. There were hundreds, thousands, of entries listed. The mysterious circumstances of Amy's death had clearly fascinated people for centuries. Lizzie deliberately chose a modern interpretation of events to try to counterbalance the blatant prejudice she had read in Hugh Tighe's nineteenth-century version.

Amy Robsart, she discovered, had died on 8th September 1560. Her body was found at the foot of a staircase at Cumnor Place. Amy had been living there as the guest of one of her husband's friends whilst her husband of ten years, Robert Dudley, had been up to various high jinks with the Queen back in Windsor. The circumstances had not initially been considered suspicious; in fact, the implication was that it might have been suicide rather than murder. The servants said that Amy had been in a strange mood that morning, very insistent that they all go to the fair in Abingdon and leave her alone. When some of them refused because it was unseemly on a Sunday, she became angry with them. There were also plenty of acquaintances ready to come forward to say how unhappy Amy had been, that she had been ill and depressed, that she was suffering as a result of Robert's neglect because his only interest was spending time with the Queen.

Lizzie winced. Guilt pricked her. She and Dudley might not have had exactly the same sort of relationship as Elizabeth and Robert but there were sufficient similarities to make her feel very uncomfortable.

She read on. *On the other hand,* the author of the article reported austerely, *there are historians who have pointed out that Amy's letters were cheerful and positive, that she had bought some new clothes and that she seemed excited about something.*

"Conflicting evidence," Lizzie muttered, "is clearly nothing new."

"It most certainly is not," Avery said, from behind her. "Only think of the different theories about the Princes in the Tower."

"Oh hello, Aunt Avery," Lizzie said, smiling. "I didn't see you there." She gestured to the chair next to her. "Would you like a glass of that lovely lemonade you left for me? Have you slaughtered the Leylandii to your satisfaction?"

She went to fetch a glass whilst Avery laid her gardening gloves and secateurs on the table and eased herself into the cushioned seat.

"You're studying that poor child Amy Robsart," Avery said, when Lizzie came back. "Did she fall, was she pushed or did she jump?"

"Something of the sort," Lizzie agreed. "It would be heartbreaking to think that she took her own life because she was so unhappy." She felt another jolt of guilt remembering the Z-list celebrities who had crawled out of the woodwork to say the same when Amelia had died.

"Suicides were denied burial in consecrated ground in those days," Avery said sombrely. "It was considered shameful and wrong in the eyes of the church. By all accounts Amy Robsart was well liked. I doubt anyone would have wanted her memory besmirched by the church's condemnation. If she did take her own life, they would probably have covered it up."

"That's an interesting idea," Lizzie said. "You would have thought that a verdict of suicide would suit Robert

Dudley best, though. That way no one could accuse him of murdering Amy to get her out of the way so he could marry the Queen."

"Yes," Avery said, "but perhaps even Robert couldn't face condemning Amy's immortal soul, no matter how little he cared for her anymore. Certainly, he pushed for an inquest and declared he wanted there to be no doubt in anyone's mind that Amy's death had been a complete accident." She sighed. "A lot of historians feel he tried to influence the inquest jury. You certainly don't hear a word of regret or sorrow from him about Amy's actual death, though. He knew he had lots of enemies and that they would accuse him of her murder and he was determined it wouldn't be allowed to queer his pitch with the Queen. No, a complete accident was the only outcome for him because he would have been blamed for her suicide as surely as he was for her murder."

"You know a lot about it," Lizzie said. "I'm only just starting to find out the story."

"Oh, I've read about it a lot over the years," Avery said vaguely. "Poor child—Amy, I mean. Her story has a hold on the imagination. We always want to know the truth about a historical mystery even when it isn't possible to be certain."

"Amy's death does feel like an accident," Lizzie said, "because surely even the most dimwitted of murderers would realise that for Amy to die at all would be a disaster for Robert Dudley's reputation, and from what little I've read about him I'd say that Robert Dudley was many things but not a fool."

"You're talking with the benefit of hindsight, Elizabeth," Avery pointed out. "We know now that Amy's death forever ruined Robert Dudley's chances of marrying the Queen but that might not have been apparent to him at the time. He was dazzled by ambition and drunk on the life he was living. Nothing and no one was going to get in the way of him achieving all that he wanted. He lived in a bubble far removed from reality, I think, and that sort of existence warps your reality."

"Just like being a celebrity," Lizzie agreed, with a grimace. "What happened after Amy's death?"

"She was buried at St Mary's Church in Oxford," Avery said. "It was a lavish funeral but Robert Dudley didn't attend."

"That looks bad," Lizzie said.

"It wasn't unusual in the Tudor period," Avery said, "and perhaps it was fortuitous because when the vicar gave his sermon, he referred to Amy being 'so pitifully murdered' which he then tried to pass off as a slip of the tongue."

"Oh God," Lizzie said, "how awkward."

"Amy's tomb is long gone," Avery said. Her blue eyes were distant. "It was dismantled in the late eighteenth century leaving only a plaque in the choir to commemorate her death."

"It feels as though they were trying to tidy her away," Lizzie said, "as though it had never happened."

"Certainly, I think Robert Dudley wished he could forget about it," Avery said drily. "It haunted him forever after. When Amy's half-brother John Appleyard expressed concerns that her death had never been properly explained and that he was sure it was murder he was imprisoned and questioned by the Privy Council. He very quickly changed his mind."

"That sounds like intimidation," Lizzie said. A thought occurred to her. "What did Arthur Robsart have to say about Amy's death?" she asked.

"He never expressed any doubt over the legitimacy of the inquest's findings," Avery said, "so one can only assume that he believed that it was an accident. Whether Arthur liked his brother-in-law or not was a different matter, I imagine, but Arthur Robsart always was..." she paused "...discreet."

"So Johnny was the one who stirred up trouble then as now," Lizzie said thoughtfully. "The parallels seem endless."

"But the pattern is always different," Avery said. "Each time it happens it changes."

Despite the warmth of the early autumn sun, Lizzie shivered. "You mentioned before that there was a repeating pattern. Have other people died?"

"Three times, to my knowledge, Elizabeth dear," Avery said. "There was an Amyas Latimer who was a clerk in holy orders in Oxford in the seventeenth century. The details are vague because it was a delicate case under the civil and ecclesiastical laws of the time but it seems he was involved in a love triangle with two of his fellow scholars—both male. He died in a fall down the tower stair in the Church of St Mary by Amy's tomb. It was ruled to be an accident but there were questions raised of both suicide and murder. It was quite a scandal at the time despite the attempts of the authorities to hush it up."

"How horrible," Lizzie said. "And the other ones?"

"Well, there was Amethyst Green," Avery said. "That was the case that first caught my attention because it happened at Oakhangar when I was a child. She was the scullery maid; she fell from the roof of the Hall. My family spun the story to look like a sad tale of a servant who had got herself into trouble and committed suicide in a fit of despair, but even as a child I guessed it was probably a lot more complicated than that. There were hints of a love triangle with two of my uncles." She pulled a face. "It's impossible to be sure what really happened, though, when the testimony at the time was heavily influenced by what people were paid—or persuaded—to say."

"I'm so sorry," Lizzie said fiercely. "The injustice of it is awful, Amy and all the others whose voices weren't heard because the rich and powerful were able to silence them."

"They even tried to silence Amy's ghost," Avery agreed. "There are stories of her haunting Cumnor and other places. Have you read the tale of the clergymen from Oxford who tried to confine her spirit to the Citrine Pool?"

"No." Lizzie shuddered. She drew her tablet towards her. "I must read about that."

"It feels as though it is time to end Amy's unhappiness," Avery said. She put her hand over Lizzie's. "I rely on you, Elizabeth. I have great hopes. You could have turned your back on Johnny Robsart and refused to help him but you did not. That was the first change to the pattern. Now it is up to you to break it completely and prevent this tragedy repeating again."

Lizzie stared at her. "Do you really believe that?"

Avery nodded. "It's been hard," she said, almost to herself, "to be no more than a witness all these years, hoping and praying that somehow, someone would be brave enough to break the curse."

"I don't know how to do it," Lizzie confessed. "I feel completely out of my depth."

Suddenly Avery looked tired, Lizzie thought, older and frailer. Her energy and exuberance so often eclipsed the fact that she was very elderly indeed. Lizzie felt a pang of fear; she had only just found Avery again and she didn't want to lose her.

"We all feel that at times," Avery said quietly. "The only advice I can give you, Elizabeth, is to remember that truth is so often a matter of perception. It is very easy to be misdirected, especially if we want to be. I cannot tell you what will happen; there are always different futures. I can only hope you will choose the right one."

Avery picked up her gardening gloves. Lizzie handed her the secateurs and saw that her gaze was bright again, that sharp, blue glance that had seen so much and knew so much.

"You should never be afraid of your gift, Elizabeth," Avery said gently. "You are strong. You always have been. When the time comes, you must use it to the full." She kissed Lizzie's cheek and wandered away down the steps towards the gap in the Leylandii hedge, leaving Lizzie wondering exactly what gifts Avery possessed herself.

The phone rang shrilly on the table beside Lizzie's tablet. She blinked as it pulled her back to the moment. She didn't really want to answer. She wanted to sit here and think, and enjoy the timeless peace of The High, which was starting to feel properly hers, her home, her place of belonging, her past but also her future.

The phone rang, on and on. She picked it up.

"Hello?" she said.

"Lizzie." It was Johnny's voice. "Lizzie, I'm back at Oakhangar Hall. Please will you come over? I need to talk to you."

24

Amy: Cumnor Place, 8th September 1560

WE HAD LAID our plans very carefully for the day of my death. Anthony, having made all the arrangements, had absented himself from Cumnor. It was vital that no suspicions should attach to him for later he would be the man who identified the body as mine. Richard Varney, the most thuggish of my husband's entourage, was the man who was providing a fresh corpse. Backstreet alley murders were of no consequence to him. Robert had already bought him out of prison twice for stabbing a man to death. If I had the slightest qualm for the poor woman whose fate would enable me to fulfil mine, I repressed it. I asked no questions of how she might meet her end in a manner that would fool any inquest jury. I did not want to know.

There was a fair in Abingdon that day. I gave the entire household permission to attend. More than that, I encouraged it, offering them some coin as an inducement. I thought that with money in their pockets, none would decline, but that was where I faced my first problem for two of Sir Anthony's servants, Mrs Owen and Mrs Odingsells, refused to go. Mrs Owen was elderly and Mrs Odingsells pious and both were as awkward as two old women could be.

"No Christian woman should attend the fair on a Sunday," Mrs Odingsells told me sharply. From the start she had resented my place in the household, usurping the authority and the status of her mistress, Sir Anthony's wife. "Mrs Owen and I shall stay in the solar."

"You may do as you wish," I said with a shrug. I knew they would be playing at cards, which was as reprehensible as going to the fair. I would not argue though. There were more important matters to attend to.

I went to my chamber and started to pack my travelling bag, one case only, for I needed to travel quick and light. That was why I did not see her when first she came; I was too preoccupied in choosing between two pairs of gloves, which to take, which to leave behind. It was such a quandary.

She slid into the room like a snake, silent, a darker shadow against the darkness of the day. It was only when I turned to throw Robert's letters on the fire, to remove all trace of our plan that the flames leaped up and it was their flare of light that illuminated my sister Anna's figure against the white wall.

I jumped and spun around.

"What are you doing here?"

My greeting was not fond, but I was astonished to see her. After our mother's death I had, to my shame, neglected Anna badly. Whilst my brothers had benefited from Robert's influence, Antony, Anna and their papist household had been left to make shift as best they could. Sometimes I had imagined Anna in her new manor house in the country, the house that Antony had rebuilt in the ruins of Sawston Hall. I tried not to think of it, though, because Robert's violence on that night when he had been thwarted in his capture of Queen Mary still sickened me. It was far easier to try to forget it and to pretend that Antony and Anna did not exist.

"Amy." Anna came forward into the light. She looked old, worn, a ghost of our mother, or perhaps a diminished version of me. I had always been the prettier. I felt a sense of irritation. I could not see her now. I had too much to do.

"Anna," I said. I tried to erase the annoyance from my voice. "You should have written—"

"I wanted to see you."

She came close to me, reached for my hands. Her faded blue eyes searched my face. I tried not to shrink from her. There was something at the same time vacant and intense in her expression that scared me.

"I need to talk to you," she said.

"Of course," I said, all the while thinking how ill-timed this was and how I might be rid of her. "But—"

"It's about Robert," she said.

This was sufficiently surprising that it silenced me. I stared at her, baffled, wondering if she was mad. Her jaw was set and there was a determined glint in her eye now, and as I watched her hand slid down protectively over her belly in a gesture that made me feel a lurch of fear and sickness. For one mad moment I thought that surely, *surely* Robert had not got her with child. The thought that my husband might have given my sister the child that he and I could not have repelled me utterly, more than any thought of him as the Queen's lover. Yet even as the suspicion started to form in my mind, I knew that it was false. Robert had not been faithful to me over the years but he would never have looked twice at Anna. There was something else here, something more sinister and dangerous than a mere affair.

The church clock, striking the hour, reminded me that I had no time to waste on Anna, no matter her grievance. Richard Varney would be here soon and I must vanish in the same moment. Any delay might spell disaster to my plan. Mrs Owen, deaf as a post and indifferent to everything about her, was no threat, but Mrs Odingsells was also downstairs and her sharp nose would twitch at any sign of trouble. I could only hope that Anna, like Richard, had entered by the back stair without being seen.

"I can't talk now," I said. I gestured towards the trunk. "I am going on a journey."

It was as though she had not heard me. She sat down on the end of the bed. Her legs were so short that they did not touch the ground and she swung them back and forth like a child.

"I never told you that I met Robert at Sawston," she said. "Do you remember that year? The year King Edward died and your husband tried to put the traitor Jane Grey on the throne?" That myopic blue stare pinned me to the spot. "Antony gave Queen Mary shelter and for that Robert burned Sawston to the ground."

My throat was suddenly dry. "I remember," I said. "I'm

sorry for it, but…" I hesitated. "Anna, we were on oppos-ing sides. It is the fortunes of war. Your husband got Mary to safety and later he was rewarded for it." I waited but she said nothing. "It was a long time ago," I said lamely, "and no one died. Time has passed. We have a different queen now. Surely all can be forgotten?"

"I have not forgotten," Anna said. "I never forgot."

I hesitated. I did not know what else to say. "I had not realised you were at Sawston at the time," I said weakly. "I'm sorry. It must have been very distressing for you."

A bitter smile touched Anna's mouth, no warmth in it. "The whole of Antony's family was at Sawston that night. We were celebrating because I was expecting another child after three miscarriages. The babe was healthy and I felt well. It was a miracle."

Horror and confusion made my brain run slow. "But you have no children," I said, stupidly. "You are child-less like me."

Anna's chin came up. "I am not like you, Amy," she said scornfully. "I conceived, more than once. And then I lost my child when we were forced to flee in the panic and confusion of the fire. We were all terrified. I was running and I fell." Once again, her hand rested protec-tively over her belly. "I hated Robert for that," she added. Her conversational tone made the chilling words all the more shocking. "Every day I would pray that Queen Mary would execute him."

"I'm sorry," I said. "I had no idea." I felt helpless. How could I appease her? How could I get rid of her before it was too late? My mind was running feverishly along the two parallel paths; how to calm Anna and send her away and how to be ready, for any moment Richard Varney might come…

"Mother said you were not to be told," Anna said. She was not looking at me now but gazing at a point far distant, a point in the past, I guessed, and yet still vivid and painful in the present. "She said that Robert would one day become a powerful man and that it was in the interests of us all, whatever our creed, to put personal feelings aside and ally ourselves to him for the good of the family. She said I would have more children, and not to fret."

I blinked. It was hard advice, pragmatic though, from a woman who was not only protective of her family but who had also experienced a number of miscarriages herself. I remembered the unsentimental way in which Mother had sent me recipes for herbal medicines to try to help me conceive and the unvarnished words that if I did not, I would be a woman with nothing: no place, no influence.

"It happened again," Anna said, "over and over, I would conceive and lose the babe and now the physician has told me I must not try again for fear it will kill me. Antony tells me it does not matter, but it does." She lifted her gaze to mine. Her face was drained of all animation, all spirit, except for the startling hatred I saw beneath the surface. It was that which kept her alive.

"You blame Robert," I said. "You think it is his fault that you have lost all your babes and your hope for the future."

She nodded. "I do. I do blame him. I always will. I lost the last child two weeks ago and I can bear it no more. I had to tell you. You had to know."

I went down on my knees beside the bed and took her

cold hands in mine regardless of the shudder of revulsion that went through me. It was like grasping a corpse.

"Anna," I said, "I am so very sorry. I know how hard it is to be childless—"

Her gaze snapped. "You do not know what it is like to *lose* a child."

I swallowed the hurt and the words that bubbled up. It was a different sorrow to fail to conceive. That grief was mine.

"No, I do not," I said carefully. "And I do understand why you feel Robert is to blame for your misfortunes. What can I do?" I shook her hands gently. "How can I help you?" I did not know what she wanted and I did not want to be so crass as to offer money for a loss that could never be compensated. "What do you want of me?" I repeated.

Her hands tightened cruelly on mine. "I want you to kill him," she said.

For a moment I was frozen into shock and then I started to laugh. It was so unexpected that I could not help myself. The sound came bubbling up and I could not prevent it bursting out. Anna let go of me as though I had the plague and leaped to her feet, leaving me kneeling there on the floor.

"I'm sorry." I scrambled up, trying to stifle my mirth. "It's the shock... I was so surprised—"

She looked at me with loathing. "I might have known that you would not care," she said.

"I'm sorry," I said again, sobering. "But... To kill Robert? How could I possibly accomplish that? And why would I want to do so?"

"Not just for me," she said, turning away so that her expression was in shadow, "but for both of us. Surely you cannot bear the way he humiliates you? You are a laughing stock, Amy. Your name is synonymous with cuckoldry throughout the entire land."

It was unkind but I had schooled myself to withstand far worse in the ten years that I had been Robert's wife. All urge to laugh had flown now; I was acutely conscious that time was running out and that I must simply get rid of her.

"You are crazed," I said coldly. "Your mind has been turned by grief and I am sorry for it. But I will not kill Robert. He may well prefer to spend his hours with the Queen than with me but he provides well for me. I lack for nothing. I am unlikely to kill the goose that lays the golden eggs."

She came very close to me. "You lack for nothing but freedom and respect. Aye, I will give you that. And you also lack generosity and love. Your material comfort has been built on the blood of those that Robert has wronged."

I turned away, tired of her now. Time was running out. I thought I heard the sound of a latch lifting, a step on the stair below. It was time for me to go. I snapped the trunk closed and swung around, heading to the door.

"Go home, Anna," I said, over my shoulder. "Go back to Antony and listen to him. He can comfort you. And if you are in material need, write to me and I will ask Robert to provide for you too." I knew that was a lie but in that moment, I would have promised anything to be free of her.

I should not have turned my back on her. I realised it too late. I had walked out of the room without a backward look at her and paused at the top of the stair, expecting to see Richard Varney below. He was not there. No one was there.

I heard the patter of Anna's running steps behind me.

She grasped my sleeve, tugging on it, spinning me about. Her face was a mask of fury.

"Do not walk away from me," she shouted, shaking my arm. "Do not turn your back on me and dismiss me like a servant!"

I was afraid that all the commotion would disturb Mrs Odingsells. I tried to free my sleeve from Anna's grasping fingers but as I turned, I caught the heel of my slipper in my gown. Such a small thing, but my head spun and I felt myself teeter dangerously on the top step.

"Amy!" Anna's voice was loud in my ears. "Amy!"

I lost my footing.

I seemed to fall so slowly. I had so much time and yet so little.

I saw horror replace the anger in Anna's face. She screamed, her mouth wide with fear.

A man came running. I recognised Richard Varney. Within the jumble of terror and despair that possessed me, I felt one last glimmer of hope.

Richard could have saved me. It would have been a simple matter for him to step forward and catch me. Instead he stepped aside. I had time to see his face, to see the calculation in his eyes, the satisfaction. And then I knew. Robert had double-crossed me. There had never been a plan where I would be free to start a new life. It would have been too much of a risk. Robert needed to make sure he was truly free.

Richard did nothing to save me. He, like Antony Forster, like William Hyde, like all the others, was Robert's man, bought and paid for. And Robert, of course, was the Queen's man. He had never been mine, not even in the beginning in Norfolk when we had been young and in love. Elizabeth had always come first, his sun and stars, the centre of his world, his inspiration and his life.

Hope died. I felt the rush of air against my face and the lightness of empty space beneath me. I felt fear, screaming inside my head. Then it was over.

25

Lizzie: Present Day

"I DON'T BELIEVE IT." Lizzie sat in the kitchen at The High that evening, a cup of tea ignored at her side, and bit hard into an almond croissant. "I don't believe it," she repeated with her mouth full. "He can't just have been visiting the seaside, or seeing a friend, or whatever else he says he's been doing. It isn't possible."

She remembered the conversation she'd had with Arthur about Johnny being in Peru or Scotland. It seemed that Arthur hadn't been far off the truth after all.

"I know it's annoying, Lizzie," Jules sounded irritatingly reasonable to Lizzie's ears, "and it's thoughtless of him and he's caused you a lot of trouble, but you said yourself that Johnny's just a boy and he's been through a lot—"

"I know." Lizzie cut her off shortly. "Sorry, Jules…"

She saw her cousin's expression. "You're right, of course, and I am glad he's safe—of course I am—it's just..." She stopped. She couldn't articulate to Jules that it wasn't actually about the problems Johnny had caused her, it was simply that Johnny's reappearance, as sudden as his disappearance, felt incongruent and wrong.

At first when she had heard the news, she had felt nothing but relief. Johnny was home, he was safe. Arthur, when she had spoken to him, had sounded overjoyed and that had made her even happier. It was only later, when the reality of Johnny's return had started to sink in, that Lizzie's feelings had also changed. For a start, she felt an utter fool. At what point had she and Arthur bought into some kind of shared delusion about Johnny's whereabouts? She was angry, with Johnny, but mostly with herself, for doing exactly what she had accused the police of and building up a case that fitted her version of the facts. It had all been based on no more than conjecture and wild imagination, and it had led her into spinning some kind of supernatural explanation for something that was a great deal simpler. Johnny, grief-stricken and depressed, had wanted some time alone to deal with his feelings. He hadn't been on any kind of quest. She had imagined the whole thing. Lizzie felt so stupid, so gullible, and in an odd way it felt as though everything that had happened to move her life forward in the intervening two weeks had been cancelled out and she was back where she had started. She'd thought all along that her dependence on psychometry was wrong and something to be ashamed of. Now she saw just how far it had misled her. She'd even started to believe that time travel was possible because Johnny had somehow normalised her gift and encouraged her to believe, and then she had taken it way too far. Perhaps she had seen a vision in the stone when she had touched the stone of Baynard's Castle, just as she saw visions from other objects. It didn't mean that she had actually *been* there and nor had Johnny.

Jules was still talking. "…So, there are gaps in the CCTV record, but there's no doubt he was seen in Oxford and various other places, just like he said, and one of his friends said they'd met up…"

So near, Lizzie thought, and yet so far.

"The police have checked it all out as far as they are able," Jules said, "and Johnny's agreed to go for some counselling. Physically he's fine, just a bit hungry."

"Johnny wants to meet up," Lizzie said. "He asked me to go over to Oakhangar Hall today but Arthur thought he'd better have a bit of time to settle back in first. He wants to apologise."

"I should think so," Jules said, sounding like a strict teacher. "It's the least he can do for all the trouble he's caused you."

"I'll go over tomorrow," Lizzie said. She tried to shake off the sense of uneasiness she was feeling. Two almond croissants and three mugs of sweet tea hadn't helped. Something felt out of kilter; she didn't know what. Perhaps it was simply that she didn't know where she and Arthur went from here. It had all been so intense, so wrapped up with what had happened to Johnny, that now that was all over it felt as though her relationship with Arthur was finished too, before it had properly started. Her night with him, so emotional and right at the time, so much a part of the connection she had thought they had, now seemed almost incomprehensible for someone as guarded as she had always been.

"I'm going to bed," she said, getting up and wishing the pastry and the misery together were not weighing so heavy on her stomach.

"Would you like me to come with you tomorrow?" Jules asked. She looked suddenly anxious, and Lizzie felt a rush of affection for her. She went over and hugged her cousin. "I'll be fine," she said. "You've done so much already; you're the best. I'll come and see all of you soon, and we can get together in London as well and I'll treat you to the Mayfair Chocolate Tour as a thank you."

"The kids will love that," Jules said.

"Me too," Lizzie admitted.

After Jules had gone, she went upstairs and took a long hot shower. It did nothing to banish the shadows that clung to the edges of her mind like cobwebs. She realised that she would need to hire a car to get to Oakhangar Hall. It felt good to grasp some sort of practical plan rather than let her mind meander through all the puzzles and confusion, so she turned out all of her bags looking for her driving licence, eventually finding it in the pocket of one of her jackets. She put it on the bedside table so she wouldn't forget it in the morning, and in doing so she caught a flash of silver illuminated in the lamp's glow.

She stooped to pick it up. It was a thin silver chain with a little silver phoenix symbol dangling from it. She remembered seeing it in the Land Rover when Arthur had given her a lift home. It had hung from the driving mirror, sparkling in the light. Turning it over in her hand Lizzie saw the initials JG engraved on the reverse. The chain had snapped. She touched the misshapen links.

Immediately her mind clouded with images, blurred by sun and water droplets and a sort of dizziness that filled her up and made her feel languid and warm and slow. She could hear loud music and laughter but it was eclipsed by the roaring of water in her ears. Panic and fear edged out the warmth in her mind, like a cloud across the sun, but it was too late, too late to start fighting, too late for the struggle. She burst through the surface and heard the sound of screaming—and Dudley's name. And then the water closed over her head again and it was easier to let it take her, to sink beneath the surface where it was gentle and dark…

She came to herself kneeling on the floor, gasping and retching, as though her lungs were full of water. In the palm of her hand it felt as though the phoenix burned against the scar. She dropped it sharply and it clattered against the base of the cabinet.

When she got her breath back, Lizzie hoisted herself up onto the bed and sat there for a little, waiting for her spinning thoughts to settle. The phoenix charm had belonged to Jenna, Arthur's fiancée. She had known that, felt it as soon as she had touched the silver links. But if the phoenix had been Jenna's then the watery plunge and the hideous death by drowning were also hers, and Dudley had been there at the time too…

She hugged herself close. She was sure that Kat had told her that Jenna had died from anorexia so perhaps the vision had been wrong. Yet it had felt so vivid, exactly like Amelia's fall had.

Lizzie remembered the story of Amy Robsart's spirit being trapped in the waters of the Citrine Pool, that descent into darkness, the binding of her soul. There were so many parallels and so many echoes. Could they really be no more than coincidence, and Johnny's disappearance had no link to it at all? There had been his notebook, full of the ancestry of the Robsart family and his research into Amy, Robert and Elizabeth. He had even checked out stone tape theory and she was certain that at Baynard's Castle he had been testing her gift to see if she could connect with the memory of stone.

She remembered Avery's words: *"Truth is so often a matter of perception. It is very easy to be misdirected, especially if we want to be..."*

Supposing Johnny was misdirecting them about where he had been? Arthur in particular would want to accept Johnny's words at face value because the only thing he cared about was having his brother safely home. Johnny knew that Arthur was not comfortable with the supernatural and would be inclined to believe him when he said he had just wanted time alone to think. Lizzie was not so sure, though. She was also not sure that Johnny had given up his hope of saving Amy and changing Amelia's fate.

Her phone rang. To her surprise she saw it was Dudley. She almost let it go to voicemail but in the end, she decided to answer. At the very least she could ask Dudley for the details of what had happened at Oakhangar Hall the day that Johnny and Amelia were playing their disappearing tricks.

"Lizzie!" He sounded so pleased to speak to her that Lizzie felt slightly sick. "Hey, how are you? The police told me Johnny's turned up. Hopefully they'll drop the investigation into Millie's death and then we can unfreeze her and get on with our lives. I can't wait." There were voices in the background and the clink of bottles. Lizzie realised that Dudley was drunk. It sounded like a big party and she was suddenly fiercely glad she was nowhere near it.

"I can imagine," Lizzie said. "Did you want anything in particular, Dudley?"

"Just to find out when you're coming back to London," Dudley said, a little plaintively. "It's boring here without you."

"But you've got Letty to play with now," Lizzie said. "I heard she'd moved in with you."

"Oh, Letty..." Dudley sounded vague as though he'd already forgotten. "Yeah, well she's no fun to be around. She's sick all the time."

"I hear that can happen when you're pregnant," Lizzie said coldly. "You should be supporting her, Dudley. Surely it's the least you can do."

"Whatever." Dudley sounded sulky now. "I'd rather see you, Lizzie. You were always more fun." His tone lifted. "You're coming back, right?"

"I've got a few things to sort out," Lizzie said briskly. She knew that even if she did go back to London it would never be to the same world, least of all to hang out again with Dudley. "Listen, Dudley," she said, wanting to capture him whilst he was still in the good mood phase, "can you just remind me of something? We were talking a while ago about the time you were at Oakhangar with Johnny and Amelia—"

"Little shit," Dudley said randomly, suddenly vehement.

"And you said something about him being an emo kid, saying weird stuff and always appearing and disappearing like a ghost," Lizzie said. She wondered suddenly if the police were tapping Dudley's phone—or hers, for that matter. Well, they could make of this what they wanted.

"Yeah..." She could tell Dudley's attention was slipping away.

"What did you mean?" Lizzie said. "About the appearing and the disappearing?"

"Fuck, Lizzie, how should I know?" Dudley said. "I can't remember last week never mind something that happened years ago at Oakhangar."

Lizzie was used to this. She waited and after a moment Dudley sighed heavily. "All I remember," he said, "was that Johnny came to visit us for a weekend at Oakhangar a few years after Amelia and I were married. School holidays or something. It was fucking awful, if you want the truth—he was about eleven and into stuff like history and religion, and Amelia said I had to spend time with him so I tried, I really did. We played football together but he was useless and there was nothing to talk about, you know, and then I'd turn around and he'd just vanished like I was the most boring person in the world... I was really mad; Amelia and I rowed about it after it happened a second time and I told her he was weird."

"You mean he walked out whilst you were talking?" Lizzie said. Her mouth was suddenly dry.

"Nah," Dudley said. "He literally disappeared. I mean, he must have slipped out when my back was turned but it was like he just vanished. That was why I said he was like a ghost. Fucking weird kid."

"Right," Lizzie said.

"They're all bad news," Dudley said. "Anna's nearly as bad. I'm sure I saw her that day at Oakhangar, when Amelia—" He stopped.

"When Amelia what?" Lizzie said.

"Nothing," Dudley said. He sounded frightened suddenly. "I dunno. I haven't seen Anna. I'm confused."

Lizzie had never been able to read Dudley's mind in her

entire life, but she knew that in that moment he had been about to say "when Amelia died." A whisper of fear crept down her spine. She felt colder than she ever had before. Had Dudley been at Oakhangar that day? Had Anna? Whatever had happened, she knew she'd get no sense from him now. Dudley would admit nothing.

She could hear the roar of the party behind him and the sound of Dudley's breathing and the moment hung on a knife's edge.

"You take care, Dudley," Lizzie said carefully. "I've got to go now."

She cut the connection and dropped the phone on the bed. Then she sat down next to it, took the little silver phoenix charm in her hand and tried to work out what she had to do.

Lizzie drove slowly through Oakhangar village, mindful of both the twistiness of the road and her unfamiliarity with the car. She was glad she hadn't fallen for the sales-girl's talk and hired herself something flashier. She liked sports cars but they weren't great on country roads and she hadn't driven for years. It had been scary enough simply getting from the hire company in Witney to Oakhangar, twelve miles away.

Oakhangar village was pretty but not in the chocolate box way Lizzie had come to expect from further west in the Cotswolds. The stone was greyer here and the build-ings looked colder and more austere than the honey gold cottages of Burford. Even though the sun was shining and the day was tranquil and warm, Lizzie felt chilled but that was hardly surprising. The anticipation of what she was about to do was like ice in her blood. She took a left turn by the Barley Mow pub, passing a high wall. Ahead of her the lane opened up to a parking area beside a stone arch in the wall. ALL SAINTS CHURCH was carved at the top of the wooden noticeboard. An uneven flagged path led to the church door.

On impulse, Lizzie stopped the car and got out to read the plaque by the gate. It was exactly as Avery had told her: the information board stated that both All Saints Church and Oakhangar Hall had been extensively rebuilt by Lord Basing in the early nineteenth century using stone from his ruined manor at Cumnor, a few miles away. The archway to the left of the plaque had come from the chapel at Cumnor Hall. A carved stone angel with luxuriant wings clasping a harp looked down on Lizzie benignly.

Lizzie got back in the car and turned right, following the lane towards some huge metal gates that were very firmly closed. The name Oakhangar Hall was picked out in gold on a black wrought iron nameplate. Lizzie didn't really remember any of this from the last time she had been there for Dudley and Amelia's wedding. She'd had a car and a driver that day and she'd spent the journey listening to her latest album on headphones. She smiled a little wryly at the memory.

She got out and pressed the bell. She'd expected there to be the usual crowd of journalists about but perhaps news of Johnny's return hadn't yet got out.

The intercom on the gate crackled but there was no response. A second later, however, the gates swung open silently and she drove through and they shut behind her. Lizzie had the oddest sensation of a trap closing. She'd always been a bit claustrophobic, wary of being penned in.

A short drive led to the house. She sat for a moment

looking at it before she put the car into gear. Her main feeling was surprise; she'd forgotten how ugly it was with its pointed window arches, spiral chimneys and quaint little turrets. Amelia had clearly done some more work on it in the years since the wedding; large windows created a wall of glass on the west side of the courtyard and the stables were clearly new but in a style that copied but did not quite pull off the character of the original. It was all a bit too much for Lizzie, a mad mixture that shouted, "Look at me!"

She pulled up in front of the main entrance. Four grotesque carved faces, a lot less friendly than the stone angel at the church, adorned the door embrasure and did nothing to make her feel welcome. She felt spiky and unsettled enough to make her almost turn tail and run.

"Hi." Arthur was waiting for her. His smile was warm and it made Lizzie feel a little bit sick in anticipation of what she was about to do. She'd lain awake a long time the previous night trying to decide whether to tell Arthur what she knew, but in the end, had decided against it. It was Johnny she needed to talk to, not Arthur. Johnny held the key to the mystery.

"Thanks for coming," Arthur said. He kissed her and for one long moment Lizzie closed her eyes and blotted out what was to come and let the warmth and the pleasure of it unfurl in her.

"Hey," Arthur said softly, when he let her go. "It's good to see you." He drew her into the hall. "Come and meet Sam. Anna's here too," he added. He saw Lizzie's quick glance. "It's OK—" he touched her arm briefly, a fleeting reassurance "—she's just so glad to have Johnny back that I'm sure she won't cause any trouble."

The hall was even more grotesque than the outside of the house. Lizzie remembered the huge stone gothic vaulting and stained-glass windows. She glanced towards the staircase.

"Was that where Amelia fell?" she asked.

"No." Arthur gave her a faint smile. "Amelia's accident happened on the back stairs."

Lizzie was relieved to find that that the kitchen was brand new, light and much more normal. Anna and an older man whom she assumed must be Sam Appleyard were sitting at the stripped pine table which was littered with newspapers and empty mugs. The air smelled warmly of baked bread and coffee. Sam got to his feet and came around the table to shake Lizzie formally by the hand.

"Hi, I'm Sam. We're grateful to you for coming over." He had short, salt-and-pepper hair and a deeply tanned and lined face. His accent was US west coast and his grip firm. He gave Lizzie an impression of durability that she thought was probably an essential quality for someone who disappeared off into the wilds for months at a time. His manner was gruff but she liked him.

Lizzie nodded to Anna, who gave a dip of the head in acknowledgement. She looked younger now and more vulnerable than she had when she had marched into Lizzie's flat, bristling with suspicion and aggression, but not much friendlier.

"Take a seat." Sam waved Lizzie to an empty chair next to Anna, who rather ostentatiously moved further away. "Would you care for a cup of coffee?"

"Thanks," Lizzie said.

Sam placed a mug of coffee in front of her and Arthur

pushed the biscuit tin across the table towards her. She cupped her hands about the mug and inhaled the scent.

"Hey, Lizzie." The door opened and Johnny ambled in. He looked just the same; lanky, cadaverous, his blue eyes tired. He seemed to vibrate with the same repressed energy Lizzie had sensed in him from the night he'd come to the flat. He kissed her cheek. "Thanks for coming," he said. "I don't deserve it but I really appreciate it."

"You owe her an apology," Anna said grudgingly. "We all thought she'd pushed you in the river or something."

"Yeah…" Johnny's gaze slid away from Lizzie's and he blushed. "I'm really, really sorry about that." He held the door open. "Can we talk?" He looked pointedly at the others. "In private?"

"I don't think that would be a good idea," Arthur said. "Lizzie might not want that after you abandoned her on the Embankment."

Johnny's blush deepened. "I've said I'm sorry," he mumbled.

Lizzie almost pitied him. She would have done if she hadn't been expecting this, hadn't suspected that Johnny would try to get her on her own again so that he could exploit her ability to read the memory of stone like he had at Baynard's Castle.

"It's OK," she said. "It'll be fine." Her nerves were strung so tightly that she could feel herself shaking. She grabbed her coffee and a couple of biscuits and followed Johnny out.

"This house is a warren," she said as they recrossed the hall. "I couldn't live somewhere like this. I'd rattle around like a marble." She tried to sound as normal as she could.

She didn't want to confront Johnny until she was absolutely sure of what he had planned.

"It's so weird that it's mine now," Johnny said. "Did Arthur tell you? Millie left it to me. I can't decide..." He let the sentence hang.

"Where are we going?" Lizzie was trying not to spill her coffee on the carpet. She was trembling so much she suspected she was leaving a trail of biscuit crumbs like Hansel and Gretel. Johnny didn't seem to have noticed, fortunately. He was concentrating only on what he needed to do. Lizzie felt a burst of compassion for him. He was so intense, so driven to save Amelia. There was no room in his mind for anything else.

"I thought we'd go to my room," Johnny said. "There's something I want to show you, to try to explain..." The sentence trailed away as he started to climb the grand stair, slowing his loping stride to match Lizzie's shorter one. The steps were broad and shallow, and at the top the landing spread out on either side like a huge gallery. The light was multicoloured, refracted through the panes of the stained-glass windows. Lizzie paused, remembering her vision of Johnny standing there as a child on the day of Dudley and Amelia's wedding, peering through the mahogany bannisters. It felt as though the shadow of Oakhangar Hall hung over everything, including Avery, who had warned her not to go back...

"This way!" Johnny called, and Lizzie hurried after him, down a side corridor. It felt colder here, even less friendly than in the gallery. Lizzie's skin prickled a warning. She was so attuned to the house now, to its moods and its memories, that it almost felt as though she could hear it breathing. Its presence wrapped about her, cold and claustrophobic.

Johnny was waiting for her at the end of the passage. They ducked beneath a low arch that was decorated with another of the Oakhangar stone angels, went down a couple of steps and suddenly they were on a small landing. It was diamond-shaped with mullioned windows and the ubiquitous stone angel over the arch at the top of a narrow flight of stone stairs. She felt the atmosphere as soon as she stepped through the door. It felt close, stifling, a blanket of grief and misery. The sensation was so strong and repellent that she took an instinctive step back, bumping clumsily into Johnny, missing her step and dropping the coffee mug. It smashed on the flagstones, splashing everywhere, but Johnny didn't seem to notice. He caught her arm and steadied her.

"I like this part of the house," he said. "It feels very close to the past." He smiled at Lizzie. "Don't worry. It can't hurt you. It's only the memory in the stone. I think it holds all of Amy Robsart's grief and regret, and that's what you are feeling." He ran a gentle hand over the smooth plaster of the wall. "This part of the house reuses the stone from Cumnor Place. Its very fabric is created from the place where Amy Robsart died."

"I know," Lizzie said. Her voice came out as a whisper. She cleared her throat. "Johnny," she said. "Johnny, this is the flight of stairs where Amelia died."

Johnny was staring down into the shadows of the stairwell below. "Just a little step back in time," he said, almost to himself.

"No!" Lizzie said. Her head was buzzing with dark shapes and patterns. She wanted to run away. "Johnny, you can't bring Amelia back," she said. "I understand what you're trying to do, but time doesn't work like that. It can't."

"I've got to save Amelia," Johnny said, as though he hadn't heard her. "I couldn't save Amy. She wouldn't listen. You have to help me." He turned to Lizzie and the suddenness, the urgency, made her draw back. He looked heartbreakingly young and hopeful. "I knew you would work it all out," he said. "I knew you were different. I need you to call up the memories in the stone like you did at Baynard's Castle. Then I can cross time."

"No," Lizzie said. "I won't do it." She tried to back away from the top of the steps but the swarm of dark shadows in her mind was clamouring for attention. There was something here that was too powerful for her to contain and it was terrifying. It was so strong that it dominated everything, filling all the spaces in her head. She fought to hold on to her own thoughts so that she would not be completely subsumed. Dizzily she put out a hand to steady herself against the wall only realising when the touch of the cold plaster seemed to burn her palm that it was the last thing she should have done. The memories in the stone had been set free.

The images were coming thick and fast now, like a jerky silent film, the figures jostling on the screen. Lizzie couldn't breathe. She was drowning in sorrow. Her lungs were full of it. She could taste it in her mouth. Images spun through her mind, animated with sound as well as movement now.

"It's not Amy," she said. "It's not Amy whose grief we can feel here. Amy had hopes and plans. She was excited, happy. She was going to escape and start anew..." She took a deep breath. "There's someone else here," she said. "Amy calls her Anna. It's Anna whose grief we can sense, Anna who is broken with guilt. She never meant for it to happen. She did not want Amy to fall. It was an accident—"

The images shifted abruptly and Lizzie saw not Amy Robsart but Amelia, in one of her long, flowing dresses, her blonde hair loose about her shoulders, standing at the top of the stone stair, suitcases scattered about her. She was looking back at someone and she was smiling, but it wasn't a warm smile, it was edged with impatience and spite. Lizzie could feel Amelia's emotions, the irritation and the exasperation. Amelia wanted to get away and someone was calling her back...

"Anna! No!"

It was Johnny's voice and the shout was so loud that it broke Lizzie from the trance. She opened her eyes, saw the dark stairs yawning below her and teetered on the edge for one sickening moment. She waited for the push in the small of the back, the fall, the rush of air and the clutch of terror, everything she had felt in her visions, the fate that had lain in wait for Amy Robsart and for Amelia and now for her. Out of the corner of her eye she saw a hand raised and instinctively put up an arm to protect herself. The blow glanced off her shoulder, giving her a momentary excruciating pain and Lizzie stumbled back, jarring her arm again as she fell clumsily. She lay still for a moment with her cheek pressed against the cold stone of the floor whilst the darkness swirled through her mind and started to clear and the pain receded. Far away, as though in a dream, she heard the splintering crash of stone.

"Anna," Johnny said again, and there was a whole world of anguish in his voice. "It was you. You killed Amelia."

Pushing herself upright, Lizzie saw Anna Robsart, and behind her Arthur, who was breathing as though he had run a mile. His eyes met Lizzie's and she saw the moment he realised what had happened. She saw the horror swamp him and felt his despair. Arthur turned away and Lizzie felt the link between them shut down.

Far below them, on the turn of the stair, the stone angel lay smashed into shards, just as the gazing ball had done so many years before.

26

"YES, I DID IT," Anna said. "I pushed Amelia down the stairs."

They were back in the kitchen, amidst the breakfast debris. There was an air of complete unreality about everything. The papers, the cold pot of tea felt like a relic from another time, from before. Arthur had his arm around Johnny. They both looked completely ashen. Lizzie felt like an interloper; she wanted to reach out to Arthur, to try to comfort him, but she knew there was nothing she could say. There was no comfort anyone could give.

Anna's blonde hair fell across her face like a curtain, sheltering her expression from view. "I killed Millie," she repeated. "We were arguing about the divorce. I wanted Millie to take Dudley for all he had. It was the least he owed her after the way he had behaved." She shot Lizzie a look. "But Millie wasn't interested. She was running away, planning a new life. She was all excited and glowing and happy and I—" Her voice cracked. "I was still so full of anger and resentment and hate. I couldn't understand why she would let Dudley off the hook like that. I told her I thought she was weak and stupid, and she looked at me with pity." She clutched convulsively at the mug, wrapping her hands about it, searching for fading warmth. "Pity from Millie, of all people! I couldn't stand it. She was the one who broke down when Mum died. I was strong—I hid how I was feeling to be there for everyone else! I didn't deserve to be patronised like that." She gulped down a mouthful of cold tea. "Well, I told her that if she wouldn't do it for herself then at least she should make Dudley pay for what he did to Mum."

She looked defiantly and deliberately from face to face. "Basically, Dudley killed Mum," she said. "When he refused to pay for her cancer treatment, he condemned her to death. He had so much cash in those days he wouldn't even have noticed but he wouldn't do it. And Amelia was complicit in that because she could have made him pay for Mum to go to America for treatment but she just gave up. When he refused, she let him get away with it."

"Anna…" Sam shifted in his seat, placing one of his hands over hers. "We talked about this at the time," he said. He sounded lost, despairing. "I thought… We all thought you agreed the treatment would have made no difference. Jessica said so herself. It was too late."

"You can't know that." Anna was shaking now. Lizzie could see how thin was the veneer of her self-control. "How can anyone know? You could at least have *tried*."

Her voice splintered on the last word and she started to sob in great gulps and gasps, her whole face contorted and her shoulders heaving with the weight of grief and anger.

"Amelia said she understood why I was still angry but that I had to let it go, that I had to let Mum go..." Anna said. She raised her chin. "She said she had moved on with her life and that I should too. But I couldn't." Her voice shredded into despair. "I didn't want to! Millie was bustling about packing her bags all the time we were talking, like I was just an irritant to be brushed away. I snapped, I suppose. When she carried the first bags over to the top of the stairs, I followed her and said she couldn't just walk out in the middle of our discussion. She laughed and said the discussion was over, and I grabbed her arm and screamed at her not to turn her back on me... And then..." She stared. "I pushed her. I was so angry I wanted to kill her. She fell down the first flight and hit her head the wall—I heard the crack—and then she sort of rolled over and fell down the second flight too."

No one said anything at all. Johnny was slumped against Arthur's shoulder, eyes closed. Arthur looked ashen. A muscle moved in his cheek.

After a second Sam got clumsily to his feet, the scrape of his chair shockingly loud in the quiet. He put his arms about Anna. She did not move into his embrace but neither did she push him away.

"It will all be all right," Sam said, and he sounded as though he was trying to convince himself. "We have to go to the police, Anna, you do understand that? We'll tell them it was an accident. It'll be all right."

Lizzie was reminded of Anna comforting Johnny that day at her flat, because how did you ever make anything right when it was so wrong, so messed up, so painful? She had no idea.

"I don't want you to tell them it was an accident." Anna pulled herself free of Sam's grip. She raised her chin, staring him down defiantly. "I've told you I did it. I don't mind admitting why. I want everyone to see what a conniving cow Amelia was and what an utter sleaze Dudley is and always will be."

Sam was looking shattered, old and exhausted. "What has Dudley got to do with this?" he said.

"It's all about Dudley in the end," Anna said bitterly. "It always was about him, selfish, self-centred, stupid, feckless Dudley. No one could resist him, could they? Not Amelia, not Letty Knollys, not even me." She glanced up for a moment, her blue eyes dull. "To think that in the beginning I thought Dudley was God's gift. I practically *begged* for his attention." She shook her head violently. "I hate him and I hate myself."

Lizzie remembered the wedding, and how both Letty and Anna had been part of the screaming, giggling pack of girls fawning over Dudley in the pool that afternoon. Anna had been so young then—sixteen—younger than Amelia, her sister, Dudley's bride. But evidently that hadn't stopped him. She felt sick.

"I saw Dudley when I was leaving that day Amelia fell," Anna said. "I was in such a horrible state I didn't stop to speak to him and I don't think he saw me. I don't know what he was doing here but later, when he pretended that he'd been miles away and he didn't know anything about it, I knew he was lying. I think he'd come to talk to Millie about the divorce and got the wind up when he realized she was dead."

"And what about Lizzie?" Arthur's voice was hard. He didn't look at Lizzie but kept his full attention on Anna. "You hit her. You could have killed her too."

"I didn't mean to," Anna said. "I thought she was going to pull one of her weird mind tricks and tell Johnny what had happened. I just wanted to stop her." Despite the words, the glance she shot Lizzie was laced with malice. "You kept causing me problems," she said to her. "I wanted to keep Johnny away from you but he liked you and so did Arthur." She shook her head. "You're as bad as Dudley in your own way. I really wish I could have pinned the whole thing on the two of you. I tried, when I gave Johnny a lift to your flat that night in Arthur's car and he left his phone behind. I planted it in your flat. But it wasn't enough."

Lizzie looked at her. Anna met her eyes defiantly but behind the bluster and bravado, Lizzie could see another Anna Robsart, the one who had hidden her grief when her mother had died, whilst her hatred and resentment festered because she thought no one else cared enough, no one had done enough to save her. She saw the Anna who loved Johnny fiercely and had tried to comfort him, and the girl who had never meant to kill her sister but had lost her temper because, as Arthur had once said, she sometimes went way too far.

"I truly didn't mean it to happen," Anna said, and in that moment, she crumbled, and her voice shook, and Sam gave a muttered curse and got up to pull her into another clumsy hug.

Lizzie stood up as quietly as she could. She wanted to slip away, unwilling to spectate on this family tragedy anymore. It felt horrible and intrusive. She knew the police would want to question her but that could wait. She already knew she wouldn't press charges against Anna. The whole hideous mess would hardly be helped if she did; as it was, Anna would have to live with what she had done for the rest of her life.

Arthur looked up and for a moment their eyes met but he said nothing, nothing at all, and Lizzie turned and walked away, out into the daylight that felt like another world.

Back at The High, Lizzie found both Jules and Avery waiting. She took one look at them and burst into tears.

"I'll run you a bath," Jules said. She couldn't deal with tears; it was left to Avery to enfold Lizzie in her arms and soothe her like a child while she poured out the whole story.

"Is it over now?" Lizzie finally pulled away from Avery, pushed the hair back from her hot face and wiped her eyes. "It has to be over because otherwise how can it have been worth it?"

Avery, her face full of sorrow, stroked Lizzie's hair just like her grandmother had done when she was a child. "I don't know," she said regretfully. "I hope so."

Later Arthur rang. The police had come, he said, and Anna had broken down completely. He and Johnny were bearing up as well as they could. They both wanted to see her, but in a little while, when Johnny was stronger.

"Any time," Lizzie said. She could barely breathe, it felt as though there was so much she wanted to say. "Come any time."

A fortnight went by. Lizzie went to the local art class. She was worse than even she had anticipated, utterly un-

able to draw anything recognisable though she had better success with abstract painting. No one seemed to care,
though. They were just pleased she was there, which she
found rather nice. She went to yoga, which wasn't at all
like the class at her London studio but was absolutely fine
all the same. She found a piano tuner and a gardener, neither of whom posted photos of her on social media. Avery
suggested that she should get some exercise by walking a
dog for the Blue Cross shelter nearby. Lizzie chose a miniature spaniel with sad eyes called Perry whose previous
owners had had to give him up when they had twins.
Two days later, Perry moved into The High. The two of
them got into a routine of sorts; Lizzie found it soothing.

And then, one afternoon, Arthur was there. Lizzie was
playing with Perry in the garden when the dog gave a tiny
yip and barrelled over to the gate where he then sat, tail
wagging in the leaves, begging for attention.

"Your dog is very well trained," Arthur said. He let
himself in, bending to stroke Perry's velvety head. The dog
promptly rolled over, begging for his stomach to be tickled.

Arthur straightened. "I never imagined you as a dog
person," he said.

"I grew up with dogs," Lizzie said. Her throat was dry,
her heart beating fast. "At least when I was staying with
Jules's family." She felt a pang of nostalgia. "I wanted a
dog when I moved to London," she said, "but I was too
busy. It wouldn't have been fair."

"You could have got your assistant to look after it," Arthur said, "or found one that fitted into a handbag."

"Kat doesn't like dogs," Lizzie said. "The clue is in
her name." She smiled at Perry. "Besides, if I have a pet
I want to look after it myself otherwise what's the point?

He's not just an accessory." She raised her gaze to Arthur and sighed. They could carry on talking about dogs forever or they could be brave.

"Would you like to come in?" she asked. "There's some coffee—or lemonade. Avery makes it for me."

Arthur followed her over to the terrace and into the kitchen, Perry trotting along behind. "You seem…settled… here," he said. There was a question in his voice.

"It's early days," Lizzie said, "but I think I may be." She gestured him to a chair and poured lemonade from the painted jug. Her hand shook a little, spilling drops of liquid onto the table. "Arthur—" she said, but she didn't know how to continue, what to say.

"I thought you'd like to know how Johnny's getting on," Arthur said. He sounded distant. Lizzie's heart ached.

"Yes," she said. "Please. I hope he's doing OK."

"He's pretty subdued," Arthur said, "but he's back at school and he's seeing a counsellor and I think he'll be fine in a while." He stretched his legs out, sitting back. "He wanted to come with me today, actually, but I told him I needed to talk to you alone first. He says he's got a lot of explaining to do and he hopes you'll forgive him. He really means it this time."

"Right," Lizzie said. She scrubbed at the spilt juice, avoiding his gaze.

"Lizzie," Arthur said. "It's not your fault. Johnny took advantage of all of us in different ways because he was so obsessed with breaking the pattern and bringing Amelia back. There was no space in his life for anything else. And the truth of what Anna did would have come out even without your involvement. None of this is your fault."

"I know," Lizzie said. She swallowed hard. "I know that

really. It's just…" She took a breath. "I feel as though my actions shattered what was left of your family," she confessed. "Even though I never intended it."

When Arthur didn't deny it or reassure her, she felt a little bit sick. She wanted to tell him how sorry she was that they had barely started to know each other and now they were strangers again. She wanted to ask if they could try again but that sounded both needy and selfish, and she shied away.

"How is Anna?" she asked instead.

Arthur grimaced. He took a mouthful of the lemonade.

"They've charged Anna with manslaughter," he said evenly. He moved his glass in slow circles of the table. "Her defence team think they can get her off, though, by explaining how affected she was by Jessica's death. They're calling Amelia's fall an accident that happened in the heat of the moment." For a moment he was very still, then he sighed. "I'm not sure Anna wants to be found innocent, though. She's broken down completely."

"I'm very sorry," Lizzie said. "Your family had already gone through so much," she said. "It feels almost unbearable, except of course somehow you have to bear it."

"We'll get through it," Arthur said. "We're strong enough. It's better to know the truth anyway. Like I said, secrets have a way of coming out in the end."

"Yes." Lizzie's heart sank as she remembered the last secret of them all. She went over to the dresser, sliding open the drawer and taking out the little silver phoenix that had hung on the driving mirror in Arthur's car.

"I have something of yours that I need to give back," she said. "I found it in my bedroom. I think it must have fallen on the floor of your car when the chain broke and somehow got snagged on my coat."

Arthur was very still. He didn't take it from her outstretched hand so after a moment she put it on the table. "It had the initials JG in it," Lizzie said. "I guessed it had belonged to Jenna, your Jenna."

"I didn't realise I'd lost it," Arthur said. He cleared his throat. "I kept it in the car like a little talisman. It was just a stupid, small thing, a present I gave Jenna when we got engaged. The phoenix is supposed to signify endurance and eternal life. I was into all that spiritual stuff at the time and I thought it was a nice way to show I'd love her forever without sounding too sentimental about it."

He looked at Lizzie. "You read it, didn't you?" he said. "You read its history."

"I didn't do it deliberately," Lizzie said. "I wish I hadn't but you know how this works—I have no warning. Sometimes I see things and sometimes I don't. It's fickle, this gift. It's one of the reasons I don't like it. I didn't want to read the talisman." She stopped. "It felt private," she said. "I didn't want to know."

Arthur was silent. She couldn't tell what he was thinking. When it came to reading Arthur, it only worked when he wanted her to do it. She thought it was only fair that he should be able to deny her that insight but his reserve, his impenetrability, made this doubly difficult. She couldn't leave it unsaid, though. She was committed now. This was the last secret between them and it had to be laid to rest, no matter what happened afterwards.

"I always wondered why you hated Dudley so much," she said slowly. "I sensed it in you from the very first. I knew you disliked me, and I thought that was because you believed I was having an affair with Dudley, but you hated Dudley even more. I thought it was because of what had happened to Amelia. That was a part of it, of course, but it wasn't the real reason. The real reason was Jenna." She waited, but Arthur said nothing. Still she could not read any of his emotions. That door was slammed in her face but she could feel the tension coming off him like static.

"Avery said that there were three other cases she knew of that mirrored in some way Amy Robsart's death," Lizzie said. "There was Amethyst Green, the serving maid at Oakhangar, and there was Amyas Latimer, the clerk in Oxford. There was Amelia, of course. But there was a fourth, someone called Mia."

"Mia was Jenna's real name," Arthur said. His voice sounded dull.

"Yes," Lizzie said. "I didn't work it out straight away because of the names, but of course Jenna Gascoyne was her stage name; her real name was Mia Roberts." She took a gulp of the lemonade. It felt cool and sweet, soothing.

"Avery told me that Jenna couldn't cope with the pressures that came with her work," Lizzie said. "You told me yourself that she was messed up and you did everything you could to help and support her. Everyone says the same; that Jenna developed anorexia and her life spiralled into depression and drug-taking and she died. What the reports don't say—" she cleared her throat, "what I saw when I touched the phoenix, was that Jenna had been partying with Dudley's band, with Call Back Summer, just before she died. It was Dudley who gave her the drugs—and was too pissed to save her when she fell in the swimming pool at Oakhangar. It was an accident, but in so many ways he was culpable all the same."

Arthur stirred at last. "The band's management hushed it up because it would have been too damaging," he said. His voice was rough. "It would have finished them. I only found out two years ago. Millie told me. She said Dudley had let slip one night that Jenna had died in the pool at Oakhangar. Millie had been away at the time because it was whilst Jessica was ill. She badgered the whole story out of him." Arthur ran a hand through his hair. "It was the beginning of the end for them really. I don't think Millie ever thought Dudley was faithful to her but the thought of him getting high with her brother's fiancée whilst she was away with her dying mother…" His face twisted. "It was pretty horrific. It sounded like some mad orgy of drink and drugs and by the end of it Jenna was dead and everything was a godforsaken mess." He looked at Lizzie properly for the first time. "I guess Dudley never told you?"

"Dudley never said a word to me," Lizzie said. "If he had, do you think I would have hidden it from you?"

"I don't know," Arthur said. He sounded tired. "After all, I hid it from you. I could have told you, but I didn't."

Lizzie swallowed the hurt. Of course Arthur had hidden it from her. It had been devastating, shattering his life. And she had been Dudley's friend. Arthur would never have confided.

Arthur shifted slightly, angling his body towards her. "I loved Jenna," he said, "properly loved her, I mean. Yes, we were young and it might have all gone wrong in time but to me at that time it felt real and mature and more important than anything."

Lizzie nodded. "I can't say I understand," she said, "because I've never experienced that sort of first love. I've always protected myself against feeling too much. But I understand that it could be like that for you."

"What hurt the most when I found out," Arthur said after a moment, "was realising that Jenna hadn't felt the same about me as I did about her. When I heard about the party... That she'd been sleeping with Dudley..." He shook his head. "I'd been so grief-stricken when she died and it felt as though I'd never known her. It felt like such a betrayal; it almost killed me."

"Perhaps Jenna did love you as much as you loved her," Lizzie said. "We all make mistakes, Arthur, and we can all be self-destructive when we're unhappy."

Arthur looked up. He gave her his heart-shaking smile and for the first time, Lizzie felt a shred of warmth.

"That's a very generous thing to say," he said, "and I think I've come to terms with it now, but—" he shrugged "—for the last couple of years, since I found out, it just about ate me up." His gaze focussed on her, sudden and intent. "When I met you, I could see it happening all over again," he said. "Another crazy, mixed-up girl—" he gave her a wry smile "—whom I really, really liked and wished I didn't."

Lizzie's heart stuttered and then started to race.

"You said you knew I disliked you," Arthur said. "That was the least of it. I knew there was a connection between us but I didn't want to get involved with you. Why would I? You were Dudley's friend, maybe more than just a friend, and I'd already lost two people I loved as a result of Dudley's selfishness. He was never directly culpable and yet it always came back to him in some way. So I thought it best to steer clear of you."

"I understand," Lizzie said. She swallowed hard. "I

guess," she said, struggling for lightness, "that it wouldn't have worked between us anyway. I mean, we may have been following some sort of pattern laid down in the sixteenth century, but Queen Elizabeth I never had a thing going on with Amy's brother Arthur Robsart, did she? From what I've read of her it sounds as though she spent the rest of her life alternatively pining for Robert Dudley and trying to make him jealous with other men, which sounds pretty ghastly to me but hey, she had to do what she had to do."

"We don't have to follow the sixteenth century pattern too closely," Arthur said. The underlying thread of humour was back in his voice. "I don't think Robert Dudley did too well out of it either. He might have been loaded with money and titles but he didn't get to marry Elizabeth, and his enemies used Amy's death as a stick to beat him with for the rest of his life. I came across a particularly cutting epitaph to him the other day." He took a breath and quoted wryly: *"Here lies the constant husband whose love was as firm as smoke."*

"Ouch," Lizzie said. "That's harsh but probably deserved."

Silence fell. The peace of The High seemed to flow around them, soft and timeless. Perry, curled up at Lizzie's feet, twitched in a dog dream.

"I hope he'll get on with Charlie and Lola," Arthur said, looking at Perry. "My dogs," he added, smiling at Lizzie. "I'm sure he will." He stirred. "I want to finish this, Lizzie," he said. "Once and for all. I want to be sure it's over."

"You mean the recurring pattern of Amy's death," Lizzie said cautiously, "not…"

Arthur looked horrified. He reached across the table and took her hands in his. "No! God no. Sorry. No, not us." He smiled at her. "We've only just begun," he said softly. "But I don't want us, or Johnny, or anyone else's life overshadowed by this again. We have to end it now."

Lizzie nodded. "I've been thinking about this," she said. "Now the truth is out that Anna killed Amelia, Amy Robsart's spirit may be appeased and the curse broken. In every other instance the truth was hushed up—Amy's death, and Amyas Latimer, and Amethyst Green…" She tightened her grip on Arthur's hands. "And Jenna," she said. "We don't know exactly what happened to all of them," she said, "and probably we never will. The story was similar but different every time, but now at least the truth is free."

She stood up, pulling Arthur to his feet too. "I have an idea," she said. "I need to talk to Avery and I need a little time." She reached up and kissed him. "Come back tomorrow," she said.

Arthur put his arms about her and joy swept through her, wrapping itself around her heart. It felt good.

"I'll go," he said, kissing her again. "But I will be back."

"For a crazy, mixed-up girl you never wanted to get involved with," Lizzie said. Her eyes filled with tears. "Oh, Arthur…"

"Hey…" Arthur brushed away her tears with the pad of his thumb. "We can do this."

"Yes," Lizzie said. Her fragile heart was just starting to believe it. "I'm used to being on my own," she cautioned. "I'm not good at relationships. It was always easier to manage by myself. I guess—" she swallowed hard "—perhaps I never felt that lovable."

"I'll show you that you are," Arthur promised. He

rubbed his cheek against her hair. "Besides, you have Jules and Avery and Johnny as well as me." He nodded to the snoring dog. "And Perry, of course."

Lizzie giggled. "It's nice having people—and dogs—you love in your life."

"I'll take that as a declaration," Arthur said. "I love you too. But you know that—" He gave her a wry smile. "You can read me like a book."

"I can't promise to stop doing that," Lizzie said, "but I reckon you understand me pretty well too, psychic gift or no psychic gift. Just don't expect me to read the memory of stone if we visit any historical houses together," she added. "I'm done with all that. You can buy a guide book like everyone else."

27

Lizzie: Present Day

IT WAS A beautiful autumn day in the Cotswolds. The sky was the pale translucent blue of a winter sea at dawn and the sun hung low over the horizon. The fallen beech leaves crunched beneath their feet as Lizzie and Arthur walked along the footpath to the Citrine Pool. There was the slightest hint of frost in the air.

"I expected the water to have a yellow tinge to it with a name like that," Arthur said as they stood on the edge of the pool, "but it's dark."

"According to legend," Lizzie said, "the waters turned black when they trapped Amy Robsart's wandering spirit and confined it to the pool. Before that it had been a greenish-yellow colour because of the rare quartz in the rock."

"I expect there's a biological explanation for the change in water colouration," Arthur said, "but it's a good story." He looked at her. "So this was where it happened. This was where the priests of Oxford locked Amy up for perpetuity."

"Yes." Lizzie shivered as a breath of air blew little eddies across the pond. "This is where they captured her and tried to bind her soul, and once she was trapped, the pattern kept on repeating." She touched Arthur's arm gently. "The pattern is broken now, but to finish this we need to set Amy's spirit free. So many wrongs have been done to her in life and the afterlife. We're closing the circle, showing her that it is over."

Arthur looked around. The willows bent low over the edge of the pool and trailed their bare branches in the water. "It's probably just my imagination," he said, "but I don't like it here. There's a bad feeling in the air."

"Yes," Lizzie said. She'd felt it from the moment she had seen the dark water glittering in the low sun.

"I almost expect to see a flash of lightning and an apparition from a horror film," Arthur said. He dug his hands deep into the pockets of his coat and hunched his shoulders. "Poor Amy," he said. "What a horrible fate."

Lizzie put down the cardboard box she had been carrying and lifted the lid. Inside was a wreath of leaves and flowers that she had created that morning with Avery's help.

"It's *Quercus robur*," she said, in answer to Arthur's quizzical look, "the English oak. It's strong and beautiful." She touched the petals of the pink flowers she had laid on top of the entwined oak stems and dark green leaves. "These are carnations," she said. "They're the descendants of the pinks and clove gillyflowers that people grew in Tudor times. They were a symbol of undying love."

"I recognise them from Amy Robsart's wedding portrait," Arthur said. "She was wearing a brooch with oak leaves and gillyflowers."

"Yes," Lizzie said. "It's a symbol from a time when Amy had both great love and great hope in her life," she said. "I wanted her to know that she is not forgotten and that hope can rise again."

Lizzie held the wreath in her hand for a moment and then she took a step back and threw it overarm into the deep water. She heard the splash and saw the ripples spread and then fade.

"Nice throw," Arthur said.

"I was in the school netball team," Lizzie said. She put her hand in his and they stood side by side.

She watched the garland settle on the water. She felt the spiral of love and grief rise up from the waters then, felt it flare into life and die down, until it was washed away and a shaft of sunlight cut through the overhanging willows and danced across the surface of the pond, reflecting shades of green and gold and citrine onto the oaken and gillyflower wreath.

"I think," she said, "that the best way to break the destructive patterns of the past, of any past, is to write a different future. We can do that now."

EPILOGUE

Amy Robsart, The Citrine Pool

FROM THE OTHER side of the pool I watch them, Elizabeth and Arthur, joined now through time and destiny. This is a different Elizabeth from the one I had known. She is as brave as the first Elizabeth, but she is kinder and more generous. She has changed, and in doing so she has altered the course of fate and the futures of those who are to come.

Elizabeth, my enemy, you were the only one who could help me. You saw that the truth needed to be told. You broke the pattern.

Yet in the end it is your kindness that heals me. Kindness cannot alter the past but it can change the future. It can bring peace.

I watch with them as the sun falls brilliant and bright on the oak and gillyflower wreath and the waters of the pool dazzle in shades of green and gold. I feel my spirit expand as it touches freedom.

They turn to leave. His arm is about her, her head against his shoulder. They love. They will always love. This, I know.

My time is done now. I can leave too, slip away and be gone, with love and hope in my heart. I am no longer trapped. I can go where I will and be free. It is a beautiful day.

★ ★ ★ ★ ★

ACKNOWLEDGEMENTS

The mystery of the death of Amy Robsart is one of the most enduring puzzles in English history. Amy, whose husband Robert Dudley was a childhood friend and favourite of Queen Elizabeth I, died at Cumnor Manor in Oxfordshire on 8th September 1560. The subsequent scandal forever destroyed Robert Dudley's chances of marrying the Queen.

Amy has fascinated me for years, perhaps because, like the other historical women who have inspired my books, her story so often gets lost in a bigger one, in this case the relationship between Elizabeth and Dudley. Last year on a particularly wet and windy autumn afternoon, I made the trip to Cumnor to the site of the lost manor house, and from there to Oxford, to the University Church of St Mary the Virgin where Amy had been buried. Her tomb has also been lost.

This book is a very personal one for me, springing as

it does from a love of Tudor history engendered in me by my beloved grandmother and I am as always immensely grateful to my family for their enduring love and support for my writing. For this book I am particularly indebted to my wonderful editor Emily Kitchin, whose ideas and suggestions inspired me to bring out the best in this story, and to Jon Appleton for his insightful copy-editing. A huge thank you too, to the teams at HQ in the UK and Graydon House in the US for all that they do to bring my stories to readers.

As always, I am most grateful to my readers. Thank you!